PEGASUS IN HARNESS
Victorian Publishing and W. M. Thackeray

VICTORIAN LITERATURE AND CULTURE SERIES

Karen Chase, Jerome J. McGann, *and* Herbert Tucker,
General Editors

———◦⟨∞⟩◦———

PEGASUS IN HARNESS

Victorian Publishing
and
W. M. Thackeray

———⌽———

Peter L. Shillingsburg

UNIVERSITY PRESS OF VIRGINIA
Charlottesville and London

THE UNIVERSITY PRESS OF VIRGINIA
Copyright © 1992 by the Rector and Visitors
of the University of Virginia

First published 1992

Library of Congress Cataloging-in-Publication Data
Shillingsburg, Peter L.
    Pegasus in harness : Victorian publishing and W. M. Thackeray /
Peter L. Shillingsburg.
        p.   cm. — (Victorian literature and culture series)
    Includes index.
    ISBN 0-8139-1397-7
    1. Thackeray, William Makepeace, 1811–1863—Publishers.
2. Authors and publishers—Great Britain—History—19th century.
3. Literature publishing—Great Britain—History—19th century.
4. Novelists, English—19th century—Economic conditions.
I. Title.   II. Series.
PR5633.S5   1992   92-2805
823'.8—dc20   CIP

Printed in the United States of America

TO THE MEMORY OF
William Shillingsburg 3rd
1903–1991

Contents

Acknowledgments

Specific debts to particularly helpful librarians and scholars are indicated in notes throughout the book, but several persons have been an inspiration and encouragement beyond specific, detailable instances.

James B. Meriwether was initially responsible for this book by encouraging me to work on Thackeray and by giving me a copy of the first American edition of *Pendennis* on the day I passed my qualifying examinations at the University of South Carolina. His influence as a teacher is evident to me on every page of the book. James L. W. West III has had a gradual and growing influence on it, by providing an example in his own work and by reading, approving, criticizing, and occasionally borrowing ideas over the years. He chaired the conference session in which I read the first paper relating to this project. He read one whole draft of this book, leading me to many changes. Edgar F. Harden has been another influential friend and scholar, leading the way with extensive studies of Thackeray's compositional habits and writing articles on *Henry Esmond* and the *Miscellanies* I was sorely tempted to appropriate wholesale. He, too, read and improved a draft of this book. John Sutherland has led us all into the world of nineteenth-century author-publisher relations. Over ten years ago he complained to me that I should have finished this book already. His work on the Smith contracts made it clear years ago that a treasure trove of information awaited further exploration. Much of this book has been written with the sinking feeling that it will not measure up to his expectations. Robert Patten, by writing the model work on the relations between one author and his publishers, has made me work much harder than I originally intended. He, too, read portions of the manuscript of this book to my benefit. Gordon Ray, by editing the collected letters and writing the major biography of Thackeray, did most of the groundwork that makes a book like this one possible to undertake. But, in addition, he must have been more than instrumental in my appointment as a Guggenheim fellow to work on this project in 1982. I hope this book is better now these many years later than it would have been had I been more prompt in fulfilling the goals of that fellowship. Harry Heseltine, by providing a congenial work schedule, made possible the final push to complete the manuscript at University College, Australian Defence Force Academy. Two travel grants from the Office of Research and Graduate Studies and three semesters with a slightly reduced teaching load in the English Department at Mississippi State University have also been useful in this project and are gratefully acknowledged.

Other scholars have had important, though less sweeping, roles in promoting the work represented here. Jane Millgate enabled me to write the first published results of my investigation of the Bradbury and Evans ledgers. Nicholas Barker's encouragement led me to complete the study of *The History of Samuel Titmarsh and the Great Hoggarty Diamond*. Paul Eggert proved an invaluable discussion partner for ideas developed in chapter 6. He also read and commented on the first three chapters.

None of these people is responsible, of course, for the flaws in this work or for the fact that there are more details than conclusions. From my point of view, however, the book is incomparably better than it would have been but for them.

I wish to thank the editors and publishers of the following journals for permitting me to incorporate all or parts of articles first published by them: "The First Edition of Thackeray's *Pendennis*," *Papers of the Bibliographical Society of America* 66 (1972):35–49; "Thackeray and the Firm of Bradbury and Evans," *Victorian Studies Association Newsletter*, no. 11 (March 1973):11–14; "The Printing, Proof-reading, and Publishing of Thackeray's *Vanity Fair:* The First Edition," *Studies in Bibliography* 34 (1981):118–45; and "Publishers' Records and Analytical Bibliography: A Thackerayan Example," *Book Collector* 29 (1980):343–362. A part of chapter 6 has appeared also in *Editing in Australia* (Sydney: Univ. of New South Wales Press, 1990) and in Philip Cohen, ed., *Devils and Angels: Textual Editing and Literary Theory* (Charlottesville: Univ. Press of Virginia, 1991).

For permission to quote from unpublished material I thank Mrs. Belinda Norman-Butler, the representative of Thackeray's literary estate. For access to manuscript materials and to rare printed matter not otherwise available to me I thank Gordon Ray, Nicholas Pickwoad, William Baker, and Edgar Harden. For cooperation in using materials, both printed and manuscript, under their guardianship I thank the staffs of the Berg Collection and the Rare Book Room at the New York Public Library, the Beinecke Library at Yale University, the Houghton Library at Harvard University, the Parrish Collection at the Princeton University Library, the St. Bride's Printing Library in London, the British Library, the National Library of Scotland, the Trinity College Library at Cambridge University, the Henry E. Huntington Library at San Marino, California, the Butler Library at Columbia University, the Fales Collection, Bobst Library at New York University, the Pierpont Morgan Library, the Australian National Library, the Mitchell Library in Sydney, the Library Company of Philadelphia, the Pennsylvania Historical Society, the Bradbury, Agnew Publishers, the Smith, Elder Archive at John Murray, Publishers, the Forester Collection at the Victoria and Albert Museum, and the rare-books rooms at the University of California at Berkeley, Duke University, the University of North Carolina at Chapel Hill, the University of South Carolina, and Mississippi State University.

For her encouragement, her criticism, and her suggestions upon reading the last draft of this book, I am deeply grateful to Miriam Shillingsburg.

A Note on Sources

References to Thackeray's published letters, cited simply as *Letters* with a volume and page designation, are to *The Letters and Private Papers of William Makepeace Thackeray,* ed. Gordon N. Ray, 4 vols. (Cambridge: Harvard Univ. Press, 1946).

Unless otherwise noted, all references to Thackeray's works are to first editions. See Appendix B.

The following location references are used for manuscript materials. Unpublished materials are used by permission of the repositories and printed by permission of the Thackeray estate, represented by Mrs. Belinda Norman-Butler:

Berg	Henry W. and Albert A. Berg Collection, New York Public Library
Beinecke	Beinecke Rare Book and Manuscript Library, Yale University
Bodleian	Bodleian Library, Oxford
Bradbury, Agnew	Bradbury and Evans Archives, Bradbury, Agnew Publishers, London
Bradbury Album	Punch Office, Bradbury, Agnew Publishers, London
Butler	Butler Library, Columbia University
Houghton	Houghton Library, Harvard University
Huntington	Henry E. Huntington Library, San Marino, California
Morgan	Pierpont Morgan Library, New York
Murray	Smith, Elder Archives, owned by John Murray, Publishers, London
NLS	National Library of Scotland, Edinburgh
NYPL	New York Public Library
NYU	Bobst Library, New York University
PHS	Pennsylvania Historical Society, Philadelphia

Transcription symbols
< >   canceled matter
↑ ↓   inserted matter

PEGASUS IN HARNESS
Victorian Publishing and W. M. Thackeray

A literary man has often to work for his bread against time, or against his will, or in spite of his health, or of his indolence, or of his repugnance to the subject on which he is called to exert himself, just like any other daily toiler. When you want to make money by Pegasus, (as he must, perhaps, who has no other saleable property,) farewell poetry and aerial flights: Pegasus only rises now like Mr. Green's balloon, at periods advertised before-hand, and when the spectator's money has been paid. Pegasus trots in harness, over the stony pavement, and pulls a cart or a cab behind him. Often Pegasus does his work with panting sides and trembling knees, and not seldom gets a cut of the whip from his driver.

Do not let us, however, be too prodigal of our pity upon Pegasus. There is no reason why this animal should be exempt from labour, or illness, or decay, any more than any of the other creatures of God's world. If he gets the whip, Pegasus very often deserves it, and I for one am quite ready to protest with my friend, George Warrington, against the doctrine which some poetical sympathisers are inclined to put forward, viz., that men of letters, and what is called genius, are to be exempt from the prose duties of this daily, bread-wanting, tax-paying life, and are not to be made to work and pay like their neighbours.

Pendennis, vol. i, chap. 37

Introduction

LAMENTING THAT LITERATURE ever became a profession, though acknowledging its inevitability, A. S. Collins remarked in 1982 that "when we speak of the trade or profession of letters, we mean the pursuit of literature as a means of living, independent of all others, and if we speak of it now as a profession, and now as a trade, it is only to mark off those like Southey who worked for high ideals, from those hacks and compilers whose aim was merely the day's wage." The thrust of these remarks is that the necessity of bread caused much writing to be done to order, with an "exhausting and a cramping effect" upon the author's mind. The alternative to the profession of literature was a free application to the Muse as "my staff but not my crutch," as Sir Walter Scott put it before necessity and debt caught up to him, so that "the profits of my literary labour, however convenient otherwise, should not, if I could help it, become necessary to my ordinary expenses." Collins saw a marked difference between writing in response to the "pressure of occasion," which might include the incentive of money, and to the "pressure of living," the unrelenting need for bread. The purpose of these distinctions was to suggest that, for the most part, the need for bread caused writers to compromise their ideals, to look to the short-term purpose of satisfying the publisher and public rather than the long-term satisfaction of literature. "Those who have been greatest in the practice of letters have rarely been those to whom letters was their supporting profession," wrote Collins, citing among the poets who did not write for money Wordsworth, Coleridge, Shelley, Keats, Byron, Rogers, and Scott and noting that in prose the situation in the romantic period was that all the best-known writers then are forgotten now.[1]

While there might be some truth in the idea that desperate need is not conducive to the production of writing of lasting value or in its converse, that freedom from desperate need allows development of literature, it cannot be sustained as a blanket observation. One might cite among those

---

[1] A. S. Collins, *The Profession of Letters: A Study of the Relations of Authors to Patron, Publisher, and Public, 1780–1832* (London, 1928), pp. 7, 8; John Lockhart's *Life of Scott,* quoted, ibid., p. 138.

authors who relied upon independent means but who burdened literature with less than the best Charles Lever, Edward Bulwer Lytton, Robert Smith Surtees, Edward Fitzgerald, Lady Blessington, Mrs. Gore, and, depending on whom one listens to, Coleridge and Wordsworth themselves, whose reputations are often said to rest on a fraction of their output. These writers either inherited independent livelihoods or obtained them through marriage, pensions, or government posts in which a comfortable living involved "nothing to do," as Charles Lever observed about his post as British consul to Trieste. On the other hand, of few writers can it be said that they did not so burden literature. The whole exercise of connecting the greatness of the literary output to the monetary motives for its production is as misguided and ideological as John Ruskin's attempt to relate the greatness of Gothic architecture to the independent spirit and moral fiber of the artisans.

All the same, a considerable mythology about writing has developed around words like imagination, fancy, creativity, genius, inspiration, the Muse, and artistic integrity. Simultaneously, the independence or autonomy of the artist has come to be thought traduced by insolent and insensitive patrons or by screwing publishers and booksellers. Such a mythology demands of authors that they conceal the sweat. Fits of creative passion, bouts of wrestling with the Muse or of striking with white heat upon her anvil are images passing muster, but daily discipline, writing to deadlines of time or space, exchanging one's soul for money are infra dig. In Thackeray's *Pendennis,* Warrington, a baronet's son and a "gentleman," admits: " 'I write. . . . I don't tell the world that I do so,' he added, with a blush. 'I do not choose that questions should be asked: or, perhaps, I am an ass, and don't wish it to be said that George Warrington writes for bread.' "[2] After looking at some of George's articles for a law review, Pen remarks: " 'I can't fly upon such a wing as yours.' 'But you can on your own, my boy, which is lighter, and soars higher, perhaps,' the other said, good-naturedly. 'Those little scraps and verses which I have seen of yours show me, what is rare in these days, a natural gift, sir. You needn't blush, you conceited young jackanapes. You have thought so yourself any time these ten years. You have got the sacred flame—a little of the real poetical fire, sir, I think; and all our oil-lamps are nothing, compared to that, though ever so well trimmed. You are a poet, Pen, my boy' " (1:312).

Thackeray's portrait of Pendennis here says much about the mythol-

---

[2] *The History of Pendennis,* 2 vols. (London: Bradbury and Evans, 1849–50), 1:311.

ogy of writing. Pen falls so easily for the rhetoric that George has to correct the pretensions: "You don't suppose that you are a serious poet, do you, and are going to cut out Milton and Æschylus? Are you setting up to be a Pindar, you absurd little tom-tit, and fancy you have the strength and pinion which the Theban eagle bear, sailing with supreme dominion through the azure fields of air? No, my boy, I think you can write a magazine article, and turn out a pretty copy of verses; that's what I think of you." When they have sold Pen's first verses to the publisher of the *Spring Annual,* Pen exults, "I can make my own way," and George remarks, "Well, you may get bread and cheese, Pen: and I own it tastes well, the bread which you earn yourself" (1:317). Having disposed of the inflated myth of romantic writer and sorted out the discrepancy between Milton and a writer of light verse for the magazines, Thackeray had Doctor Portman signify "his approval of Pen's productions, saying that the lad had spirit, taste, and fancy, and wrote, if not like a scholar, at any rate like a gentleman" (1:349). By contrast, Pen's "fellow laborer," Mr. Bludyer, reviews books according to which publishing house produces the magazine he writes for and then sells the review copy to buy brandy.

The real distinctions between writers as poets, versifiers, scholars, gentlemen, and Grub Street literary hacks can be put in the context of Thackeray's own immediate experience. His own mentor in magazine writing was William Maginn who wrote like a scholar but was no gentleman. Editor of *Fraser's Magazine,* Maginn was the impecunious prototype for Captain Shandon in *Pendennis,* but unlike Shandon he was a learned, though self-educated, man. Thackeray himself was a fair versifier and in many regards, like Pen himself, soared on a lighter wing—if it can be called soaring to write desperately for bread.[3] Thackeray's need to support himself was a deal more acute than Pen's. Thackeray's fellow writer on *Punch,* Douglas Jerrold, could write both the light verse and the political article but did not pretend to be either scholar or gentleman. Another of Thackeray's friends, writing like both a scholar and a gentleman, was Thomas Taylor, who, though a fellow contributor to *Punch,* had earned a first in the classical tripos at Trinity College (where Thackeray had had his own brief and unsuccessful flash of pleasure and education) and had been elected fellow and awarded an M.A. by 1843. He was appointed professor of English literature at London University in 1845 and was called to the bar

---

[3]Charlotte Brontë accused (I think that is the right word) Thackeray of being Warrington rather than Pen, but Thackeray found writing in George's style for the *Morning Chronicle* less to his liking than writing in Pen's for *Punch* (*Letters* 2:784–85, 225).

in 1846. In short, he was a man who succeeded brilliantly in the very competitions that Pendennis (and Thackeray) had found too rigorous or formally restrictive to endure. Though Taylor's father was a brewer and self-made man and consequently "of no family," Thomas had made his own way into the worlds of literature, medicine (he was secretary to the Board of Health from 1854 to his retirement in 1871), theater (he was an avid and prolific playwright), and the periodic press where for years he wrote regularly for the *Times,* the *Morning Chronicle,* the *Daily News,* and *Punch,* which he also edited from 1874 to his death in 1880.[4]

The point of this little digression is that Thackeray's personal experience of the profession of letters, his extensive acquaintance with other members of the profession from the top to the bottom,[5] and his personal dealings with a range of publishers on a commercial basis for his livelihood allowed him to examine at first hand the realities and pretensions of literature as a calling, a mission, a vocation, and a trade. His circle of acquaintance among writers ranged from Thomas Carlyle, Alfred Tennyson, and the Brownings to Douglas Jerrold, George Augustus Sala, Mark Lemon, William Maginn, Harrison Ainsworth, and Charles Lever and to Mrs. Gore, Lady Blessington, Richard Bedingfield, and William Carleton. His reaction to this diversity and the development of his own response to the profession is one subject of this book.

Certainly he had moments of creative satisfaction. Thackeray's excitement at discovering a title for *Vanity Fair* ("I jumped out of bed and ran three times round my room, uttering as I went, 'Vanity Fair, Vanity Fair, Vanity Fair' ") and his satisfaction with the description of Rawdon Crawley flinging Becky's diamonds at Lord Steyne and scarring his forehead "to his dying day" ("When I wrote the . . . sentence, I slapped my fist on the table and said '*that* is a touch of genius' "), for example, can be seen as tastes of the rewards of creative genius.[6] But he had moments of professional pride as well. His satisfaction at hearing that *Notes on a Journey from Cornhill to Grand Cairo* would be his first book to require a second edition (*Letters* 2:558–59) and his delight in George Smith's offer of £1,000 for a

---

[4]*Dictionary of National Biography.*

[5]It is useless to classify authors in a single scale; social, economic, educational, and aesthetic standards conflict with one another as do the measure of popular success and the range of self-deception and pretension held by or attributed to each.

[6]Kate Perry, *Reminiscences of a London Drawing Room,* quoted by Edgar Harden, *The Emergence of Thackeray's Serial Fiction* (Athens, Ga., 1979), p. 332; James Hannay, *A Brief Memoir of the Late Mr. Thackeray,* quoted in Gordon N. Ray, *Thackeray: The Uses of Adversity* (New York, 1955), p. 438.

novel[7] were token rewards of a trade well conducted. The interplay of these points of view, popularly conceived as opposed to one another, is more intricate and extensive than is usually acknowledged. The interplay certainly was complex in the case of Thackeray, whose experience was akin to Thomas Campbell's when he boasted that "necessity, not inspiration, was the great prompter of his Muse."[8]

Samuel Johnson once remarked, "Sir, there was a good public, and liberal booksellers, and you should not let yourself be seduced by a pension."[9] Thackeray eventually adopted this attitude perforce. His acquiescence was perhaps philosophical, for in his middle years he attempted and failed to get a sinecure—as assistant secretary in the Post Office in 1848—and he stood unsuccessfully for a seat in Parliament for Oxford in 1857. In 1850 he wrote to William Allingham, a poet receiving income as a customs officer in Belfast, "You're lucky to have a trade and live out of this turmoil" (*Letters* 2:711). He was called to the bar in 1848 and had his name added to the door of Thomas Taylor's chambers, but nothing came of these attempts to secure a financial competence outside the profession of letters. Addressing the Royal Literary Fund dinner in June 1859, Thackeray alluded to this fact: "I have no claim to appear before you as a representative of letters at all, except on this account, that for nearly a quarter of a century I have been a struggling literary man of no other profession than that, getting on as best I could."[10] Thackeray often referred to his publishers as liberal and fair, and he eventually found the public to be good. In fact, he made the public—not the reviewing public, but the book-buying public—into an article of faith for his profession when he wrote to William Aytoun asking that *Vanity Fair* be reviewed in *Blackwood's Magazine* and then retracting his request on the grounds that "puffs are good and the testimony of good men, but I don't think these will make a success for a man and he ought to stand as the public chooses to

---

[7]See below, chapter 3.

[8]Collins, *Profession,* p. 127. One might note, however, that Campbell has also been credited with the remark that Barabbas was a publisher (James Hepburn, *The Author's Empty Purse and the Rise of the Literary Agent* [London, 1968], p. 4).

[9]Collins, *Profession,* p. 127. It is perhaps ironic that Johnson, who is often credited with being the "first writer in English to depend truly on the literary marketplace," actually "depended heavily on a royal pension that rewarded him for some political work—work sinister enough to place Johnson's name not on the civil list but on the crown's secret service list" (R. Jackson Wilson, *Figures of Speech* [New York, 1989], p. 99).

[10]Lewis Melville, *William Makepeace Thackeray: A Biography Including Hitherto Uncollected Letters and Speeches and a Bibliography of 1,300 Items,* 2 vols. (London, 1910), 2:117.

put him" (*Letters* 2:267). All this points to a question, taken up in chapter 6, about the extent to which the writing was shaped or even determined by social and economic exigencies. Did the author bow to the "pressures of living" and compromise the Muse? One wonders if the question is legitimate, suggesting as it does that some writings might not be shaped by their social and economic milieus.

Thackeray's reputation has had its ups and downs, lagging behind, then surpassing, and lagging once again behind that of Charles Dickens, the other great professional writer of the mid-century. But no one questions his position as one of the foremost English novelists of the period. Are his achievements to be understood outside of A. S. Collins's lament that anyone should write for a living? Are we to understand Thackeray and Dickens, as Collins did Robert Southey, to be exceptions to a rule that assumes real literature is written for its own sake, not for bread? Thackeray would have denied there was such a rule; Dickens would more likely have believed that there was and that he himself might be an exception to it. The picture Collins drew ends in 1832, a great year for reform but a very bad year for literature. The next year Thackeray purchased and began editing the *National Standard,* an enterprise he undertook on the strength of an inheritance of approximately £17,000. A year later he had lost both periodical and inheritance.

Since the days of Pope and Johnson, who are often said to have begun the "profession of letters" in England, the prospects for making a living with the pen had increased dramatically. The nation of readers that Johnson referred to in the 1780s doubled and tripled again by the 1830s, and the cost of book production and taxes on paper were reduced. In consequence, the place for a profession of letters, for a viable means of getting a living by one's pen, existed in Victorian England as it never had before. On the other hand, the competition was far stiffer, with more writers than ever before vying for a place in the sun.[11] Furthermore, from the end of the eighteenth century can be traced the development of publishing as a profession separate from printing and bookselling; there was, therefore, a new breed of middlemen between the author and public to be supported by the increased literary trade.

---

[11]The editors of *The Wellesley Index of Periodicals* (ed. Walter E. Houghton and Esther Rhoads Houghton, 5 vols. [Toronto, 1966–89]), in the process of indexing just forty of the hundreds of Victorian periodicals, identified over 12,000 different contributors. An estimate of the total number of authors represented in nineteenth-century English periodicals must at least double that figure.

As James Hepburn has pointed out, however, the fault for the "author's empty purse" was not wholly to be laid at the feet of greedy publishers and booksellers. Many authors themselves had traditionally regarded writing as a hobby or a calling or an avocation and had regarded themselves as gentlemen if not actually guardians of the sacred flame above the ruck and rout of commercial life. There was little tradition of authors with a strong sense of the monetary value of the products of imagination. Copyrights had long been thought to be vested in the printed book—product of the endeavors of printers and booksellers—rather than in the imaginative content—product of the author's work. The lines between plagiarism and influence and borrowing have never been firmly established, as celebrated cases in our own century demonstrate, but they were especially loosely drawn in the gentlemanly circle of dabblers in literature, whose borrowings and influences suggested perhaps that a published work was in a sense fair game in the public domain. For good or ill, something of this notion of community property or gift to the world provided the most attractive models for the myth of "the author" with his mind and goals above petty merchandise. But the situation was much changed in actual fact and practice by 1832. The opportunity for petty skulduggery by printers, booksellers, and publishers—and, toward the later part of the century, by literary agents—abounded, of course, but so too did the opportunity for equitable professional dealings and mutually beneficial contracts and long-standing business relationships. The fact is there was a lot of money to be made in publishing, and one would need more than the fingers on two hands to count the Victorian authors, let alone publishers, who left estates in five figures earned entirely from writing.[12]

On the other hand, a longer list could be made of those authors who died in poverty or whose lot it fell to benefit from the temporary assistance of the Literary Fund. Fear of the wolf at the door was always present for professional writers—or at least such was the popular conception. Established in 1790 and renamed the Royal Literary Fund (RLF) in 1842 under the patronage of Prince Albert, it named among its beneficiaries Coleridge, Chateaubriand, Peacock, Leigh Hunt, and Richard Jefferies.[13] Among other applicants (whether successful or not, I do not know) were William Maginn, George Augustus Sala, William Carleton, the widow of Mark Lemon (*Punch* editor), and scores of others. But the idea that

[12]See Hepburn, *The Author's Empty Purse*, p. 96.
[13]Nigel Cross, *The Royal Literary Fund, 1790–1918* (London, 1984), p. 4.

literature was a viable means of livelihood is not belied by these instances, nor by the lamentable case of Gilbert à Beckett who died in 1856 leaving no estate and a wife and children with no means of support because he had failed to insure his life. The fact is à Beckett had one child in university and another in an expensive public school; he had achieved these things through writing (*Letters* 2:617).

The aspiring literary hack's struggle to fulfill the role of poet/priest or of heroic man of letters was dramatized in a literary controversy over how to best lend a helping hand to the writers of England without betraying the dignity of literature. Thackeray was at the center of the debate. He was toasted and responded in recorded speeches at the annual fund-raising dinners of the Royal Literary Fund in 1848, 1849, 1851, 1852, 1857, and 1859. In his response for 1851 he remarked in reference to the laudatory toast that "in my profession we get immense premiums, and amongst them is this one which has exhibited itself so nobly to-night, and for which I do feel most sincerely and proudly grateful." He went on to claim that the degraded and downtrodden author was a thing of the past:

> Literary men are not by any means, at this present time, the most unfortunate and most degraded set of people whom they are sometimes represented to be. . . . certain persons are constantly apt to bring forward or to believe in the existence, at this moment, of the miserable old literary hack of the time of George the Second, and bring him before us as the literary man of this day. I say that that disreputable old phantom ought to be hissed out of society. I don't believe in the literary man being obliged to resort to ignoble artifices and mean flatteries to get places at the tables of the great, and to enter into society upon sufferance. . . . As for pity being employed upon authors, especially in my branch of the profession, if you will but look at the novelists of the present day, I think you will see it is altogether out of the question to pity them. . . . Of course it is impossible for us to settle the mere prices by which the works of those who amuse the public are to be paid. I am perfectly aware that Signore Twankeydillo, of the Italian Opera, and Mademoiselle Petitpas of the Haymarket, will get a great deal more money in a week for the skilful exercise of their chest and toes than I, or you, or any gentleman here present, should be able to get by our brains and by weeks of hard labour. We cannot help these differences in payment; we know there must be high and low payments in our trade, as in all trades; that there must be gluts of the market and over-production; and there must be successful machinery, and rivals, and brilliant importations from foreign countries; that there must be hands out of employ, and

tribulation of workmen. But these ill-winds which afflict us blow fortunes to our successors. They are natural evils. It is the progress of the world, rather than any evil which we can remedy; and that is why I say this society acts most wisely and justly, in endeavouring to remedy, not the chronic distress, but the temporary evil; that it finds a man at the moment of the pinch of necessity, helps him a little, and gives him a "God-speed," and sends him on his way. For my own part, I have felt that necessity, and bent under that calamity; and it is because I have found friends who have nobly, with God's blessing, helped me at that moment of distress that I feel deeply interested in the ends of a Society which has for its object to help my brother in similar need.[14]

Though sentiments expressed on public occasions of ceremony might not be the most candid, Thackeray was expressing the side of an argument about the profession of letters that had been brewing for several years between himself and Charles Dickens. Thackeray pictured the author in a natural world beset by natural evils, fighting the same fight that other tradesmen fought, and like them capable of self-reliance and economic competence, though perhaps occasionally in need of a hand when things got especially rough. This view differed radically from that of Dickens and John Forster, who saw the temporary aid of the RLF to the absolutely destitute writer as too little too late. The official notice of purpose for the RLF states that it "is to assist authors and their families who are in distress. Before their needs can be considered, all applicants must have published work of approved literary merit (which may include contributions to periodical literature). . . . The Fund does not offer grants to writers who can earn a living in other ways; nor provide financial support for writing projects. It exists to sustain authors who have, for one reason or another, fallen on hard times—illness, family misfortune, or sheer loss of writing form; all of which can afflict an established author and deprive him/her of that peace of mind necessary for work."[15]

Dickens saw the abject poverty of many young or ill or old writers and the mind-cramping work of many literary hacks who under other circumstances might produce better work and concluded that the dignity of literature was dragged down. Thackeray, on the other hand, saw in literature a fair means of gaining a livelihood and in the pensions Dickens and Forster were proposing an admission that literature did not provide

---

[14]Melville, *Thackeray: A Biography* 2:71–75.

[15]Cross, *Royal Literary Fund*, p. 4.

the dignity of a living. To accept such a pension for writing was to lose the
dignity of honest effort and the rewards available in the marketplace. "I
have been earning my own bread with my pen for near twenty years now,"
Thackeray wrote to a French critic in 1854, "and sometimes very hardly
too, but in the worst time, please God, never lost my own respect" (*Letters*
3:390). That there was reason and justice on both sides seems clear, but the
verdict of history, so to speak, sided with the work of the RLF. The
Literary Guild established by Dickens was a star-crossed endeavor that
never succeeded, in part because its establishment was linked to a hostile
attack on the RLF and in part because its goals were far too ambitious for
its financial resources.

Thackeray's relations with his publishers have produced a small crop of
classic stories—some true, some apocryphal, like the tale of *Vanity Fair*
being rejected by five or six publishers before finally finding a home in the
Punch Office or the story his last publisher, George Smith, told of Thackeray entering his office from time to time with empty pockets pulled inside
out in a gesture of need. More significant episodes are made famous by the
scholarly controversies that have been waged over them. What, for example, were Thackeray's relations with William Maginn, the brilliant, hard-
drinking, easy-spending Irish editor of *Fraser's Magazine,* and when did
Thackeray actually start writing for *Fraser's*? What were the full reasons
for Thackeray's break with *Punch Magazine,* and why did he never again
publish in *Punch* after 1854? And what were Thackeray's relations with the
American reprinters of his books?

It is, in part, my aim to push beyond and to answer such questions.

Some of Thackeray's publishers' account books still exist, as do some
of the contracts for books both written and unwritten. And some of the
correspondence between Thackeray's publishers concerning the posthumous disposition of the copyrights survives. The production ledgers of
the Bradbury and Evans Company and the Smith, Elder Company survive with very few—and therefore very tantalizing—gaps. The Chapman
and Hall records seem to have been destroyed. But a large part of the
picture can be clearly seen.

For example, one can follow in the ledgers Thackeray's income from
his books. In 1847 he made £780 from books published by Bradbury and
Evans. In 1850 Bradbury and Evans paid him £1,200, but in 1852 he got
only £113 from that company. Combining with the account books what
can be determined from contracts and letters, it is clear, however, that 1852
was not a bad year for Thackeray. He earned an undeterminable amount

by lecturing that year (approximately £4,500 by Thackeray's own estimate); he got £1,200 from Smith, Elder for *Henry Esmond;* he received an undetermined amount from Smith for the publication of his lectures (probably about £95 on the first edition and £146 on the second edition, but perhaps not collected until 1853); and he got $1,000 from Harper and Brothers for the American publication of the lectures; Appleton and Company gave him £100 in December 1852 for an introduction to its pirated reprint series of his work; and Smith, Elder paid an advance of £200 for a book Thackeray never wrote. Total for 1852: somewhere between £1,700 and £5,000.

The ledgers also reveal print orders and the rate of sale for the books. It is interesting to watch *Vanity Fair,* which began in January 1847 with a print order of 5,000 copies for the first monthly number, take an early spurt to 6,000, and then drop back to 4,000 for numbers 7 through 11, and finally climb back to 5,000 for the last five numbers. That is not a great record, comparing pretty evenly with Robert Smith Surtees's *Mr. Sponge's Sporting Tour* three years later, which began at 4,000 copies, dropped to 3,500, and ended at 6,000, or with Charles Dickens's *Oliver Twist* in 1845–46, which began at just under 5,000 and fluctuated between 5,750 and 3,750. But *Vanity Fair* had staying power, and over the next twenty years there were continuous demands for reprints, so that by 1868, 10,500 copies of the first edition had been printed and sold. In 1853 a cheap edition of *Vanity Fair* was printed with an initial print order of 5,000 copies, and 22,000 had been printed and sold by 1865. Comparisons with Thackeray's other major books also reveal interesting facts. It took seven printings to produce the 10,500 copies of the first edition of *Vanity Fair.* It took five printings to produce the 9,500 copies of his next book, *Pendennis.* It took four printings to produce 14,000 copies of *The Newcomes,* and it took only one printing of the serialization in 1857–59 to produce 13,000 copies of *The Virginians,* about 700 of which remained unsold in 1865.

The ledgers are an invaluable source of bibliographical information, revealing previously unknown editions, the existence of tipped-in title pages for reissues of leftover stock, and a number of reprintings that have otherwise escaped notice. Furthermore, the ledgers reveal enough about the materials from which the books were made to reveal the production processes. They show pretty accurately for some of Thackeray's works just how the manuscript became a book and in what ways Thackeray was able to influence the process and in what ways the process influenced the texts. There is no need to resort to vague generalizations about production modes and assumed social contracts to determine the influence of social and economic forces on Thackeray's works. This is not to say that there are no unsolved mysteries, but there is more evidence extant than one might suspect regarding production.

In some ways, however, the most interesting documents concerning Thackeray's relations with his publishers are the contracts he signed with George Smith of Smith, Elder, and the correspondence between Smith and Thackeray's other publishers after the novelist's death in 1863. While Smith was rather careful, shrewd, and meticulous about his contractual dealings with authors, other of Thackeray's publishers were casual. Chapman and Hall had to admit that the firm did not have contracts relating to the copyrights it claimed to own, nor had it registered its titles in the Stationers' Hall. Bradbury and Evans had at least two contracts (only one survives) and had entered all but one title in the Stationers' Register, but casual arrangements were apparently common. Charles Lever remarked that only "great publishing people" require contracts.[16]

Thackeray's years as Smith's author, 1860–63, were the most lucrative of his life. Not only were his old copyrights finally producing a cumulative substantial annual income, his new contracts with Smith kept him close to the £500-per-month level. R. Jackson Wilson has remarked that in one way of looking at the profession of writing, authors produce words as commodities and publishers purchase them as goods.[17] This model might be of some use in understanding Thackeray's relation to Smith, who preferred, it seems, to pay high premiums for full (though usually temporary) use of the copyrights. And while one effect of Smith's contracts was to give the publisher total control of reprints and foreign rights and to relieve the company of any requirement to open its books to the author, another effect was to take care of all the "tawdry business deals" and to leave the writer well taken care of and with hands clean of trade. Thackeray seems to have sunk more or less comfortably into this romantic authorial role, but that is not the role he developed during the twenty-six years preceding his final adoption by Smith. With all Thackeray's other publishers, particularly after the publication of *Vanity Fair,* author and publisher were partners, together courting the favor of a mutual patron, the public.

In recent years it has become fashionable to reject the romantic image of the autonomous writer-genius and to acknowledge, instead, the deter-

---

[16]Quoted by John Sutherland, *Victorian Novelists and Publishers* (Chicago, 1976), p. 54.
[17]Wilson, *Figures of Speech,* p. 63.

mining confluence of social, economic, and ideological factors that used the writer to produce the commodities needed by the market. There is enough balderdash in the former and enough insight in the latter to account for the attractions of this fashion. The differences these two views offer of the relations among the writer, his work, and his society highlight the fact that historical reconstructions reflect the present ideologies of the historian as well as the evidence under review. The construct of Thackeray's business relations, the account of his attitude toward his profession, and the discussion of the nature of Thackeray's texts presented in this book must also demonstrate this aspect of historical writing. Insofar as I can be aware of the underlying predispositions of this work, then, I would warn the reader (in what must appear to be an old-fashioned authorial intrusion) that I reject the romantic view of the autonomous author and the fortuitous notions of artistic integrity it entails, because its support appears to me patently rhetorical rather than evidential. Likewise, I reject the social deterministic interpretation of the writer's function, because it tends to define too rigidly the influences on human acts by the limitations of social, economic, political, and indeed linguistic structures within which "creative" acts take place. If it is true that the writer is not free to do anything he or she likes, it seems to me also true that the writer is free within limits and may occasionally be subversive not just to the consciously imposed conventionalities of a society but to the very limits of determinism itself.

I retain sufficient respect for Thackeray's genius to prefer explanations of evidence that redound to his credit rather than indicate his weakness or helpless acquiescence to the pressures of convention. As Anthony Trollope once remarked, "I do not think that we yet know how great that man was."[18] On the other hand, I retain sufficient respect for rational thought to be suspicious of the hagiologist's stance. Thackeray indeed had weaknesses and acquiesced to the pressures to compromise, but he did not claim to be more than an ordinary mortal, just a gentleman who strove to tell the truth as he saw it. That many people of his own age and ours have chosen to see the truth otherwise would not upset or surprise him, for as he said at the RLF dinner in 1852, "Long after the present generation is dead,—of readers and authors of books,—there must be kindness and generosity, and folly and fidelity, and love, and heroism, and humbug, in all the world; and, as long as they last, my successors, or the successors of the novelists who come long after us, will have plenty to do, and plenty of

---

[18]Quoted in Cross, *Royal Literary Fund*, p. 21.

subjects to write upon."[19] Historians are such novelists, too, somewhat more determined but no less free to construct their narratives.

In this book I have tried to consider a large variety of aspects of Thackeray's professional career. While I began with a concern for contracts and ledger accounts of costs, profits, and circulation, I have tried to explore the personal and business relations between the author and his publishers. Furthermore, I have tried in the first chapter to follow the implications of these data to Thackeray's projections of authorship both in the cultivation of his own image and in his fiction. The next two chapters narrate the history of Thackeray's career as a professional writer, showing in detail the development of his writing persona and his changing relations with publishers. Chapter 4 explores the book market and shows how copyrights were worked through reissues, reprints, new editions, foreign rights, and translations. The fifth chapter represents, historically, the research foundation for this book. It traces the textual significance of production, an area so little known and so complex that its details can be suggested only through specific examples. Chapter 6 deals with the implications of the whole enterprise—the biographical, social, economic, and production complex—to textual questions. What is the text; which is the text; how can it be read; how can it be edited? Chapter 7 shows how Thackeray revealed in his prefaces his own conflicting roles of author and writer, trying both to "tell the truth" and to sell goods. Appendix A provides transcripts of all extant contracts for Thackeray's books, and Appendix B provides a checklist and census of locations for Thackeray imprints though 1865. Appendixes C, D, and E provide supporting details for the arguments of chapter 5.

This book began as a description of the Bradbury and Evans publishing-house ledgers as they related to the bibliographical description of Thackeray's works. It developed into a narrative of the relations between Thackeray and his publishers. And it became, finally, an analysis of Thackeray as a professional writer and a discussion of how the trade of book publishing impinged on the writer and how that might affect our approaches as readers and editors to Thackeray's texts. It is intended as a contribution to the study of authorship, described by Robert Patten, that integrates "theory, history, biography, and sociology with an understanding of how a literary text is created, published, and marketed and how its utterance might be shaped by the cultural conditions of its creation."[20]

---

[19]Melville, *Thackeray: A Biography* 2:78.

[20]Robert Patten, review of Nigel Cross's *The Common Writer in Review* 9 (1987): 4.

I

The Man of Business

AMONG THE professional Victorian writers who made a living, or even a fortune, from writing without the aid of outside sources of income, there were a fair number who were incompetent businessmen. Of those who made a fortune, Thackeray probably has the reputation of being the least businesslike. He is known as a lucky, careless genius, a lazy giant with great powers and equal weaknesses. Although he squandered a considerable part of his £17,000 inheritance through a weakness for gambling and in two ill-fated investments in periodicals, the *Constitutional* and the *National Standard,* the loss that threw him absolutely upon the resources of his pen appears to have been a bank failure in India—no fault of his own. Having struggled back to fiscal competence from his initial ruin, he invested £500 in the railroad mania in which he lost again in the general collapse of 1845. The success of *Vanity Fair* made his life easier but did not restore his lost fortunes. His lecture tours in America netted approximately £5,000, which Thackeray invested in American railroads and sold out during the Civil War for only £3,895 (*Letters* 3:275). Nevertheless, he left his daughters an estate nearly equaling the £10,000 apiece that he repeatedly said was his goal.

Explaining the differences between Thackeray and Dickens as professional writers, Anthony Trollope—certainly one of the most businessmanlike of authors—wrote:

> The one was steadfast, industrious, full of purpose, never doubting of himself, always putting his best foot foremost and standing firmly on it when he got there; with no inward trepidation, with no moments in which he was half inclined to think that this race was not for his winning, this goal not to be reached by his struggles. The sympathy of friends was good to him, but he could have done without it. The good opinion which he had of himself was never shaken by adverse criticism; and the criticism on the other side, by which it was exalted, came from the enumeration of the number of copies sold. He was a firm reliant man, very little prone to change, who, when he had discovered the nature of his own talent, knew how to do the very best with it. It may almost be said that Thackeray was the very opposite of this.

Unsteadfast, idle, changeable of purpose, aware of his intellect but not trusting it, no man ever failed more generally than he to put his best foot foremost. Full as his works are of pathos, full of humour, full of love and charity, tending, as they always do, to truth and honour and manly worth and womanly modesty, excelling, as they seem to me to do, most other written precepts that I know, they always seem to lack something that might have been there. There is a touch of vagueness which indicates that his pen was not firm while he was using it. He seems to me to have been dreaming ever of some high flight, and then to have told himself, with a half-broken heart, that it was beyond his power to soar up into those bright regions. I can fancy as the sheets went from him every day he told himself, in regard to every sheet, that it was a failure. Dickens was quite sure of his sheets.[1]

It is not quite clear if Trollope was aware of the potential double meaning of that last assertion, but Thackeray was. In any case, this passage is the sort of realistic fiction for which Trollope is justly famous. But though it is misleading, if not an outright falsehood, Trollope's Thackeray has stuck in the popular mind. The image Trollope evoked corresponds generally with the one promoted by Thackeray himself in such things as his vignette drawing of a printer's devil waiting at the door to carry his manuscripts to a presumably impatient printer and by stories like the one James T. Fields told of Thackeray coming to one of his own dinner parties well over an hour late with ink on his fingers announcing the completion of the last sheet of *The Virginians*.[2]

It is indisputable that Thackeray produced much of his work under the pressure of deadlines. That need not mean he was lazy. John Sutherland has argued that Thackeray may even have written better under pressure than at leisure.[3] Thackeray spoke often in his letters of living, eating, drinking his novels to the exclusion almost of his own daily life. He relished the creative pressure induced by deadlines, though he also knew the pace would wear him out. It has been altogether too easy to overplay Thackeray in the role of procrastinator, the would-be gentleman of leisure, and to lose sight of the facts concerning Thackeray the businessman and professional writer. This part of the picture can be filled out from two other sources: his comments in his fiction on the craft of writing and the facts of his relations with his publishers revealed in letters, contracts and publishers' account books.

---

[1]Anthony Trollope, *Thackeray* (London, 1879), pp. 19–20.

[2]James T. Fields, *Yesterdays with Authors* (1871; rpt. Boston, 1925), pp. 17–18.

[3]John Sutherland, *Thackeray at Work* (London, 1974).

A key episode in establishing the image of Thackeray's view of his profession, its rank, rights, and responsibilities, took place in 1850. Thackeray brought the wrath of John Forster upon his head when, in *Pendennis,* he had George Warrington remark to Pen on their way home from a dreary publisher's party, "And now that you have seen the men of letters, tell me, was I far wrong in saying there are thousands of people in this town, who don't write books, who are, to the full, as clever and intellectual as people who do?" Thackeray went on in the voice of his narrator, "And it may be whispered to those uninitiated people who are anxious to know the habits and make the acquaintance of men of letters, that there are no race of people who talk about books, or perhaps, who read books, so little as literary men" (1:346).

Forster's objection, printed in the *Examiner* for 5 January 1850, was directed against Thackeray for disparaging literary men as a whole by presenting the Shandons, Waggs, and Bunions of the party as representative of all literary men and women. Forster attributed Thackeray's "attack" to a desire to curry favor with the nonliterary classes. In defending himself, Thackeray gave one view of the professional writer. He claimed never to have "been ashamed of his profession, or (except for its dulness) of any single line from his pen." He considered the charge that he was currying favor among the nonliterary classes absurd, since in his experience people honored writers, and he would gain nothing through the supposed stratagem of which he was accused. Finally, he defended his portrait of the literary world on the grounds that it was true. Why, he asked, "are these things not to be described . . . if such exist, or have existed, they are as good subjects for comedy as men of other callings" (*Letters* 2:630, 634). Forster would not let the subject alone, showing himself totally unmoved by Thackeray's explanations. He distinguished between identifying humbug in a profession and identifying humbug with a profession. Here the public debate lapsed into silence without a winner. It is quite likely that Forster was predisposed to pick a fight with Thackeray over this issue because of a long-standing and fundamental difference between them, friends though they had been, concerning the status of professional writers and their role and responsibility in society. Forster and Dickens, as has been suggested by Craig Howes, represented the author in a romantic light, as a dignified, inspired artist. The author's role, according to this view, was that of inspirer and castigator—as social conscience for the betterment of society.[4] Michael Lund has cited various nineteenth-

---

[4]Craig Howes, "*Pendennis* and the Controversy on the 'Dignity of Literature,'" *Nineteenth Century Literature* 41 (Dec. 1986): 269–98.

century versions of this view suggesting that authorship is not work like other trades or professions but rather a gift or inspired avocation.[5] Thackeray, on the other hand, had long been speaking and writing from a different perspective, emphasizing the trade relations, admitting the work involved, and making fun of pretentious writing and pretentious writers. Thus, the controversy over the dignity of literature boils down to one side trying to uphold an ideal and a social responsibility (which they see as doing good) and the other side trying to be honest and unpretentious (which they see as being true). The object of fiction for the one is to change society; for the other, to understand it. There is no resolution for such a controversy.

Privately, in a letter to his friend Abraham Heyward, Thackeray admitted, however: "The words in Pendennis are untenable be hanged to them: but they were meant to apply to a particular class of literary men, my class who are the most ignorant men under the Sun, myself included I mean. But I wrote so carelessly that it appears as if I would speak of all, and even if it were true I ought never to have written what I did" (*Letters* 2:636). Yet this apology expresses regret for having written carelessly, not for having thought the thought. Thackeray did not change his mind about writers; rather, he was sorry to have stirred up this particularly fruitless controversy.

In the novel Pendennis goes on to become a successful novelist, serving first a sort of apprenticeship writing reviews. He later becomes the author of Thackeray's *The Newcomes,* in which he gives the following description of the profession of authorship:

> *The drawbacks and penalties attendant upon our profession are taken into full account, as we well know, by literary men, and their friends. Our poverty, hardships, and disappointments are set forth with great emphasis, and often with too great truth by those who speak of us; but there are advantages belonging to our trade which are passed over, I think by some of those who exercise it, and for which, in striking the balance of our accounts, we are not always duly thankful. We have no patron, so to speak—we sit in ante-chambers no more, waiting the present of a few guineas from my lord; in return for a fulsome dedication. We sell our wares to the book purveyor, between whom and us there is no greater obligation than between him and his paper-maker or printer. In the great*

---

[5]Michael Lund, "Novels, Writers, and Readers in 1850," *Victorian Periodicals Review* 17 (Spring-Summer 1984): 15–28.

towns in our country, immense stores of books are provided for us, with librarians to class them, kind attendants to wait upon us, and comfortable appliances to study. We require scarce any capital wherewith to exercise our trade. What other so called learned profession is equally fortunate? A doctor, for example, after carefully and expensively educating himself, must invest in house and furniture, horses, carriage, and men-servants, before the public patient will think of calling him in. I am told that such gentlemen have to coax and wheedle dowagers, to humour hypochondriacs, to practise a score of little subsidiary arts in order to make that of healing profitable. How many many hundreds of pounds has a barrister to sink upon his stock in trade before his returns are available? There are the costly charges of university education—the costly chambers in the Inn of court—certain expenses all to be defrayed before the possible client makes his appearance, and the chance of fame or competency arrives. The prizes are great, to be sure, in the law, but what a prodigious sum the lottery ticket costs! If a man of letters cannot win, neither does he risk so much. Let us speak of our trade as we find it, and not be too eager in calling out for public compassion.[6]

This description of the author's life and work emphasizes one aspect at the expense of others. Pendennis, as the narrator of *The Newcomes,* has constantly to remind himself not to think in inflated terms about authorship. This litany of the trade relations and modest requirements reveals that authorship is open to one and all who care to risk the chance of publication. Elsewhere, Thackeray emphasized other requirements, most notably the need to develop, through extensive reading, a sense of history. The comparison with the professions of medicine and law both elevate and deflate the picture being presented. It is not so difficult nor so lucrative as those relatively bourgeois professions; but if it is like a trade involving paper sellers, printers, and booksellers, it yet also has freedoms and responsibilities unlike those trades which made it nonetheless a profession. Among those responsibilities Thackeray included the moral one of avoiding inflated language and slipshod moral implications—the two main butts of his humorous attacks in *Novels by Eminent Hands.*[7]

Like Thackeray's celebrated redefinitions of *snob* and *gentleman,* his view of the professional writer as tradesman is a double one reconciling in itself traditionally opposing views. Just as a middle-class or poor gentle-

---

[6] *The Newcomes,* 2 vols. (London: Bradbury and Evans, 1854–55), 1:321–22.

[7] Also known as *Punch's Prize Novelists* and first published in *Punch* 22–23 (1847).

man seemed a contradiction in Regency terms, so too the poet as tradesman seemed contradictory in romantic terms. Both Dickens and Forster
remonstrated with Thackeray for his failure to hold high enough the
dignity of the profession—their arguments smacking of conventional
notions of the smudge of trade. There is a tawdry irony in the notion of
Dickens and Forster, both with tradesman connections in their back-
grounds, and particularly Forster, who besides writing was a paid em-
ployee of a publisher, objecting to Thackeray's portraits of writers as
tradesmen. But Thackeray's view cuts through the pomposity and cant
about the dignity of literature to the heart of the ideals of his profession—
to love and truth,[8] upholding the ideals without losing sight of the
mundane business facts of authors writing for money, relying on and
being relied upon in turn by publishers in much the same way that the
printers and the paper sellers rely on one another in the business transactions that make books and periodicals. To admit that the author is one in a
line of necessary manufacturers and purveyors of literature that includes
the publisher, printer, stationer, and bookstall vendor is to pursue truth
where there seems to be nothing to gain except the miserable satisfaction
of knowing it. In fact, however, that view is subversive to establishment
conventions—a fact that goes a long way toward explaining the disagreement between Forster and Thackeray. Of course, this truth is not the
whole truth any more than is that other much better known image
Thackeray created of the novelist as the preacher in cap and bells.[9] That is
to say, Thackeray was not just an exposer of sham, nor was he just a
satirist.

Thackeray's double view of the word trade as it applied, without
shame, to his own profession, is reminiscent of his similar treatment of
trade in *Vanity Fair* where poor Dobbin in school is the butt of all the jokes
because his father, a grocer, pays his bill in goods. Dobbin gains respect by
beating Cuff in a fight, but the narrator notes that the lordly little George
Osborne's grandfather was a tradesman too. Dobbin's father becomes a
respected alderman albeit none too refined a man, and Dobbin is unques-

---

[8]It is customary to assume that the Victorians adopted a certain stance when using the phrase
"love and truth" and that in their minds they generally capitalized the words and thought of
absolute ideals. Although it would be hard to argue that Thackeray clearly articulated to
himself the idea that truth and love were merely pragmatic relative concepts, he was keenly
aware that most talk about them was cant. His own assertions of an unsophisticated
allegiance to them as ideals probably did no more than claim to reject hypocrisy.

[9]See Gordon N. Ray, "*Vanity Fair:* One Version of the Novelist's Responsibility," *Essays by
Divers Hands* 25 (1950): 87–101.

tionably the real gentleman of the book. If authorship and publishing have the taint of trade, they also can have the honor of trade. And where there is honor, there is the risk of dishonor. The ideals of the profession could be traduced not only by inflated rhetoric but by dishonest shows of learning or of sentiment. In an early review Thackeray complained of writers who sugared their instructions in manners and morals and academic subjects by putting them into fiction, but at the same time he firmly believed in the novelist's responsibility, even in the guise of a clown's cap and bells, to instruct—not with moral platitudes, of course, but with the lessons inherent in what he thought was unvarnished truth.[10] To the editor of *Punch*, Mark Lemon, he wrote on concluding the "Snobs of England": "A few years ago I should have sneered at the idea of setting up as a teacher at all, and perhaps at this pompous and pious way of talking about a few papers of jokes in Punch—but I have got to believe in the business, and in many other things since then. And our Profession seems to me to be as serious as the Parson's own" (*Letters* 2:282).

One need not agree with Trollope that the vagueness or ambivalence in Thackeray's work reveals lack of commitment or conviction or strength. What some of his contemporaries thought of as a feigned "want of earnestness," an "undervaluing of his art," a carelessness about details, plain ineptitude, or tired repetitions in narrative structures may better be understood as the deliberate manifestations of a cast of mind that rejected, or at least suspected, the values represented by earnestness and narrative order. Thackeray's narrative technique undermines surface realism and the sense of certitude and stable values implied by authorial omniscience. I think it likely that Thackeray deliberately undermined such values because he did not believe in them, because he thought the danger lay in overvaluing art. Thackeray saw more clearly than most of his contemporaries the problems of trying to create or capture "reality" in "fiction," and he knew more clearly than many a historian of his day that the coherence created by the orderly arrangement of historical data, commonly taken for "truth" in "history," is an illusion. Jack Rawlins has recognized and described in some detail Thackeray's habit of undercutting the fictional realities he had created, but Rawlins seems not to have understood the implication of the narrative strategy, deploring Thackeray's refusal to adopt the novelist's

---

[10]"If we want instruction, we prefer to take it from fact rather than fiction" (Thackeray, "Lever's *St. Patrick's Eve*—Comic Politics," *Morning Chronicle,* 3 April 1845, rpt. in *Thackeray: Contributions to the* Morning Chronicle, ed. Gordon N. Ray [Urbana, Ill., 1966], p. 71).

responsibility to impose a moral order beneficial to society.[11] In this regard Rawlins agreed with Forster.

From time to time scholars, noting the "lapses" in Thackeray's "artistic values," explain them as carelessness or as the inevitable, though lamentable, results of a hectic mode of production. John Sutherland, in *Victorian Authors and Publishers,* and N. N. Feltes, in *Modes of Production of Victorian Novels,* have turned this argument on its head as a means of praising *Henry Esmond,* which was produced under circumstances different from those attending any other Thackeray work; it is the only novel Thackeray finished before it was published. However, the very same kinds of disruptions of realism occur throughout that book, as a multitude of readers have noted, particularly Elaine Scarry.[12]

John Sutherland has remarked that "the mode of production confirmed in Thackeray a kind of narrative opportunism. One always feels that he has reserved the right to switch the course of his narrative whenever and however it suits him. He alludes jokingly to the arbitrariness of his power over plot in the preface: 'Perhaps the lovers of "excitement" may care to know that this book began with a very precise plan, which was entirely put aside. Ladies and gentlemen, you were to have been treated and the writer's and publisher's pocket benefited, by the recital of the most active horrors. . . . Nay, up to nine o'clock this very morning, my poor friend, Colonel Altamont, was doomed to execution, and the author only relented when his victim was actually at the window.' "[13]

Sutherland opined that this was "high-spirited nonsense" and the "element of truth" about Thackeray's work was the lamentable one of "narrative opportunism." That particular interpretation is apparent only to persons committed to the tradition of English fiction adhering to Jamesian inevitability, to Trollope's insistence on the novelist's right (and need?) to be able to adjust the beginning to the end, to a Joycean refining of the author out of existence. But it is not "nonsense," high-spirited or otherwise, to anyone willing to face the possibility that these "lapses" (they seem rather too frequent and to come in too strategic locations to be lapses) are, if not deliberate, at least characteristic gestures reflecting a point of view about history, fiction, and reality that is controlled by a value system rejecting the Jamesian striving for realism precisely because realism is a contrived illusion.

[11]Jack Rawlins, *Thackeray's Novels: A Fiction That Is True* (Berkeley, Calif., 1974).

[12]See below, chapter 6, on the editorial implications of the book production process.

[13]Sutherland, *Victorian Novelists and Publishers,* p. 103. Sutherland's quotation is from the preface to *Pendennis.*

The particular example of "opportunism" in question is from *Pendennis*. It illustrates the carefully planned contrivance of this illusion, for the "communicating leads" and window box that make Altamont's escape possible were first planted, so to speak, 330 pages earlier (2:38) and had already been used (2:260–61) by Colonel Strong to escape a bailiff. No reader finding Altamont cornered in the same apartments could be surprised by the escape. To accuse Thackeray of opportunism—that is, to take seriously his remark about relenting at the last moment—is both to underestimate the control he had over his materials and to misunderstand his deliberate exposure of the illusion of reality in order to make his point.

For Thackeray, fiction was fun, and the illusion of reality was fascinating. All his sympathies were on Dobbin's side, for example, when on a school half-holiday the boy sits under a tree, carried away by a book into the world of the Arabian Nights. But he continually insisted that that world was not real; reality obtrudes for the reader of Thackeray's fiction in the form of his "lapses" just as surely as it did for Dobbin when the altercation between Cuff and George Osborne broke in on his fictive Arabian world. Thackeray addresses the reader, laughs in his sleeve, imagines Jones yawning over the number, and "reserves the right to switch the course of his narrative whenever and however it suits him" because, much as he likes creating the illusion of reality, he likes more reminding his readers that in actuality he, Thackeray, is telling the reader, sitting in a chair, a story. That is realism with a significant philosophical point: that the author, like the reader, is subject to human limitations of knowledge and judgment. Authors may have a keen view of human foibles but are no better at prescribing for the world than any other reader. Thackeray refused to set himself up to be the hero as man of letters. And for all that, paradoxically, there is more of truth in his sheets than in the pages of many a self-proclaimed regenerator of the age.

Thackeray's realism is one that his contemporaries and, it seems, many later generations of Thackeray's readers have been unprepared to see or accept. Thackeray must have known that, for he introduced his disruptions of fictive realism gently; they can be dismissed as "lapses" or the eccentricities of genius. Perhaps it has been too easy for readers to miss the implications. Thackeray's sardonic view of aristocratic airs, his tracing of meanness and snobbery from top to bottom of the social scale, his "failure" to produce a moral framework within which the indeterminacies can come to moral closure have variously been explained as gentlemanly detachment, as declining to be the moral enthusiast, or as a weakness of spirit or lack of moral fiber. Among Thackeray's most enthusiastic fans, these matters have been, at worst, irritations to be ignored. Thackeray was, to my mind, deliberate and committed in this fundamental point from his early writings throughout his life. But he was not prepared to make the point at the expense of his livelihood or the fortune he intended to make and leave for his daughters. He was very much aware of the commercial exigencies of novel writing, and it was not his aim to disrupt profits by focusing attention on his private beliefs and values. But there was good and ample reason for him to introduce into his fiction those elements that so irritated John Forster and Charles Dickens and that apparently disappointed Trollope and John Sutherland. In such passages as the one in *Philip* where Thackeray discussed the amount of money the paragraph he was writing would earn him or the closing of *Vanity Fair* where the emphasis falls so heavily on the show and contrivance that his puppets "really are," he reminded his readers that the illusion of realism is created in the reality of storytelling. The neat wrapping up of loose ends where villains are punished and heroes vindicated and rewarded, Thackeray knew, is an illusion. Reality is ambiguous and indeterminate. The true realist does not know enough to pass out poetic justice justly. So Thackeray reminds his readers constantly and truthfully that the puppet show is not real. He forces an ultimate realism upon his readers by denying the possibility of honest satisfaction in fictive endings. To him, the truth about the world included the truth about writing fiction for a living.

Thackeray's methods expose the sham realism in which the author pretends to know not only what his characters think and do but by what moral standards characters should be measured. Thackeray's tentativeness, his apparently cynical view of good, and his supposedly infirm or sentimental stance on evil resulted, I believe, from honesty, humility, and simple acknowledgment of the true limits of authorial knowledge.

Henry Dodd Worthington's description of his father in James Gould Cozzens's *Morning Noon and Night* suggests something of what I am trying to identify in Thackeray's character.

> *Then there was that manner of his. You could not say it was shy, but you felt some lack of self-assertion, by most people associated with weakness, infirmity of purpose. . . . What these were plain signs of I can now see. They were signs of deep and thorough skepticism. That I then didn't see it wasn't, I think, just boyish imperceptiveness, I would guess that few people saw it, that few people ever thought of him as skeptical. What people expect from a skeptic is skepticism in its commoner loud, assertive form of scorning, challenging, contemptuously rejecting. This kind of skepticism will often be superficial, professings of men who basically are cynics, men of shallow thinking and loose feeling. My*

father's kind of skepticism made no show. It worked as a sort of silent patient withholding of judgment, almost as though his mild steady distrust of all appearances or supposed certainties went so far that when he felt serious doubts about anything those very doubts had to be held open to doubt.[14]

To many of his contemporaries, Trollope and Carlyle particularly, Thackeray was a weak man, indecisive, lacking positive force. I believe they mistook his distrust of certainty.

The other extreme response to Thackeray, typified by Charlotte Brontë's remarks in the dedication of the second edition of *Jane Eyre,* calling Thackeray "the first regenerator of the day" who resembled Henry Fielding "as an eagle doth a vulture," is a corrective that goes too far. Reacting to Thackeray's bold cutting through the cant and hypocrisy of the upper middle class, Brontë and other admirers tended to see in him a prophet whose attack on conventional values established an alternative foundation of values enshrining duty, loyalty, humility, and social responsibility. When upon meeting him Brontë discovered that Thackeray was no Carlyle, her disappointment arose from a misunderstanding not far removed from Trollope's. Alike, they failed to recognize and admire the profound honesty of Thackeray's aversion to overconfident assertions of values. Intense assertion of values was a common Victorian stance, but it was not Thackeray's.

Thackeray's respect for the "uncertainty principle," the humility with which he declined to be sure, is, of course, not peculiar to him, though it was a rare enough position in Victorian England. The position has had its influential manifestations, notably following periods of rigid or excessive authoritarianism. It played roles in the decline of the Spanish Inquisition and the rejection of Puritan rigidity following the excess of the Salem witch trials. But it can be seen also in the tremendous variety of human foibles tolerated without authorial condemnation in Shakespeare and in the attitudes revealed in Fielding's *Tom Jones,* Sterne's *Tristram Shandy,* and Keats's *Odes*—all hesitating to judge too finely or too finally and, consequently, all creating problems for earnest moralists. In Thackeray's case it is particularly necessary to distinguish, also, between a mere dislike of rigidity or discipline (which he indeed had) and a deeply felt suspicion of certitude (which I think he also had). The former results from an irritable or sensitive personality, the latter from a philosophical position.[15]

---

[14]James Gould Cozzens, *Morning Noon and Night* (New York, 1968), p. 287.

[15]In recent years, Robert Colby has described at least one source for that position, which he

In his own day Thackeray's satiric view of the romantic ideals of his profession made him appear weak, ambivalent, his own worst enemy. And that view, with a hefty boost from Trollope, has carried over into the image of Thackeray as an undisciplined craftsman, leading more than one critic to characterize him as a "careless putter forth" or hasty or even lazy improviser.[16] And this unflattering view extends to the image of Thackeray the businessman or, as he implied with characteristic deflation, tradesman.

The word *tradesman* in Victorian England denoted, as it still to some extent does, an outlook and a rank in life that were incompatible with imagination and beauty, which were central to the concept of artist, poet, or even novelist. One equates tradesman in Victorian England with Mr. Pumblechook in *Great Expectations* and Mr. Polly in H. G. Wells's *History of Mr. Polly* or, on a higher economic—though not sensibility—scale, Mr. Freeman in John Fowles's *French Lieutenant's Woman,* whose industrial and commercial sensibilities are impervious to art. But Thackeray was a practical man who had learned, from more than one penniless crisis, the reality of writing for money. That reality was a fact to be honestly acknowledged. If authorship had certain high ideals, it included, on the other hand, the mundane practical details of the trade of writing. By using the loaded word *trade* for the artist, Thackeray undercut both the social snobbery and the mystical trappings of *artist,* which some writers cultivated.

The social snobbery probably was an unconscious outgrowth, rather than a desired aim, of earlier proponents of the mystical view. The Victorian version of that view derived at least in part from the notions of poet or artist promulgated by Wordsworth in the preface to *Lyrical Ballads,* where the poet's sensibilities above the common run of men is claimed, and by Shelley's "Defense of Poesie," where the poet's position as an unacknowledged legislator of the world is proclaimed. But perhaps the strongest impetus to view the writer's calling in a special light with special capabilities and privileges was Thomas Carlyle's portrayal of the "Man of Letters" in *On Heroes, Hero Worship, and the Heroic in History.* Thackeray's early send-ups of Dr. Lardner and Sir Edward Bulwer Lytton as pompous

---

calls eclecticism, in the French philosopher Victor Cousin (*Thackeray's Canvass of Humanity* [Columbus, Ohio, 1979], pp. 18–53). Catherine Peters, too, in her perceptive and appreciative discussion of *Vanity Fair,* explores Thackeray's detached, suspended judgment as a strength (*Thackeray's Universe* [London, 1987], pp. 143–70).

[16] The phrase comes from George Saintsbury's Introduction to *Pendennis* (London: Oxford Univ. Press, [1908]), in which he also called Thackeray a shrewd reviser.

snobs playing off their roles as artists in social settings is an indication of his suspicion of the role. As a practicing writer, he turned to the trade rather than the calling in order to deflate the aggrandized view.

Thackeray became, in fact, an able and a reliable businessman who expected publishers and illustrators to fulfill their commitments with equal promptness. To his publishers, Bradbury and Evans, Thackeray wrote in May 1854 to complain of Richard Doyle, the illustrator Thackeray himself had chosen for *The Newcomes:* "However much I may regard Doyle as a friend it is clear that as men of business we cannot allow our property to suffer by his continual procrastination. The original agreement with Doyle, made between Bradbury myself & him was that the blocks & plates for the ensuing month should always be supplied by Doyle on the 15th of the month current. I have now written to him, to say that I shall hold him to his agreement & that if by the 15 June the plates & blocks of No 10 of the Newcomes are not in your hands I shall employ another designer" (NLS). It would have been the height of arrogance and insensitivity for Trollope's Thackeray to require promptness and commitment from another man—holding Doyle to standards too rigid for himself. But Trollope's Thackeray was a fiction. The real Thackeray was a reliable professional masked by a public image. The popular concept of a harried Thackeray dashing off the last lines of the monthly number for the printer just in the nick of time is a romantic misunderstanding of serial publication.

In thirty years of professional writing, Thackeray failed to meet only three deadlines that seriously affected a publisher. Only one of these commitments lay within his power to fulfill. The October 1844 installment of *Barry Lyndon* was delayed one month for lack of copy, and even then there were mitigating circumstances. He mailed off the October installment on 23 September from Smyrna while on his Eastern tour (recounted in *From Cornhill to Grand Cairo*), and it arrived too late in London for the October number of the magazine. He finished the book on 3 November.[17] In September 1848 he become so ill he had to suspend the writing and publishing of the monthly numbers of *Pendennis* for three months, and in August 1859 he was too ill to write a complete final double number for *The Virginians,* providing instead a one-part number 23 and a one-part final number in September.

Thackeray's sense of the business requirements of authorship was hard won. Though he had earned his livelihood by journalism for ten years

---

[17]Ray, *Adversity,* p. 343; *Letters* 2:153–54, 156.

when he began *Vanity Fair,* he was in 1846 still very much a petitioner appealing to the largess of the proprietors of *Punch* and other publishers, and he was dependent on their valuation of the goods he brought for sale. But by 1854 the author of *The Newcomes* saw himself as coproprietor with the publisher. The change is dramatic, and the composition, production, and financial success of *Vanity Fair* mark the watershed of Thackeray's career as a businessman, transforming him from the investor/gambler, the writer waiting upon publishers with his goods, into the propertied tradesman who built himself a debt-free mansion at 2 Palace Green, Kensington.

Five chapters of *Vanity Fair* were written by early spring 1846. Thackeray announced to his mother that serial publication would begin on 1 May, and in March or April the first five chapters were set in type.[18] Production problems immediately became apparent: when the corrected galleys were paged, it was discovered that the fourth chapter reached page 28 and the fifth chapter extended to the middle of page 35. Serial publication, however, required exactly thirty-two pages, no more and no less. The first of May passed with no publication. The type for chapters 1–5 was knocked down and redistributed to the typecases, while Thackeray eked out his living with "The Snobs of England" and "Novels by Eminent Hands"—contributions to *Punch* lasting beyond the publication of the revised initial number of *Vanity Fair* in January 1847.

What Thackeray learned during the eight-month delay in the publication of *Vanity Fair* can only be surmised from the regularity of his serial numbers from 1 January 1847 to the end of his life (except in the fall of 1848 and August 1859 when illness, not lassitude, prevented the professional fulfillment of his commitments to the public). The process he worked out was fairly simple but has only recently been understood by scholars. Except when he wrote *The Newcomes,* a few numbers of *Philip,* and *Denis Duval,* Thackeray never completed a monthly installment before the month it was due at the print shop. His contract for *Vanity Fair*—written and signed, curiously enough, on 25 January 1847 as the second installment was being printed—specifies that he was to submit copy by the fifteenth of each month. According to his letters, however, often on about the twenty-fifth of the month he would write that he had "just ended his number." Such statements, along with his frequent self-accusations of

---

[18]The manuscript with imbedded fragments of proofs from the first typesetting is in the Pierpont Morgan Library. The discovery of the nature of those proof fragments was first revealed in the *Thackeray Newsletter,* nos. 6 and 7 (1977), and expanded in the Textual Introduction to my edition of *Vanity Fair* (New York: Garland, 1989).

procrastination and the picture of the sleeping printer's devil waiting at the door, combine to give the superficial and false impression of a writer who could not meet his contracted deadlines. In fact, the process was a smooth, if hectic, coordination of writing, typesetting, proofreading, correcting, and printing responsibilities.

The reason Thackeray "ended" his numbers on the twenty-fifth or so is that serial publication does not lend itself to the submission of a finished manuscript on the fifteenth. The first time Thackeray tried that, his installment would have occupied either twenty-eight or thirty-five pages had it been published. Instead, he would submit about three-quarters of an installment to the printer—probably by the twentieth or earlier—to be set in type. With as many as five compositors working on a single installment (their names are on the manuscripts), typesetting twenty to thirty pages could be completed in a day or less. The printer's devil would then carry proofs to Thackeray, who corrected them and measured them with a string corresponding in length to a page of the printed book.[19] Arriving at a fairly accurate estimate of the amount of text still required to fill the number, he would revise and augment or cut as necessary. A printer's boy or the mails would then return the corrected and augmented proof to the printshop. Second proofs with page headings and page numbers embedded would be ready in another day or so, making it possible for Thackeray to read proofs and make final adjustments in length by the twenty-fifth or twenty-sixth of the month. The printers and binders then usually had about five days to get an installment ready for distribution by the last day of the month.

This coordination of production effort lends itself to the concept of writing as a trade. The artist's fancy is not free; the grinding schedule of production curtailed the craftsman's time and forced his energies in ways which Thackeray is on record as both appreciating and lamenting. The conditions of serial novel writing were not very different from newspaper journalism or the scheduled inches of letterpress Thackeray was responsible for in *Punch*. Novel writers of Thackeray's standing today may have a fellowship or an advance from the publisher and a full year or eighteen months to write the novel. Not so Thackeray. Yet the pressure was

---

[19]Thackeray explained the measurement in a letter to Doyle, 5 June 1854, *Letters* 3:372. Alternatively, Thackeray could have counted words as is indicated in his October 1854 letter to Mark Lemon explaining why he would no longer work for *Punch* at the new rates they proposed, "A page of Newcomes contains 47 lines of 56 letters = 2612 letters. 4 pages = 10448" (photocopy supplied by William Baker).

invigorating; he lived, talked, ate, slept his fiction up until deadline time. Thackeray's enthusiasm for the invigorating aspect of the engines of journalism shows in George Warrington's praises of it in *Pendennis:*

[1:308]   *There she is—the great engine—she never sleeps. She has her ambas-
sadors in every quarter of the world—her couriers upon every road. Her
officers march along with armies, and her envoys walk into statesmen's
cabinets. They are ubiquitous. Yonder journal has an agent, at this
minute, giving bribes at Madrid; and another inspecting the price of
potatoes in Covent Garden. Look! here comes the Foreign Express
galloping in. They will be able to give news to Downing Street tomorrow: funds will rise or fall, fortunes be made or lost; Lord B. will get
up, and, holding the paper in his hand, and seeing the noble marquis in his
place, will make a great speech; and—and Mr. Doolan will be called
away from his supper at the Back Kitchen; for he is foreign sub-editor,
and sees the mail on the newspaper sheet before he goes to his own.*

The mock-heroic tone of the adjective "ubiquitous," of the exclama-
tion "Look!", and of the juxtaposition of bribes in Madrid with the price of
potatoes in Covent Garden introduces a faint distrust of the enthusiasm
but does not belie the excitement Warrington feels for the press. The
positive part of the passage echoes the spirit of historic significance that
prompted the 1832 pressmen's parades in London, complete with a working press carried in a cart producing ink-wet pamphlets on freedom of the
press for the crowd. But Warrington's detachment, echoing Thackeray's
own balances the sentiment with the dash and the pun on Mr. Doolan's
mundane diurnal oscillation between the printed sheets and his bed sheets.
The double view suggests that the situation is too complex to be captured
by one feeling or one attitude. That same sleepless engine is also the
inexorable, insatiable engine which fed on the writer and caused the haste
and the drain of energy which sapped the health of more men than just
Thackeray.

Thackeray's sense of the economic realities of publishing was acute—
won at the price of two failed literary magazines and years of journalistic
hand-to-mouth work. His image of Pegasus drawing a wagon and his
unaristocratic equation of the literary profession with the trades are of a
piece with his mockery of inflated self-importance in any calling in life.
These self-deprecatory remarks cannot be taken to mean more than they
do—that literary men must work hard, must meet their deadlines, must
accept the consequences of the responses of publishers as merchandisers
and readers as the market for art: they must write what will be published
and purchased. Thackeray's remarks on his profession do not mean that he

held it in low regard or that he had no sense of the dignity of literature. For Thackeray the dignity of the profession lay in the integrity of presenting the world he knew as he saw it—including the business of authorship. In a letter to John Forster he indicated what humbug he thought lay at the root of attempts to assert the dignity of literature by any other means: "I don't believe in the Guild of Literature I dont believe in the Theatrical Scheme; I think *that* is against the dignity of our profession,—but you are honest and clever men and free to your opinion (thank you for nothing say you) well, believe that mine's loyally entertained too."[20] Thackeray was saying that the artist cannot with honesty or true dignity hide behind cant about a high calling.

Thackeray's position is neither starry-eyed or simpleminded. He knew the plight of many literary men who could be said to want the dignity of a bare living; his purse was frequently open to them.[21] With similar honesty he acknowledged the ambiguity of good and evil, a view which more positive men took to reveal weakness. Nor is his position uncomplicatedly open and without subtlety of its own. A chapter of Thackeray's life remains to be written by someone who can see beyond or beneath the surface and untangle the remark in John Chapman's diary for 14 June 1851: "I find that his religious views are perfectly free, but he does not mean to lessen his popularity by fully avowing them, he said he had debated the question with himself whether he was called upon to martyrise himself for the sake of his views and concluded in the negative. His chief object seems to be the making of money. He will go to America for that purpose. He impresses me as much abler than the lecture I heard, but I fear his success is spoiling him."[22]

Thackeray's net worth when he died unexpectedly on 23 December

---

[20]It appears that this letter may not have been sent; the original is with Smith's correspondence from Thackeray (NLS), who may have been content with showing it to his publisher.

[21]This seems particularly true in his days as editor of the *Cornhill* when, perhaps because his "brother authors" knew his ship had come in, they wrote asking for various kinds of help. One letter from Thackeray with a draft for £10 remains among George Smith's papers (NLS), for Smith intercepted and effectively canceled that bit of Thackeray's generosity.

[22]Manuscript diary, Beinecke. Chapman had met Thackeray after one of his lectures on Richard Steele two days earlier, at which time Thackeray expressed an interest in purchasing "at the 'trade price' some of my 'atheistic' publications." In his 14 June meeting at Chapman's, Thackeray declined an invitation to write a review of "Modern Novelists for the Westminster Review" because he could get more for his prose elsewhere and because he thought himself unprepared to do such an article. He also "complained of the rivalry and partizanship which is being fostered, I think chiefly Fo(r)ster'd, in respect to him and Dickens by foolish friends." Though Thackeray suggested that Charlotte Brontë write the proposed article, Mary Ann Evans objected, and George Lewes finally agreed to do it.

1863, at age fifty-three, attests for our material age his business success. His house was sold for £10,000. His furniture and personal effects sold for £2,000; his wine for £400. His copyrights brought his daughters £5,000. A total of about £18,000—one thousand more than his father had left him.

It is difficult to understand in modern terms the meaning of £18,000 or of an annual income of £2,000 to £4,000, which Thackeray was making in the last six or seven years of his life. An exchange rate does not help much because buying power changes as goods and services go up or come down. According to an article on the Royal Literary Fund in the *Smithsonian Magazine* (May 1985), London postmen made £50 a year in 1839. Of Anthony Trollope, John Sutherland has said, "With a bit of scrimping £250 was a tolerable annual salary."[23] Another source claims that £250 was the minimum required to be a gentleman. By such meaningless standards the man who wrote a chapter of *Vanity Fair* called "How to Live on Nothing a Year" was twelve times a gentleman.

---

[23]Fred Strebigh, "Keeping the Hacks and Geniuses Out of Debtors Prison," p. 126; Sutherland, *Victorian Novelists and Publishers,* p. 16. See also Robert Patten's interesting worry with this question in *Charles Dickens and His Publishers* (Oxford, 1978), p. 3. R. V. Jackson's "The Structure of Pay in Nineteenth-Century Britain," *Economic History Review,* 2d ser., 40 (1987): 563, notes a variety of "nominal annual earnings in skilled service occupations" for 1851 within the civil service: schoolmasters £81 a year, clergy £167, surgeons and doctors £200, and as top pay for solicitors and barristers £1,837.

II

The Literary Tradesman

Breaking into Print

HOW THACKERAY BECAME A WRITER has been the subject of many books
and articles, but recounting the story (with some new material) emphasizes the connections between his experiences as writer and the point of
view about the writer's trade presented in the preceding chapter. It illustrates how a romantic youth developed into a young dilettante; how,
without a "useful" education, Thackeray was thrown rather summarily
upon the resources of his pen to survive and to support a young and
trouble-ridden family; how years of hackwork and dogged determination
won for him a combination of pride in his journalistic achievements and a
humility or at least unpretentiousness about art; and how, when the laurels
of fame and fortune finally became his, he found the dignity of literature in
the economic and social rewards for hard labor rather than in the mantle of
the hero as man of letters.

His contributions as a schoolboy at the Charterhouse to the *Carthu-
sian,* as a teenager in 1828–29 to the *Western Luminary* (a newspaper at
Ottery Saint Mary's), and as a college student in 1829–30 to the *Snob* and
Gownsman (literary newspapers conducted by students at Cambridge)
have been described in detail by Harold Strong Gulliver,[1] an account still
worth reading, though corrections as well as new material can be found in
Gordon Ray's *Thackeray: The Uses of Adversity.*[2] In some ways, the best

---

[1] Harold Strong Gulliver, *Thackeray's Literary Apprenticeship* (Valdosta, Ga., 1936).

[2] The present retelling emphasizes the professional, trade, and economic aspects of the story
at the expense of the personal biography which is relevant but so readily available and so
often emphasized that there is no point in telling it again. Despite recent biographical
accounts by Anne Monsarrat (*An Uneasy Victorian: Thackeray the Man* [London, 1980]) and
Catherine Peters (*Thackeray's Universe*), both of which add some new material, the basis for
any account of Thackeray's life remains Gordon Ray's four-volume collection of *Letters and
Private Papers* and his two-volume biography, *Thackeray: The Uses of Adversity* and *Thackeray: The Age of Wisdom* (New York, 1955, 1958). Monsarrat and Peters bring enthusiasm
and appreciation to an old story which they augment minimally, the former occasionally
making mistakes that undermine the work, though both are well-written and serve the
purpose of introducing new readers to Thackeray. My own account is, of course, based
largely on the *Letters and Private Papers* and Ray's biography, but I also have used 370 letters
from Thackeray to his various publishers that are not in *Letters,* though some of these were
available to Ray when he wrote the biography.

account of these activities and of Thackeray's attitude toward the Muse and literary work at this time is his own fictional account of young Pendennis. As important as these ventures were in whetting Thackeray's appetite for literary work, they cannot be seen as the beginnings of his professional career. These literary endeavors, on a par with his contributions in 1831 to Ottilie von Goethe's Weimar literary paper, *Chaos,* were works of amateur enthusiasm. They were not undertaken for pay, nor were they part of any endeavor to forge a literary career, whether "for a living" or as the work of a gentleman of the world, which Thackeray could have been but for his weakness for gambling and, more importantly, the bank failures in India in late 1833 that virtually wiped out his considerable inheritance.

On his return from Weimar in March 1831, having chosen to forgo the rest of his education at college, where he had lost £1,500 at play, he sampled with distaste the rigors of reading for the law, turned twenty-one on 18 July 1832, dissipated in Paris for three or four months, and tried his hand for three months as a bill discounter. By May 1833 he was ready to invest his money in something more congenial to his tastes and talents. He purchased a periodical, the *National Standard,* thereby making himself a publisher. He was also the editor and chief contributor. His motive was only partially economic, as is perhaps clear from the oft-quoted self-satire he printed thirty years later in *Lovel the Widower* where Mr. Batchelor gave himself "airs as editor of that confounded Museum, and proposed to educate the public taste . . . and made a gabby of" himself.[3] The *National Standard* lasted till February 1834, by which time Thackeray had learned of the Indian bank failures and knew himself to be a poor man, the bulk of his remaining inheritance having evaporated, for though the estate may still have amounted to £7,000, it was encumbered by annuities which left Thackeray financially hobbled.[4]

Even before this misfortune, while still Paris correspondent for the *National Standard,* Thackeray had undertaken the formal study of art in Paris as "an independent man who is not obliged to look to his brush for his livelihood."[5] But by the end of 1833 all that changed. Thackeray first thought to repair his condition by pursuing with serious intent the calling he had chosen from inclination at a better time; however, he knew by the summer of 1835 that he could not succeed as a painter. From need he

---

[3]*Lovel the Widower* (London: Smith, Elder, 1861), chap. 1.

[4]Ray, *Adversity,* pp. 162–63.

[5]Ibid., p. 167.

sought out literary assignments, selling at least one article to *Fraser's Magazine,* working for *Galignani's Messenger* in Paris, projecting and abandoning a "Picturesque Annual" for which he would both write and draw, producing *Flore et Zéphyr,* a book of lithographs from which he apparently made nothing, and perhaps starting, editing, or at least working for a Paris rival to *Galignani's.*

Like painting, writing was a high-risk speculative venture without guaranteed returns. *Flore et Zéphyr,* Thackeray's first book, has no text beyond captions to the lithographs. It was published in April 1836 in London by John Mitchell while Thackeray was in France. Thackeray's letters to Mitchell betray the confusion characterizing this effort: "I cannot understand from yr. notes what is the drawing wanted," and the next day, "I do not know whether you propose to publish any letter-press with the drawing, will you allow me to see it, before its appearance" (*Letters* 1:299–300). The publication of *Flore et Zéphyr* was financed by Thackeray's wealthy friend John Bowes Bowes, who held an interest in *Galignani's Messenger* in Paris and who later wrote Thackeray that he thought Mitchell had fudged on the accounts "and put a lot of money in his pocket."[6] Whether Mitchell made any money is not known, but Thackeray and Bowes did not, though it may not have mattered much to the latter. (Time heals all wounds, it seems, for in 1851. Mitchell reappears in Thackeray's affairs as the manager of the London lectures on eighteenth-century humorists [*Letters* 2:783].)

Thackeray's depression over blasted hopes as a painter was alleviated somewhat by his meeting and falling in love with Isabella Shawe, an event with financial implications requiring an even more assiduous pursuit of literary work. Thackeray found that writing for a living, which he could do with some success, was far more demanding than writing occasional pieces for fun and glory. So when in early 1836 the opportunity arose to become involved with a politically radical literary paper, the *Constitutional and Public Ledger,* which was supposed to have a broadly subscribed economic base, Thackeray persuaded his stepfather, Major Carmichael-Smyth, to help him by subscribing the venture and serving as chairman of the company. Thackeray's salary was set at eight guineas a week.[7] In the flurry of setting up the company and gathering a staff, Thackeray wrote to Isabella that he was to have £450 per year (*Letters* 1:306), and serious

---

[6]Ibid., pp. 184, 467.

[7]Ibid., p. 185; Gulliver, *Thackeray's Literary Apprenticeship,* p. 54, said £400 a year without citing a source.

courtship and plans for marriage became possible in spite of the obstacles provided by his future mother-in-law, Mrs. Shawe. Thackeray's writings for the *Constitutional* began appearing in September, one month after his marriage. The account given by Ray of those next months suggests that Thackeray thought himself arrived at stability and contentedness, with the leisure to secure and execute additional jobs as illustrator.[8] But the whole project collapsed by July of the next year, crippling Major Carmichael-Smyth financially and throwing Thackeray once again upon the resources of his free-lance pen, this time with a wife and child to support. Thackeray would not again enjoy the leisure and stability of those few months as Paris correspondent for many years to come, but he had broken into print, he knew how to do it, he had developed some confidence in his abilities, and he set about his work with vigor.

When in 1833 Thackeray had commented to his mother that the *National Standard* was "very rapidly improving, & will form I have no doubt a property" (*Letters* 1:268), he was still the investor seeking to acquire and improve a property ready made; now he was to discover that he had "no other saleable property" than his writings.

Odious Magazinery

It cannot be said that Thackeray deliberately set about to build a property. He knew full well in July 1837, as the last number of the *Constitutional* was being printed, that his property was in the inkwell. But life came at him too fast and furiously for him to think beyond the present. For the next ten years Thackeray encountered one disaster after another, justifying his recollection years later of "the wife crazy and the publisher refusing me 15£ who owes me £13.10 and the Times to which I apply for a little more than 5 guineas for a week's work, refusing to give me more" (*Letters* 4:271). But with the publication and growing success of *Vanity Fair* in 1847–48, Thackeray awoke to discover that he had a property, one he had been building all along.

From the failure of the *Constitutional* in July 1837 to the start of *Vanity Fair* in January 1847, Thackeray was a journalist, writing for his life at a job—one hesitates to call it either a trade or profession—that he spoke of as "odious magazine-work wh. wd. kill any writer in 6 years" (*Letters* 1:459). During that period he contributed nearly 450 pieces of original work to at least twenty-two different magazines, newspapers, or other periodicals. The major vehicles of his magazinery were *Fraser's Magazine,*

[8]Ray, *Adversity,* pp. 188–89.

the *Times, New Monthly Magazine, Foreign Quarterly Review, Morning Chronicle,* and *Punch.* From these Thackeray expected and got regular work for at least several months together. *Fraser's* was his first regular means of support, and *Punch* sustained him and launched *Vanity Fair,* which bore as the imprint on the monthly wrappers not Bradbury and Evans, the staid publisher and printer, but "Published at the Punch Office."

The incredible number of Thackeray's contributions to periodicals during those ten years and especially the fact that so much of his work appears in six apparently friendly magazines may mask the desperate difficulties and repeated rebuffs he endured from publishers in the early years. There are a number of letters in 1837, for example, from Thackeray to John Mitchell Kemble, his friend from Cambridge days and at the time editor of the *British and Foreign Review,* asking for work and proposing articles and reviews, but after two acceptances Kemble apparently decided against any more of Thackeray's "light" articles and, in spite of Thackeray's pleas for more work, evinced enough coolness toward his college friend that Thackeray gave up on account of Kemble's "airs."[9] In February 1841, having recently concluded that his wife's mental condition demanded professional care, he wrote from France a plaintive letter to Jane Carlyle asking her to forward three letters for him, one to the *Times,* one to James Fraser, editor of *Fraser's Magazine,* and a third to an unknown correspondent, possibly Richard Bentley, whom Thackeray mentioned in his cover letter. He further asked her to intercede with the *Times* and with John Forster to help promote the sale of *Comic Tales* by writing good reviews. The letter reveals a man desperate for cash though he asked only for help in getting his work published and sold. A month later on 20 March, he wrote Mrs. Carlyle again, this time in a slightly more relaxed tone, thanking her for the success of her intervention with Fraser (with whom Thackeray had had "a slight coolness") and remarking that Fraser and Bentley had "stuff enough to keep my dear little woman where she is for 3 months to come." Although Fraser published Thackeray's work, Thackeray had to write Bentley on the first of June to turn his manuscript of *The History of Samuel Titmarsh* over to another publisher, Hugh Cunningham.[10] And there is no record of an acceptance from the *Times* in that year.

---

[9]H. B. de Groot and Walter Houghton, "The *British and Foreign Review;* or, *European Quarterly Journal,* 1835–1844: Introduction," *Wellesley Index to Victorian Periodicals* 3:68; *Letters* 1:420.

[10]Edgar Harden, "Thackeray and the Carlyles: Seven Further Letters," *Studies in Scottish Literature* 14 (1979): 168–70; Ray, *Adversity,* p. 478.

Short series and occasional items continued to be equally necessary to his livelihood, and in addition to writing for the "big six," Thackeray contributed sporadically to fourteen other periodicals, including the *Calcutta Star* (contributions which have yet to be traced, listed, and reprinted) and *Corsair* (an American enterprise operated by N. P. Willis which Thackeray apparently abandoned for nonpayment of fees). Thackeray also illustrated works by Douglas Jerrold, John Burrow, and Charles G. Addison, as well as providing drawings for the *Anti-Corn Law Circular* and *Punch,* where the text, if any, was supplied by others. He also tried and failed to get work illustrating novels by Charles Dickens and William Harrison Ainsworth. But his attempts remind us of his real ability as an artist who chose to illustrate many of his own works because he was talented enough to do so.

Magazine work was, of course, more odious some times than others, and Thackeray's relatively stable staff status with *Fraser's,* the *Morning Chronicle,* and *Punch* provided him with income he did not readily give up when he became a top book author. His magazinery, moreover, included apprentice fiction that one day would earn him both more money and more reputation than the struggling author at first thought. During the ten years preceding *Vanity Fair,* he wrote as serials *The Yellowplush Papers* for *Fraser's* (November 1837–August 1838), *Major Gahagan* for *New Monthly* (November 1838–February 1839), *Catherine* for *Fraser's* (May 1839–February 1840), *A Shabby Genteel Story* for *Fraser's* (June–October 1840), *The History of Samuel Titmarsh and the Great Hoggarty Diamond* for *Fraser's* (September–December 1841), "Miss Tickletoby's Lectures" for *Punch* (July–October 1842), "Fitzboodle's Confessions" for *Punch* (October 1842–November 1843), and *The Luck of Barry Lyndon* for *Fraser's* (January–December 1844). All these, of course, were paid at odious magazine rates, about ten to twelve guineas a sheet (sixteen printed pages). Though he had little success, throughout these years his aim was to produce books, from which, as he said rather too optimistically in 1840, he could "get 300£ for my 3 months work instead of 120 wh. the Magazines wd. pay" (*Letters* 1:459).

Book Work

Thackeray had lost his fortune in 1833; he married in 1836 on the strength of a position that failed him within a year. His needs and his production were prodigious, but in 1840, after seven years in the profession, he still had not published a book. He was still learning the lesson that had to be learned by any person "with no other saleable property," that Pegasus "does his work with panting sides and trembling knees," and that to survive the artist must "hit the public" with what it wants. Success was slow in coming; it entailed a shift from the view of a romantic artist to that of a professional tradesman.

The bibliographies usually tout *The Yellowplush Papers* (Philadelphia: Cary and Hart, 1837) as Thackeray's first published book, but he had nothing to do with its production and received not a penny from it, for Cary and Hart lifted it without so much as a by-your-leave from *Fraser's Magazine*. But *Yellowplush*'s rapid transformation from periodical to book form is ample support for thinking Thackeray's early assessment of his work was right when he wrote on 5 March 1839 to Fraser:

[*Letters*
1:351–52][11]

I hereby give notice that I shall strike for wages.

You pay more to others, I find, than to me; and so I intend to make some fresh conditions about Yellowplush. I shall write no more of that gentleman's remarks except at the rate of twelve guineas a sheet, and with a drawing for each number in which his story appears—the drawings two guineas.

Pray do not be angry at this decision on my part; it is simply a bargain, which it is my duty to make. Bad as he is, Mr. Yellowplush is the most popular contributor to your magazine, and ought to be paid accordingly; if he does not deserve more than the monthly nurse or the Blue Friars, I am a Dutchman.

I have been at work upon his adventures to-day, and will send them to you or not as you like, but in common regard for myself I won't work under prices.

Well, I dare say you will be very indignant, and swear I am the most mercenary of individuals. Not so. But I am a better workman than most in your crew and deserve a better price.

You must not, I repeat, be angry, or because we differ as tradesmen break off our connection as friends. Believe me that, whether I write for you or not, I always shall be glad of your friendship.

This letter is important as an early indication of Thackeray's realistic attitude toward his occupation and his place in it. It indicates furthermore the personal relationship he shared with many of his publishers. Thack-

---

[11]Anne Monsarrat, quoting this letter, omitted the last paragraph and asserted throughout her account of Thackeray's relations with Fraser that Thackeray felt superior to and acted haughtily toward Fraser (*An Uneasy Victorian*, pp. 90–91). The only evidence she cited is the analogy of Warrington's behavior toward Bungay in *Pendennis*.

eray's assumption of equality, evidenced in his right to strike, is equaled by the publisher's right to decline. The reference to publisher and author as fellow tradesmen and the assumption of a value for the friendship aside from pounds, shillings, and pence reflect Thackeray's easy acceptance of the real conditions of his position as a professional writer in the commercial world of letters. He was no snobbish "gentleman" condescending to a bookseller. Any appreciation of his desperately precarious financial condition would dispel that notion.

Another candidate for Thackeray's first book resulted from a similar episode in 1840 with perhaps a less happy ending involving another publisher friend, Sir Henry Cole, for whom Thackeray in 1839 had supplied illustrations for the *Anti-Corn Law Circular*. In 1840 he dealt with Cole for an article on George Cruikshank for the *Westminster Review*. The article, a long one, appeared in June 1840; work on it may well have helped delay the work on *The Paris Sketch Book*, which also appeared in June. Thackeray's attitude toward the work he was doing on this essay can be seen in his correspondence with Cole. In April he noted that "after thinking and thinking I am come to the determination that the Ck. article MUST have several vignettes introduced into the pages, and this not for money's sake." Here a sense of what is required professionally outweighs money considerations. The next month he sent in the finished article, saying: "Amen, and as I think it over, and over, the hours of toil which have been spent in its composition I cannot but give it as my candid opinion that you have had all things considered a pretty good bargain for your money. . . . I know not how far the article may extend but I request you as speedily as you possibly can to transmit to its author that trifling remuneration for which in a moment of weakness—of imbecile delirium he engaged to supply you with his composition."[12] Called "George Cruikshank's Works" and signed "Θ", the article took up sixty pages of the June issue. Cole decided to reprint the article separately and must have communicated with Thackeray some proposition, for on 31 July Thackeray wrote Cole, "If the Cruikshank article is to be published in the shape of a pamphlet, I would humbly suggest to you—that the author who was paid ½ price in the first instance, should be paid something for his name and his permission to use his writing. I have spoken with him on the subject & he says, by Jove, he will not otherwise consent to the appearance of the publication" (Houghton). In an undated note that must have been written in August, a much

---

[12]Two letters to Cole, in Henry S. Van Duzer, *A Thackeray Library* (1919; rpt. New York, 1965), p. 45 (not in *Letters*).

subdued Thackeray wrote Cole: "I suppose Cruikshank is useless by this time—indeed I take shame to myself for not having earlier answered your note concerning him. But I was out of town when it arrived only came back to be in a great deal of bustle and anxiety and be off again, and indeed forgot all abt. the Cruikshank matter till this very morning of my return. Of course you may do exactly as you like with the article—and put my name to it if it is the least use."[13] Thackeray's name was not used in the reprint, and he may well have missed out also on any added remuneration.

Though Thackeray's review of Cruikshank's works in the *Westminster* may have appeared before the publication of *The Paris Sketch Book,* its book form postdated the larger book, making Thackeray's first real book *The Paris Sketch Book* (1840).[14] It came only after seven hard years of labor as a journalist, and the success it represented bore little resemblance to his anticipated £300 for three months' work. The burden was scarcely eased from Thackeray's panting sides. Thackeray first mentioned *The Paris Sketch Book* as a project in January 1837 in a letter to John Macrone, its eventual publisher, for whom Thackeray was trying (and failing) to provide illustrations to William Harrison Ainsworth's *Crichton.* Though Macrone died in September 1837, his name appeared on the publisher's imprint for *The Paris Sketch Book* in 1840, by which time Hugh Cunningham was running the business. When Thackeray first approached Macrone in January 1837, that new, enterprising, and nearly insolvent publisher had just published Charles Dickens's *Sketches by Boz,* second series. Though Macrone had been best man at Dickens's wedding in the spring of 1836, he was no longer on speaking terms with Dickens, the result of contract disputes over a new edition of *Sketches.*[15]

That sort of problem seems not to have affected Thackeray's brief relations with the publisher, perhaps because, unlike Dickens, Thackeray did not suddenly and unexpectedly become a best-selling author. Next to a trial title page surrounded by a decoration vaguely resembling a fiddle case, Thackeray wrote to Macrone:

[*Letters*   *Will you give me £50 20 now for the 1st Edition of a book in 2*
1:328–29]   *Wollums. with 20 drawings. entitled Rambles & Sketches in old and new*

---

[13]Houghton; not in *Letters.* The work was reprinted from the *Westminster Review* as *An Essay on the Genius of George Cruikshank* (London: Henry Hooper, 1840).

[14]The earlier *Flore et Zéphyr* (1836) has captions but is otherwise devoid of text, and the ostensible but never confirmed publication of *Major Gahagan* by an unidentified American publisher occupies if anything the same position as the pirated *Yellowplush.*

[15]See Patten, *Dickens and His Publishers,* pp. 28–44.

Paris by ☙ *I have not of course written a word of it, that's why I offer it so
cheap. but I want to be made to write, and to bind myself by a contract or
fine.*

*Think now about the advantages of this offer (I mean the one in the
fiddle case)—I want something to do—& wd. be right glad to do this.*

Thackeray obviously was quick to realize that he produced better
under the pressure of a sure publication than at leisure on uncommissioned
work. This letter was not just a ploy for an advance of £20 (which we do
not know if he got) but a deliberate attempt to impose work deadlines,
something Thackeray sought for the rest of his life—including during the
flush times of his later career—and which he hoped would lift him out of
the round of magazinery to the status of an author of books. By December
1839, nearly three years after his first proposal to Macrone, the project was
still pending, and Thackeray referred to the *Sketch Book* as "this horrid
book" which would be finished in six weeks and "be tolerably pleasant"
(*Letters* 1:397). But by 3 March 1840, it was still not ready and only "half of
Vol. I. is at the printers" (*Letters* 1:425). In April his book had "not got on
much" though he was writing furiously on it and several other projects,
particularly the Cruikshank article (*Letters* 1:437). *The Paris Sketch Book* for
which he had wanted a £20 advance and contract in January 1837 was
finished (presumably final page proofs read) on 1 June 1840. Thackeray
produced such a lot of other material in that time (including *Yellowplush,
Gahagan,* and *Catherine*) that it is probable Macrone had not advanced the
£20 Thackeray had requested. Macrone may have done no more than
encourage Thackeray, who seems to have worked occasionally for the
publisher as a reader and editor as well, reading and recommending
extensive changes in a book by Colonel Francis Maceroni (July 1837,
Letters 1:344). *The Paris Sketch Book* contract offer may have been the
experience where Thackeray learned the advice he was later to pass on to
another aspiring author: that a writer "must first do the books & then its 5
chances to 1, that he sells them," for publishers do not "buy a pig in a
poke" (June 1847, *Letters* 2:305).

By the end of July 1840, Thackeray's glee was apparent in a letter to
his mother announcing that 400 copies of *The Paris Sketch Book* had been
sold: "Enough to pay all the expenses of authorship printing &c. and to
leave 500£ profit to the publisher if the rest are sold" (*Letters* 1:459). If,
indeed, Thackeray sold the first edition to the publisher for £50, and if
Macrone actually stood to earn £500, Thackeray, now the author of his
first book, and that a publisher's success, was not about to gripe at his

share.[16] He knew well enough that the sales figures made him a desirable property for other publishers. Longman, book publisher and proprietor of the *Edinburgh Review,* and Chapman and Hall, at the time Dickens's main publisher and proprietor of the *Foreign Quarterly Review,* were reported "very willing to enter into treaty with me" (*Letters* 1:459). The time would come when the author would make more money than the publisher from each new book, but for the moment what was good for Thackeray's publisher was great news for the author himself. Desperate for cash, Thackeray was happy with the new visibility.

Capitalizing on Apparent Success

Although Thackeray closed no deals with Longman until five years later, within two months he made a £385 contract with Chapman and Hall for "Titmarsh in Ireland" (eventually *The Irish Sketch-Book*). His star may have been a faint one yet, but it was definitely rising. The contract, or "fine," he had begged of Macrone in 1837 was delivered into his hand in September 1840 by Chapman and Hall, complete with a due date for an illustrated two volumes by 31 December!

The silver lining, however, had a dark cloud. Though the ante this time seems to have jumped from £20 to £120 "to be paid down this day" (*Letters* 1:471), there lurked in the background of the contract an arrangement with Chapman and Hall revealed only in Thackeray's letters to his mother asking Miss Mary Graham, his cousin and adoptive sister, to sign a letter of surety for Chapman and Hall in case of Thackeray's default; moreover, Thackeray left his plate-chest with the publisher who held it until 1846 (*Letters* 1:468, 473). Three weeks earlier Thackeray had returned from Belgium to discover his wife in a deep depression he still hoped was temporary. On 12 September, Thackeray took his family to Ireland where he hoped to write the book and see if Cork air and a visit home would restore Isabella's wandering mind and spirits. Neither endeavor was successful. On the trip to Ireland, Isabella's depression manifested itself as insanity. She threw herself into the sea where she was found twenty minutes later "floating on her back, paddling with her hands." The Thackerays' sojourn in the Emerald Isle lasted just a month, during which Thackeray nursed his wife, chafed heavily under the tyranny of his mother-in-law, and worked intermittently on an unidentified play. His exit from Ireland

---

[16]Though at the time neither Thackeray nor his potential publishers could know it, *The Paris Sketch Book* would be remaindered at a coffeehouse auction in 1842 (Leonard Huxley, *The House of Smith, Elder* [London, 1923], p. 66).

on 11 October 1840 was something of an escape or retreat from Isabella's mother. By the end of November, Isabella was institutionalized in France at J.-E.-D. Esquirol's Maison de Santé, and Thackeray could spend more and calmer time writing.[17]

Among his first concerns was *The Shabby Genteel Story*. On 3 December he wrote James Fraser from Paris: "I left purposely the Shabby Genteel Story in such a state that it might be continued in the magazine or not as you and I liked best. Would you like it to be continued? In that case I should like to write the whole story off, and of course be paid for it on delivering over the MSS. Some 4 sheets I think would complete the affair. Please let me know whether I shall proceed with it, for though I can't afford to begin any new articles at your prices this one had better be gone through with if you think fit." Then, assuming that Fraser would authorize the continuation, he added, "I shall probably publish the whole tale wh. has a very moral ending in a volume with illustrations" (*Letters* 1:488). The plan reveals again Thackeray's increasing desire to see his magazine work in book form. Fraser, however, declined; a continuation, as such, was never written, though Thackeray briefly considered it in 1856 when searching for copy for volume 2 of *Miscellanies* to fill a vacuum caused by a miscommunication with his publisher. The incomplete story was first published in book form by Appleton in New York in 1852.[18] But there was plenty more to keep Thackeray busy.

On 15 December 1840 Thackeray witnessed the celebrations connected with the arrival of Napoleon's body from St. Helena for burial in Paris. He claimed to have written *The Second Funeral of Napoleon* in four days and the appended "Chronicle of a Drum" in a week. Published by Hugh Cunningham in London in January 1841, it made a small book of 122 pages—one of the quickest productions of his career. He wrote to friends that he was to receive 7½ pence for every copy sold and claimed by 21 January to have earned £3.2.6 from the sale of 100 copies (*Letters* 2:4, 7). By March he groused that the total sold was only 140 copies.

In spite of his disastrous personal circumstances at the end of 1840, or perhaps because of them, Thackeray was intensely committed to the production of new works. The initial success of *The Paris Sketch Book* in mid-1840 had made *The Irish Sketch-Book* contract possible, but when work on that scale proved impossible under the circumstances, Thackeray produced shorter pieces (*A Shabby Genteel Story* and *The Second Funeral*)

---

[17]See Ray, *Adversity*, pp. 255–60.

[18]Thackeray did return to the story when he wrote *The Adventures of Philip* (1862).

and projected more by the end of the year. Cunningham advertised two new books by Titmarsh: *The Second Funeral* and *Dinner Reminiscences: The Young Gormandizer's Guide at Paris.* The latter work was never issued, though parts of it may survive in "Memorials of Gormandizing" in *Fraser's Magazine,* June 1841. Cunningham may have waited to see how *The Second Funeral* would do, deciding not to try another book in the same format when that one failed in the marketplace, or he may have decided that *Comic Tales,* a new two-volume venture already planned, was as much as he dare invest at one time in the as yet little known author.

Long before the first manifestation of his wife's illness and before dealing with Chapman and Hall for *The Irish Sketch-Book* in September, Thackeray had already planned a collection of his earlier magazine fiction, *Comic Tales,* to be published with Cunningham. The idea was first mentioned in surviving letters in December 1839, and by December 1840 he remarked to James Fraser his intention to republish *A Shabby Genteel Story*[19] and added, "I have got a very decent price from Cunningham for a republication of my comic miscellanies" (*Letters* 1:489). That decent price is not known, but by then he had signed with Chapman and Hall for a new work at £385 and had begun to appreciate the market value of his work. Serious work and new illustrations were undertaken in February and March 1841, and *Comic Tales* was published in April in two volumes (*Letters* 2:9).[20] The only new text in the book was Thackeray's preface clearly indicating that the American appearance of *Yellowplush* and the rumored but never confirmed republication of *Gahagan* had spurred preparation of the collection. Both those works appeared in *Comic Tales.* No evidence exists to confirm that Thackeray was instrumental in having *Yellowplush* published that same year by Baudry in Paris in tandem with Dickens's *Master Humphrey's Clock,* but the Baudry text derives from the *Comic Tales* edition, not the *Fraser's* text, and Thackeray was in Paris off and on during the year and may have collected a modest amount for the republication there. If so, he was tasting the first fruits of having a literary property out of the inkwell.

During the six months after Isabella's entry to the Maison de Santé for treatment (December 1840 to May 1841), Thackeray was very produc-

---

[19]*A Shabby Genteel Story* was not republished until the *Miscellanies* in 1856.

[20]In his 20 March 1841 letter to Jane Carlyle, Thackeray remarked: "Yellowplush's republication has been delayed by the accursed dilatoriness & clumsiness of the copper-plate printers here, who spoiled half the work that I was obliged to do again" (Harden, "Thackeray and the Carlyles," 170).

tive, as Gordon Ray has pointed out. He wrote *The Second Funeral* in December and *The History of Samuel Titmarsh* in January and February, began and abandoned eight chapters of the never completed historical novel "The Knights of Borsellen" between January and April, saw *Comic Tales* through press in March, and wrote "between February and May a dozen magazine articles and stories."[21] Such a flurry of activity was made both possible and necessary by the emotional crises and the increased financial burdens of the last year's ending. But Thackeray's almost single-minded application to writing at the same time was developing in him ideas about his profession—about the cold trade relations existing between all persons making a living out of writing, printing, publishing, and bookselling as well as about the unpredictable nature of literature's new patrons, the public. This is the period in which he wrote the two letters to Jane Carlyle from France, the first full of desperate need, the second of cheerful but, as it turned out, misplaced hope. *The Second Funeral* was a failure, and *Comic Tales* cannot have done well; not only did Cunningham never publish anything else by Thackeray, remaindered sheets from the 1841 *Comic Tales* were reissued with a new title page in 1848 to take advantage of the popularity of *Vanity Fair*. "The Knights" was abandoned, and the publisher Bentley ignored the manuscript of *The History of Samuel Titmarsh*. The rising star so quickly blighted by Isabella's illness had flared once more only to die back, Thackeray eking out his living with the usual magazine work.

The manuscript of *The History of Samuel Titmarsh* languished with Bentley from late February to the first of June when Thackeray wrote angrily to have it turned over to Hugh Cunningham. It is a notable letter revealing both frustration and a new confidence in his status that did not mind offending a publisher: "& next time your obedient Servant sends you an article you may set him down without fail to be you understand what [sketch of a donkey] yours & whatdyecallem W M Thackeray."[22] But Cunningham did not want *Samuel Titmarsh* either, and it was published at magazine rates in *Fraser's* from September to December 1841.[23]

---

[21]Ray, *Adversity,* p. 261.

[22]Ibid., p. 478.

[23]*Fraser's* was paying £12 a sheet, or 15s. 9d. per page. Thackeray got £385 for *The Irish Sketch-Book,* or about 12s. 2d. per page. However, *Fraser's* double-column format accommodated approximately twice the text required to fill a page of the book, so that in effect Thackeray's rate of pay for the book was nearly double the magazine rates. In addition, the total payment for the job was much more and, when it finally came, came in lump sums. *Punch* paid Thackeray two guineas per page, but its pages held even more than *Fraser's.*

During these years of hand-to-mouth existence, Thackeray entered many tentative and aborted relations with publishers, some of several years' duration or occasional renewal. His relations with Richard Bentley seem to have begun with the publication of "The Professor," a short story in *Bentley's Miscellany*, September 1837. That was also the end of their business together, although they both came up with other proposals. It was probably on the strength of an interest Bentley had shown that Thackeray began writing "The Knights of Borsellen" early in 1841,[24] and it is just as probable that his anger with Bentley and break with him in June 1841 influenced him to abandon it. Nearly a year later, still casting about for any work he could get, Thackeray approached Bentley again, offering the translation of a French novel ("strange to say it is not at all indecent") and suggesting that it "would answer for 3 volumes or for the Miscellany" (NYU). Apparently Thackeray had already translated two volumes, but the project came to nothing. We do not even know what novel it was. Three years later, Thackeray began translating a Eugène Sue novel, for which he also failed to find a publisher after having done a good deal of the work.

Later, while writing *Vanity Fair,* Thackeray wrote to Bentley asking for a copy of the six-volume edition of Horace Walpole's letters edited by John Wright in 1840 and offering to pay for it by writing for Bentley's *Miscellany*. Bentley, according to Thackeray's recollection, declined the deal but offered to pay for any of Thackeray's contributions at the rate of £12 per sheet. Thackeray apparently did not respond at the time. After the successes of *Vanity Fair, Pendennis,* and *Esmond,* it was Bentley who wrote proposals to Thackeray and the novelist who turned them down. In 1853 Bentley suggested, probably because of the success of Thackeray's first lecture series, that he reedit Walpole's letters. Two more volumes, edited by the Reverend J. Mitford, had been added in 1851, and Bentley wanted a uniform and chronologically arranged eight-volume work. Thackeray responded, "The task wh. you propose is one wh. I should be glad enough to undertake provided we could agree upon terms." He reminded Bentley of his earlier offer of £12 per sheet and concluded, "I'm sure that you are going to make me better proposals than the above: and awaiting them, am, very faithfully yours, W M Thackeray."[25] Though this was a far more polite closing than the "Yours & whatdyecallem" of twelve years earlier,

---

[24]Ray, *Adversity,* p. 268.

[25]NYU. By comparison, three years later Thackeray noted to Mark Lemon, editor of *Punch,* that his going rate for contributions to *Blackwell's* was £28 per sheet.

no terms were agreed upon. Bentley tried once more in 1857 when, probably because of the success of Thackeray's second lecture series, he wrote to propose a work on the eighteenth-century artist and caricaturist William Hogarth. Aside from having "my own hands quite full at present," it happened that Thackeray had inside information on a project in progress answering Bentley's description exactly. In September 1855 George Augustus Sala had first spoken to Thackeray and then written to him of his work on Hogarth. Thackeray had recommended Sala to George Smith and apparently put it out of his mind until Bentley's proposal reminded him of it. Interestingly, Thackeray, who was in Paris at the time, sent his response first to George Smith to be forwarded to Bentley, writing Smith a note at the same time on the back of Bentley's proposal (NLS). Sala's work on Hogarth appeared first as nine installments in Smith's *Cornhill Magazine* (February–October 1860) and as a book under the Smith, Elder imprint in 1866.

Meanwhile, in June 1841 *The Irish Sketch-Book* remained unwritten, Chapman and Hall holding the plate-chest and looking very like bankers making a loan instead of publishers paying an advance. Indeed, Thackeray seemed in no hurry to redeem his plate, offering instead to write a serial fiction for Fraser that might be turned into a book:

[*Letters* 2:29–30]

> *I have in my trip to the country, found materials (rather a character) for a story, that I'm sure must be amusing. I want to write & illustrate it, and as you see how Harry Lorrequer succeeds both in the Dublin Magazine & out of it, why should not my story of* BARRY-LYNN *(or by what name so ever it may be called) answer in as well as out of Regina. Suppose for instance you were to give a sheet & a half per month that sheet and a half could be stretched into two sheets for the shilling number by transposing (or whatever you call it) the type: and the book would thus make a handsome saleable volume at the end of the year. My subject I am sure is a good one, and I have made a vow to chasten and otherwise popularize my style. Thus I could have 20 guineas a month from you and a farther chance of profit from the sale of the single numbers. Were we to come to a bargain I would not of course begin until 3 numbers of the tale were in hand: with the plates &c.*

Here for the first time we see Thackeray planning a work as "a property" with a view to its value beyond its first appearance. And we see him acknowledging the need to write first and close deals second, offering to have three installments done on the basis of encouragement alone from the publisher. In the event, however, Thackeray wrote *The Irish Sketch-Book* first.

Thackeray had removed Isabella from the Maison de Santé in early April 1841, and she seemed so much better that he spent a considerable amount of time with her over the next few months, taking her for water treatments at a sanatorium on the Rhine in August. While they were there, two unforeseen events altered his financial situation: his half sister died, freeing to Thackeray £500 of inheritance that had been entailed while she lived, and his cousin Mary Graham, now married to Charles, Major Carmichael-Smyth's brother, lent him another £500 (*Letters* 2:34). The Thackerays continued the water treatments in Boppard until October when Isabella ceased to improve, and by February 1842 she was placed under the residential care of Dr. Puzin in Chaillot (*Letters* 2:41).

Over that winter Thackeray continued producing articles for *Fraser's* and *George Cruikshank's Omnibus,* but no progress seems to have been made on *Barry Lyndon* or *The Irish Sketch-Book* until February 1842 when Thackeray wrote of his impending return to Ireland (*Letters* 2:42). As that spring progressed, references to the Irish book came more and more into Thackeray's letters, including several to Chapman and Hall for whose newly acquired *Foreign Quarterly Review* he was writing two major articles totaling fifty pages (perhaps as a bid to become its new editor). Payment for these articles was separate from the advance (or loan) Chapman and Hall had made for *The Irish Sketch-Book.* After suggesting that the ordinary rate for his article on France was too little, considering the time for research it required ("The restoration alone cost me 6 weeks labor, & the reading of many scores of books" [*Letters* 2:51]), he concluded that the continuation on Louis Philippe would "bring no profit" and would be done "for reputation's sake" (*Letters* 2:65).

Thackeray at the same time had been busy with his first serial contribution to *Punch,* "Mrs. Tickletoby's Lectures." By 19 September 1842 nine installments had appeared, and Thackeray awaited payment from *Punch's* publisher, Bradbury and Evans.

[Bodleian]   *You may remember that when I spoke to you regarding Punch, you were ready to promise as proprietors of the journal that any articles wh. I wrote for it should be paid. My stipulations with the editor of the paper were that my contributions should be paid at the rate of 2 guineas a page, and the only article for wh. I have recd payment was at that rate.*

   I have now been writing for nearly 3 months (the printers have some more of my MS in their hands) I wrote a fortnight since to Mr. Landells

requesting him to communicate with Mr. Lemon, and beg the latter to
send me what was my due, according to the account; wh. I have not kept
myself but wh. can easily be arranged by reference to Punch from wh. this
year I have received nothing.

I did not receive an answer from Mr. Landells & then wrote to Mr.
Lemon I have likewise no reply from that gentleman.

Will you have the kindness to let me know where I am to apply, in
the first place for answers to my letters, and secondly for payment for my
contributions? and may I beg an answer either with or without money by
return of post?

Thackeray's letters to Landells and Lemon have not survived. But by
27 September, Thackeray had received £25 and the bad news that the
publisher was not pleased with Thackeray's contribution. Evidently two
more installments had been sent off already, for it appears that Thackeray
broke off immediately: "I have no wish to continue the original agreement
made between us, as it is dissatisfactory to you and, possibly, injurious to
your work; and shall gladly cease Mrs. Tickletoby's Lectures, hoping that
you will be able to supply her place with some more amusing and lively
correspondent" (*Letters* 2:82).

Judging from Thackeray's letters to his mother during his Ireland
tour, which lasted from July to 1 November 1842, he was also writing
steadily on *The Irish Sketch-Book*. Even before finishing it, however, he
proposed, in January 1843, a new work, "FAIRY BALLADS by W. Thackeray," to Chapman and Hall and continued to write book reviews for that
publisher's *Foreign Quarterly Review* (*Letters* 2:92). One can only imagine
Chapman's response to this new proposal, with old ones pending long
overdue, for there is no further reference to it in extant letters. But two
weeks later Thackeray asked Mark Lemon to submit anonymously to the
actor Macready a tragedy he had worked on while in Ireland (*Letters* 2:93).
Apparently nothing came of the effort. In February, Thackeray reported
reading proofs for the first two sheets of *The Irish Sketch-Book,* noting
"they've spoiled my first chapter for me though . . . by making me
withdraw some personalities, agst. the Catholics wh. might certainly have
been dangerous" (*Letters* 2:94, 96). This remark should, however, be read
in the context of a comment he made to his mother from Ireland: "A man
coming here as I did with a strong disposition in favor of the Catholics,
priests & all can't fail to get indignant at the slavish brutal superstition of
the latter, and to become rather Toryfied so far. So I shall be abused by the
Catholic Press for abusing the priests, and by the Tory papers for being a
liberal" (*Letters* 2:78).

Oddly, though he was reading proofs by 20 February, Thackeray waited until 11 March to complain, mildly, to Chapman and Hall about the type size and page size of the book: "I find I am done out of no less than 50 pages by the size of the type &c. I bargained for 25 lines of 40 letters, and our page is 26 lines of 43" (*Letter* 2:98). While there was no stipulation in the contract for a certain number of pages, the book was "to consist of two volumes of the size . . . of the Paris Sketch Book." The Paris book consisted of two volumes of 304 pages and 298 pages; the Irish work turned out to be 311 pages and 327 pages. In spite of his hope that Chapman and Hall's "perspicacious generosity will bear this fact I'm sure in mind," apparently Thackeray found himself obliged for the extra pages, some of which may have been fleshed out with added illustrations. Perhaps because of Chapman and Hall's insistence on the full complement of pages, Thackeray recovered from a genial attitude toward what the publishers were doing to his book. Earlier, complaining mildly to his mother that "they have called it Rambles in Ireland wh. I think is a foolish name," he added that he was too lazy to do anything about it, but in the end he must have balked.[26]

On 29 April 1843 Thackeray sent unbound sheets (all but the one containing the front matter)[27] to his friend Percival Leigh asking for a quick review in the May issue of *Fraser's Magazine:* "Not a puff you understand, hit as hard as you like but in a good natured way and so as not to break bones." He explained that "the book is dedicated to Mr. Lever: and the preface says that it was to have been called the Cockney in Ireland but for the remonstrances of the publisher wh. were so pathetic that the author was obliged to give way. In a *second edition* it is to be changed" (*Letters* 2:106). The facetious tone of these remarks is familiar. The title probably was an item of discussion and perhaps contention between author and publisher, but in fact there is no preface in the book and the

---

[26]*Letters* 2:100. Thackeray probably had forgotten that he himself had once proposed "Rambles and Sketches in Old and New Paris" as a title for *The Paris Sketch Book*. The contract for the Ireland tour called the book "Titmarsh in Ireland"—a title proposed by Thackeray. The sequence of titles includes, in addition, "Rambles in Ireland," proposed by Chapman and Hall and temporarily acquiesced in by Thackeray (March 1843); "The Cockney in Ireland," presumably proposed by Thackeray in the projected but apparently never written preface (April 1843); and *The Irish Sketch-Book,* agreed upon by both parties and actually used as the title. John Gordan noted a fifth title, "Irish Sketches," in *William Makepeace Thackeray: An Exhibition* (New York, 1947), p. 12, but he cited no source, and Catherine Peters noted a sixth, "Cockney Travels in Ireland," also citing no source (*Thackeray's Universe,* p. 105).

[27]It was customary, indeed necessary, to print front matter last, particularly if there was to be a table of contents with page references to the body of the work. Prefaces are usually the last part of a work to be written.

dedication does not mention the alternate title. On the same day that Thackeray wrote to Leigh, he sent a similar request for a review to Laman Blanchard, saying, "It is dedicated to Mr. Lever, and the author will say in the preface that it was to have been called 'The Cockney in Ireland,' but for the pathetic remonstrances of the publishers" (*Letters* 2:106). The future tense may be telling; it is conceivable that Thackeray had not yet read the proofs or settled finally on the content of the front matter. Furthermore, the reference to a second edition, as if one were already planned, was entirely facetious. Though *The Irish Sketch-Book* was Thackeray's greatest success to date, the 1845 "second edition," two years later, was nothing more than leftover first-edition sheets reissued with a new title page, and not with Thackeray's jocular title.[28] No new negotiations and no additional payment came to Thackeray from that reissue.[29] The next true English edition of *The Irish Sketch-Book* was not required until 1857.

A Man of Experience

It is perhaps easy to make too much of the tone with which stray remarks are written in casual correspondence, but it is interesting to note an apparent shift in Thackeray's self-portrayal in his letters to Chapman and Hall and Bradbury and Evans in the months following the appearance of *The Irish Sketch-Book*. On 15 May 1843, from Brighton, he wrote the former, "I came down here to be alone, & avoid good dinners and do some magazine work" (*Letters* 2:111). The letter is otherwise about reviews of, and advertisements for, the Irish book. In August, just before setting out on a tour of the Low Countries, he wrote Chapman and Hall again, lamenting briefly that an article he wrote for the *Foreign Quarterly Review* did not appear, asking for any money due to him, and devoting the bulk of his letter to proposing a German sketchbook:

> *I wish I could persuade you to think that Titmarsh in Germany devoting himself to the consideration of the fine arts there, and with a score or two of ballads to decorate the volumes, and plenty of etchings and a great deal of*

---

[28]I thank Mr. Nicolas Barker for confirming, by examining the two copies at the British Library, that the "1845 edition" of *The Irish Sketch-Book* is merely a reissue of the 1843 sheets with canceled title pages. I have seen two other privately owned copies that indicate the same.

[29]Gordon Ray, probably following Melville's bibliography, mistakenly called the 1845 reissue of *The Irish Sketch-Book* the first of Thackeray's books to go into a second edition (*Adversity*, p. 315), but that distinction belongs, if one discounts unauthorized foreign reprints, to *Notes of a Journey from Cornhill to Grand Cairo*, which reached a genuine, negotiated second edition in 1846, the year of its first publication.

> *fantastical humour and much nurture of the poetical and the ludicrous—I*
> *say I wish you would think such a book popular, and offer me the same*
> *terms for it as the Irish book. People (as I hope and trust) have only to*
> *become better acquainted with Titmarsh to like him more and the success*
> *of a German Sketch Book would help off very likely the few remaining*
> *copies of the Irish one. I am also in "the interesting situation" with respect*
> *to a novel: but I want to produce a very good one and a good work of art,*
> *and such a w[ork] demands a deal of time and thinking.*[30]

To Bradbury and Evans he wrote in February 1844:

> *I do not know whether you pay anything extra for great services (as all*
> *wise persons do) but I should not be surprised at hearing that any sum of*
> *money had been paid to my bankers as a reward for the astonishing late*
> *enclosed.*
>
> *If you publish it again in a little book there will be a deal of extra*
> *profit for all of us.*[31]

In short, Thackeray now fancied himself primarily an author of books who also wrote for the magazines, and he now often thought of the potential book version of his magazine contributions.

Though nothing ever came of the German sketchbook,[32] it is interesting to note Thackeray's warning to the publisher that "such a w[ork] demands a deal of time and thinking"—this from the man who on 10 September 1840 signed a contract to deliver by the end of December a two-volume work which he had not even started. The professional author had learned some things from the fact that serious work on the Irish book took four months of touring and writing in Ireland and four more months of writing, illustrating, and proofreading. His expenses from July 1842 to March 1843 (estimated by himself for an account to his mother and therefore, like Pendennis's accounts of college expenses, probably conservative) were £370, including £110 spent in Ireland. His income, not counting the £120 advance that had long since been spent, came to £110 for magazine work and under £200 for the book, which seems to have sold fairly well. Although for the purpose of the account to his mother Thackeray counted the £120 advance and figured his income on the book to be

---

[30]Original in possession of Peter Rhodes, Esq.; transcript supplied by Nicholas Pickwood.

[31]Bodleian. Possibly "The History of the Next French Revolution" published in *Punch*, February–April 1844, in nine installments; it was not republished separately.

[32]Three months later, on 10 Nov., Thackeray mentioned the project again, to no avail (*Letters* 2:126).

near £300, he did have to admit that the "childrens' nest egg is broken in upon as you say" (*Letters* 2:100). The pressure was clearly still on; and while a visible property was accumulating, Thackeray's fortune was still largely in the inkwell.

Another indication that Thackeray's sense of his profession and of his own position in it had come to a turning point after *The Irish Sketch-Book* and after agreeing with *Fraser's* for twelve installments of *Barry Lyndon* comes in a December 1843 letter of advice to his cousin Richard Bedingfield, who recently had published a book called *The Miser's Son*. It was advice which Thackeray clearly drew from his own experience and which was given as from one "old in the trade now."

[*Letters* 2:136–37]   *I sent on Tuesday week last a very pressing note to Jerdan regarding the "Miser's Son," with a little notice which I myself had written so as to save him trouble.*

It was, I need not tell you a favourable one as the story deserved; it has a great deal of talent of a great number of kinds, and many a man has made a fortune with a tithe of the merit.

But in spite of this, Jerdan has not inserted my article. Have you ever advertised in his paper or elsewhere? A laudatory paragraph here and there will do you no earthly good, unless the name of your book is perpetually before the public. The best book I ever wrote I published with an unknown publisher, and we got off two hundred and fifty copies of it, and this was after the success of the Paris book, with some thirty pounds of advertisements, and hugely laudatory notices in a score of journals. Shakespeare himself would not get a hearing in Gray's Inn Lane.

Unless your publisher actually offers you money for a future work, I beg you to have nothing to do with him. Write short tales. Make a dash at all the magazines; and at one or two of them I can promise you, as I have said, not an acceptance of your articles, but a favourable hearing. It is, however, a bad trade at the best. The prizes in it are fewer and worse than in any other professional lottery; but I know it's useless damping a man who will be an author whether or no—men are doomed, as it were, to the calling.

Make up your mind to this, my dear fellow, that the "Miser's Son" will never succeed—not from want of merit, but from want of a publisher. Shut it up without delay, and turn to some work that will pay you. Eschew poetry above all (you've had too much of it), and read all the history you can. Don't mind this patriarchal tone from me. I'm old in the trade now, and have lived so much with all sorts of people in the world that I plume myself on my experience.

Bedingfield followed Thackeray's advice, but a new work eighteen months later fared no better than the first with Thackeray, who wrote, "I can suit the magazines (but I can't hit the public, be hanged to them), and, from my knowledge of the former, I should say you will never get a good sale for commodities like these . . . your system may be the right one and mine wrong, but I'm sure I'm right as *to the state of the market*" (*Letters* 2:193).

In mid-1843 Thackeray's literary accounts stood thus: two substantial travel books (the Paris and Irish sketchbooks—the second an actual success); one collection of novellas and short stories (*Comic Tales*—not a success); three ephemeral pamphlets (*Flore et Zéphyr, An Essay on the Genius of George Cruikshank,* and *The Second Funeral of Napoleon*—all of greater critical than financial note). *Catherine* and *The History of Samuel Titmarsh* had been written with book publication in mind, but the former never got beyond magazine publication, and the latter was not published at all until after *Vanity Fair.* The odious magazine work was still the mainstay of his professional income. Within three years he would be the author of *Vanity Fair;* but for the present art criticism, travel, and observations on manners, dished out periodically, seemed his forte. The latter two veins of his genius would be extended in *From Cornhill to Grand Cairo* (1845–46) and "The Snobs of England" (1846–47). But at the same time Thackeray was gearing up for greater things. *Catherine* (1839) and *Barry Lyndon* (1844) develop the satiric fiction; *A Shabby Genteel Story* (1840), *Samuel Titmarsh* (1841), and *A Legend of the Rhine* (1845) develop the sentimental pathetic line. All these elements would find their way into *Vanity Fair.*

Though Thackeray had not produced a best-seller, he was steadily gaining attention. *The Irish Sketch-Book* was reprinted in America, the pirate being J. Winchester of New York. It became, in 1844, Thackeray's second American book, but like the first, it added nothing to Thackeray's coffers.[33] The most substantial property to come from Thackeray's pen in the remaining months of 1843 was the serial form of *Men's Wives* by George Fitzboodle in *Fraser's.* And in January 1844 the first installment of *Barry Lyndon* under the same pseudonym appeared in the same magazine. Though *Men's Wives* seems to have grown in response to favorable reactions to Fitzboodle's *Confessions* of late 1842, *Barry Lyndon* was a deliberate

---

[33]The Winchester edition is undated, but James Grant Wilson dated it 1844 (*Thackeray in the United States 1852–3, 1855–6,* 2 vols. [London, 1904]), as does the catalogue at the New York Public Library, where there are two copies. Henry Van Duzer (*A Thackeray Library*) dated it 1843. No one explains how the date was determined.

attempt to write a novel for eventual book publication. Despite the success of *The Irish Sketch-Book,* however, *Wives* and *Lyndon* both finally became books with no help from, and no immediate benefit to, Thackeray when in 1852 they became parts of a series of small books pirated by Appleton and Company of New York to take advantage of the publicity surrounding the author's first lecture tour of America. In the short term, however, *Barry Lyndon* gave Thackeray a steadiness of income he was not used to: "It is a comfort to think that there is a decent income arranged for 1844 (please God my health hold good) and actually a prospect of saving money at the year's end. . . . I have begun a story wh. is to last through the year in Fraser, and am to have my own way with the worthy Mr. Punch, whose pay is more than double of that I get anywhere else" (*Letters* 2:134–35).

It was with the confidence instilled by this financial prospect, as well as the assurance in his "experience," of which he had written Bedingfield, that one month later he declined to sign a contract for £108 per year with an American periodical publisher (a man named Henry Wikoff whose periodical has yet to be identified) because it required that Thackeray stay in Paris to write two articles a month on Paris and France. Unwilling to "sacrifice my liberty," Thackeray offered instead that "as I take your word for the payment of the articles you must please to take mine for supplying them." He outlined a plan for the American to pay a monthly salary and for himself to submit the two monthly articles, concluding: "I am a bad man of business, and only settle with you as I would with any other publisher. If I don't hear from you I shall conclude the negociation at an end" (*Letters* 2:158–59). Thackeray's account book for 1844 shows receipts of £4 and £3.10 for "India & American letters" in January and February and 4*s*. 10*d*. for an American letter in February; none of these has been identified. We hear no more of the American publisher but need not conclude Thackeray was right to characterize himself as a bad businessman. True, he did not close a deal with Wikoff, but neither did he commit himself to a course he could not or would not follow. Though Thackeray was still in a sense "writing for his life" and still occasionally had to remind friends that he was a "poor day-laborer in the vineyard and must work often when I would like to be taking my diversion" (*Letters* 2:138), he was not clutching desperately at every chance of work as he had been only a year earlier.

Thackeray's conception of himself as a bad businessman stemmed in large part from his sense of his own lack of steady, disciplined, organized work habits. Capable of enormous work binges, he thought himself lazy for procrastinating. And he could not shake the effects of the unfortunate experiences with the *National Standard* and the *Constitutional*. His "failure" to close with Wikoff may have contributed to that sense, as perhaps did also his failure four days later to get the publisher Giraldon to pay for his translation of Eugène Sue's *Mystères de Paris,* a work he threw over because he was not paid.[34] But the same evidence shows a businessman who knew, perhaps from bitter experience, when to cut his losses and who had a clear sense of himself, his profession, and what he was and was not willing to do. The letters to Wikoff and Giraldon were not written in financial complacency; in spite of the steady work on *Barry Lyndon* and the *Punch* contributions, Thackeray wrote the same month offering Fraser a burlesque originally titled "The Childe of Godesberg";[35] he proposed substantial reviews for Chapman and Hall's *Foreign Quarterly Review* (only one of which was accepted) and asked if they would "send me to any other country to travel" (*Letters* 2:161–62); and he wrote Bradbury and Evans proposing a collection of his shorter pieces (*Letters* 2:162–63). He was prompted to write to Bradbury and Evans under the mistaken notion that *Comic Tales* had been sold out, though in fact the 1848 reissue of *Comic Tales* was an attempt to sell off remaining copies of the 1840 impression with a new title page. At the same time he offered to edit a new gentleman's journal with "a decided air of white kid gloves . . . I know of no man in Europe who would handle ⟨it better⟩" (*Letters* 2:163).[36]

The tone of these proposals has changed: the appeals with side references to family obligations and friendship that suggested an undercurrent of desperate need are gone. The letters now have an air of "take it if you will; don't if you won't," suggesting perfect willingness on the author's part to face reality with equanimity. He was grateful, it is true, that Bradbury and Evans approved of his latest *Punch* contribution, "The History of the Next French Revolution," and he thanked the firm for its remittance, but at the same time his friendly and familiar relations with the publisher are revealed in his mock serious tone when, on reading the first

---

[34]Thackeray had reviewed *Mystères* in the *Foreign Quarterly Review* for April 1843 and noted various stints of translation in his diary for January 1844. On 2 Feb. 1844 Thackeray stipulated to the publisher M. Giraldon that he would do no more without payment (*Letters* 2:159). His account books show that he received £4 in January and 100 francs in February from Giraldon (ibid., 2:841); the translation was never finished.

[35]See *Letters* 2:141 n. 12, 160. Thackeray's account book shows receipt of £12 in January and £5 more in February from George Nickisson, editor of *Fraser's,* for "Godesberg," but it was not published by that magazine (Ray, *Adversity,* p. 338). It appeared as *A Legend of the Rhine* one year later in George Cruikshank's *Table Book,* June–December 1845.

[36]The angle brackets indicate a conjectural reading by Ray.

installment in print, he complained: "Having confided to you a few chapters of my forthcoming work on the next French revolution—you are bound in justice to print my words fairly—and I protest in the most solemn manner against several liberties which have been taken with my text. What is a historian without accuracy? A mere romancer and I hold such a creature in the utmost contempt" (*Letters* 2:163). He pointed out three specific errors, which because "The Next French Revolution" was never reprinted in Thackeray's lifetime have never been corrected.[37]

While Thackeray began as an enthusiastic amateur, a gentleman/author, and had become, because of financial and domestic disasters, a desperate literary hack dependent on the largess of relatively powerful publishers, nevertheless the relations between author and publisher by 1844 had become those between equals, literary tradesmen in the best meaning of the term as Thackeray had redefined it. This relationship did not characterize only Thackeray's dealings with Bradbury and Evans; he wrote in the same tone to Henry Colburn on 15 May, "Here is a very little article but in revenge I think a very good one" (*Letters* 2:169), and Colburn printed it.

The point is worth emphasizing, for it contradicts another misapprehension that has grown up about Thackeray's relations with publishers. Sir William Fraser, recollecting Thackeray years after the author's death, wrote:

> *Thackeray's resentment towards the trade of Publishers was deeply rooted. I believe that sixteen publishers refused him the pittance required to print his immortal work,* Vanity Fair. *Not one of them was capable intellectually of appreciating it.*
>
> *He pours out the vials of his wrath upon them in* Pendennis: *painting them to the world as the most stupid, the most selfish, and the most vulgar, class of tradesmen. . . .*
>
> *Calling on a publisher Thackeray waited with a friend, who told me the story: the carpet of the drawing-room was of a gaudy design of red and white: on the host appearing, the author of* Vanity Fair *said, "We*

---

[37]"In the first place there were not a *hundred* and twenty-four forts round Paris but twenty-four. . . . Secondly I never called H. M. Louis Philippe a Prince among Sovereigns which is absurd: but in reference to His Majesty's great age named him a PRIAM among Sovereigns. . . . Third. The two paragraphs beginning with the words 'Charenton the great lunatic asylum' and ending 'the Government alarm' should be inserted after"; the remainder of the letter is cut off, though Ray surmised the sentence to have ended: "the paragraph ending 'your countersign, Valmy'" (*Letters* 2:164).

have been admiring your carpet: it is most appropriate! You wade in the blood and brains of authors."[38]

Aside from the exaggeration represented by sixteen publishers without the brains to appreciate *Vanity Fair* and the distorted overstatement of Warrington's characterization of publishers, both of which reveal more about Sir William than about Thackeray, the final anecdote can be seen as typical of Thackeray's ironic humor rather than as the bitter commentary Fraser obviously took it for. Other commentators refer to Thackeray's haughty attitude toward publishers and usually point to the portraits of Bacon and Bungay in *Pendennis* as indications of Thackeray's general attitude. But if one can see Bentley and Colburn in these two portraits, one cannot see Chapman and Hall, Bradbury and Evans, or George Smith in them. I doubt if one can see James Fraser, John Macrone, or Hugh Cunningham there either, though there is precious little factual material with which to build a picture of Thackeray's personal relations with these three publishers.

The Climb to the Top

With *Barry Lyndon* in progress, "The History of the Next French Revolution" completed, and a multitude of short magazine articles keeping him from trouble with the bankers, Thackeray was still far from any peak in his career. To his mother he wrote, "It seems to me there is no time for anything here—The day occupied with nothings that must be done—and a fresh labor for almost every day—This is not very conducive to fame, nor to money somehow though it ought to be, and there's no reason why with regular labor I shouldn't make 1200—BUT somehow it doesn't go beyond 65 or 70 a month—and in that occasional failures" (*Letters* 2:170). Ten days later he still felt that "there's no use in writing about my professional business wh. is very incessant though paltry—I don't do above 20£ a month for the Chronicle instead of 40—but it is my own fault—the fact is I can't write the politics and the literary part is badly paid" (*Letters* 2:172).

Consequently, it should strike one with no surprise that Thackeray continued to be willing to try anything that came along. Between interviews and visits to locate a place in England to which he could bring and settle his wife, he agreed to write a biography of Talleyrand. Perhaps

---

[38]Sir William Fraser, *Hic et Ubique* (1893), except rpt. in Philip Collins, ed., *Thackeray Interviews and Recollections*, 2 vols. (London, 1983), 1:140.

having forgotten the lesson of the contract for *The Irish Sketch-Book* in 1840, Thackeray wrote Chapman and Hall on 16 July 1844: "I will engage to write the volume 'the life of Talleyrand, and to have the MS. in your hands by the 1 December—health permitting. and will sign an agreement to that effect if you will have the goodness to prepare one" (*Letters* 2:174). The contract, if there was one, is lost, but two weeks later he was rushing off to London from Liège where he had been spending time with his family to find books he needed in his Talleyrand research (*Letters* 2:175).

Then on 20 August he had an offer he couldn't refuse—free passage to the Middle East. "I thought the chance so great that Ive accepted," he explained to his mother; "I'm to write a book for 200£ for C&H. [Chapman and Hall] on the East first, or that Cockney part wh. I shall see—then to do Talleyrand" (*Letters* 2:176–77). The next day he boarded ship in Southampton, devoting himself to continuing *Barry Lyndon* for *Fraser's*, sending periodic travel accounts to *Punch* from "Our Fat Contributor," and writing the Cockney's Eastern book for Chapman and Hall.

Over two months later, his tour ended at Malta on 28 October, but his return to England was delayed by quarantine and a sojourn in Rome where a mix-up at "the dd dd-dd-ddd-ddd post office" kept him from his mail and his money for, he claimed, thirty-five days (*Letters* 2:185–86). By 10 January 1845 he wrote Chapman and Hall to say the book "is all but done," and he promised to "go tooth and nail at Talleyrand directly I reach England" (*Letters* 2:185). However, by the end of March, "Talleyrand is put off sine die"—never to be heard of again—and the "Eastern book just going into hand" (*Letters* 2:190). At the same time he hinted at a project, possibly *Vanity Fair*, "wh. is projected and of prodigious importance, This is a scheme by wh I expect to make a great deal of money it is to be called—but never mind what until it is ready" (*Letters* 2:190). A month later he wrote George William Nickisson, at *Fraser's*, "between ourselves I believe I am in a career of most wonderful money getting" (*Letters* 2:191). It is generally supposed that "the commencement of a novel" which Thackeray had earlier sent to Henry Colburn at the *New Monthly Magazine* and then retrieved from William Harrison Ainsworth who replaced Colburn as editor was an early draft of *Vanity Fair*. But it would be eight more months before the beginning of that novel was first set in type and eight more after that before it began publication.

In the meantime, *A Legend of the Rhine*, written as "The Childe of Godesburg" in early 1844, finally saw the light in *George Cruikshank's Table Book* (June–December 1845). *Mrs. Perkins's Ball*, begun at least as early as November 1844, projected for Christmas 1845 and nearly finished, was eventually delayed till December 1846 (though its imprint says 1847). And in July 1845 the Eastern book still needed work ("I want to fill two blanks in my chapter" [*Letters* 2:199]). The delays may account in part for Thackeray's request to Bradbury and Evans on 9 July: "May I ask you for 100?—my funds are getting very low, and I should be very glad of a supply" (Bodleian). It is probable that Bradbury and Evans owed him some of that already and soon would owe the rest, judging from the number of Thackeray's contributions to *Punch* in that year: eighty-four— of which eleven appeared in July. That compares with fifty-four contribu- tions in 1844 and seventy-two in 1846.[39] However, on the very same day he sent Chapman and Hall £55 they had lent him previously, at the same time trying to sort out the terms of agreement for publishing what he still referred to as "the Eastern Book": "I have been thinking over the bargain regarding the Eastern Book, and think you are rather hard upon me. The trip was a very expensive one. I was offered my own terms elsewhere— and I assure you undertook the book for you with the full conviction that it would be paid at the price of the other volume on wh. I am engaged for you—viz two hundred guineas. I shall rely on your justice confidently however" (*Letters* 2:201). It is understandable that there was no firm agreement to turn to, since whatever passed between author and publisher on 19 August 1844, when Thackeray decided to go to Egypt, must have taken place hastily.

It is worth digressing to follow the fortunes of *Notes of a Journey from Cornhill to Grand Cairo* and the continued negotiations between Thackeray and Chapman and Hall; for in the next surviving reference to it, Thackeray equated the original agreement for the book with the agreement for *The Irish Sketch-Book:* "I . . . am glad to hear that at last I am to have the fortune of a second edition. Our bargain for the first edition was made upon the notion that it was a half guinea book on the same terms as the Irish book— I certainly ought to have my share of the 1400 odd shillings wh. the book has brought in and suggest accordingly that division." But a look back through surviving letters shows that Thackeray skipped over the inter- vening negotiations for the biography of Talleyrand and that that was the book agreed upon with reference to the Irish book. Thackeray, in the rush of embarking for the Orient, had understood that Chapman and Hall would take the Eastern book on the same terms as Talleyrand. Now, in the latter half of 1846, operating on that understanding, he couched his

---

[39]See M. H. Spielman's checklist in *Hitherto Unidentified Contributions of W. M. Thackeray to Punch* (1900; rpt. New York, 1971).

demand for fair treatment in the self-deprecatory language so characteristic of his relations with publishers. "But I was always a bad hand at accounts," he continued, "and put myself honestly into your hands as men of business to deal fairly with me." He did not stop there: "We will ask Forster tomorrow whether or no I am right in my claim to the 1400 sixpences" (*Letters* 2:258–59). The Talleyrand book was not finished, and there is no record of Thackeray's income from the Eastern book.

In August 1845, because of remonstrances by his mother, he "cancelled" the chapter on Jerusalem, which he found very difficult to replace, partly for lack of time, partly for trying to tread lightly between a heterodoxy that might offend the public and a hypocrisy that would offend himself. Work on it dragged through the autumn and into December— mostly neglected while he wrote for *Punch* (*Jeames's Diary* began appearing in November), but on 22 December he sent in the dedication and preface, and *Notes on a Journey from Cornhill to Grand Cairo* finally appeared in February 1846.

Another small episode, beginning a new stage in Thackeray's relations with his publishers, occurred at this time. Thomas Fraser, foreign correspondent in Paris for the *Morning Chronicle,* wrote asking him to act as go-between for another author and the firm of Chapman and Hall. From this time on, such letters became frequent. In those days before literary agents, well-known authors were constantly being asked by unknown authors to act as agents. In the same letter in which Thackeray fulfilled this task to Hall, he submitted an article on behalf of Mrs. Colmache, which he seems finally to have succeeded in placing with Ainsworth's *New Monthly Magazine* (*Letters* 2:219, 230, 232). Like other informal agents he was frequently unsuccessful; he explained to one friend that not only could he not help with the *Morning Chronicle* but was himself not helped there by a letter of reference from Arthur Buller (*Letters* 2:252). Over the years Thackeray did what he could as literary agent, though he sometimes refused for lack of time or for lack of belief in the marketability of the writings sent to him. He expressed himself perhaps most frankly to his mother, who sometime in 1847 sent him one of her own compositions to place:

[*Letters* 2:330] *I will send your wonderful story to Chapman & to Smith & Elder who will send it back again. It may be from an angels pen and I doubt if you will get a publisher to bring it out except at the author's charges. As for getting money by it is a vain hope—and to suppose it will succeed because it will do people good—is as green almost as my horse-dealings.*

The publishers don't care a straw for a friend of mine, but for what will put money in their pockets—and consider, will your tale cover an outlay of 60 or 70£ and give them a return for their risk and trouble? say 100£ of a half crown book sold at 1/6d to the trade, costing 6d let us say to produce they would require to sell 2000 to pay £100—& how many books do you think sell 2000? not one in as many 100.

American interest in Thackeray's work continued to grow. In addition to its London appearance in two genuine editions in 1846, the Eastern book was pirated by Wiley and Putman in Philadelphia. The same year saw another of his books issued in America with no economic benefit to the author: *Jeames's Diary* was lifted from *Punch* by William Taylor and Company of New York, Philadelphia, and Baltimore. At home *Mrs. Perkins's Ball,* dated 1847, actually appeared in time for the 1846 Christmas trade, published by Chapman and Hall. Unlike the other books, however, *Mrs. Perkins's* was "a great success—the greatest I have had." On 23 December he reported that it was selling "very fast near 1500 are gone out of 2000 already—and this is a great success for the likes of me" (*Letters* 2:258). At the end of May the next year, finding himself pressed for money to pay for railway shares gone sour, he wrote Chapman a plea for cash he hoped was resulting from the second edition of *Mrs. Perkins's Ball.*[40]

In 1846 Thackeray was quite busy contributing on a regular basis to *Punch* (seventy-two articles) and to the *Morning Chronicle* (eighteen articles). He had time for only five *Fraser's* pieces that year. The most memorable work of the year was "The Snobs of England" in *Punch,* a series which "hit the public," not only as a social satire but as a popular success.

His projections for 1846 had been "so good, that I calculate on laying by at least 500 next year. I am engaged to write a monthly story at 60£ a number [*Vanity Fair*]—I have besides 700£ between Punch & the Chronicle: though I don't calculate on the latter beyond the year as I am a very weak & poor politician only good for outside articles and occasional jeux-d'esprit—The 400 may subside possibly into 2 or 300 but you see there will be enough and to spare."[41] His resignation from the *Morning Chronicle* in February, before anything he may have written for it that year was

---

[40]*Letters* 2:290. The first edition is undated; the second is dated 1847 and says "Second Edition" on the cover. Thackeray never kept close tabs on how much publishers owed him, and a letter like this one asking if any money was owed reflected his awareness that he may already have received as advance or loan the amount due.

[41]Letter to his stepfather, *Letters* 2:225.

published, was short-lived and may have been, like his striking for wages against *Fraser's* in 1837, part of a negotiation. From March through October his work appeared in the *Morning Chronicle* regularly. Or his brief resignation may have been connected with the proposed commencement of *Vanity Fair* on the first of May. However, work on that great book could not have occupied much of his time since he clearly had not progressed beyond the five chapters that Bradbury and Evans set in type in April. And, in any case, the serial publication of the novel was delayed until January 1847.

Moonlighting

From January 1847 through June 1848 Thackeray's major work and single largest source of income was *Vanity Fair*. From October 1848 through November 1850 his major work was *Pendennis*. Such work would be a full-time occupation for many an author, but in the same four-year period Thackeray produced chapters 44–52 of "The Snobs of England," twenty-one installments of *Punch's Prize Novelists*, fifteen installments of "Travels in London," six installments of *A Little Dinner at Timmins's*, a Christmas book called *Our Street* (December 1847, dated 1848), eighteen installments of *Mr. Brown's Letters to a Young Man about Town*, another Christmas book called *Dr. Birch and His Young Friends* (December 1848, dated 1849), seven installments of "The Proser," and over one hundred other magazine contributions, primarily to *Punch*. His primary "employers" were William Bradbury and F. M. Evans, partners in a large printing firm that had begun publishing in the early 1840s and proprietors of *Punch*, who were for a short time the primary publisher for both Thackeray and Charles Dickens. Bradbury and Evans, riding a rising tide out of the recession of the mid-1840s, seemed content to let Thackeray write and publish elsewhere as much as he liked, so long as the monthly installment novels continued on schedule and his *Punch* contributions stayed up.

Thackeray's ship had finally come in. Evidence is seen in the book-form issue in 1848 of *Vanity Fair, Dr. Birch,* and *The Book of Snobs*. Plans began in June 1848 for the reissue of *The History of Samuel Titmarsh*, though a pirated American edition in November or December (by Harper and Brothers) preceded the English edition, which did not come out until January 1849. Cunningham also took advantage of the rising popularity of *Vanity Fair* to reissue *Comic Tales* with a new title page. In 1849 the English edition of *Samuel Titmarsh* made its appearance, sold out, and a second edition was produced;[42] the first volume of *Pendennis* appeared in England

---

[42]A detailed account is given below in chapter 5.

and Germany (by Tauchnitz), *Vanity Fair* appeared in America (pirated by Harper and Brothers) and in Germany (paid for by Tauchnitz); a first volume of *Miscellanies* appeared in Germany (Tauchnitz); and *Rebecca and Rowena* (dated 1850) appeared in England and France. In 1850 the second volume of *Pendennis* was published in England as well as in Germany; *The Kickleburys on the Rhine* appeared in December (and required a second printing in January); and *Stubbs's Calendar* was reprinted without authority in New York (by Stringer and Townsend). Throughout these three years Thackeray also contributed occasional drawings and illustrations to works other than his own.

Thackeray said he was "at the top of the tree," and it may appear that that was the case, but somehow he yet felt keenly his precarious economic condition. It took a while for *Vanity Fair* to catch on with the public. Though Thackeray remarked in a letter in July 1847 that "the publishers are quite contented" (*Letters* 2:311), he noted in October that "it does everything but sell, and appears really immensely to increase my reputation if not my income" (*Letters* 2:318). In December he reluctantly wrote a dunning letter to Edward Chapman: "Will you send me the remaining 60£ by the bearer if you please. Indeed I'm sorry for everyone's delays and misfortunes" (*Letters* 2:326). One month later he lamented to his mother that "on going to the publishers to draw my money tother day I was met with a smiling reference to some old books by wh. it appears I had overdrawn them 120£ 2 years ago—about wh. fatal circumstance I was quite ignorant" (*Letters* 2:333).

Although his own finances occasionally caught him by surprise, Thackeray seemed well aware of the risk and venture that publishing involved. He wrote in May 1848 that "the publishers are at this minute several hundred pounds out of pocket by me, that I know for certain—and I try to keep down any elation wh. my friends praises may cause me, by keeping this fact steadily before my eyes" (*Letters* 2:378). It was not until August 1848, two months after the appearance of the last installment, that Thackeray could write with real confidence, "Vanity Fair is doing very well commercially I'm happy to say at last. They have sold 1500 volumes wh. is very well in these times of revolution and dismay" (*Letters* 2:420).

Thackeray's increasing income seemed, however, insufficient to meet his needs. In 1847 he took a house big enough to accommodate his daughters and parents, and during 1848 he was keenly bent on clearing away his stepfather's debts, thereby enabling his mother to move to England and be with the children. In addition, he had invested and lost over £500 in the railroad mania that year. His efforts to get his parents back to England reached a peak in the summer of 1848, when in June he negotiated with Bradbury and Evans for the book publication of *The History of Samuel Titmarsh*. Before a final agreement was reached, he wrote his mother, "I am to have 100£ for the reprint of The Hoggarty Diamond, perhaps today, (but I don't like to dun). . . . I am to have another 1000 a year for my next story [*Pendennis*] and with Punch & what not can do very like 700 or 750 more it is good income," and at the end of the same letter he added optimistically, "I have just seen Evans he can not give me an answer about the H.D. for 2 or 3 days but will tell me—indeed you may consider the matter as done and come as soon as you like to us all" (*Letters* 2:382–83). At about this same time in an undated letter to Evans, Thackeray pressed his proposal, with particular attention to the money: "If money is scarce could not a bill at 6 weeks be made out bearing your venerated signature? My bankers I believe would let me pay it in as cash and in that time I should have discharged my part of the obligation to you regarding the great Hoggarty Diamond by completing the 10 blocks for that work. How much are you to give me? 100 or 150? You said you would see—Let me have the just sum: and I'm sure you'll see that I ought to have 100 a month for the Pendennis" (Bodleian). And on 18 July he wrote to Chapman asking for "50£ in advance of the Kickleburys abroad" in order to pay a bill for his stepfather (*Letters* 2:399). The same day he paid the bill, which came to £30, the last outstanding debt preventing his parents' return to England. The other £20 probably went, at least in part, for the expenses of his birthday party the same day. Although his parents visited London in October and then again on several occasions, including one trying four-month stay in 1857, they did not move to England until 1859, when they set up an establishment of their own.

The rising success of *Vanity Fair* and the continued popularity of *Punch* led to two celebrations by publishers and authors. On 20 June 1848 the staff of *Punch* signed a sort of declaration to William Bradbury calling for the celebration of the seventh year of publication of *Punch* (Morgan). The celebration itself may have been the dinner given at Greenwich for William Bradbury to which Thackeray referred in an undated letter to one of the *Punch* illustrators (*Letters* 2:396). Apparently there was also a dinner to celebrate the completion of *Vanity Fair,* and it may have been to it that Thackeray referred in another undated letter to F. M. Evans in the summer of 1848, saying: "Please to send me per bearer the little ready money we spoke about yesterday. The bill for 120 Gnas at 6 weeks. and 1 dozen small knives for the dinner today. I shall look for you at 7+" (Bodleian).

As is apparent from a variety of letters already cited, Thackeray left the daily accounting of financial obligations between himself and his major publishers entirely to the publishers. He did negotiate occasionally for the sale price or profit-sharing percentage, but when it came to second editions and the slow accumulation of profit-sharing dividends, he was, as most authors are, at the mercy of the publisher's accounting. Thus he applied to publishers for money according to his needs rather than according to the goods he had for sale. That is because his back list was beginning quietly to produce small but long-term profits which he had no other way to monitor than by asking for the money.

Thackeray's years of struggle, or "adversity" as Gordon Ray denominated them, would soon end. He had had two golden years of gentlemanly, leisurely pursuit of the Muse, followed by fifteen years of steadily beating the flanks of harnessed art in order to reach a plateau of economic security and restored financial competence. In 1847 Thackeray finally could see real prospects of restoring a fortune for his daughters equal to that he had received and lost.

The annals of nineteenth-century English literature do not sport many comparable tales. Instead, authors like Byron, Irving, Scott, Edward Bulwer Lytton, Edward Fitzgerald, and even Robert Smith Surtees cultivated the role of gentlemen amateurs, hiding their disciplined application to the work behind anonymous publication or romantic tales of tossing off the fruits of inspiration in their spare time. Every one of these men had income from other sources, either inherited estates or government posts or pensions. Thackeray may have aspired to a similar image in his early days, though while still independently wealthy he openly entered the editorship of the *National Standard* as an investor and educator of public taste. All that was brushed aside by ill fate and necessity; the amateur genius or dilettante became the literary tradesman, proud of his professional accomplishments and disdainful of the pretensions of inspiration. Thackeray did not mind showing that he had to earn his living by the sweat of his brow.

On the other hand, the largely unsung history of nineteenth-century English writing is full of instances of persons with less initial luck and worse continued bad luck, folks with little but their brains and determination to carry them on—men like Douglas Jerrold, Gilbert à Beckett, John Leech, Richard Doyle, and George Augustus Sala (to name a few of Thackeray's colleagues on the *Punch* staff), or like George Henry Lewes, Leigh Hunt, and William Carleton who died in poverty and left no estate.

Thackeray's story is more akin to that of Charles Dickens and Thomas Carlyle whose economic competences were also wrung from their writings, though neither of them could look back upon lost patrimonies or aspire to a restored level of social acceptance. Matthew Arnold, John Henry Newman, Anthony Trollope, and T. H. Huxley all had income from other work to keep the wolf from the door. It made a difference in one's assessment of the Muse and Pegasus if literature was an add-on rather than the mainstay of livelihood. Yet, Thackeray's view was diametrically opposed to those of Dickens and Carlyle. Dickens's insistence on the dignity of literature seems to me based in part on a romantic view of the artist as aesthete, in greater part on Carlyle's view of the hero as man of letters, and finally but unprovably in part on a realization that the dignity of literature was the only prop he had to lean on for a place in the English social structure. Carlyle, likewise a social outsider, disdained all standards of value outside the morally useful heroic or prophetic, perhaps because he too had no other toehold for approval by a Victorian audience. But Thackeray, equally dependent with Dickens and Carlyle on the proceeds of his writing for economic survival, had other resources for his place in society. Little as Dickens or Carlyle would have envied Thackeray's social graces or manners, the self-confidence these provided Thackeray enabled him to view with less charity or self-interest the romantic and heroic visions of the artist in society. Though his view of writing as a trade was susceptible to the charges laid at his door by John Forster of denigrating his profession to gain status with the "non-literary classes," I choose to think, instead, that his view of the profession was more realistic and less histrionic, as his writing is also more realistic and less histrionic, than that of Dickens or Carlyle.

III

The Writer as a Literary Property

DURING THE YEARS OF STRUGGLE to establish himself as a writer, Thackeray can hardly be said to have "had a publisher." Each new book had to find a home, often with a new publisher because his last book had failed to make money. By 1847 Thackeray's works had been published in book form by ten different publishers, of which four (Chapman and Hall, Macrone, Cunningham, and Hooper) are known to have paid him money. Another (Mitchell) published by agreement with him but claimed that returns did not even cover production costs, so there was no payment to the author. The other five (Taylor, Baudry, Berford, Cary and Hart, and Winchester), publishing unauthorized reprints, definitely did not pay.[1]

Chapman and Hall

Of the four who did pay, Chapman and Hall alone stuck with the author over a significant period of time. Indeed, the firm acted as Thackeray's bankers as well as publishers in the early 1840s. Then, for four years running (1846–49), Thackeray was able to count on them to publish his Christmas books.

Thackeray's relations with the Chapman firm in the second half of the 1840s was carried on as between equals in a business venture. In the turbulent revolutionary year 1848, Thackeray wrote Chapman suggesting the projected Christmas book, *Kickleburys on the Rhine,* be dropped in favor of a purely domestic and politically safe story (*Letters* 2:444–45). *Dr. Birch and His Young Friends* became the season's offering that year. On the other hand, when Charles Lever parodied Thackeray as Elias Howle in the next month's installment of *Roland Cashel,* Thackeray's protest to Chapman that *his* publisher should not be "the office for this dreary personality" apparently made no difference. Yet Thackeray's business relations with Chapman and Hall proceeded on a professional level; subsequent letters deal with the production problems and illustrations for *Dr. Birch* (*Letters* 2:466).

Rebecca and Rowena was Thackeray's last book published by Chapman

---

[1]Baudry is a possible exception, but there is no evidence one way or the other.

and Hall. On 17 September 1849, while he concerned himself primarily
with producing *Pendennis,* Thackeray twisted his ankle badly enough to
put him in bed for a few days. As luck would have it, he came down at the
same time with a case of what may have been cholera, the worst of the
illness coming on the night of 3 October. Obviously, he failed to prepare
the next number of *Pendennis* for October; and though he pulled through
and was declared out of danger by 15 October, he did not resume publication of *Pendennis* until 1 January 1850. He spent the end of October in
Brighton to convalesce with "Dr. Sea Breeze," and on 7 November he
began work, with Eyre Crowe's help, on the texts for Louis Marvy's
Sketches after English Landscape Painters to be published by David Bogue in
1850. Bogue had very recently taken over the business of Charles Tilt,
who had published Thackeray's *Stubbs's Calendar* in *The Comic Almanac for
1839.* Bogue wished both to build on Tilt's past interest and to take
advantage of Thackeray's new popularity, so he wrote to Thackeray
proposing republication of *Stubbs's.* On 21 November Thackeray replied:

[*Letters*   *The story of Stubb's Calendar has been already reprinted by me, in the
2:610–11]   "Comic Tales & Sketches" published by Cunningham in 1840—It is my
                copyright, as all my works have been by verbal agreements with the
                publishers for whom I wrote, with the exception of certain contributions to
                the "Heads of the People" about wh. I forgot to make a stipulation:
                though I am advised that I can with perfect safety republish these latter in
                case I shd. think fit so to do.
                    I regret that I cannot consent to the republication of the Stubbs story,
                under the present circumstances.
                    I am working at the text for M. Marvy's engravings, & hope very
                shortly to deliver it to you. Nothing but illness wd. have prevented me
                from executing this task before now.*

By 3 December Thackeray was well enough to accept a dinner
invitation from George Smith, publisher of Charlotte Brontë's *Jane Eyre.*
The two men had not met, but Brontë had asked Smith for a meeting with
Thackeray. There is nothing in George Smith's recollections[2] or Thackeray's own to suggest any lingering effects of his illness. Yet in December,
Thackeray had to write Joseph Cundall to explain the delay in completing
the text for Marvy's book. Cundall, remembered primarily as a writer and
publisher of children's books in the 1840s and 1850s, had previously been
employed by Charles Tilt and had copublished several books with David

---

[2]Quoted from Leonard Huxley's *House of Smith, Elder* in *Letters* 2:611n.

Bogue. He had just suffered bankruptcy and was continuing his publishing activities only in conjunction with other publishers when he apparently inquired on Bogue's behalf concerning the text Thackeray was preparing.[3] Thackeray wrote:

[*Letters*   *The gentleman whom I had engaged to get some biographical notices for*
2:612–13]   *Mr. Marvy's sketches is gone to France, hence my delay during the last*
              month—but this month at any rate I promise you that the work shall be
              done, and always keep my promises.
                       I hope Mr. Bogue will settle with Mr. Marvy—what is it that I am
              to be paid for my contributions? It is a very difficult task to perform.

It may be that in November, while Eyre Crowe was in France, Thackeray worked on *Rebecca and Rowena,* the 102-page continuation of the romance of Ivanhoe. Whatever the case, it was already December when he sent the manuscript to Chapman, at the same time asking to be paid £50 and saying, "The book has cost me more time than all the rest" (*Letters* 2:613). That left little time for publication, and it is perhaps understandable that mistakes should have been made, particularly with the title and preface, which are always the last to be prepared. Thackeray sent the preface together with copy for an advertisement to the publisher, who mistakenly assumed the preface was part of the ad. The whole apparently appeared together, for Thackeray wrote the publisher correcting the subtitle from "A Romance on Romance" to "*or* Romance on Romance" and adding: "What the devil have you gone & done? Why the devil didnt you send me proof You have gone & printed the preface with the advertisement—spoiled my point: offended Dr. Elliotson & annoyed me beyond measure."[4] A partially corrected advertisement appeared in the *Examiner* on 1 December, without the preface but still sporting the erroneous subtitle, prompting Thackeray to write again: "The title as I wrote, and rewrote and recorrected is R & R or Romance on Romance not A [Romance on Romance]" (*Letters* 2:614). On 22 December the *Examiner* ad miscorrected the subtitle to "Or A Romance on Romance," but the book itself never was corrected. Since the title page is a wood engraving, one wonders if perhaps the illustrator, Richard Doyle, might have initiated the problem.

---

[3]Ruari McLean, *Joseph Cundall: A Victorian Publisher* (Pinner, 1976), pp. 1, 18, 22.

[4]*Letters* 2:613–14. This episode is described in detail in Edgar Harden's "Thackeray: 'Rebecca and Rowena': A Further Document," *Notes and Queries* 24 (1977): 20–22. Three manuscript pages with advertisement copy and preface are at the John Rylands Library, Manchester. The published advertisement has not been located.

Such irritations may seem minor, but there is an evident coolness on both sides that attends the almost gentlemanly duty Thackeray fulfilled when he offered Chapman and Hall his next Christmas book, the one that had been scheduled for two years earlier when *Dr. Birch* was substituted. It is likely, too, that Thackeray's new stature as author of two successful major works made him less tolerant of Chapman and Hall's decidedly genteel, informal, and occasionally sloppy business practices. On the other hand, Thackeray himself tended to be informal about business agreements, as is suggested by his reference to the "verbal agreements" about copyrights in his letter to Bogue.

In August 1850 Thackeray dutifully broached the subject of *The Kickleburys on the Rhine,* his fifth Christmas book, offering Chapman and Hall an edition of 3,000 copies for £150. "I think," he wrote, "I have a right to a shilling per copy of a 5/ & often 7/ book: and intend to stipulate for that sum with my publisher" (*Letters* 2:687). Chapman's reply on the back of Thackeray's letter was:

[Hunt-   *I find that there are about 350 copies of Rebecca [the 1849 Christmas*
ington]   *book] now on hand out of the 3000 printed and I know that there are also a*
                 great many [illegible word] with the country booksellers. I don't think
                 that a sale of more than 2500 could be depended on for the new book.
                     Under these circumstances, I could not, I am sorry to say agree to
                 your proposal with any chance of profit to myself.
                     I am obliged to you for mentioning your intention to me before
                 applying elsewhere & shall be sorry to lose the ⟨advantage⟩ ↑ value ↓ of
                 your name, but it would be useless for me to undertake a speculation by
                 which I feel assured I should lose.

How wrong Chapman was and how right Thackeray was to hold out became evident soon enough. Chapman and Hall lost whatever hold the firm may have had on Thackeray. The relationship, however, had been a long and generally friendly one; and, although Thackeray's written correspondence with Chapman and Hall seems virtually to have ceased in 1850, his letters to others contain references to his having met and conversed with one or another of the partners from time to time for the rest of his life.

If Chapman and Hall was Thackeray's publisher in any proprietary way—Thackeray had assured the firm when offering it *The Kickleburys* in 1850 that he had spoken to no other publishers—it did not try very hard to hold him. Chapman obviously made his decision without reading any of the manuscript, and his change in wording from "advantage," which has a positive meaning, to the ambiguous "value," suggests Chapman may not have been as sorry as he said about losing Thackeray. In any case, two other publishers were ready to take Thackeray away. The first was Bradbury and Evans. *Vanity Fair* became that company's publication almost by default. Thackeray had thought, when he first became a *Punch* writer for Bradbury and Evans, that he was associating himself with a less respectable magazine, but by 1846 this connection was not only economically important but one Thackeray had come to take seriously as a means of satire and ridicule against political and social evil. Yet to have his first major book published from "THE PUNCH OFFICE," after being rejected by at least one and possibly four other publishers, is an indication that he was settling for a familiar, somewhat lower class publisher. (Dickens, publishing his first work, *Dombey and Son,* with Bradbury and Evans at the same time, had no reference to *Punch* in the imprint of his numbered parts.) And once Bradbury and Evans had carried *Vanity Fair* through the risky part of its production to success and had offered Thackeray increased pay for his next novel before a word of it was written, he became a Bradbury and Evans author.

That was not, however, an exclusive arrangement. The other publisher wooing Thackeray from Chapman and Hall did so far more deliberately and intentionally. With Chapman and Hall's release of its courtesy claim to his next Christmas book, by declining to pay £150 for it, Thackeray was free to offer it to George Smith of Smith, Elder, and Company, who immediately sent him a check for the full amount.[5] Thackeray replied in August 1850, "I went out of town early on the mg. of the 25th or I should sooner have acknowledged your letter, & the enclosed cheque for 150£: the price of the Copyright of 3000 copies of my Xmas book for 1851 [i.e., December 1850]" (NLS). The first edition of 3,000 copies sold out immediately. On the day Smith wrote Thackeray with this news (and, by the way, enclosing a £50 bonus check), the *Times* printed an unfavorable review (later attributed to Charles Lamb Kenny). Thackeray's response, "An Essay on Thunder and Small Beer," appeared in the second printing of *The Kickleburys,* announcing itself as a "Second Edition," dated 1850. Two more reprints, the second called a "Third Edition," were issued in 1851. The printer's records for Smith, Elder no longer exist for the years preceding 1853, but it is clear that Chapman and Hall turned down a chance to make a tidy profit and thereby also lost any chance of enlarging

---

[5] John Sutherland, "The Thackeray-Smith Contracts," *Studies in the Novel* 13 (1981): 171.

its share in an increasingly valuable literary property.[6] Chapman and Hall's dealings with Thackeray had begun with caution, the formalities of contracts, and the proffer of advances in exchange for a security, the deposit of the family plate. These formalities later were dropped, and there were no written contracts for the Christmas books and no formal registration of titles with the Stationers' Register, facts discovered by George Smith in 1865 when he was trying to gain control of all Thackeray's copyrights.[7] Nevertheless, the Chapman and Hall firm seems to have paid its small profit-sharing dividends regularly, relying on gentlemen's agreements.

Bradbury and Evans exhibited a similar tendency toward informal agreements, and the company's hold on Thackeray was never a very firm one. It never stipulated for anything except the work it was about to publish. Anything else Thackeray undertook at the same time was none of its business or concern. With Smith, Elder, for example, Thackeray published *The Kickleburys* in 1850, *The History of Henry Esmond* in 1852, and *Lectures on Eighteenth Century English Humourists* in 1853, but in fact he was primarily a Bradbury and Evans author from 1847 to 1859.

Bradbury and Evans

William Bradbury and Frederick Mullet Evans had gone into partnership as a printing firm in 1830. The company became the primary printer for the publisher and bookseller Moxon and later for Chapman and Hall. In the late 1840s and 50s it appears to have done much of Smith, Elder's printing until that firm acquired its own printing works in 1857. Bradbury and Evans began, then, as a printer, not bookseller and publisher. When the partners purchased *Punch* in 1841, they launched a publishing career that seems to have been extraordinarily lucky rather than expert or self-assured. Charles Dickens considered a long while and turned down several offers from Bradbury and Evans because he was not convinced the firm knew enough about advertising and book distribution to make the most of his works.[8] Thackeray's connection with Bradbury and Evans had begun, of course, with his contributions to *Punch* in 1842 and included occasional pieces in such *Punch* Office publications as *George Cruikshank's Table-Book* (1845) and *Punch's Pocket Book for 1847*. Perhaps like Dickens, Thackeray

---

[6]We do not know how large a printing the second edition was, but in 1853 approximately 550 copies were left, and in 1863, 173 copies were left.

[7]MS correspondence between Smith and Chapman, used by permission of John Murray, Publishers, the present owners.

[8]Patten, *Dickens and His Publishers*, p. 141.

distrusted his *Punch* employers as book publisher, for he tried other publishers with his first truly ambitious book before settling with their firm.
The first number of *Vanity Fair,* issued on 1 January 1847, was the first
Thackeray title published separately by Bradbury and Evans, and it
marked the beginning of eleven years during which the firm was Thackeray's primary publisher. This relationship ended in 1859 with the purported failure of *The Virginians* and the successful wooing of Thackeray by
George Smith, which bore fruit in the *Cornhill Magazine.* By then Bradbury and Evans had published Thackeray's four longest novels and three
of the four volumes of *Miscellanies* collecting many of his better early
productions. Thus, Bradbury and Evans continued to exercise publication
rights in the majority of Thackeray's work until July 1865, when Smith,
Elder and Company purchased the unsold stock, stereotyped plates, and
copyrights from all other interested parties.

Thackeray's business association with Bradbury and Evans can be
detailed rather fully because the firm's account books are still extant, and
while the various records seem incomplete and do not always agree on
amounts, especially in accounting for the distribution of copies printed,
the archive provides what is in the main a faithful picture of the financial
relationship between author and publisher. Sales figures provide a clue to
the circulation of Thackeray's works; the size and number of printings
suggest the development and decline in the popularity of individual titles;
a clearer view is gained of the financial "failure" of *The Virginians;* and a
previously unknown edition of one of his books is revealed.[9]

Although *Vanity Fair* (1847–48) earned Thackeray less money
than any of his other parts–issued novels (£3,006.3.3, compared with
£3,207.18.1 for *Pendennis* and £4,561.3.9 for *The Newcomes*), it was his
most widely circulated book. Of the two editions published by Bradbury
and Evans, 32,500 copies were printed, and only 931 of these remained in
stock in June 1865. Most of the sales were of the cheap edition, which was
printed eleven times between 1853 and 1865 to produce 22,000 copies.
Aside from the fact that Thackeray received only £60 per number as initial
payments for *Vanity Fair,* production costs kept it from earning much on
the profit-sharing system, and although the total number of copies of the
first edition (10,500) exceeded that for *Pendennis* (9,500), it required twice
as many printings to reach that figure. The obvious reason for this was
that *Vanity Fair* was written by a relatively unknown author for whom no

---

[9]A detailed analysis of the ledgers as clues to production is given for *Vanity Fair* and *Esmond* in
chapter 5 below.

publisher would be likely to risk large printings, whereas *Pendennis* (1848–50) was written by the author of *Vanity Fair*—a fact which had a considerable bearing on the size of the initial printings (9,000 per number for *Pendennis* compared to an average of 4,500 per number for *Vanity Fair*).

After *Vanity Fair* Thackeray's most purchased books were *Pendennis* and *The Newcomes* (20,000 copies printed of each with only 500 copies of *The Newcomes* and 423 of *Pendennis* left in stock in 1865). For both publisher and author *The Newcomes* (1854–55) was a bigger money-maker than *Pendennis* because it sold more copies in the more expensive first edition and because production costs were slightly lower (fewer and larger reprints); for Thackeray himself *The Newcomes* had the additional advantage of initial payments £50 per number higher than those for *Pendennis*. *The Book of Snobs*, riding the rising wave of popularity developed by *Vanity Fair*, also had a large circulation. In two separate editions (1848 and as an "off-print" of *Miscellanies*, vol. 1, in 1855) *Snobs* circulated 11,750 copies. When this figure is added to the 10,000-copy printing of the first volume of *Miscellanies*, which contained it, it appears that *Snobs* may have reached a higher circulation figure than *Pendennis*. However, the records do not indicate clearly how many copies of each volume of the four-volume *Miscellanies* were included in the total of 1,600 copies left in stock or unaccounted for in 1865.

Although the *The Virginians* (1857–59) was recorded by Bradbury and Evans as a financial failure, it was Thackeray's greatest financial success while with that firm. No contract survives to tell us the details of Thackeray's agreement with Bradbury and Evans, but on 10 September 1856 he wrote to his friends Mrs. Elliot and Kate Perry that he was to receive £6,000 for the novel (*Letters* 3:616). He repeated that information to his mother in December (*Letters* 3:655). Since *The Virginians* is a twenty-four-part novel, like *Pendennis* and *The Newcomes*, this figure averages out at £250 per month. As late as February 1857, however, Thackeray referred to it as "that novel expanded into 20 or 4 numbers wh. ⟨wd⟩ ↑ was to ↓ have been the continuation of Esmond—embracing the American War" (NLS). Thackeray seriously contemplated making it a twenty-part novel, like *Vanity Fair*, for he mentioned to William Bradford Reed in May 1857 that he was to receive twice as much for *The Virginians* as he had gotten for any other publication (*Letters* 4:44). His highest previous payment was for *The Newcomes*, for which he had received £150 per month. Thackeray used the same phrase to Baron Tauchnitz on 12 November 1857: "my publishers here pay me twice as much as for the *Newcomes*."[10] The first

---

[10]*Der Verlag Bernhard Tauchnitz, 1837–1912* (Leipzig: Tauchnitz, 1912), p. 123.

installment appeared on 1 November, but sales were not as high as expected. Thackeray wrote to his American friends the Baxters in that month, "I tremble for the poor publishers who give me 300£ a number—I don't think they can afford it and shall have the melancholy duty of disgorging" (*Letters* 4:56). And sure enough, on 21 December he wrote to John Blackwood: "We don't sell 20000 of the Virginians as we hoped, but more than 16000 and should have done better but for the confounded times. I have thought proper to knock 50£ a month off my pay from Bradbury & Evans till we get up to a higher number—For you see Sir my publishers have always acted honestly and kindly by me and I don't want any man to lose by me" (Morgan). It is tempting to speculate that the novel was extended from twenty to twenty-four numbers, as *Pendennis* had been, so that while Thackeray's pay dropped from £300 to £250 per month, the total initial payment remained at £6,000, but that might just be an ingenious way to reconcile the varying figures in the surviving correspondence.[11]

It had been Bradbury and Evans's practice with *Pendennis* and *The Newcomes* to record the firm's own share of income as one of the costs of production. The split on *Pendennis* was £100 to Thackeray and £75 to the publisher, and the split on *The Newcomes* was £150 to Thackeray and £112.10 to the publisher. Both of those books began showing a profit over and above these initial payments to author and publisher within a year of publication. But in accounting for *The Virginians,* the publisher did not figure in its share as a cost of production. According to the records, then, the author received his £6,000 while the publisher was still showing a deficit of £3,257.2.3 in 1865. There never were any profits to share from the first edition of *The Virginians*. Two reasons for the publisher's alleged predicament emerge from the records. First, it grossly overestimated the sale of the book: of the first number, 20,000 copies were printed; the print order was immediately reduced to 16,000 each for numbers 2 and 3, and reductions continued until, finally, only 13,000 copies each were printed of numbers 18–24; even this was too many, for in 1865 there were still 16,000 parts (equivalent to 690 copies of the book) left in stock. Second, the publisher agreed to pay more for this novel than Thackeray ever earned from a single title during the entire period of the company's connection with him.

---

[11]One piece of evidence that does not fit this explanation is the fact that in November, Thackeray told the Baxters he was to get £500 from Harper for the book, and the next month he acknowledged that Harper paid $100 per month (*Letters* 4:55, 60). At the then current exchange rate of £1 to $5, it would have taken twenty-five months to make £500.

Every commentator on the financial fortunes of *The Virginians,* Thackeray included, has believed that Bradbury and Evans lost money on the book. They point to the fact that Thackeray agreed to a £50 per month reduction in pay and to the fact that Bradbury and Evans let Thackeray go to Smith without protest. In fact, however, Thackeray never stood to earn more than £6,000 in initial payments for the book, all of which he received, and a look at the records shows that the publisher's loss was a loss of expected profits, not a loss of capital outlay. By December 1857, after three numbers of *The Virginians,* there was a £66 deficit after paying production costs and after paying Thackeray but before paying Bradbury and Evans. By December 1858, after fifteen numbers, there was a surplus of £546 after paying production costs and author. The surplus continued to grow, Bradbury and Evans enjoying the fruits of it but not recording the firm's share until January 1863, when the surplus recorded was £1,199. At this point Bradbury and Evans credited the company with £4,500, which would have been its share in profits if the book had made enough to pay that share. By December 1863 the account showed a loss of £3,291, which really means that Bradbury and Evans made a little over £1,200 on the book. The firm recovered, through sales, all the costs of production, including all the money it had paid to Thackeray, and paid itself just over £1,200 in real money from profits. The deficit reported represents the amount required to pay the company its share of the proceeds from the book before the bookkeeper would declare the account balanced and proceed to ring up profits for sharing with the author. Since Bradbury and Evans apportioned to the company only £4,500 to Thackeray's £6,000, it appears, in the absence of any surviving contract, that the profit-sharing arrangement for *The Virginians* was to have been three to four, very slightly less for Thackeray than the two-to-three agreement in effect for the *Miscellanies.* Since Bradbury and Evans earned only a fourth of its three-sevenths share on the first edition of *The Virginians,* the deal was the worst it had made with Thackeray, earning it a profit of just over one half what it had made from the first edition of *Vanity Fair. The Newcomes* (1853–54), the second highest money-maker for Thackeray, had netted him only £4,561.3.9 by 1865, but it was a far more satisfactory bargain for the publisher, showing a profit within a year of the novel's completion in July 1855. To show a profit in that case meant the publisher had been able to pay itself as much as it had paid Thackeray.

The History of Samuel Titmarsh and the Great Hoggarty Diamond (circulation about 15,000) almost equaled the sales of *The Virginians* (about 15,500), but both lagged behind the *Ballads,* a sleeper of which 18,000 copies were printed (8,000 in a separate edition requiring nine printings and 10,000 as part of the first volume of *Miscellanies*).

The relationship between Thackeray and the firm of Bradbury and Evans was for the most part a pleasant and fruitful one. The records show the publisher always increasing remunerations to the successful author: initial payments for parts-issued novels climbed rapidly from £60 per number for *Vanity Fair* to £100 for *Pendennis*, £150 for *The Newcomes*, and finally to the supposedly disastrous £250 for *The Virginians*. Likewise, in profits Thackeray's share, usually a half, became three-fifths for the *Miscellanies* (1855–57) and four-sevenths for *The Virginians* (1857–59).[12]

Thackeray's relations with Bradbury and Evans were personal as well as professional. The weekly Saturday *Punch* dinners for the magazine staff promoted both camaraderie and business, as is apparent from Henry Silver's diary recording the conversation at the table.[13] Bradbury and Evans gave Thackeray a punch bowl, engraved as from the publisher of *Vanity Fair* and *Pendennis*, in May 1849 (*Letters* 2:530); in May 1852, in a letter to Evans asking if the agreement for *Pendennis* had not specified his share to be four-sevenths rather than one-half, Thackeray also asked both cheekily and deferentially for a couple of commemorative cups "that my children might have after me—the Dobbin cup and the 'Warrington' say. 20 might buy them; and they would slave who knows at what sideboards when you and I are passed away—" (Bradbury Album). It would seem that there was no contract for *Pendennis* to which Thackeray could appeal for support of his memory of the agreement, and the profit sharing for that book proceeded at half for the author, half for the publisher.

What Thackeray seems not to have known when he wrote his complaint, but which might have been told to him in person, is that Bradbury and Evans had undertaken a sacrifice on his behalf, which the firm probably felt was sufficient to satisfy the author. The publisher routinely charged 10 percent of gross income as a commission. This overhead cost was assessed as a cost along with production and in the case of *Vanity Fair* meant that Bradbury and Evans earned nearly £700 more than Thackeray did from the first edition of that book, which was published on a half-share

---

[12]Four-sevenths is slightly less than three-fifths, but the original agreement for *The Virginians* had been for £50 per number more. If that were extrapolated for twenty-four months, it would have meant a total of £7,200, which would have been a 5-to-8 ratio. In any case, the precedent set with the *Miscellanies* seems to have helped increase Thackeray's share for *The Virginians* over what it had been for earlier parts-issued books.

[13]Quoted by Ray, *Wisdom*, p. 347, and transcribed by Constance Smith, "The Henry Silver Diary: An Annotated Edition" (Ph.D. diss., St Louis Univ., 1987).

contract. In December 1851, after having charged the *Pendennis* account £787.13.10 for the publisher's commission, Bradbury and Evans seems to have had a change of heart, for it restored the full amount to the credit side of the ledger, pushing the *Pendennis* account from a deficit to a profit and enabling the first profit-sharing check to be drawn. It was that check which prompted Thackeray's letter of complaint about his portion. Bradbury and Evans never charged a publisher's commission again on *Pendennis* or on Thackeray's two other serial novels.

It was inevitable, of course, that the relationship would have its low points. One instance, more a case of panic than crossness, interrupted the otherwise smooth production of *The Newcomes*. Thackeray had a hard time getting Bradbury and Evans to deal expeditiously with Sampson Low for the sale of advance sheets to Harper and Brothers. In the end he lost about £150 by the company's failure to press the matter.[14] Perhaps more important was the sharp tone used by Thackeray concerning Richard Doyle's tardy work in illustrating *The Newcomes*, but here Thackeray's irritation was shared with Bradbury and Evans, not directed against it.[15]

Serious problems and a near rupture in the relationship occurred, however, early in 1855. In December 1851 Thackeray had resigned from *Punch* because of political disagreements, primarily with Douglas Jerrold. His last contribution to *Punch* as a regular staff member appeared in that month. The break was not without its tense feelings, but it seems not to have been personal between Thackeray and the publisher. In 1853 and 1854 Thackeray again contributed a few occasional pieces to *Punch*, apparently taking little heed to the rate of payment until, having dunned the editor, Mark Lemon, for back pay, he noticed in October 1854 that his rate of pay had been reduced. In a humorous but restrained letter to Lemon, Thackeray calculated the relative rates of pay for *Punch*, *The Newcomes*, and *Blackwood's* by adding up letters per line, lines per page, and pages per sheet, demonstrating in that way that he could no longer afford to work for *Punch*. It is clear also, however, that he was miffed.[16]

These money matters, just the current irritation, were easily exacerbated by a series of events beginning in December 1854. Thackeray wrote an article about *Punch* in the *Quarterly Review* which he said was intended to be good-natured but in which he praised John Leech, the illustrator, at the expense of all other contributors. Other staff members were under-

---

[14]More details are given in chapter 4 below.

[15]Further details are given in chapter 1 above.

[16]Undated letters to Mark Lemon, privately owned, photocopies supplied by William Baker.

standably upset, though Douglas Jerrold in particular was predisposed to resent any remark Thackeray might make. The first result of the ensuing tempest was that Thackeray, who had been proposing to George Smith that he start a periodical called *Fair Play* with Thackeray as editor, decided he could not undertake such a task. To Smith he wrote:

> *another incident has occurred to put a spoke in Fair Play's wheel; and I must give up all idea of the paper.*
>
> *I wrote an unlucky half-line in the Quarterly about the Punch men saying that Leech was Punch, and that without him the learned gentlemen who wrote might leave the thing alone—an opinion wh. true or not, certainly should not have been uttered by me, and has caused the saddest annoyance and pain amongst my old comrades[.] I had quite forgotten the phrase until it stared me in the face on my return home. Jerrold had attacked me about it, and with perfect reason calling me a Snob & flunkey—and on the face of the matter I think I was a Snob—but thats not the question.*
>
> *I wrote to confess my fault to my old friends the Publishers & Editor and passed ½ the night awake thinking of the pain I had given my kind old companions. This is for ½ a line written in an article intended to be entirely good-natured—Don't you see the moral?*
>
> *If in writing, once in 5 years or so, a literary criticism intended to be good natured, I manage to anger a body of old friends, to cause myself pain and regret, to put my foot into a nest of hornets wh. sting and have their annoyance too, to lose rest and quiet, hadn't I better give up that game of Fair Play wh. I thought of, stick to my old pursuits, and keep my health and temper?*[17]

To Bradbury and Evans, Thackeray explained: "you know how carelessly I read my proofs over that is all I can say. Phrases pass under my eye, and I don't see them. And I am obliged to go back constantly to my own back numbers; and find new blunders every time I take them up" (Bradbury Album).

But that was not the end. Rumors and allegations (no longer, if ever, existing in writing) began circulating concerning the original reasons for Thackeray's resignation from *Punch* in 1851. Clearly the remarks on Leech opened festering wounds, and Thackeray found to his surprise that his old friends Bradbury and Evans were not willing to back him in a dispute with

---

[17]*Letters* reprints this letter from the Centenary Biographical Edition; my text is from the original, NLS.

their magazine's continuing staff. In March 1855 Thackeray wrote Evans one of his rather frequent dunning letters for payments on *The Newcomes*, then added:

> *I met Murray the Publisher the other day, and cannot help fancying from his manner to me that there is some screw loose with him too about that unlucky Leech article. Lemon answering one of my letters said that he previously complained that my account of my leaving Punch was not correct.*
>
> *There was such a row at the time and I was so annoyed at the wrong that I had done, that I thought I had best leave Lemon's remonstrance for a while and right it on some future occasion.*
>
> *I recal now to you and beg you to show to him and to any other persons who may have recd. a different version of the story—what the facts were. I had had some serious public differences with the conduct of Punch—about the abuse of Prince Albert & the Crystal Palace on wh. I very nearly resigned, about the abuse of Lord Palmerston, about the abuse finally of L. Napoleon—in all wh. Punch followed the Times, wh. I think and thought was writing unjustly at the time, and dangerously for the welfare and peace of the Country.*
>
> *Coming from Edinburgh I bought a Punch containing the picture of a Beggar on Horseback in wh. the Emperor was represented galloping to Hell with a sword reeking with blood. As soon as ever I could, after my return, (a day or 2 days after) I went to Bouverie St. saw you and gave my resignation.*
>
> *I mention this because I know the cause of my resignation has been questioned at Punch—because this was the cause of it. I talked it over with you and Leech saw me coming out of your room and I told him of my retirement.*
>
> *No engagement afterwards took place between us; nor have I ever been since a member of Punch's Cabinet so to speak. Wishing you all heartily well I wrote a few occasional papers last year—and not liking the rate of remuneration wh. was less than that to wh. I had been accustomed in my time—I wrote no more.*
>
> *And you can say for me as a reason why I should feel hurt at your changing the old rates of payment made to me—that I am not a man who quarrels about a guinea or two except as a point of honour; and that when I could have had a much larger sum than that wh. you give me for my last novel [*The Newcomes]*—I preferred to remain with old friends, who had acted honorably and kindly by me.*

> *I reproach myself with having written a ½ line regarding my old Punch Companions, wh. was perfectly true, wh. I have often said—but wh. I ought not to have written. No other wrong that I know of have I done. And I think it now about time that my old friends and publishers should now set me right.*[18]

But Evans declined, it seems, to arbitrate or to support Thackeray, who on April 3 wrote Evans again:

[Bodleian]   *I have copied out from my letter to you of 24th. March the statement I then made respecting my retirement from Punch and have forwarded it to Lemon. As my Punch arrangements were always made with you and not with him, I am sorry you cannot help me in confirming a fact to which you and I alone were privy—but for which I luckily have an out-door witness in Leech.—*

I am at a loss to think how you should imagine that my contributions to Punch continued up to my departure for America.[19] *My successor Mr Shirley Brooks came on, if I remember aright, very soon after I went off. I remember to have contributed nothing but a Ballad for which I never asked or received any payment, and that point must be set at rest by the certainty that if I had sent any contributions wh. were paid to me at a less rate than that for which I had been accustomed to write I should assuredly have "struck work"; as I did when we came to our last unlucky little settlement of Punch Accounts.*

Will you have the kindness to pay into my bankers the sum due to me for the current number? According to my Banker's Account there is still a month of last year owing to me.

The crisp concluding reminder lacks any of the humor usually attending such requests; it is clear that the friendship had been strained. And yet Thackeray's business relations with Bradbury and Evans survived four and a half years longer. Much of the interaction between the author and publisher, of course, is not represented in surviving letters, for the next letter, undated but obviously not much later, is in a much kinder tone and

---

[18]*Letters* reprints this letter verbatim from Marion H. Spielmann's *History of Punch,* which prints an editorially revised version of the last, awkward sentence; my text is from the original, Bodleian.

[19]Eleven months elapsed between Thackeray's last appearance in *Punch* and his departure for America in November 1852; he had resigned from *Punch* in December 1851, his last contribution having appeared the month previous. He contributed some occasional material again in 1853 and 1854.

regretfully declines a dinner meeting with the *Punch* staff because of a prior engagement. Thackeray concluded, "Commend me to all my friends & believe me yours always" (Bodleian).

One might have thought that Thackeray's 1851 resignation from *Punch* or his 1855 controversy with the *Punch* staff in which Evans betrayed his trust would have led to a clear rupture, particularly since George Smith was perpetually in the wings offering to be Thackeray's publisher. But the facts, as Thackeray saw them, were that Bradbury and Evans had launched him when he was unknown and that the firm's dealings with him were always honest and ever improving. By August 1855 the relationship was back to normal: Thackeray dunned Bradbury and Evans for back pay and raised the question of a cheap edition of *Pendennis*—an idea that saw the light in October of the same year (Bodleian).

From the completion of *Pendennis* on 1 December 1850 to the commencement of *The Newcomes* on 1 October 1854, Thackeray published no new works with Bradbury and Evans outside *Punch*. Three new works written during this period went to Smith, Elder (*Kickleburys, Henry Esmond,* and *English Humourists*) and a fourth (*Rose and the Ring*) would be published by that firm in December 1854, and yet Thackeray considered Bradbury and Evans to be his primary publisher. Why this should be so is open to question, for in fact Thackeray published as many titles with Chapman and Hall and with Smith, Elder as he did with Bradbury and Evans. But it is evident from his letters and the amount of his magazinery published in *Punch,* as well as from the coterie of *Punch* writers to which he belonged, that in the late 1840s Thackeray's most substantial financial and personal connection with publishers was with William Bradbury and F. M. ("Pater") Evans. Further, though *Vanity Fair* and *Pendennis* may have represented only one working contract each and can be listed in a bibliography in just two entries, they were the major continuing writing obligation of Thackeray's life from January 1847 to December 1850—four continuous years of service, producing the two works which made the difference for Thackeray between "odious magazinery" and the "fight at the top of the tree." And yet, as well as Thackeray seems to have gotten on with Bradbury and Evans and as loyal to the company as he felt with regard to his next serial fiction, Bradbury and Evans had not been his first choice as publisher for *Vanity Fair;* he did not turn to the firm with his Christmas books when Chapman and Hall declined to meet his price; and he turned easily to George Smith with *Henry Esmond* and the lectures. What George Smith had that Bradbury and Evans did not was a certain air of substance, perhaps even elegance, attached to the publisher's imprint, which was associated with works of scholarship in zoology, astronomy, art history, and geography and with elegant illustrated works.[20] These matters may have weighed as much with Thackeray as Smith's purported generosity with money, for which he became known as the "Prince of Publishers."

A third factor, however, must have been the personal attraction between the two men. If Smith was, after all, a "mere tradesman," he was also intelligent. Smith had been asked to leave his boarding school at age fourteen not because he was a poor scholar (he was academically one of the top three students in his class) but because he was, to put it politely, too energetic. He immediately was apprenticed to his father's new partner, Patrick Stewart, where he learned all aspects of bookselling, stationery, trade with India, and banking. He continued his reading in history, science, religion, and fiction and could read French and Latin well. Furthermore, Smith, like Thackeray, was an avid theatergoer. He was over six feet tall, of slender, not athletic, build. Thackeray might well have found these abilities and characteristics congenial in a businessman publisher who was not only energetic but was cultivated enough to be a successful host for literate people in social settings.[21] The personal relationship is attested by the fact that Thackeray seconded Smith's bid in 1861 to become a member of the Reform Club (NLS). Though Thackeray had been on friendly terms with his previous publishers, he was not on such a footing with them as he developed with George Smith.

An Interlude with Smith, Elder and Company

Where Bradbury and Evans had been casual about contracts and nonexclusive in its "proprietorship" of the author, Smith did business another way. Thackeray had first met George Smith in November 1849, when the publisher invited the author to meet Charlotte Brontë at the publisher's home. Smith already had a long-standing admiration for Thackeray and

---

[20]Among the Smith, Elder titles of the early 1840s were Ruskin's *Modern Painters* (1843), Darwin's *Structure and Distribution of Coral Reefs* (1842), the five-volume account *Zoology of the Beagle Expedition,* and an illustrated selection of Byron's poems called *The Byron Gallery.* It is true that the firm, under the direction of Alexander Elder, had tried to establish a series of cheap fiction reprints called *The Library of Romance,* which was discontinued after fifteen titles; and the firm was committed to publish G. P. R. James's novels as he wrote them according to an open-ended contract from which Smith extricated the firm only after nine titles. (Sutherland has claimed James had wrangled the contract "with the twenty-year-old George Smith, just after he had taken over the family firm" [*Victorian Novelists and Publishers,* p. 88], but Smith was twenty-two when he took over the firm and terminated James's contract the next year.) Among George Smith's own early acquisitions were R. H. Horne's *New Spirit of the Age* and Leigh Hunt's *Imagination and Fancy.* See Jenifer Glynn, *Prince of Publishers: A Biography of George Smith* (London, 1986), pp. 27–30, 35–36.

[21]The information for this sketch comes from Glynn, *Prince of Publishers,* pp. 16–21.

no doubt on this occasion expressed a willingness to entertain a proposal from Thackeray.[22] Had such an offer come earlier, Thackeray might have jumped at the chance, but having spent years importuning and cajoling publishers, he found himself suddenly in 1849 all but overcommitted. To his friend Mrs. Sartoris he confided one year later the frustration of having too many deadlines: "My young one said to me just now Papa how will you get through your plates and your Punch and your Xmas book and your Pendennis? 'Why do you ask me that question? says I, flinging out of their school room. I've been writing all day" (*Letters* 2:701).

It is not clear how early George Smith decided to make Thackeray "his author" and build a part of his publishing empire on Thackeray's works. From the way he originally approached Thackeray for *Henry Esmond* and the *Lectures on the English Humourists,* it is evident he had something of the sort in mind by 1851, but he may have thought of it earlier. He responded eagerly to Thackeray's offer of *The Kickleburys on the Rhine* in August 1850, paying the whole amount asked, £150, four months before publication and then sending a bonus £50, apparently unasked, when the whole edition sold out immediately. Thackeray was unused to that kind of treatment from Chapman and Hall and Bradbury and Evans.

Thackeray finished *Pendennis* at the end of November 1850 and saw *Kickleburys* through the press in December; he then turned his attention immediately to reading for *The English Humourists,* which he projected for a lecture tour in America. He spent January with his family in Paris. There is no evidence to suggest what schemes Thackeray may have discussed with publishers in the first half of 1851, but he began delivering the lectures in London on May 15. It seems fair, therefore, to conjecture that he was concentrating on the lectures and as yet was only thinking about his next novel, which he had mentioned without name in late November: "I've got a better subject for a novel than any I've had yet" (*Letters* 2:708). In a January 1851 letter he referred to the novel as "a story biling up in my interior, in wh. there shall appear some very good lofty and generous people" (*Letters* 2:736).

With the lectures scheduled to complete their first run on July 3, Thackeray was quite ready to commit himself to his next project, and he signed for *Esmond* with George Smith on June 27. Thackeray's daughter Lady Ritchie later gave an account of the author and publisher's agreement for *Esmond:* "One day my father came in, in great excitement. 'There is a

[22]Smith recalled how in the early 1840s he had gone to a book auction to mark his catalogue with the prices realized in the sale; he found a copy of Thackeray's *Paris Sketch Book,* became engrossed, and missed all the prices (Huxley, *House of Smith, Elder,* p. 69).

young fellow just come,' said he; 'he has brought a thousand pounds in his pocket. He has made me an offer for my book, it's the most spirited, handsome offer, I scarcely like to take him at his word; he's hardly more than a boy, his name is George Smith."[23] No date is given for this supposed occurrence, but if the tale is accurate in its details, it cannot have taken place in 1851. Thackeray had met Smith too many times already, had dined at the publisher's house in 1849, and had entertained Smith and Brontë at his own home with his daughters in 1850, a year before signing the contract for *Esmond* (*Letters* 2:673).[24] When, in November 1849, Smith first invited Thackeray to his home, the two men had never met before. One can only conclude that this meeting took place in November 1849 and that Smith offered to publish a book, probably a three-decker, for £1,000 at the same time that he invited Thackeray to dinner. The alternatives are to believe that the episode never happened or that the account of it is totally distorted.[25]

George Smith's own account, written years after the event, states that Thackeray "had mentioned the work to me and I had expressed my anxiety to publish it. 'But I shall want four figures for it,' said Thackeray. This proved no obstacle."[26] The two accounts from recollection appear contradictory, but they obviously refer to two occasions separated by nearly two years, Anne Thackeray recalling an event in November 1849 and Smith recalling another, probably in May or June 1851. Thackeray dined at Smith's home, again in company with Charlotte Brontë, on 13 June 1851 (*Letters* 2:784), and there must have been many other opportune moments for the exchange Smith recalled.

In November 1849 the author was in no position to respond to an offer from Smith—he was just recovering from a nearly fatal illness, he had half of *Pendennis* yet to write, and he was busy with *Rebecca and Rowena* (already committed to Chapman and Hall) and the joint project with Louis

---

[23]George Smith, *Chapters from Some Memoirs* (London, 1894), p. 130, quoted by Huxley, *House of Smith, Elder*, p. 69, and in *Letters* 2:804.

[24]Jenifer Glynn, in retelling this episode, placed the meeting Anne recalled in 1851 (*Prince of Publishers*, p. 119), in spite of the fact that Anne said it was the first occasion on which she heard Smith's name; 1849 is a much more plausible date for that.

[25]Edgar Harden, realizing the historical difficulties with the story, called it an "apparently figurative account" ("Historical Introduction," *The History of Henry Esmond* [New York: Garland, 1989], p. 393).

[26]George Smith, "The Recollections of a Long and Busy Life," 2 vols. (typescript), vol. 1, chap. 10, p. 6, quoted by Edgar Harden, "The Writing and Publication of *Esmond*," *Studies in the Novel* 13 (1981): 80–81.

Marvy on English landscape painters (already committed to Hugh Cunningham). The next project Thackeray was free to offer Smith was *Kickleburys*—which he first felt obliged to offer to Chapman, who fortunately declined it. Doubtless Smith's earlier magnificent offer lingered in Thackeray's memory as Henry Esmond's story was "biling up in [his] interior" in the spring of 1851.

Thackeray did not receive a £1,000 advance for *Esmond*. The contract indicates his advance was £400. He signed the contract on 27 June 1851, at first agreeing to submit the completed manuscript for a three-decker novel on the first of November. (Thackeray had tried to lock himself into that kind of agreement before.) The word "November" was canceled in the contract and "December" substituted probably at the time Thackeray signed it; later postponements of the due date are not reflected in further changes in the contract. Upon submission of the manuscript, Thackeray was to receive £400 more, and on publication he would get a final £400, for a total of £1,200. Smith was to get the entire profits from the first edition, which was not to exceed 2,750 copies.

Smith must have thought Thackeray could produce a three-decker from scratch in six months; further, Smith believed he could produce and publish one in two months, for in October he announced that the novel would appear in January 1852.[27] Thackeray had not meant to relax his writing pace in spite of the windfall income from the lectures. On 9 October he wrote to Dr. John Brown that he intended to invest his lecture income and not "touch the proceeds of the lectures myself (beyond actual travelling charges). . . . In order to [achieve] this end you see I must work as if nothing had happened, and am under stringent engagements to write a novel" (*Letters* 2:804). But Thackeray was unable to lecture and write at the same time, and he apparently was already lagging behind in writing the book (though he did not immediately inform Smith), for in the same month, Thackeray wrote to the Tauchnitz firm saying publication would take place not in January as Smith had advertised but in February (*Letters* 2:806). On 10 November he was hoping to finish *Esmond* by the end of January (*Letters* 2:810). But then on 26 December, Thackeray, who had been delivering his lectures all fall in Oxford, Cambridge, and Edinburgh, wrote the inevitable plaintive letter to Smith: "I have so far bad news to give you that I have not advanced 5 pages whilst I was in Edinburgh. It was impossible to write. And if it doesn't interfere with your plans much I am

---

[27]Advertised in *Publishers' Circular*, as noted by Sutherland, *Victorian Novelists and Publishers*, p. 108.

glad of the delay—Every month is of importance toward effecting a cure of a complaint wh. would have made the book dismal & a failure."[28] At about this same time, Thackeray resigned from *Punch* (*Letters* 2:823). Delay followed delay, and Thackeray finally finished the manuscript on 29 May 1852, five months over schedule.

Smith's estimate of the time it would take to publish the novel was also quite unrealistic. It was not, however, from inexperience in publishing three-deckers, but from his inexperience in publishing books requiring special old-fashioned type. According to Eyre Crowe, the delays in getting proofs to Thackeray were the result of insufficient type stock, which meant that the type used to print the first part of the book had to be cleaned and distributed for use in subsequent parts of the book.[29] No one has determined how much type was involved or how large a part of the book could be printed at once, but Thackeray received proofs in portions approximately 100 pages long at weekly intervals from 15 August through 13 October (*Letters* 3:69, 72, 661).

It seems fairly clear that Smith was anxious to get Thackeray to write for him. Further, it is clear that though young, Smith was no boy. He began publishing on his own within his father's firm at nineteen in 1846 and took over his father's work completely in 1848. He soon discovered his former mentor and partner, Patrick Stewart, to have embezzled approximately £30,000 from the firm. By 1851 Smith was a very mature young man, whose overload of work apparently showed in his thin face but not in his business relations, which were thriving.[30] Nevertheless, that early business catastrophe must have had its influence on the contract for *Esmond,* which is cautiously protective of the publisher's rights. In addition to the stipulations concerning manuscript submission, the contract specifies that Thackeray "will not print or publish any serial or other work within six months of the date of publication of the above mentioned work" (NLS; see Appendix A). No other publisher is known to have exacted such a promise from Thackeray. Had the prohibition been levied at any earlier point in his career, Thackeray would have either worked

---

[28]NLS. The complaint almost certainly is a reference to his break with the Brookfields, an episode in his love life reflected throughout *Henry Esmond.* See chapter 6 below, and Gordon N. Ray, *The Buried Life: A Study of the Relation between Thackeray's Fiction and His Personal History* (Cambridge, Mass., 1952).

[29]Eyre Crowe, *With Thackeray in America* (London, 1893), p. 7.

[30]Glynn, *Prince of Publishers* p. 70. Apparently, as he recovered from the financial crises, Smith also more than recovered his looks, becoming by the mid-1850s what Elizabeth Gaskell called "too stout to be handsome" (ibid., p. 90).

night and day on the novel or starved. The contract seems to mean primarily that Thackeray should not undertake any large work after accepting the £400 advance, but it may have meant he was to cease all other publications. Lending support to the latter view is the fact that Thackeray did not publish anything in 1852 except *Henry Esmond.*

John Sutherland has concluded that "altogether Thackeray was led by the terms of his arrangement for *Esmond* to do two things which were unusual for him personally and the Victorian novelist generally. These were to think in terms of 'plans' for his career, and to pay attention to the completeness of the work in hand."[31] He contrasted this work with *Vanity Fair,* which he assumed was under threat of termination at any time if the publisher thought it unsuccessful (thus rendering long-term plans by Thackeray for the book less likely), and with *Pendennis,* which was extended from twenty to twenty-four numbers in midstream. Edgar Harden assessed the matter similarly: "Thackeray was committing himself to a dual task he had never undertaken before—both completing a novel before publication and, by implication, working on it more or less exclusively."[32] These assessments seem only partially correct. In June 1851, as Thackeray was signing this commitment and collecting the first install-ment of £400, he was also putting away £500 in earnings from the first round of London lectures.[33] He planned to repeat his lectures in the fall in England and Scotland and intended to take them to America in the new year. His check from Bradbury and Evans for profit sharing in *Pendennis* had come in May (£66), and he must have sincerely believed he could finish *Henry Esmond* by December and collect the next £400 of the purchase price. In fact, if Thackeray and Smith could have fulfilled the schedule they imagined the contract called for—submission of the manuscript on 1 December and publication in January 1852—Thackeray would have made £1,200 in eight months, or £150 per month, £50 a month more than Bradbury and Evans had paid for *Pendennis.*[34] In addition, far from com-

---

[31]Sutherland, *Victorian Authors and Publishers,* p. 111.

[32]Harden, "Historical Introduction," *Esmond,* p. 394.

[33]Ray, *Wisdom,* p. 168.

[34]Sutherland's assessment of Thackeray's attitude toward the financial arrangements for the book seems based on the assumption that £1,200 for *Esmond* was only half as much as the £2,400 for *Pendennis* (*Victorian Authors and Publishers,* p. 107), but it had taken Thackeray twenty-seven months to write *Pendennis,* while he projected only seven or eight months for *Esmond.* Thackeray probably, then, did not see *Esmond* from the time of signing the contract as a work done for art's sake rather than for money; he must instead have thought he was embarking on the best deal he had ever had. However, another way to assess Thackeray's income from the novel is to figure the rate per page. Had *Esmond* been printed in the same

mitting him to exclusive attention to *Esmond,* the contract left him free to pursue the lecture circuit, which he called "the easiest and most profitable business" he had ever done.[35] Furthermore, he continued sporadic contributions to *Punch* through September 1851, slowing down his contribution rate at least as much because of a growing alienation from the political stance of the magazine as because of the pressure of time caused by concentrating on *Esmond.* He resigned from *Punch* in December 1851 primarily because of political disagreements, not pressure from George Smith or stipulations in the contract for *Esmond.*

So, on 27 June as he signed the contract, it must have appeared to Thackeray the most lucrative arrangement of his blossoming career. Since, however, neither Thackeray nor Smith was able to meet his projected deadlines, sixteen months elapsed between the first and third payments, making Thackeray's effective income from *Esmond* £75 per month. Yet, that can have had little to do with Thackeray's attitude toward the book while writing it, since he could not have anticipated the delays of the production process and since his own delays were caused by his being busy making relatively easy money lecturing. In addition, it is probable that the thing that most put Thackeray off from his proposed schedule on *Esmond* was the traumatic rupture in his relations with the Brookfields in September 1851. Briefly, in August Thackeray's long but apparently platonic affair with Jane Octavia Brookfield led to or exacerbated an argument between Jane and her husband William, one of Thackeray's college friends. On or about 22 September, Brookfield forbade Thackeray to visit his home again (*Letters* 4:428). That was most likely the complaint needing time to cure to which he referred in his December letter to Smith asking for an extension.

It is not clear from the contract precisely which six months were intended as the period during which Thackeray should not "print or publish," but it really did not matter. The lecture circuit, with its necessary social obligations, kept Thackeray too busy to write anything else. It remains a matter of critical controversy whether the mode of production stipulated by the contract for *Esmond* and the differences in schedules and work rhythms between serial publication and three-decker novels significantly influenced the style, tone, structure, or meaning of the novel.[36]

---

format as *Pendennis,* it would have been just under 400 pages compared to just under 700 for the larger book. By that measure, Thackeray was slightly underpaid by Smith.

[35]Ray, *Wisdom,* p. 169.

[36]My own contribution to this question is in chapter 6 below.

Esmond was submitted to the publisher in May 1852 and was published in October just as Thackeray sailed on his long-delayed tour to America. He had already made approximately £2,500 from the lectures in England; he would make that much and more in America. There is nothing to suggest that Thackeray was in any way dissatisfied with his new publisher. His next book, the lectures themselves, went to the same firm.

It is interesting to see the remarkable difference between Thackeray's relations with George Smith and with any previous publisher. In every other relationship to date, Thackeray had been dependent on the current work for financial solvency. For the most part his publishers were not much better off, unable or unwilling, in any case, to brook many delays or leave advances unrecovered for long. With Smith in 1851–52, author and publisher were both engaged in an enterprise that could be delayed, improved, and embellished because neither was financially dependent on a quick return. It is no wonder they got on well. Surely that fact went into the decision to print the book in Queen Anne–style type font, a decision that delayed publication but apparently did not frazzle any nerves.

A further indication of Smith's desire to keep Thackeray as his author and of Thackeray's contentedness to be courted by Smith can be seen in a contract they signed on 3 June 1852, one week after Thackeray finished writing *Esmond,* for a Continental travel book the size of *From Cornhill to Grand Cairo* (i.e., about 40,000 words, less than half the size of *The Irish Sketch-Book*). The plan was to do the work in four months, and Thackeray left for the continent a week and a half later. Smith gave Thackeray £200 on the spot as an advance. Had Thackeray not lost half of the money when his purse was stolen a few days later and had he actually written the book, it would have been published under a most liberal and innovative contract. Although the contract specifies that the book would be like the Eastern book, "containing no less matter" than that one, the rest of the agreement tacitly acknowledged that whatever Thackeray came back with would have to do, for it specifies that upon the manuscript "being placed in the hands of Smith Elder & Co an estimate is to be made by them of the cost of printing, paper, engraving, binding, advertising and other necessary expenses" (NLS; see Appendix A). In other words, both parties would have to wait and see what turned up before any hard figures could be determined. Then, "the above mentioned estimate being made up, Smith Elder & Co are to pay Mr Thackeray the difference between the amount of Four Sevenths of the estimated profit of the First edition & the Two Hundred Pounds already received by him." Both men knew that if the book was not done by the time Thackeray sailed to America in October, it probably would not get done. Here was a contract in favor of the author. He was allowed to bring in a manuscript that might not exactly conform to the specified goal, he was given a substantial advance, and he was to be paid a share of estimated, not realized, profits. Furthermore, his share, four-sevenths, was higher than anything he had been offered to date. There are some safeguards for the publisher, but on the whole this remarkable contract reflected Thackeray's power and George Smith's trust in it. Unfortunately, the book was never written, and Thackeray lived under the cloud (not an ominous one) of his debt to Smith until the 1854 publication of *The Rose and the Ring*.

Why that debt lingered unpaid until 1854 is not at all clear, for when the first edition of *Esmond* sold out in less than two months, a second was published and produced £101 profits each for author and publisher within six months, and *The English Humourists* was published in the spring of 1853, likewise producing profits—Thackeray's first share coming to just over £190. Thackeray, however, remained under the impression that the £200 advance for the travel book was overlooked and unpaid, so on 28 August 1854 he asked Smith to take £150 of it out of the fee for *The Rose and the Ring* (NLS). But the ledger accounts for that book do not show any charge against it for back debts. There is, however, a charge for £200 "cash on account" in a statement of accounts to Thackeray for 1852–53, which covers some transactions in the period for which ledgers no longer exist.[37] It seems possible that Smith did not dun Thackeray because the debt was already paid. In the statement of accounts for 1853, Smith indicated that he still owed Thackeray over £75 in their various dealings (i.e., not specifically attributable to any one book).

George Smith gained a reputation for being a careful and shrewd, though also generous, businessman. At age twenty-two he took an established business that was severely rocked by an embezzler and turned it into a thriving concern, and he launched a publishing business that fostered some of England's best writing talents. He is famous for the advances and payments he made to authors; and, as with *Esmond,* he spelled out fairly detailed terms in his contracts. And yet one wonders why no contracts survive for three books he published by Thackeray: *The Kickleburys, The English Humourists,* and *The Rose and the Ring*. The publishing arrangements for these books are accessible through letters and the ledger books; they show the precision of Smith's professional dealings, and they show

[37]MS owned by Gordon Ray, now at the Pierpont Morgan Library.

him scrupulously honest with his author. It is hardly surprising that there seems to be only one story of a good but disgruntled author leaving Smith, as they always left Newby, Bentley, Colburn, and even Chapman and Hall and Bradbury and Evans, with feelings of suspicion and anger.[38]

The Kickleburys was a success, requiring and getting a second edition within two weeks of first publication. The surviving ledger accounts for that book begin in 1853 when only 236 copies of the second edition remained unsold. Thackeray made at least £200 off the first edition; his share for the second edition is unknown. Smith presumably made an equal amount for himself.

For the *English Humourists* there is no surviving record of agreement. On 21 October, just ten days before sailing to America, Thackeray wrote Smith in such a way as to indicate that an agreement for the publication of the lectures had already been made: "Whatever the notes may be to the Lectures; the Text may be printed at once & in a large type say, to wh. the notes could be afterwards subjoined. I write to Mr. Hannay by this day's post, who knows the Lectures, & is conversant with the literature of the period; & I should be very glad if he could help me" (NLS). In fact, the notes were done by James Hannay who, according to a statement of accounts to Thackeray made out in 1853 by George Smith, received £40 for his services. The same accounting makes it possible to figure out the main features of the agreement. A first printing of 2,500 copies was made in February 1853 at a total cost of just over £445. All but 97 copies had been disposed of by July 1853, netting £333.11.3 in profits. Thackeray got four-sevenths and Smith three-sevenths, making Thackeray's portion £190.11.8. There was apparently no advance, unless Smith's reference to £200 cash in his account to Thackeray of his income in 1852–53 was an advance for the *English Humourists* and not for the travel book.

Publication of *The English Humourists* did not go smoothly. In January Thackeray wrote from New York to say haste in publication was unnecessary to forestall piracy, for he had closed a deal with Harper and Brothers, the "chief buccaneers," for publication in America; consequently, he wanted a chance to read over proofs for the English edition and to make changes and corrections—no doubt a result of his continuing to tinker with the lectures as he gave them (NLS). This request was ignored or came

[38]Sutherland, *Victorian Authors and Publishers*, chap. 1. See Patten, *Dickens and His Publishers*, for accounts of Dickens's disputes with the latter two publishers. The one exception in Smith's case was John Ruskin, who quarreled with Smith after thirty years of friendly and productive relations (Glynn, *Prince of Publishers*, pp. 104–11).

too late, for the book with Hannay's notes was printed and a prepublication copy sent to Thackeray in April.[39] He responded in a tone of irritation: "I have not had leisure to look carefully through the Lectures; but am sorry to say I have seen faults enough already in glancing through the pages to make me wish that they had not been printed without my supervision. One page (193) contains a blunder of my own making, wh. will require the cancelling of the sheet; & I shall send you a list of errata by the next packet." The letter actually goes on to four pages and the errata list is included: "—for Almanza: read:—Barcelona: at page 193. line 14.—that page must be cancelled & the sheet likewise if necessary. The book must *on no account* be published with such an error."[40] Upon his return to London in May, he wrote Smith again:

[NLS]   *It is heart-breaking to read the blunders through the volume: and I am sure it would be more creditable to cancel it all than to let it go forth with all these errors.*

If you insist however—the errors marked on the next page must be amended and we must leave the rest to the just indignation of the public.

I will pay half the expenses of a new edition if they are anything reasonable—And in that case you'll send me proofs wont you.

He added a list of page numbers where changes had to be made. With that, he went off to Paris to see his daughters and parents. But on 16 May, still in reference to the first printing, he wrote again sending a marked copy of the book and calling attention especially to a change on page 199: "It is of great importance and the page as it at present stands should be cancelled" (NLS).

What happened next can be deduced from the ledger. Three "sheets" were reprinted, and the rest left to the "indignation of the public." The ledger indicates charges for the cancellation of three sheets at a cost of £31.13. Smith hired out the printing to Bradbury and Evans; hence, Smith's records are not sufficiently detailed to determine just how the book was printed. Each sheet of double crown paper would hold two gatherings of the book, but if the pressmen mounted one whole gathering,

---

[39]It is possible that Thackeray was sent a bound proof copy, which he may have mistaken for the trade edition, for only three copies are known to exist in a form corresponding to his description of the one he received; see Edgar Harden's "The Writing and Publication of Thackeray's *English Humourists*" *PBSA* 76 (1982): 203.

[40]NLS. The underscoring was added in a different ink and may have been added by another hand. The letter itself is in Eyre Crowe's handwriting, obviously written from dictation. Thackeray may have added the underlining when proofing the letter, or Smith may have underscored the instructions that led to the extra charges for the three canceled gatherings.

outer and inner forms, on the press and printed by the work-and-turn method, then each sheet would hold two copies of one gathering. If, on the other hand, they mounted one form each from two separate gatherings, each printed sheet would produce two gatherings. It is not immediately apparent, therefore, whether "three cancelled sheets" represents three gatherings (forty-eight pages) or six gatherings (ninety-six pages) in the book. Further, it is not clear whether the canceled gatherings were consecutive or from various parts of the book. Finally, although the ledger shows that enough paper was used in the cancels to replace all 2,500 copies of three double-gathering sheets, the printing cost was charged at exactly half the rate charged for printing the whole book. Collation of the various surviving states of the book and comparison of Thackeray's notes with the published book indicate that the three canceled sheets probably contained six book gatherings, for there are significant changes in the first three gatherings (through page 48), the sixth gathering (pp. 81–96), and the thirteenth (pp. 193–204).

Clearly, Smith was unwilling to waste a whole edition of 2,500 copies, though he could have; it would have cost him only about £115 to correct and reprint the whole book. Instead, he paid an extra £31.13 for correcting and reprinting six gatherings and went ahead with publication. Economically, it was a good decision, for the first printing sold out in the first month, netting Thackeray £190.11.8 and Smith £142.19.7 in profits. Furthermore, none of the reviewers seem to have noticed anything untoward in the printing of the lectures, though several objected to Thackeray's opinions and judgments—particularly about Swift.[41] A second printing being wanted immediately, it was produced with extensive alterations made in the standing type from the first printing. Since a new setting of type was not involved, the printing cost was half of that for the first printing (£114.3.9), and the profits should have been correspondingly higher. Thackeray wrote to Smith in September asking to see an accounting for the lectures: "I hope that the first Edition will yield me more than 200£; calculating that we should go shares in the proportion of 3 for me and 2 for you: and take half profits upon the second edition" (NLS). Had the share been three to two, Thackeray's cut would have been over £200, but it was only four to three. Perhaps that is why Smith figured Thackeray's share in the second edition at four to three also, instead of the one to one Thackeray suggested.

---

[41]Dudley Flamm, *Thackeray's Critics* (Chapel Hill, N.C., 1967) provides an extensive, though not complete, list of reviews and contemporary notices.

In response to Thackeray's request, Smith had two account statements drawn up, one for each printing.[42] The first statement shows
Thackeray's earnings of £190 from the sold-out printing. The second
estimates the total cost and profits for the second printing if it sold out.
According to that accounting the second printing would net £511.8.9, of
which Thackeray's share would be £292.5 and Smith's £219.3.9. However, a memo indicates that half of the profit sharing would become due
only when two-thirds of the copies printed had been sold. The ledger
entries for the second printing show Thackeray's first half (£146.2.6) paid
in 1853 at a time when sales had provided enough income to pay production costs and all but £8.2 of Thackeray's share. Smith's share is not
recorded then. By June 1858, 300 copies were remaindered at half price.
Income at that time exceeded expenses by a total of £217.6, which was
£1.17.9 less than Smith's share was supposed to have been. However, the
second half of Thackeray's share and none of Smith's is recorded as paid,
and the final disposition of the £217.6 is not found in the ledger. Since
the agreement called for a four-to-three split, Smith should have taken
£109.11.10 to bring him even with what had been paid to Thackeray. Then
the remaining £107.14.2 should have been divided four to three, giving
Thackeray just over £61 more, for a total income from the two printings of
approximately £397. That is probably what happened.

Perhaps the remarkable thing about these transactions is the infor-
mality of the accounting. It is astonishing enough that Smith's projections
about the income would be fulfilled so closely, but his other contracts
suggest that normally Smith was a stickler for form. This entry is reminiscent of Thackeray's arrangements with Chapman and Hall and Bradbury
and Evans, which often amounted to little more than gentlemen's agreements.

The bottom line for the next book Smith undertook for Thackeray,
The Rose and the Ring (December 1854), shows Thackeray earning £250
and Smith £224.5.9, not quite a fifty-fifty split, but the agreement for this
book was rather different from that for any of Thackeray's previous
dealings with Smith. For this book Thackeray parted with the entire
copyright for one printing of 5,000 copies for £150 and then sold the entire
copyright for a second and third printing of 1,000 copies each for £100
more. Smith's entire payment to Thackeray was "up front," so the risk
was entirely his. His judgment, however, was unerring, for by 1858 he
was able to earn for himself nearly as much as he had paid the author. At

---

[42]MSS in the estate of Gordon Ray, now at the Pierpont Morgan Library.

first blush, it might seem strange that Thackeray could make £397 from 5,000 copies of *English Humourists* but only £250 from 7,000 copies of *The Rose and the Ring*, but the ledgers make it clear. The cost of manufacturing and advertising and selling 5,000 copies of the lectures was about £745 for a book that sold to the trade at 7s. and 6d. Of those 5,000 copies, over 300 were remaindered at 3s. 6d. The lecture volume had a total income of £1,815, or a profit of £1,100. On the other hand, it cost nearly £420 to manufacture, advertise, and sell 7,000 copies of *The Rose and the Ring* that sold to the trade at 3s. 6d. Of the 7,000 copies, over 300 were remaindered at 1s. 9d. *The Rose and the Ring* had a total income of £1,198.15, or a profit of £778.15. It took the sale of 2,000 copies of the lectures at the trade price to recover the cost of production, leaving 3,000 copies to produce profit. It took a sale of 2,400 copies of the Christmas book at the trade price to recover the cost of production, leaving 3,600 to produce profit. In short, therefore, although there were more "profit copies" of the Christmas book, the lectures produced profit at twice the rate that the Christmas book did. In addition, a higher proportion of profit from the Christmas book went to the publisher: total profits to Smith for the lectures equaled £695, while for the *Rose* they were £474.

Both books were unusually expensive to produce, the lectures because of the canceled sheets and editing fee, the *Rose* because of the lavish illustrations. The remarkable thing is that despite these problems, which undoubtedly would have swamped any of Thackeray's publishing efforts in the 1840s, the books were turned into moderate successes.

Return to Bouverie Street

Smith came close to being the publisher of *The Newcomes,* as seems apparent from Thackeray's 16 June letter explaining, with regret, why he had given the work to his old publisher Bradbury and Evans:

[NLS]
> *I wish this answer to your kind letter could be Yes: but my friends Bradbury & Evans have always dealt so honorably by me that I was bound in duty to them; and offered them ⟨terms⟩ the same terms about wh. I had spoken ↑ with them, ↓ on my return from America. They were not so good as those wh. other publishers I know would have given me; but having stated my own price, wasn't it my duty to abide by my words?—I think so, though I might have benefitted my pocket elsewhere.*
>
> *I hope you & I however will have many other dealings, and I'm sure you won't think the worse of me for remaining constant to old friends, who have been very kind & constant to me.*
>
> *P.S. This is a secret. Next year I am not pledged not to write a book*

about the United States; with wh. and the Warringtons of Virginia & the
4 Georges I see a tolerable amount of work before both of us.

There is a possibility that this letter, carrying no year date, was written not
in 1853 but in 1857 and refers to *The Virginians,* for which Smith may have
made a bid as well (this letter seems, in fact, to offer that book to Smith);
but a reference in a letter from Thackeray to Evans on 24 March 1855
seems to point directly to an offer from Smith for *The Newcomes.* In asking
Evans for help in straightening out misunderstandings about his resignation from *Punch,* Thackeray noted, "And you can say for me as a reason
why I should feel hurt at your changing the old rates of payment made to
me—that I am not a man who quarrels about a guinea or two except as a
point of honour; *and* that when I could have had a much larger sum than
that wh you give me for my last novel [*The Newcomes*]—I preferred to
remain with old friends, who had acted honorably and kindly by me."[43]

And so, though Thackeray's relations with Bradbury and Evans were
becoming slightly less cordial, and though Thackeray seemed to prefer
working with Smith, he thought that because Bradbury and Evans had
published his first two large, successful serial novels, his third large serial,
The Newcomes, should be offered first to that company.

The terms of his offer are not on record—there is no extant contract—but Bradbury and Evans must have given what Thackeray asked.
Thackeray wrote to the Baxters in June 1853 that he had "signed and sealed
with Bradbury and Evans for a new book" (*Letters* 3:280). The first
number appeared on 1 October 1853. Thackeray had written nothing else
for publication since his return from America on 2 May. His plan had been
to finish the whole book by the end of the year, but once again Thackeray
was being too optimistic. He had actually written four monthly installments by 1 September, and he had decided to have the illustrations done by
Richard Doyle, so there was reason to believe he could stay well ahead of
the monthly deadlines. But the work was allowed interruptions. A full
account of the composition and publication of *The Newcomes* has been
given by Professor Edgar Harden.[44] He detailed how the book was
written while Thackeray traveled in Europe, staying for a while in Rome,

---

[43]Bodleian. Jenifer Glynn speculated that the reason *The Newcomes* went to Bradbury and
Evans was that before the *Cornhill Magazine,* which began in 1860, Smith did not publish
serials and "Thackeray wanted the money that only a serial could bring" (*Prince of Publishers,* p. 120). These things may have been true, but the reason for publishing with
Bradbury and Evans instead of Smith seems to have been that an agreement had already
been struck before Smith offered.

[44]Harden, *Emergence of Thackeray's Serial Fiction,* pp. 75–137.

how Percival Leigh was employed to oversee the proofing and final adjustments in length and illustrations, and how a mix-up at the London end misplaced an extra passage that was meant for installment 6, resulting in some jury-rigging by Leigh, the illustrator, and the printer to make a short installment fill the required thirty-two pages. The extra passage has not been identified and apparently has been lost forever; it was not mistakenly added to installment 5, for that was too long already, having had to accommodate an overage from installment 4.

Thackeray finished the novel in June 1855, just a little over one month before publication of the final double number. Clearly he did not stay as far ahead of publication as he had been on 1 October 1853 when the serial began. Furthermore, his writing for periodicals had fallen off sharply: only ten contributions to *Punch* during two years and the controversial article on John Leech in the *Quarterly Review*. In addition, he wrote *The Rose and the Ring* (published by Smith in December 1854). A relatively secure financial base, illness, and a house moving seem to have combined to slow Thackeray's production, though he was putting some time into preparing the cheap editions of *Vanity Fair* (1853), *Pendennis* (1855), and the *Miscellanies* (1855–58). But Thackeray's essay on Leech, published in December 1854, was his last known prose contribution to a periodical until he began writing as contributing editor for Smith's *Cornhill Magazine* in 1860.[45]

Having finished *The Newcomes,* Thackeray wrote an exploratory letter to Smith in September 1855 offering him *The Four Georges* and perhaps a travel book. He went on to contemplate *The Virginians* but did not offer it: "I propose to sell you an edition of 'The Georges. Sketches of Courts, manners, and town life, and if I do a book of travels I shall bring it you but this is hardly likely. I shall more likely do the Esmonds of Virginia, and it will depend on the size to wh. that book goes whether it shall appear in 3 vols. or 20 numbers" (NLS).

Gordon Ray noted that "with Bradbury and Evans bidding against George Smith for his next book, the terms proposed soon soared so high that Thackeray could not refuse them,"[46] but Ray cited no source for this competition, which nevertheless may have accounted in part for the high offer Bradbury and Evans made for *The Newcomes* (£3,600 plus £500 from Harper and Tauchnitz [*Letters* 3:280]) and the even higher bid for *The Virginians* (£6,000). But the evidence of Thackeray's June 1853 letter

---

[45]"The Idler," a poem, appeared in the *Idler* 1 (March 1856): 172–73.
[46]Ray, *Wisdom*, p. 222.

suggests that whatever the competition was, loyalty to Bradbury and Evans for a time won out over higher offers. Whatever the reason was that took *The Virginians* to Bradbury and Evans, Smith must have been grateful; for though the Bradbury and Evans loss was not as bad as the firm led people to believe, it probably had effects on Smith's negotiations with Thackeray, which are visible in the contracts. Nevertheless, Smith's overall plan to acquire Thackeray as a property was undiminished.

The Final Move to Cornhill

Thackeray must have entered an early, though tentative, agreement with Smith to publish *The Four Georges* at some future date, for he apparently received an offer from another publisher in February 1857. Thackeray sent this no longer extant offer to Smith on 16 February, commenting: "Meditate the astounding offer contained in the enclosed not with the idea that I am going to think of accepting it. Having sold my horse to a good friend & for a good price how can I sell it to another dealer? But the question with me is, Is the delusion about those Lectures sufficiently great to enable us to sell them as they actually stand at a good profit. And having read them ⟨all⟩ through the country for a few months more Shall we kill the wretched goose & have done with it. Or shall we bring out not 2 but haply 6 great volumes in future ages about the Georges with a success that might be something like Stricklands.?" (NLS).

Neither man was, however, in a hurry to kill the goose. Thackeray continued to deliver the lectures as late as June,[47] after which the parliamentary election campaign in Oxford, a holiday, and then, perhaps, the pressure of deadlines for *The Virginians,* which he was eking out monthly as he had *Vanity Fair* and *Pendennis,* kept him from following through with the plan to publish. Whatever the case, no action was taken on that issue until 1859.

To Charles Lever, Thackeray commented in June 1859: "I leave them [Bradbury and Evans] (we remain perfect good friends) and go over to Smith & Elder. . . . [I]ndeed I have had every reason to be satisfied with both firms" (*Letters* 4:144). But Thackeray's profitable dealings with George Smith (*Kickleburys on the Rhine,* 1850, and *Henry Esmond,* 1852) and the fabulous offers made him by the firm of Smith, Elder to edit the *Cornhill Magazine* doubtless made him eager to part company with a publisher who claimed to be losing money on his latest book.

The give-and-take between the apparently easygoing author and the

---

[47]Ibid., p. 267.

shrewd businessman publisher can be seen best in the history of the founding of the *Cornhill Magazine*. As early as 1854 Thackeray had proposed to Smith a periodical called *Fair Play,* which he would edit. Smith took to the idea and started making plans. Then in February 1855 Thackeray cried off after his *Quarterly Review* remark that *Punch Magazine* was nothing without the illustrator John Leech drew the anger of his former writing cronies. The incident made Thackeray doubt his abilities to be an editor without inadvertently making enemies. Smith's final assault and successful siege to capture complete control of Thackeray's writing may have grown out of that aborted project. On 19 February 1859 Smith approached Thackeray with a memorandum announcing his intention to "commence the publication of a Monthly Magazine on January 1st, 1860," and offering a contract specifying "1 or 2 novels of the ordinary size" to be delivered one-twelfth at a time for monthly publication in the magazine. Thackeray would give up all rights in the novels for the magazine and one book-form publication but would share in the profits from any second or subsequent book form. He would be paid £350 each month (*Letters* 4:130). Two outstanding elements of this offer are the length of the novels and the rate of pay. Smith wanted a novel in twelve parts, each "estimated to be about equal to one number of a serial," and he was willing to pay £100 per month more than the firm of Bradbury and Evans was paying for *The Virginians,* on which it claimed to be losing money. Smith's insurance was to be all the income from foreign editions (Harper and Tauchnitz) and one separate book edition.

Two months later, 9 April 1859, an agreement was drawn up, but the stipulations had been changed. In this agreement both men honed the clauses to suit what they thought was important. Smith now insisted on submission of manuscript exactly one month before publication date; he insisted that the scenes "are to be descriptive of contemporary English life society and manners" (i.e., not a historical narrative); he increased his leeway in book publishing by claiming all the profits from two separate book issues (though the agreement is written in such a way as to preclude either of those from being a "cheap" edition, for which Thackeray reserved the right to share half profits); and he insisted that Thackeray write for no one else for the duration of magazine serialization. Thackeray seems also to have worked over the contract. He is probably the one who insisted that the serial length be increased to sixteen numbers and the one who suggested "not less than twenty four original drawings for etchings on steel" (NLS; see Appendix A). By this contract Smith secured Thackeray's services for thirty-six months and Thackeray secured the highest monthly income of his life (£350) for thirty-two of those months.

One stipulation did rankle Thackeray. On the afternoon of 14 February Thackeray signed the agreement and sent it to Smith with the following note: "I have written at the side of one paragraph a remark of wh. you'll see the bearing. You'll see I am hankering still to write a ballad or two without my name in Punch—or do something to show my old friends that Ive not quite separated from them." And the next morning he wrote a second note to Smith: "I found your note when I came home last night having meanwhile sent you from the Club the signed agreement: by wh. I propose to abide. The objections written on the other leaf may be torn off if you like; but I think I *ought* to write a Punch paper or ballad or so, to show that there is no disagreement between me & my old employers. This is a matter of minor importance however, ⟨and⟩ I consider our agreement as made" (NLS). The copy of the 9 April agreement that Thackeray signed has brackets marking the paragraph stipulating he not publish elsewhere, and the facing page has been torn away.[48] Four months later, 20 August, Smith and Thackeray signed a substitute agreement beginning: "Some of the conditions of the agreement made on 9th. of April 1859 between Mr. Thackeray and Smith Elder & Co. are to be varied as follows—" (NLS; see Appendix A). The changes were substantial; again both men were negotiating. There is still no mention of editing the magazine.

The first part of the new agreement must represent Thackeray's new demands. The starting date for beginning the first novel was postponed six months to 1 June 1860; the length of each novel was to be expandable to twenty numbers at Thackeray's option; illustrated initials would be furnished in addition to the steel engraved plates; the novels would be separate serials rather than parts of the proposed magazine; and Smith would have the full rights to only one book form in addition to the serial. No reference is made to money; so one assumes the £350 per month specified in the April contract held good. Furthermore, the new agreement makes no mention of foreign rights, a fact Thackeray picked up on in a letter that indicates he may have taken the agreement away with him to consider: "I have forgot the Agreement at Fkstone. but its all right. The American reprints are mine in this case?" (NLS). Exhausted by *The*

---

[48]Ray claimed Smith asked Thackeray to edit the magazine at this time and suggested that this letter refers to that offer (ibid., p. 294), but Smith cannot have made such an offer before the end of summer.

Virginians and unwell, Thackeray was giving himself room to breath. Four days earlier he had written to F. M. Evans concerning the last number of *The Virginians:* "I have been ill again, and am very much afraid I cant do the double number this month. The single number I can do—it is + done already. I hope the delay wont inconvenience you" (Bodleian).

Smith, however, was not losing his man. Thackeray agreed to supply a very short novel in six parts for the magazine, each only sixteen pages long, half the size of a normal serial monthly. In addition, *The Four Georges* would be serialized. Each work would belong to Smith for one book issue. The price for this magazine work was £1,500, to be paid in three installments. No date was stipulated for submission of the lectures manuscript, and in fact it began its appearance in the magazine in June after the short novel, *Lovel the Widower,* had run its course. Gordon Ray has suggested that the reduced writing load was a result of Smith's decision to ask Thackeray to become the magazine's new editor,[49] but this seems unlikely in view of the lack of any mention of editorial duties in the 20 August contract and the possible interpretation of the contract that would have put both *Lovel the Widower* and *The Four Georges* in the first issues. George Smith's own account of his decision is undated: "We were then living at Wimbledon, and I used to ride on the Common before breakfast. One morning, just as I had pulled up my horse after a smart gallop, that good genius which has so often helped me whispered into my ear, 'Why should not Mr Thackeray himself edit the magazine, and you yourself do what is necessary to supplement any deficiencies on his part as a man of business? . . . .' After breakfast I drove straight to Thackeray's house in Onslow Square, talked to him of my difficulty, and induced him to accept the editorship, for which I was to pay him a salary of £1000 a year."[50] The first clear indication in Thackeray's letters that he was the editor comes on 7 September when he reported to Smith on recruiting articles and remarked: "As I think of the editing business I like it. But the Magazine must bear my *cachet* you see and be a man of the world Magazine, a little cut of Temple Bar, or Charles I on the outside?" (*Letters* 4:149–50).

The changes in the August contract reveal some important things about the hard-nosed Smith and the easygoing Thackeray. Smith was careful in the details of each contract but apparently easily induced to

---

[49]*Letters* 4:148. I think Ray was misled by his ascribing a June date for a letter to Charles Lever that clearly implies an editorial relation (ibid., 4:143). I think it more likely to have been written later in the year.

[50]Huxley, *House of Smith, Elder,* p. 95.

change or abandon provisions at the author's request; Thackeray was fairly eager to please the man with the money but insisting on changes both for health's and for art's sake. As far as money is concerned, there is a change from £350 per month to an average of £214 per month for the first six months.[51] What Thackeray bought with these contractual changes was time—time that the tiring author felt he needed—but simultaneously he assured himself a continuing income, since the two substantial novels were merely postponed. On his side, George Smith obtained the services of one of the day's two foremost writers of fiction for his magazine and the prospect of a continuing relationship that amounted almost to ownership of the talent, for Thackeray was not allowed to publish anything with other publishers during the life of the contract.

With the addition of the editorial salary, Thackeray's monthly income came to just over £297 per month. And then in another undated contract, Smith and Thackeray agreed to include twenty-four five-page essays, *The Roundabout Papers,* for another £1,000, or about £42 per month. Then because *Cornhill Magazine* did so well, Smith doubled Thackeray's salary, bringing the total at least briefly to £422 per month.[52] In the actual event, the first of Thackeray's larger novels was postponed until January 1861; so in effect, his income for the second half of 1860 consisted of his editorial salary and payments for *Roundabout Papers*—about £209 per month. Thackeray had never been so thoroughly controlled by contracts, nor had he ever been so well and regularly paid. Smith had his literary giant, he had the grace and flexibility to change agreements, and he had the financial wherewithal to keep his giant happy.

Thackeray took to his new duties with enthusiasm and vigor. His letters to Smith in November and December 1859 are full of accounts of meetings with contributors and comments on their articles and poems. George Augustus Sala's work on Hogarth, about which Sala, Thackeray, and Smith had corresponded in September 1855, turned up as a contribution that needed extensive reworking. Thackeray wrote of operating, amputating, cutting, and correcting material for the first number, and early on he suggested that "a boy ought to be set on to call at my house at 2 o'clock every day" (NLS). Commentators on the editing of the *Cornhill* have frequently noted the powerful hand Smith maintained in editorial

---

[51]This figure assumes that all the conditions for receiving the £1,500 would be fulfilled between December 1859 and June 1860.

[52]Ray, apparently forgetting the reductions in income represented by the 9 Aug. contract, calculated Thackeray's income at this point at "almost £600 per month" (*Wisdom,* p. 296).

matters, and it is true that he exercised his right of veto to an extent only a coeditor would. But Thackeray insisted on his own decisions as well, persuading Smith to back down on his objections to articles by Robert Bell and General John Fox Burgoyne and poems by Thomas Hood for the first two numbers. But the pressure of editorial decisions and continuous correspondence with Smith soon reached a climax. "In the name of Allah let go!" Thackeray exclaimed in December. "I can't pretend to correct the other contributors proofs—and wouldnt, no not for 10000 a year. What a man that Reader is! but there must be a reason for him, as I never should have seen the notable blunder of the *Naids* until you pointed it out" (NLS). Apparently Smith was trying to get as much for his money as he could. Friction there was, from time to time, and Thackeray finally resigned in March 1862 in terms that suggest it was not only the exigencies of the job that became too much but the difficulty of working with Smith himself. But their disagreements were kept strictly in control, and their personal and business relations continued to their mutual financial benefit.[53]

By the time *Lovel* and the *Four Georges* were completed in the *Cornhill,* both men must have considered the contracts signed in 1859 to be ancient history, for instead of reverting to them for terms on Thackeray's next major novel, *The Adventures of Philip,* they drew up a new contract in December 1860, stipulating 250 guineas as the monthly rate with Smith getting all the profits from magazine and two book forms (NLS; see Appendix A). This represents nearly £100 per month less than the earlier contract specified, but with Thackeray now also receiving £166 a month as editor and £42 for each *Roundabout,* the total of over £450 must have struck the amazed author as adequate.[54] This contract stipulates the name of the novel, which suggests that its historical character was known to both parties. Earlier contracts had stipulated an unnamed novel with scenes from contemporary English life. Although the contract also specifies "sixteen consecutive numbers" as the length, Thackeray's previously negotiated option to increase the total to twenty numbers probably was omitted by oversight rather than conscious agreement, for an undated postscript on the contract, written in Thackeray's hand, adds: "The terms of this agreement apply to 'Philip' as about to be extended to twenty

---

[53]See Spencer Eddy, *The Founding of the* Cornhill Magazine, Ball State Univ. Monograph no. 19 (Muncie, Ind., 1970), for a more general account of Thackeray's role as the magazine's first editor.

[54]There is a single sheet prepared by Smith for the author accounting for Thackeray's income for 1861; it shows an average income of £470 per month for that year (Gordon Ray's collection, Pierpont Morgan Library).

numbers of the Magazine" (NLS). Other changes are also significant; the length of each installment was to be twenty-four rather than thirty-two pages, and instead of two steel engraved plates and one initial vignette, there would be one full-page illustration and two vignettes.

Publication of *Philip* concluded in the August 1862 issue of the magazine, four months after Thackeray's resignation as editor. On 4 March Thackeray wrote Smith:

> *I have been thinking over our conversation of yesterday, and it has not improved the gaiety of the work on wh. I am presently busy.*
>
> *To day I have taken my friend Sir Charles Taylor into my confidence; and his opinion coincides with mine that I should withdraw from the Magazine. To go into bygones now is needless. Before ever the Magazine appeared, I was, as I have told you, on the point of writing such a letter as this: And whether connected with the CornHill Magazine or not, I hope I shall always be Sincerely your friend W M Thackeray*

And two days later he continued in the same vein.

> *I daresay your night, like mine, has been a little disturbed: but* Philip *presses and until this matter is over, I can't make that story so amusing as I would wish.*
>
> *I had this pocket pistol in my breast yesterday but hesitated to pull the trigger at an old friend. My daughters are for a compromise. They say "It is all very fine Sir Charles Taylor telling you to do so and so Mr. Smith has proved himself your friend always."* Bien. *It is because I wish him to remain so, that I and the Magazine had better part company.*[55]

What the specific row was about, we do not know, but it concerned editorial policy, for Thackeray obviously continued both as Smith's friend and as main contributor to the magazine with *Roundabout Papers* and *Philip*.

A new contract for *The Roundabout Papers* was drafted in the month *Philip* concluded, for the twenty-four essays called for in the original contract had appeared. The new agreement reiterates the provisions of the contract signed in December 1859, but it spells out more specifically the essays covered. Some of Thackeray's occasional pieces had been published without the rubric "Roundabout Papers," and these were now included in the agreement by name; in all twenty-six essays are assumed to have been covered by the original contract. Furthermore, the rate of remuneration

---

[55]The originals of both letters are in the NLS; Thackeray copied them into his diary which is transcribed in *Letters* 4:399–400.

for any new essays is specified at £12.12, or one guinea, a page; and a seven-page limit is imposed. Far from rigorous, this contract is of a piece with the previous ones and includes an escape clause whereby "either Mr Thackeray or Smith Elder & co are to be at liberty to terminate this Agreement as far as it relates to the publication of further 'Round-about Papers' in the 'Cornhill Magazine' at any period after the end of the present year" (NLS; see Appendix A). Thackeray provided four more monthly *Roundabouts* in 1862 (skipping October), but in 1863 he wrote only five essays for the magazine.

The final contract between Smith and Thackeray concerns *Denis Duval*. Whether the terms of the August 1859 contract were still lingering in the consciousness of author and publisher can only be guessed. It had specified two novels for the magazine at £350 per month, and *Philip* represented the first of these. In his farewell letter as editor to the readers of the *Cornhill* on 25 March 1862, Thackeray anticipated his next novel: "Whilst the present tale of *Philip* is passing through the press, I am preparing another, on which I have worked at intervals for many years past, and which I hope to introduce in the ensuing year" (*Letters* 4:260). Ray suggested that the work Thackeray had in mind was "The Knights of Borsellen," a fifteenth-century romance which in fact he never completed. Having finished *Philip* in August, Thackeray did not turn his attention for some time to any new work except the *Roundabouts*. On 14 January he wrote to Smith, "I have been thinking over a story wh. might do but it had much better be in 8 numbers than in 4. No moral reflections and plenty of adventures." He then lapsed into the voice of what was to become Denis Duval and gave a 750-word sketch of the life of that hero, concluding with "and lived happy ever after but I could hardly do all this in one volume[.] Couldn't we make two of it? Of course not in Old English."[56] The name Denis Duval does not appear in this letter, nor does it appear in the contract signed nearly one month later on 11 February, where the work is referred to merely as "a story of eight parts of twenty four pages each" (NLS; see Appendix A). Smith's usual stipulation that it contain scenes from contemporary life is also conspicuously absent. Submission date for the first part was "on or before the Ist. of March," but that deadline came and went without any apparent anxiety on the part of either author or publisher. In

---

[56]NLS. Frederick Greenwood quoted the part of this letter that represents Duval's "autobiography" without noting the date. Ray reprinted from Greenwood and ascribed a September date (*Letters* 4:292). Sutherland, unaware of the original letter, astutely ascribed a February date ("The Thackeray-Smith Contracts," p. 183).

May, Thackeray wrote a partly facetious letter to a Mrs. James claiming, "I have done nothing for a WHOLE YEAR and I MUST go to my horrible pens & paper" (*Letters* 4:287).

Thackeray frequently referred, in his 1863 correspondence, to the time he spent writing for the printers, but five essays for *Cornhill* and *Denis Duval* appear to have been his only work that year. When he died on 23 December, he had completed about half of the projected eight-number or two-volume work, which appeared in four monthly installments in the *Cornhill* commencing in March 1864.

IV

Working the Copyrights

Copyrights and Contracts

TO HAVE A PROPERTY that could be "worked" required not only fertile ground but rights of property both statutory and contractual. When Thackeray began his career, the Copyright Act of 1709, as altered in 1814, was in force in Great Britain, providing the statutory framework within which contracts for the buying, selling, and leasing of copyrights could could be worked out. English copyright had evolved out of grants or monopolies engineered by and carefully protected not by authors but by printers and booksellers.[1] All the early challenges to these monopolies in court actions and in lobbying for new legislation had been conducted by printers and booksellers in order to protect their own interests and investments or to break open opportunities to share in properties they deemed part of the public domain. Even though the 1709 Copyright Act explicitly defined copyright in relation to the author by providing protection for an initial fourteen years and a second fourteen years if the author was still alive, booksellers continued to act as though copyright was designed for their benefit—as indeed, historically it had been. They even thought that they had exclusive rights to publish works they had purchased from an author after the expiration of copyright—until in 1774 the last in a series of court cases including appeals to the House of Lords ended the concept of booksellers' monopolies except as specified explicitly in the copyright act.

The 1814 alteration in the law extended copyright protection to an initial period of twenty-eight years and then, if the author was still alive, continuation until his death. By the terms of this statute, *The Paris Sketch Book,* published in 1840, was protected until 1868, five years after Thackeray's death. A new copyright act was passed in 1842 granting copyright for forty-two years from publication or for seven years after the death of the author, whichever was longer. By these terms *The Irish Sketch-Book,* published in 1843, was protected until 1885. Further, the 1842 act codified

---

[1]Detailed histories of copyright legislation are given in Sir Frank Mackinnon's "Notes on the History of English Copyright," *The Oxford Companion to English Literature* (London, 1967), pp. 921–31, and Simon Nowell-Smith's *International Copyright Law and the Publisher in the Reign of Queen Victoria* (London, 1968).

for the first time the author's "right" in perpetuity to the publication of unpublished material by making the "copyright" in such material an explicit part of the author's estate.

Today it may seem an unremarkable thing that copyrights "belong" to authors for a copyright relinquished through deliberate sale or inexperience in publishers' contracts now automatically reverts to the author or his estate after a certain period or after another owner's inactivity regarding it. But the concept of authors' copyright as opposed to printers' or booksellers' or publishers' copyright was relatively new in the nineteenth century, and not all authors had learned to prize or use the possession. An author's ability to hang on to and improve the value of his copyrights depended—as possession of all valuable commodities do—on the author's economic strengths and weaknesses. A hungry or naive or careless author might sell his rights in perpetuity, not anticipating their potential increased value. Among authors who seem to have preferred the outright sale of their copyrights were Charles Lever and, for a time, Anthony Trollope.[2] Trollope may have been right in his instinct to sell outright, for the "wisdom" of such a move depended on the long-term value of the property. *The Small House at Allington,* for example, could have brought him £3,500 in 1861 had he sold it outright, but by then Trollope was aware of possible long-term values and chose instead to sell a limited license for eighteen months for £2,500. Under the terms of his contract he did not earn any additional money from editions produced in that time: a serialization in *Cornhill Magazine* and a two-volume book edition. When the eighteen-month period expired, Trollope entered an unknown arrangement with the publisher to continue selling the work in two volumes and a cheap edition, issued in 1864. Then sometime before 1878, Trollope purchased back for £500 whatever part of the copyright he had given up, perhaps to allow inclusion of the work in Chapman and Hall's Chronicles of Barsetshire, a series that became an economic failure.[3] The answer to the question would be in the Smith, Elder records, but it is difficult to believe that Trollope made £1,500 from the cheap editions of the novel; he probably would have been better off accepting Smith, Elder's

---

[2]On 17 Dec. 1872 Trollope wrote to Baron Tauchnitz concerning the foreign rights to his works: "Latterly in order that I might avoid the trouble of many bargainings I have sold my novels with all the rights of copyright to the English purchaser—and have, therefore, given over to him the power to do what he pleases as to foreign editions. . . . As to the future I will arrange that the German republication shall be with you" (*Der Verlag Bernhard Tauchnitz,* p. 124).

[3]Michael Sadleir, *Trollope: A Bibliography* (1928; rpt. London, 1964), pp. 279, 245.

original offer for the entire copyright. Trollope's experience dramatizes the difference between copyright protection set up by statutory law and the practical function of copyright as an economic commodity in an open market. Rights, like real property, can be sold or leased; it is in this sense that copyrights are "a property" that can "be worked."

Author/publisher contracts could be arranged in a variety of ways. Initially the author came to a publisher owning the manuscript and the right to publish it. But because most authors lacked the capital, machinery, expertise, or connections required to produce and market a book, they had to part with something in order to entice a publisher, printer, or bookseller to undertake the business for them. For wealthy or otherwise financially capable authors, there has always been the option of paying for the whole operation. There are very few success stories of authors adopting this method, but among them are Lewis Carroll and *Alice's Adventures in Wonderland*. Such arrangements usually were undertaken by the publisher on commission, with production and promotion costs borne by the author while the publisher raked off a standard commission on gross income (10% in the case of *Alice*). This appears to have been the arrangement under which John Mitchell published Thackeray's *Flore et Zéphyr*, though production costs were borne by Thackeray's friend John Bowes Bowes rather than the author himself.[4] How Mitchell justified paying no return in a situation like this remains as mysterious today as it was to Thackeray and Bowes in 1836; the experience, in any case, seems to have cured Thackeray of ever undertaking that sort of agreement again.

Another arrangement common in the nineteenth century was called half profits, in which profits were split equally by author and publisher. But here again a variety of options existed. Initial costs of production and promotion might be underwritten by either author or publisher, all income going to defray those expenses before profits for sharing were declared. If a book did not earn back the cost of production, the loss might or might not be shared, depending on the contract agreement about who stood the risk of the publishing venture. Obviously, publishers were more willing to bear this risk on some books and some authors than on others. Again Trollope provides a good example of this and, incidentally, reveals the snobbery that could obscure the real issues in author/publisher relations. He wrote in his *Autobiography*:

> *When I went to Mr. Longman with my next novel,* The Three Clerks,
> *in my hand, I could not induce him to understand that a lump sum down*

---

[4]Morton N. Cohen and Anita Gandolfo, eds., *Lewis Carroll and the House of Macmillan* (Cambridge, 1987), pp. 14–15; Ray, *Adversity*, pp. 184, 467.

was more pleasant than a deferred annuity. I wished him to buy it from me at a price which he might think to be a fair value, and I argued with him that as soon as an author has put himself into a position which insures a sufficient sale of his works to give a profit, the publisher is not entitled to expect the half of such proceeds. While there is a pecuniary risk, the whole of which must be borne by the publisher, such division is fair enough; but such a demand on the part of the publisher is monstrous as soon as the article produced is known to be a marketable commodity. I thought that I had now reached that point, but Mr. Longman did not agree with me. And he endeavoured to convince me that I might lose more than I gained, even though I should get more money by going elsewhere. "It is for you," said he, "to think whether our names on your title-page are not worth more to you than the increased payment." This seemed to me to savour of that high-flown doctrine of the contempt of money which I have never admired.[5]

Trollope declined Longman's £100, half profits, and distinguished imprint in favor of Bentley's £250 for the full copyright. It was a marvellous piece of bargaining for Bentley who made £74 from the first edition and all the profits from three subsequent editions (a total of 8,000 copies of the book) and who then sold the copyright in 1890 for £125.[6]

Thackeray, beginning as a journalist and becoming known in that way to the publishers, did not enter any agreements after *Flore et Zéphyr* in which he was liable for production costs. He was clearly writing and publishing for a living, not because he had a mission to promote or a hobby to indulge. Thackeray undertook half-profits agreements with Chapman and Hall for the Irish and Mediterranean travel books and three Christmas books, and that was the agreement he made with Bradbury and Evans for *Vanity Fair,* but in all these cases the publisher bore the initial expense of publication and promotion as well as providing the author with an advance on his share in the profits. Had any venture been a failure, Thackeray was not liable for either production costs or return of the advance; the risks were all on the publisher's side.[7] By comparison with later agreements, the *Vanity Fair* contract may sound parsimonious, but in 1847 it was a measure of Bradbury and Evans's growing confidence in one of the star contributors to *Punch.*

---

[5]Anthony Trollope, *Autobiography* (New York, 1883), p. 99.

[6]Sutherland, *Victorian Novelists and Publishers*, p. 139.

[7]Thackeray did return some money to Bradbury and Evans on *The Virginians* by taking a reduction in initial monthly payments, but at the time he considered himself overpaid and did it from a sense of concern for the publisher, not because of a contractual obligation (see chapter 3 above).

A variation on the half-profits agreement was called a joint account, which could arrange responsibility for initial costs in any way agreeable to the two principal parties but often called for those costs to be shared. In such cases the author would be liable for a share of the costs if the sales failed to recoup the investment. Thackeray never entered such an agreement.

Yet another variation on the half-profits agreement called for proportionate profit sharing other than fifty-fifty. *Pendennis* represents a variation of this sort, for Thackeray's advance of £100 per number was "matched" by the publisher's £75, though when profits began accruing they were shared on a fifty-fifty basis. When Thackeray received his first account on *Pendennis* profits, he expressed surprise at his share, having understood the three-to-four ratio on initial payments to represent the agreed proportion for sharing all profits (Bradbury, Agnew). His protest was mild, ignored, and dropped—all which suggest there may not have been a written contract to appeal to. Similar arrangements with increasingly high initial payments at share ratios more advantageous to Thackeray mark the agreements for *The Newcomes* and *The Virginians*. In most half-profit and joint account agreements I have seen, the publishers charged a 5 to 10 percent commission on gross receipts to cover returned books and unforeseen expenditures.

Another common contractual agreement between author and publisher involved the lease or limited sale of copyright. The publisher would agree to pay a specified amount upon receipt of the manuscript, underwrite all production and promotion charges, and claim for the firm all profits from a specified number of editions, or printings, or copies. This is the type of agreement Thackeray signed with George Smith for *Henry Esmond*. Sometimes the size of the edition or printing leased in this way was not specified, giving by ambiguity or omission a flexibility in the publishers' favor. If the number of copies was not specified, the publisher could stop production of a poor seller before manufacturing a specified number of copies, or better yet, it could enlarge an edition if sales went well. Such flexibility was increased in cases where, instead of specifying a number of copies or editions to be leased, the copyright was leased or purchased for a specified period of time.

It was abuses with regard to this particular type of contract that led to so much distrust of publishers by authors. All of these contractual arrangements required a certain amount of trust in the publisher to keep and report accurate accounts. Thackeray seems to have been lucky in this regard, for he seldom had reason to question his publishers' records and always declared himself to be in their hands with regard to accounts. Generally speaking he was satisfied with the accounts rendered and never left a book publisher over a money dispute. Other authors not so lucky tended to prefer an outright sale of copyright because it was a clean, once and for all, transaction over which there would be no further squabbles.[8]

It is difficult to tell for Thackeray's early books (*The Paris Sketch Book* and *Comic Tales*) what precise agreement existed between author and the publishers, Macrone and Cunningham. Thackeray received £50 for *The Paris Sketch Book,* and that appears to have covered either the whole copyright or the whole first edition. If it was a lease or limited sale, it does not matter how many copies or how long Macrone's agreement specified because the book was remaindered in 1842 (at a coffeehouse sale attended and reported on by George Smith) and was never republished in England in Thackeray's lifetime. However, if he sold the copyright outright, that may account for its failure to reappear after the author became a "hot" literary property in the 1850s when much of his other early work was collected and reprinted. Thackeray's recollection concerning *Stubbs's Calendar* in November 1849—that "it is my copyright, as all my works have been by verbal agreements with the publishers for whom I wrote, with the exception of certain contributions to the 'Heads of the People' about wh. I forgot to make a stipulation" (*Letters* 2:610)—cannot be taken as conclusive proof with regard to *The Paris Sketch Book.* Evidence suggesting that the copyright had reverted to the author lies in the fact that after Thackeray's death when George Smith was buying up all the outstanding shares in Thackeray's copyrights, for which there are extensive records, there is no mention of purchase from any publisher of rights to either *The Paris Sketch Book* or *Comic Tales,* both of which entered the public domain in 1868.

Another mystery book from the 1840s is *Rebecca and Rowena* published by Chapman and Hall in 1849. That Thackeray had published five books with Chapman and Hall on half profits is indicated by the records of Smith's purchase in 1865 of Chapman and Hall's shares in Thackeray's works (Murray). But *Rebecca and Rowena* is missing from Chapman and Hall's list, and in fact the book was reprinted by Bradbury and Evans in volume 3 of the *Miscellanies* (1856). What must have happened is that

---

[8]Of course there are exceptions, as when Charles Dickens, to extricate himself from a letter of agreement with Macrone for a new novel, agreed to sell "without reserve" his copyright to *Sketches by Boz,* second series, and then objected and threatened action when Macrone planned a new edition in imitation of the *Pickwick* format (Patten, *Dickens and His Publishers,* pp. 38–41).

Thackeray saw greater advantage to himself in selling to Chapman and Hall the right to print one edition of a specified number of copies for a fixed sum and reserving the entire copyright of any subsequent editions to himself rather than continuing the half-profits agreements of the past. He was right to do so, for the sales of the book under Chapman and Hall were so disappointing that the firm declined Thackeray's next work, which was offered to it explicitly as a limited sale or lease (one edition of no more than 3,000 copies for £150 [*Letters* 2:687]). Furthermore, when Bradbury and Evans republished *Rebecca and Rowena* in the *Miscellanies,* Thackeray's share of profits was two-thirds, while for the other books which Chapman and Hall continued to sell, his share was only a half. *Rebecca and Rowena* was the last book Thackeray published with Chapman and Hall, and it is likely that ownership of the copyright reverted to him for any subsequent editions, such as the inclusion in *Miscellanies,* without requiring permission from the original publishers.

The publishing history of *Rebecca and Rowena* highlights an aspect of Thackeray's other contracts that seems surprisingly restrictive: in most of them he signed away the right ever to move a title from one publisher to another. *Rebecca and Rowena* and the unwritten "Tour on the Continent" contracted in 1852 appear to be the only exceptions. *Rebecca and Rowena* is the only one of his books originally published by one house and later published by another during his lifetime. The clause at the end of the one surviving Bradbury and Evans contract specifies rather straightforwardly that the copyright "shall be the joint Property" of author and publisher. The Smith contracts usually have some variation of the following clause from the *Esmond* contract: "that all future impressions of the said work shall be published by Mr George Smith at such times and in such manner as he may think advantageous and that one half of the net profits derived from them shall be paid by Mr. George Smith to Mr. W. M. Thackeray." In the contract for the never-written "Tour on the Continent," it appears that Thackeray tried to stipulate freedom to move the work to another publisher after a period of time—perhaps he had in mind John Murray, the acknowledged leader in travel guide publications. Smith, however, hedged the agreement closely, reserving "the sole right of printing and publishing the work until Four Years after the publication of the First Edition," after which his firm was to "have no interest in the Copyright." He then added what amounts to a retraction of all the advantages of that part of the agreement: "Mr. Thackeray agrees not to publish or authorize the publication of any new Edition of the work until any copies that may then be in the hands of Smith Elder & Co shall have been sold" (NLS; see Appendix A).

The omission of *The Paris Sketch Book* from *Miscellanies* suggests that Thackeray's agreement with Macrone (and his successor, Cunningham) may have been an outright sale of copyright or, less likely, a half-profit partnership that fell fallow. Its absence from the Smith, Elder purchase agreements for posthumous copyrights could mean that it was a lease agreement which had already reverted to Thackeray or that the record of Smith's transactions with Hugh Cunningham or his successors is just missing from the archive. Whatever the case, Smith reprinted the work in 1866, two years before it was due to enter the public domain, so he must have acquired the rights somehow. If the copyright had reverted entirely to Thackeray, Smith got the rights in the general purchase of copyrights from Thackeray's daughters. It remains something of a puzzle, though, why it was the only one of Thackeray's 1840s books not reissued in England in the 1850s.

Reaping a Second Harvest: The English Reprints

In the 1840s Thackeray's publishers resorted to various marketing strategies to get rid of excess copies of books for which optimism had led to overprinting: *Comic Tales and Sketches* published in 1841 reappeared with 1848 title pages but reissued 1841 sheets, and *The Irish Sketch-Book* reappeared in 1845 with new tipped-in title pages. A timid first edition (2,000 copies) of *The History of Samuel Titmarsh and the Great Hoggarty Diamond* sold out immediately, and the elated publisher ordered a bold second edition (2,000 more copies) but was then forced to resort to the old expedient of printing up and tipping in new title pages in recurrent attempts to unload leftover stock (in the case of *Samuel Titmarsh* in 1852, 1857, and 1872).[9] It is true that *From Cornhill to Grand Cairo* reached a true second edition in the year of its first publication, 1846, but it is quite possible that this resulted from the same phenomenon that affected *Samuel Titmarsh,* an unusually cautious first printing.

And yet the experience of *Samuel Titmarsh* probably signals a change in opportunities and strategies for Thackeray's publishers. In the 1850s they were dealing with a known and valuable property whereas in the 1840s they had a promising but uncertain commodity. Some of the advantage of this change is not reflected in reissues and new editions but is

---

[9]Details are given in chapter 5 below.

recorded as a continuous availability of the original editions, which continued to sell with little extra effort on the part of the publishers. When in 1857 Chapman and Hall found it expedient to reset *The Irish Sketch-Book,* the new edition was made to look like the original, and it presumably sold for as much. In the same year the firm reissued *Our Street, Doctor Birch,* and *Mrs. Perkins's Ball* together under the title *Christmas Books,* but the new book looked like the original three bound together. In most of this sort of unimaginative but steady increase of wealth, Thackeray participated as the half owner of copyright and half sharer of profits. But the British book trade was set up in such a way as to maximize the publisher's potential income from initial sales of single editions. All of Thackeray's works, and one supposes this to be the common lot, fell off sharply in sales after the initial burst of enthusiasm. Therefore, initial editions were seldom cost effective as long-term steady sellers. What was needed was cheap reprints at low production costs and low retail prices aimed at a new market.

Bernhard Tauchnitz blazed the trail with the first volume of Thackeray's *Miscellanies* in 1849 and the second in 1851. What arrangement Tauchnitz had with Thackeray is unknown, but it is likely that one existed, for the baron had paid willingly for *Vanity Fair* and *Pendennis* though no law required it of him. In 1852 Appleton and Company of New York mounted a similar though more systematic and less friendly assault on Thackeray's earlier periodical works as well as his travel books. Though these ventures were clearly more advantageous to their publishers than to the author, they probably paved the way or at least hinted at possibilities for the slower-moving English publishers.

Bradbury and Evans was the first English publisher to issue a Thackeray work in a format designed to capture a second rank of English book buyers and thus cultivate a separate market rather than merely capitalize on the rising popularity of the author to flog additional copies of the original edition. In 1853 that firm issued a cheap edition of *Vanity Fair* in one volume without illustrations. It did the same for *Pendennis* in 1855 (dated 1856), *The Newcomes* in 1860, and *The Virginians* in 1863. Although there are no contracts for any of these, the publisher's ledgers indicate that each was published on a half-profits share agreement. Publisher and author each earned an average of over £70 per year for twelve years from *Vanity Fair,* £45 per year for ten years from *Pendennis,* £45 per year for six years from *The Newcomes,* and a total of £83.16.8 for the cheap edition of *The Virginians* in the two years before the copyrights were sold to Smith in 1865.

Smith, too, got on the bandwagon, so to speak, for his firm issued cheap editions of *Henry Esmond* and *The English Humourists* in 1858. Smith took advantage of the format that Bradbury and Evans had established for the cheap editions of *Vanity Fair* and *Pendennis* and also used for the *Miscellanies* by advertising *Esmond* in the *Athenaeum* as uniform with those books. Furthermore, he tried to take advantage of the popularity of *The Virginians,* currently being published in serial form, by emphasizing the link between the two stories. He must, however, have asked for Thackeray's opinion or advice on the advertisement, perhaps sensing the possible impropriety of that advantage where the author is shared between two publishers. Thackeray responded:

[NLS]   *I spoke to Evans about the paragraph you sent me and he did not ½ like it. Some such par as this might do.*

   "The Virginians" are the ⟨two⟩ twin brothers mentioned in the preface to Mr. Thackeray's novel of Esmond, where it is stated that they ⟨espoused⟩ ↑ took ↓ different sides in the Revolutionary War. Esmond (perhaps a puff from the Edinburgh or Quarterly here) is just issued in a cheap reprint by Messrs. Smith & Elder.

   Though the boy is waiting & I know this isn't good

                                            Faithfully yours

   I have not found an advertisement using Thackeray's proposed paragraph, and Smith may have contented himself with the uniformity of size and brown cover. However, Smith was not so circumspect in the promotional ads included in his own publications. The advertisement of *Esmond* at the back of the cheap edition of *The English Humourists* quoted from a review of *The Virginians* in the *Leader* saying, " 'Esmond' must be read just now as an introduction to 'The Virginians.' It is quite impossible fully to understand and enjoy the latter without a good knowledge of 'Esmond.' " The cheap edition of *Esmond* was published on half shares from which Thackeray realized £143.9 by June 1863. For reasons that remain unknown, the cheap edition of *The English Humourists* took a totally new look with black printed covers and spine on slick buff-colored cloth. Smith paid Thackeray a lump sum of £200 in 1857 and earned for his company £252 by 1864.

   Some of the publishers' efforts to reap a second harvest were conducted without firsthand assistance from the author. Thackeray's second tour of the United States began in October 1855 and lasted till May 1856. In his absence his amanuensis, George Hodder, undertook, apparently in good faith but without sufficient care, to see the second volume of the *Miscellanies* through the press. From a financial point of view the venture was a success. A first printing of 2,000 copies of volume 1 had been followed immediately with a second and then a third printing of 2,000 copies each—all within two months. In addition, Bradbury and Evans issued the contents of volume 1 simultaneously in four wrappered parts: *The Book of Snobs, Major Gahagan, Fatal Boots and Cox's Diary,* and *Ballads,* each with a first printing of 2,000 copies and a reprint within a month of 1,500 copies for the first three and 1,000 for *Ballads.* The second volume, the one "edited" by Hodder, was printed within a month of the first and had a 5,000 copy first printing. As with the first volume, the contents of volume 2 were issued simultaneously in three paper-wrappered parts: *Novels by Eminent Hands, Sketches and Travels,* and *Yellowplush Papers,* each in a first printing of 3,000 copies. Although there was no initial payment for the *Miscellanies,* Thackeray received two-thirds of the profit, which began accruing immediately; his January 1856 share on profits in 1855 came to £98.15.4, and six months later his share was £221.3.2. In the same period he got £260 more from the separate publications of the contents of those two volumes.

However, all was not well. Although it is probable that Thackeray had reviewed and approved the contents of the first volume before he left for America on 13 October, he had not reviewed the contents for the second volume, having indicated only that it should be made up from the Appleton volumes of reprints made in 1852 and 1853. George Hodder apparently thought he was to see to the publication of all four volumes, for Bradbury and Evans wrote to Thackeray in America asking him to approve proofs for a third volume, to which he replied on 18 December, "I regret very much that I cant send you corrected proofs of B. Lyndon, Shabby Genteel & Catherine: but I cannot find time to write a letter much more to do any careful & continuous work: & the publication of these must be delayed until my return, or till quieter times" (Bradbury Album). Publication of volume 3 was delayed until Thackeray's return, and *Catherine* was not included.

It was not until after this December letter that Thackeray realized volume 2 had been produced and mismanaged—to his embarrassment. John Forster evidently wrote to Thackeray (who was in New Orleans) in January 1856 to ask how he could allow such a piece as "Epistles to the Literati" to be reprinted. "Epistles" was first published in *Fraser's Magazine* in 1839 and republished twice in 1841 (in *Comic Tales* and an English reprint in France). Those were Thackeray's early struggling years when his daughters were babies, his wife's mental illness was just beginning to reveal itself, and the next meal was still in the inkwell. Thackeray did not know Bulwer Lytton apart from his writings, and that writer's pomposity seemed fair game. By 1852 Thackeray had virtually forgotten the lampoon and in any case had outgrown that sort of tomfoolery, but the lampoon surfaced in the unauthorized collected early works which Appleton and Company of New York issued in 1852–53 to coincide with Thackeray's first lecture tour of the United States. Discovering the book already printed but offered the chance (and £100) to write a preface to a subsequent volume in Appleton's series, Thackeray lamented the reprinting of "Epistles" and apologized publicly to Bulwer Lytton. He wrote in the introduction of *Mr. Brown,* "there are two performances especially . . . which I am very sorry to see reproduced, and I ask pardon of the author of the 'Caxtons' for a lampoon, which I know he himself has forgiven, and which I wish I could recal." On his return to England, Thackeray wrote to Bulwer Lytton, quoting the apology from his preface.

Circumstances and forgetfulness, however, again combined to perpetuate the piece in Bradbury and Evans's *Miscellanies,* volume 2 (1856). The instructions Thackeray left with Hodder may have been vague and in any case were misunderstood. Hodder's recollection of the event was that on the day he left, Thackeray "was enabled to attend to several money transactions which it was necessary he should arrange before leaving and to give me certain instructions about the four volumes of his 'Miscellanies' then in course of publication, and which he begged me to watch in their passage through the press, with a view to a few footnotes that might be thought desirable."[10] Thackeray recounted the events and his reaction in a letter to John Blackwood in 1858 when, as a part of the controversy over Edmund Yates's lampoon of Thackeray, the Bulwer Lytton satire—and particularly its repeated appearances—was raised against Thackeray:

> *I learn through a friend who had it from Edwin James a queer piece of news, Bulwer has been applied to (by my indefatigably kind friend Dickens I suppose,)[11] and an attempt is to be made to show "my monstrous ingratitude" to E.L.B.L.—on acct I suppose of that unlucky reprint of the Bulwer-Lardner buffoonery written 20 years ago.*
>
> *I talked to you I think about it: & of the ludicrous annoyance it must give the writer & the subject too.*
>
> *When I went first to America I found a whole edition of my works reprinted malgré moi, and among them that article: wh. I said never*

---

[10]George Hodder, *Memoirs of My Time* (London, 1870), p. 266.

[11]Thackeray had just found out that Dickens had been Yates's adviser in the controversy.

should have appeared had I had any control over the reprint, and for wh. I apologized (in a general preface) as "an unworthy lampoon." When I came home, I wrote to Sir B.L. quoting the words of this preface, and he replied, in a very civil friendly letter saying all was forgotten & forgiven—compliments on both sides—shake hands—salute—We had been introduced & spoken 20 words before, but, I think, no more.

*Bradbury & Evans now undertook a republication of my early works and a volume was published under my eyes and before I went to America for the second time (in 55, wasn't it?)—*These American reprints were the text books for the English republication, *as the works were here all to my hand,[12] and when I went away, I sent a bundle of them to B&E, by an amanuensis of mine—who if he was not one of the greatest donkeys in the wide-world, would have read that preface, and of course have cancelled the pages for wh. I myself had apologized. No arrangement was concluded for any publication in my absence and I never thought any would be made—but the publishers thought themselves authorized, the amanuensis thought he was left as the Editor of my works, & that cursed Lardner-Bulwer article made its appearance again before the public. The first word I heard of it was at New Orleans I think where I got a letter from Forster asking me how I could ever have allowed the thing to reappear? I wrote to B. & Evans to cancel it if they could: but it was too late—the mischief was done—the cup was thrown down, & all the kings horses & all the kings men couldnt mend it—and there was no use explaining or apologizing—better not—in such a matter. I was in hopes Sir EBL too had condoned it, & understood my position, when he asked me to dine at his house last year.*

I daresay a different story has been told him, and he may have been made to fancy it was of malice prepense I published the article—for wh. I am sorry not only in America but in England. If you can, & see fit, I think you might disabuse him. I am as clear of personal malice or artifice towards him, as I am towards Lord Byron: and upon my word I am more annoyed than he could be at the reappearance of that piece of unworthy personality. All this I suppose I shall have to say in the Witness-box, where Dickens, & Bulwer too for what I know, & the deuce knows who besides, may be lugged in this astounding case.[13]

Though Thackeray did not mention it, and may have forgotten by 1858 when he wrote to Blackwood, he also had written concerning the Lardner

---

[12] *The Snobs* was reprinted from the 1848 English edition, not the Appleton.

[13] Morgan; Ray quoted this letter in part in *Wisdom*, p. 286; see also Edgar Harden, "Thackeray's *Miscellanies*," *PBSA* 71 (1977): 479–508.

article to Baron Tauchnitz in Leipzig on 16 May 1856, one week after his return to England: "There is a paper about Bulwer & Lardner wh. was printed by mistake, wh. is an unworthy lampoon, for wh. I apologized in the American edition & wh. I hope you'll omit in the Leipzig."[14] His request was too late; the article appeared in the Tauchnitz edition of the *Miscellanies* in the same year.

Despite these problems the reissue in England of his 1840s works in four volumes of *Miscellanies* was by far the most ambitious and for Thackeray the most lucrative reworking of his copyrights. A total sale of 33,500 volumes by June 1865 brought Thackeray and his estate an income of £1,606.4.3. In addition each volume was simultaneously issued in yellow-wrapped fascicles selling at a shilling each—four for volume 1 and three each for the others. In this form 66,000 copies were sold by 1865 for an additional income to Thackeray of £1,064.5.0, so that his total income from reworking old copyrights in the *Miscellanies* was £2,670.9.3. By comparison the cheap editions of the four big serial novels netted Thackeray in the same period £1,779.9.1. Since the original editions continued selling just a few copies a year, the cheap editions clearly reached a different market. Comparable information on the cheap edition of *Esmond* is only partially available. A single printing of 10,000 copies was prepared, and this stock lasted until 1866 when a new printing of 1,000 copies was run off. In the first eighteen months Thackeray's share was £98, which compares with his first eighteen months' income from the cheap edition of *Pendennis* of £125. Smith charged a 5 percent commission on all sales income; Bradbury and Evans did not.

From Pirates to Partners: American Publishers

It is inaccurate to speak of Thackeray's American publishers as though there was a formal relationship, for every American edition was a reprint of material originally published in England, and until 1852 every American edition was unauthorized. Conventional analysis of American literary piracy notes that there was no international copyright law until 1891, that cross-Atlantic literary piracy was not a legal crime, and that American protectionism and isolation stood in the way of international legislation for literary rights. Cynics are fond of noting in addition that whatever effect it had on authors, the absence of the law did not hurt American publishers until such a time as there was an American literature they might be able to sell to an international market. The absence of an international

---

[14]MS, Pennsylvania State Univ. Library; the copy in *Letters* 3:607, taken from a published source, omits the quoted passage, which is a postscript.

law was not so much a cause as it was a symptom of conditions in the publishing world that prevailed on both sides of the Atlantic, but which publishers on the American side managed to enjoy for a longer time and with fewer inhibitions than did those on the English side.

The first surprising fact is that Thackeray himself found those early unauthorized American appearances of his work interesting and important. The wisdom of his way of looking at the situation is supported by the fact that he eventually came to benefit financially from an American market in spite of the absence throughout his lifetime of any copyright protection for his works in America.

Aside from the author-subsidized publication of *Flore et Zéphyr,* a book of twelve lithographs with captions produced in London in 1836, American publishers were the first to recognize in the magazinery of the struggling journalist the stuff for book work. *The Yellowplush Correspondence,* which Thackeray had written as a loosely connected series for *Fraser's Magazine* in 1837, became, early the next year, in the hands of Cary and Hart of Philadelphia, his first book. The company's "Cost Books" indicate the production of 1,000 copies at a cost of twenty-four cents per copy (PHS). That cost, of course, included no payment to the author. I have not found what the books were sold for or how many were actually sold, but there was apparently no demand for a reprint, for none is recorded.

English authors and publishers might rant and rave about American literary piracy, but Americans had, at least in the 1830s and 40s, nothing to fear and no incentive to care what the English establishment thought.[15] For his part, Thackeray began by looking with sardonic curiosity and a philosophical attitude at his American successes. He may have rued the failure to get any payment for *Yellowplush* or for the putative reprinting of *The Historical Reminiscences of Major Gahagan* (a work as yet unseen by any bibliographer), but he benefited, nonetheless, by these piracies, for he used their existence to convince his first English book publishers, John Macrone and his successor Hugh Cunningham, to publish *Yellowplush* and *Gahagan* along with a few other items in a two-volume collection called *Comic Tales.* In the preface to the collection he remarked on the popularity of *The Yellowplush Papers* in America "where they have been reprinted more than once," adding that *Gahagan* was "received by our American brethren with similar piratical honours; and the editor has had the pleasure of perusing them likewise."

---

[15]See Graham Pollard's account of English and American copyright relations for the period in I. R. Brussel's *Anglo-American First Editions, 1826–1900, East to West* (London, 1935).

Though Thackeray's journalism continued to be reprinted in American magazines, a lull in book publication set in and lasted until 1844, a condition no doubt irritating to Thackeray who was having a hard time getting anything into book form anywhere. It is possible that in 1844 J. Winchester, a New York publisher, reprinted *The Irish Sketch-Book,* without formal arrangements with its author, of course. (The Winchester edition is undated, and bibliographers have failed to find or report external evidence of the date of appearance.) In the next few years before *Vanity Fair,* American publishers in New York, Baltimore, and Philadelphia reprinted *Notes on a Journey from Cornhill to Grand Cairo* and *Jeames's Diary* with impunity.

Throughout his career, in fact, Thackeray expressed willingness to take half a loaf when there was no whole loaf to be had or to dine on mutton when there was no venison. But with the publication of *Vanity Fair,* January 1847–July 1848, Thackeray's attitude changed along with the shift in his economic situation. In the early days of *Vanity Fair,* he wrote that the book "did everything but sell, and appears really immensely to increase my reputation if not my income" (*Letters* 2:318). But when, in August 1848, he could write that "Vanity Fair is doing very well commercially I'm happy to say at last" (*Letters* 2:420), he knew he had gained bargaining power, and he quickly developed the ability and habit of persuading publishers to raise his fees.

At first this power did not extend over American publishers. Harper and Brothers was the first to cash in freely on the economic strength of the new superstar, but that firm was in no hurry. Its two-volume paperbound edition of *Vanity Fair* was published in July and August 1848, after the entire serial had run its course in England (Harper MS, Butler). In December, Harper coolly added *The Great Hoggarty Diamond* to its list by lifting it from *Fraser's Magazine,* thereby, apparently by coincidence rather than malice aforethought, predating the authorized English reprinting by three months. With *Pendennis,* as with *Vanity Fair,* there was no rush of competition among the American pirates. The first of Harper's eight-part reprint appeared on 14 August 1849, ten and a half months after the London publication of the first serial part. Surviving Harper and Brothers records show no payments to English author or publishers for these three works, though the company's record of reprints over the next twenty-five years indicates how lucrative the piracy of superstars could be.

While lack of competition for *Vanity Fair* might be attributed to the fact that Thackeray was not yet a popular author, that for *Pendennis* might have resulted, instead, from the operation of a self-imposed but not very binding "courtesy of the trade" practiced among the more established

American publishers. These large publishing houses knew that competition for marginal books was detrimental to profits. In fact, the only book by Thackeray that was published simultaneously by two American publishers was *The Virginians*. Thackeray attributed the reluctance of American pirates to publish his works to the fact that Harper and Brothers was too difficult to compete with. Probably, however, *The Virginians* was the first of Thackeray's works thought to be worth fighting over.

When, in October 1852, Thackeray met the Harper brothers in New York at their homes, he reportedly greeted James Harper's daughter with the words, "So this is a 'pirate's' daughter, is it?"[16] But on 26 November, Thackeray could write to his English publisher George Smith that "Messrs. Harper through your friend Mr. Low have communicated with me & to-night after the Lecture made me an offer of 1,000$ for the publication of my Lectures, simultaneously with the re-issue in England: I shall thankfully accept the same & keep this little sum for myself this time" (NLS). He went on to describe New York as "the only city in wh. piracy is, I think, most to be feared" (NLS). And early in January he eased Smith's anxiety about getting the English edition of the lectures in print, saying, "I should not like the Lectures to go to press without reviewing, & here & there altering them; there's no danger now of their being pirated in this Country, the Harper's being the chief buccaneers, & the perfect terror of all their brethren in these seas" (NLS). Thackeray's confidence in the honor of American publishing pirates is evident in the tone with which he declined a rival offer for the lectures from George P. Putnam of Philadelphia: "All things considered, I think it best that I should accept their [Harper's] liberal proposal. I thank you very much for your generous offer; and for my own sake, as well as that of my literary brethren in England, I am sincerely rejoiced to find how very kindly the American publishers are disposed towards us" (*Letters* 3:131). Of course, kindness may have had nothing to do with it. There were, for one thing, no printed copies of the lectures available for pirating, so any publisher in this case would have to deal directly with the author or work from transcripts made at the lectures. And in the second place, it might have been the opinion of the American publishers that while one edition of the lectures could be produced profitably, the market would not bear two. Such a judgment, combined perhaps with the workings of trade courtesy, probably kept Putnam from issuing a pirated edition. The Harper records do show payments for all of Thackeray's books beginning with *Henry Esmond*, but, curiously, they also show

---

[16]Crowe, *With Thackeray in America*, p. 66.

a December 1848 payment of £3.3 for *Dr. Birch,* a Christmas book published in England by Chapman and Hall, which Harper never published.[17]

The second American publisher to cash in on Thackeray's growing reputation was William Appleton. In 1852, under the direction of Evert Duyckinck, Appleton launched its Popular Library. Thackeray's name topped the list of proposed authors in the prospectus, and *Yellowplush* was the first of his works in the series. It is probable that the people at Appleton knew or hoped at the outset of this project that Thackeray would be coming to America in October of that year. Thackeray's first mention of a possible lecture trip to America appeared in a letter written to his mother on 3 January 1851, though one thing after another intervened to postpone the trip until the end of October 1852. The lecture series in London began in May 1851, and in June he signed the contract with George Smith for *Henry Esmond,* which was not completed until the end of May 1852. However, in May 1852 Thackeray responded to the New York Mercantile Library Association's invitation to lecture there; so, no doubt, word had by then gotten around that Thackeray was planning to come to America. The trip was actually worked out for Thackeray by James T. Fields, of Ticknor and Fields in Boston, a publishing house which failed to cash in on Thackeray until 1855 when it reprinted a small book of ballads. It seems likely then that the trip was well known far in advance and that Duyckinck planned Appleton's Popular Library with the impending trip in mind. When Thackeray arrived in Boston on 13 November, the fledgling Appleton Popular Library already contained *The Yellowplush Papers, The Paris Sketch Book* (in two volumes), *The Book of Snobs, Men's Wives,* and *A Shabby Genteel Story.* Four more volumes were announced as "nearly ready" in the week Thackeray arrived in New York, though only three of them were published (*The Luck of Barry Lyndon,* in two volumes, and *The Confessions of Fitz-Boodle and Some Passages in the Life of Major Gahagan*). In all, nine volumes were produced in the series without a by-your-leave or any planned financial arrangement with the author. Appleton, to its credit,

---

[17]One could take a substantial amount of time correcting errors of fact made by bibliographers, publishing house historians, cross-culture exchange historians, and antiquarian booksellers about the American appearances of Thackeray's works. For example, Eugene Exman, in his history of the Harper firm, conjectured that Harper paid Thackeray £100 for *Vanity Fair;* he reasoned that that seemed an average amount for the time. It is clear from the records and Thackeray's letters that no payment was ever made for *Vanity Fair* or for *Pendennis.* Exman also claimed *Pendennis* first appeared in America in *Harper's Magazine,* a periodical which began publication after the publication of *Pendennis* (*The Brothers Harper* [New York, [1946], pp. 262, 337–38). Other sometimes ludicrous bibliographical "facts" are corrected in my *"Pendennis* in America," *PBSA* 68 (1974): 325–329.

was quick to redress the moral wrong, though there had been no legal wrong committed. Of course, the redress of moral wrongs is never as expensive as that for legal ones; Appleton approached Thackeray with £100 "to edit a couple of volumes out of Punch" (*Letters* 3:121).

Thackeray recounted that while on board ship just out from Liverpool en route to Boston and before the passengers had acquired sea legs, a young man representing the firm of Appleton approached him with a publishing proposal. What the proposal was or what the outcome, Thackeray did not disclose, for at that moment the ship gave an unusually large heave and the two gentlemen were obliged to approach the rail and bring up accounts of a different nature. There can be little doubt, however, that the proposal was to make up two or three volumes from his contributions to *Punch* for the Popular Library and to write a preface. Thackeray's response as reported to his daughters in a letter home was, "So you see here is the harvest and let us reap it against the winter comes" (*Letters* 3:121). In 1853 Appleton published four new volumes of Thackeray's miscellaneous works and produced a second edition of *A Shabby Genteel Story.*[18]

Thackeray's preface to the first *Punch* volume in the Appleton series remarks on the authority of the texts and reveals fairly honestly his attitude toward the American appropriation of his work.

> On coming into this country I found that the projectors of this series of little books had preceded my arrival by publishing a number of early works, which have appeared under various pseudonyms during the last fifteen years. I was not the master to choose what stories of mine should appear or not: these miscellanies were all advertised, or in course of publication; nor have I had the good fortune to be able to draw a pen, or alter a blunder of author or printer, except in the case of the accompanying volumes, which contain contributions to Punch, whence I have been enabled to make something like a selection.

Later in the preface he adds:

> That extreme liberality with which American publishers have printed the works of English authors, has had at least this beneficial result for us, that our names and writings are known by multitudes using our common mother tongue, who never had heard of us or our books but for the speculators who have sent them all over this continent.
>
> It is, of course, not unnatural for the English writer to hope, that

---

[18]James Grant Wilson claimed Appleton sold 83,750 copies, which must be an aggregate figure for the whole series. He did not give a source (*Thackeray in the United States* 1:59).

someday he may share a portion of the profits which his works bring at present to the persons who vend them in this country; and I am bound gratefully to say myself, that since my arrival here I have met with several publishing houses who are willing to acknowledge our little claim to participate in the advantages arising out of our books; and the present writer having long since ascertained that a portion of a loaf is more satisfactory than no bread at all, gratefully accepts and acknowledges several slices which the book purveyors in this city have proffered to him of their free will.

If we are not paid in full and in specie as yet, English writers surely ought to be thankful for the very great kindness and friendliness with which the American public receives them; and if he hopes some day that measures may pass here to legalize our right to profit a little by the commodities which we invent and in which we deal, I for one can cheerfully say, that the good will towards us from publishers and public is undoubted, and wait for still better times with perfect confidence and humour.

If I have to complain of any special hardship, it is, not that our favourite works are reproduced, . . . but that ancient magazines are ransacked, and shabby old articles dragged out, which we had gladly left in the wardrobes where they have lain hidden many years. There is no control, however, over a man's thought—once uttered and printed, back they may come upon us on any sudden day.

The Appleton preface shows Thackeray as a deft diplomatist, expressing his pleasure in the evident pleasure of American publishers and public alike. Thackeray's sincerity in this regard can be measured by remarks he made at about the same time in letters to England: "Even the publishers are liberal one gives me a thousand dollars and another 500 or perhaps 1000 more for books to be republished" (*Letters* 3:132). "I have made 1200£ by coming here already—800 by the lectures and 4 by my books, money wh. I shouldn't have had had I staid home" (*Letters* 3:148). "It would have been worth my while even for my books to come out here: the publishers are liberal enough and will be still more so with any future thing I may do" (*Letters* 2:154). "Appleton Harper & others all give or offer me money. I shall be able to add something like 40 per Cent to the value of my future books" (*Letters* 3:158). To the Boston publisher Fields, Thackeray wrote from New York: "The publishers here are acting most generously with regard to my works, past, present, & to come; in fact it was a lucky Friday when I set foot in the country" (Huntington).

However, the possibility of a whole loaf remained very attractive, too. While lecturing in Washington, he dined and talked with a great many persons in government, including the incumbent president, Millard Fillmore, and incoming president, Franklin Pierce. From the American capital he wrote, "I hear the most cheering accounts (but this is a secret I believe) of the International Copyright bill, wh. upon my conscience will make me 5000 dollars a year the richer" (*Letters* 3:204). The attempt Thackeray referred to as "a secret I believe" was surely something he learned upon his arrival in Washington. The first strategy in the movement to promote an international agreement about copyright had been to jockey a copyright bill through the House of Representatives.[19] It was being promoted by John F. Crampton, British foreign minister to Washington, who had recently taken over that position and project from Edward Bulwer Lytton's brother, Henry. It was a secret because the attempts to orchestrate the necessary support just to get the bill introduced and approved at committee level were complicated, expensive, and drawn out. Its supporters did not want American book publishers, book manufacturers, and that part of the American book-buying population that thrived on low-priced, unauthorized reprintings of British writings to mount a lobby against the bill until it had gotten a head of steam. Thackeray may have known about it before, for an appeal had been made early in 1852 to English authors and publishers for financial support for the effort. Smith, Elder and Chapman and Hall had contributed £50 each; Bradbury and Evans and Charles Dickens gave £100 each. In all, a variety of authors, publishers, and booksellers contributed £1,000 to finance the legislation. Thackeray, however, is not among those recorded as contributors.

In addition to his secret efforts to promote a copyright bill in the House, Crampton was secretly negotiating an Anglo-American copyright treaty with the secretary of state, Daniel Webster. Crampton had to keep information about the proposed treaty from those involved with the House bill because a treaty, since it did not require House action, might be seen in the House as an attempt to circumvent its authority. And then, apparently to Crampton's surprise, a separate petition for a copyright bill was introduced in the Senate by Senator Charles Sumner, with the support of senators Andrew Butler of South Carolina and M. T. Hunter and

---

[19]The following account is derived from James J. Barnes's fascinating and detailed exploration of various failed attempts to establish an international agreement in America, *Authors, Publishers, and Politicians: The Quest for an Anglo-American Copyright Agreement, 1815–1854* (London, 1974), pp. 177–262.

James M. Mason of Virginia.[20] The fact was that there was considerable support in America, particularly among its writers, for a fair copyright agreement. The opposition came primarily from publishers and even more from book manufacturers—typesetters, type foundries, stereotypers, and bookbinders.

By the time Thackeray reached Washington in February 1853, Daniel Webster had died; his successor Edward Everett seemed less keen on dealing with Crampton, whom he apparently did not like; and the publishers had gotten wind of the proposed agreement and had submitted a list of objections to the copyright treaty. Thackeray met Crampton, and together they drafted a response to those objections.[21] The effect must have been good, for on 17 February 1853 Everett signed the treaty, which then had to be delivered to the Senate for ratification. Delay followed delay; the Senate adjourned for the summer; other Anglo-American treaties and crises intervened; proposed amendments were negotiated by the Americans and objected to by the British; and worse, the American opposition lobby gained momentum. In August 1852 President Fillmore had written to Harper and Brothers asking for its opinion regarding an international copyright treaty. The response was ambiguous and evasive, declining to try to influence the government on a matter affecting so many different kinds of people. In May 1853 a similarly oracular statement was published in the editor's "Easy Chair" of *Harper's Magazine:* "We may not pass by silently the new stir in relation to an international copyright. And however the question may finally be settled, we welcome the discussion, and the interest in the discussion, as so many tokens of the increased consideration which is given, both by people and by government, to the making and printing of books. Twenty odd millions of people in our commonwealth are furnishing a host of readers; and it behooves government and people to consider wisely what sort of reading is to be furnished, and what sort of pay the furnishers are to receive."[22] Having lobbed this bit of wisdom from a firm position on the fence, the editor went on to cloud

---

[20]The Butler-Sumner cooperation may seem unlikely given the hostilities between these men three years later over the slavery question, when Butler's nephew, Preston Brooks, caned and nearly killed Sumner on the Senate floor.

[21]According to Barnes (ibid., p. 296) the objections and Crampton's and Thackeray's résumé are extant in the Public Records Office, Fo5/563/312-21, London. Thackeray's memorandum relating to this transaction is in the Crampton Papers, Bodleian Library.

[22]Joseph Henry Harper, *The House of Harper* (New York, 1912), pp. 107, 117.

the issue with irrelevant arguments about whether authors could or could not make a decent living and to poke fun at Edward Bulwer Lytton for guessing at the amount of money he could have made had there been an international law. The fact is that Harper and Brothers, whose history of piracy and whose system of small payments for advance sheets from English authors must have overcome their sense of the fairness of paying full rates in a regulated trade, stood to gain nothing by a copyright treaty. The treaty failed in 1854. There would be no international copyright law until 1891.

Nevertheless, by 1853 Thackeray's power and confidence as a major economic commodity made it possible for him practically to write his own ticket with the publishers in ways unavailable to many of his contemporaries, yet that power did not mean that his relations with publishers went smoothly.

In 1851 the author of *Vanity Fair* and *Pendennis* discovered with some astonishment that the lecture circuit was more lucrative in the short run than book publication. The contract for *Esmond* had stipulated that Thackeray would not publish anything anywhere within six months of the publication of that book, but he did not publish anything except *Esmond* in the whole of 1852. Yet his income from lecturing and the sale of "moral rights" to his books in America made it the most financially satisfying year he had ever had since 1832 when he came into his patrimony.

It should not escape notice that the unauthorized Appleton editions were dragged into the mainstream of textual history when Thackeray used them as the basis for the authorized *Miscellanies* produced by Bradbury and Evans in London. And it is questionable whether Thackeray actually took the opportunity to select and correct the texts of the three volumes of *Punch* material; one can only assume that he selected or at least reviewed the selection of items for those three Appleton volumes. Two of the volumes Appleton had announced as nearly ready in November 1852 did not appear as advertised; their alterations may well have been influenced by Thackeray. Furthermore, the parody of James Fenimore Cooper in *Punch's Prize Novelists* was omitted either by Thackeray who was already embarrassed by the Bulwer satire or by Evert Duyckinck who may have been more sensitive on behalf of American than British writers. But it is known that Thackeray did little if any correcting, and he did no revising for Appleton. The text of *Mr. Brown's Letters to a Young Man about Town,* for example, differs from the *Punch* text only in spelling and punctuation. Some *Punch* errors were corrected, but a number of new errors were introduced. No change bears the unmistakable stamp of authority. Most of the alterations are neither errors nor corrections, though unlike Harper and Brothers, which systematically house-styled Thackeray's spelling and punctuation for its reprints, Appleton did not. The effect, therefore, on the authority of the Bradbury and Evans reprints of the mid-1850s, even though Thackeray did revise slightly at that time, is that of progressive minor deterioration of textual authority.

In April 1853 Thackeray returned to England and soon agreed with Bradbury and Evans, the publishers of *Vanity Fair* and *Pendennis,* to write *The Newcomes* in twenty-four monthly parts. In June he wrote to Harper that "it will appear as soon as possible after the termination of Mr. Dickens' serial, and I hope you will be inclined to treat with me for the republication of my story in America, upon the same terms wh. you give Mr. Dickens and Sir Bulwer Lytton. I do not intend to begin to publish until several numbers are completed, and propose to devote the whole of the next 12 months to this story . . . please to tell me that you have paid to my account . . . the $1000 I am to receive from you for the publication of my lectures. I hope they have been as successful with you as in London, where we sold the whole of the first edition of 2500 (at 10/6) in a week."[23] During the next few months Thackeray visited with his family, toured the Continent, and wrote four numbers of *The Newcomes* with which he returned to London on the first of September where he discovered that in his absence Harper and Brothers had offered him £10 per number.[24] Thackeray immediately wrote to Bradbury and Evans noting Harper's condition that "they could get my numbers 6 weeks before it was printed here—so unless we put off till Nov. I lose £240" (*Letters* 3:300). Bradbury and Evans did not put off the projected publication, the first number appearing in London on 1 October. Later that month Thackeray wrote Bradbury and Evans again. "I just find a letter from Mr. Low . . . proposing still to treat with me on behalf of Messrs. Harper, and to secure you." By this time his tone is plaintive, perhaps on the edge of irritation: "Could one of you see Mr. Low without delay to day if possible as a Steamer starts tomorrow wh. might take out no 3 if you so chose. They did not publish no 1. No Briton has pirated it—it is impossible that it should now be touched and I have the consolation of thinking that my [£]300 have been lost from a panic where there was no danger. Some of it however may be recovered if you'll have the goodness to go to Lowe. Do

---

[23]Robert F. Batchelder Catalogue no. 60, item 95.

[24]The exchange rate at the time was 1 to 5, so the offer (by comparison with the $1,000 Harper gave him for the lectures) was $50 per number or $1,200 for the whole book.

try to day" (Bodleian). The Harper "Priority List" of payments made to English publishers for advance sheets indicates that Harper paid only £150 ($750) for *The Newcomes* (Harper MS, Butler), which appeared in *Harper's Magazine* from November 1853 through October 1855.

Whether or not a lesson in international relations had been learned from the experience with *The Newcomes* is impossible to know, but the arrangements for *The Virginians,* which began publication in London on 1 November 1857, seem to have worked out a little better from Thackeray's point of view and worse from Harper's. As before, the negotiations with Harper's agent, Sampson Low, were carried out by Thackeray, but the business of collecting the money and sending the advance proofs was left to the publisher. When in early October 1857 news of bank failures in America reached England, Thackeray wrote to his American friends the Baxters fearful "that all the American savings were gone to smash, including the 500£ from Harper Brothers for the Virginians" (*Letters* 4:55). It was with some relief that he wrote a note to Bradbury and Evans on 3 December saying: "I hear that Messrs. Harper of New York have forwarded funds to meet their engagements in this country, and shall be glad to have payment for my 2 numbers of the Virginians. Will you or Mr. Joyce call on Messrs. Low and receive the monthly money on behalf of Yours very Faithfully W M Thackeray" (*Letters* 4:58).

Meanwhile, a sticky situation was developing for the chief of American literary buccaneers. Serialization in *Harper's Magazine* began in the issue dated December, which appeared in the middle of November. A few days later *The Virginians* reappeared in the *New York Semi-Weekly Tribune.* Harper immediately appealed to Thackeray through Sampson Low to do something; on 11 December he replied:

[Berg]   *I am sorry to hear from you that the N Y. Tribune is reprinting the Virginians, and no doubt hurting the Messrs. Harpers' Issue of the story, who pay me 100$ per month for early impression. But I do not see what good any remonstrances of mine can effect. If American houses choose to reprint our books we can't prevent them, and the Tribune will doubtless take it's own course, in spite of any objections of mine or Messrs. Harper. Could English writers have remonstrated with any effect we should have done so years ago: but I am sure an outcry at present would neither be useful nor dignified; and can only express my regret that I dont see how, in the present instance, I can be of any service to a House wh. shows itself inclined to act in a kind and friendly manner to English literary men.*

A postscript in a scribal copy of this letter notes, "I am just advised of your payment for No I & II & hope to send you no III next week" (Beinecke). This letter is barbed (which may account for why the postscript was deleted from the letter actually sent): the reference to English authors being unable to prevent American houses from printing their works and the explanation that the unhappiness of the situation was one which English writers had been frustrated about for years are pointed reminders that there was no international copyright agreement. Thackeray must have known of the Harper firm's failure to take any active role in support of the copyright initiatives in 1853–54, though the firm had assured President Fillmore in 1853 that an international copyright arrangement "becomes more and more manifest."[25] Thackeray probably could not help hinting to the company that it was merely suffering the consequences of its own complacency and receiving, besides, only what it had dished out so generously over the years in which it had gained the reputation of a pirate. On the other hand, Thackeray's letter shows his deft diplomacy in the reference to Harper's freely chosen attempts to be kind and friendly to English literary men.

Harper and Brothers continued to chaff ineffectually at the *Tribune,* accusing the newspaper of lifting the story from *Harper's* and remarking sarcastically that the *Tribune* "had been leading advocates of an International Copyright Law." The *Tribune* claimed on 26 November that the novel was "carefully reprinted from a London copy" and that readers could expect it "in the *Weekly* and *Semi-Weekly Tribune,* usually a few days in advance of its appearance in any other American publication." Harper's printed response was: "This is simply untrue. HARPER'S MAGAZINE for January was published on the 17th of December; it contained Part II of Mr. Thackeray's Novel, in which three slight corrections were made from the London copy. *The Virginians* was 'carefully reprinted,' *with these alterations* in the *Semi-Weekly Tribune* the next day. When the Editor of the Tribune receives a 'London copy,' he will be able to ascertain what these alterations are." Confronted with this damning evidence, the *Tribune* countered that the Harper's was contaminating the text and thus breaking faith with the public. The legalities were a moot point, a fact not lost on the newspaper, which had nothing to fear but a little bad publicity.[26]

---

[25]Harper, *House of Harper,* p. 107.

[26]Excerpts in ibid., pp. 115–16; Wilson, *Thackeray in the United States* 2:399.

Once George Smith had fished for and netted Thackeray, a series of complicated and restrictive contracts organized his financial fortunes from 1860 until his death in 1863. In these contracts Smith specified that the income from foreign editions would go to the publisher, and Thackeray no longer concerned himself with the proper fulfillment of these foreign agreements. But until then the frequently frantic negotiations on his own behalf which characterized Thackeray's dealings with his publishers on both sides of the Atlantic may be an indication that the absence of an international copyright law was merely a symptom, not a cause, of the turmoil and uncertainty in the transatlantic profession of authorship in the 1840s and 1850s. The cause seems to have been the laissez-faire economics that made a free-for-all in which the devil might take the hindmost on both sides of the Atlantic even in the case of popular authors. In such conditions the publishers had the upper hand; the history of copyright legislation from that time forward was the history of increased protection of authors' rights, not publishers' rights.

The European Reprints and Translations

A small but significant market for Thackeray's works also developed in Europe, in both English-language reprints and translations. *The Yellow-plush Papers* was the first to appear in Europe, as it had been in America, coming out in tandem with Charles Dickens's *Master Humphrey's Clock* in Paris, 1841, published by Baudry, a firm owned at least in part by Thackeray's friend John Bowes Bowes and for which the author may have worked briefly in the 1830s. Continental interest in Thackeray did not really begin until 1849. In that year A. and W. Galignani, publishers of *Galignani's Messenger* in Paris, for whom Thackeray had also worked "for 10 francs a day very cheerfully 10 years ago" (*Letters* 2:475), issued *Doctor Birch* and followed up the next year with *Rebecca and Rowena*. There is no extant record, but Thackeray's previous connection with the publishers makes it possible that he was paid.

The important Continental story, however, concerns the Bernhard Tauchnitz firm in Leipzig, Germany. Baron Tauchnitz's Collection of British Authors series was begun in 1846 and soon dominated the English-language fiction market in Europe; only one other European publisher besides Galignani tried to compete with the German company for Thackeray. Aggressive acquisition and marketing made possible what could not be guaranteed through copyrights; for, as in America, there was no international copyright in Europe. In 1848 *Vanity Fair* was added to the collection; *Pendennis* and the first of what would eventually be eight volumes of *Miscellanies* followed. Tauchnitz was very anxious, in spite of the absence of a legal standing for his contracts, to develop personal, amicable financial relations with his British authors. The terms of his agreement for *Vanity Fair* have not survived, but Thackeray wrote in October 1848 to the baron's English representatives, Williams and Norgate, acknowledging receipt of a check, promising to send proof sheets of *The History of Samuel Titmarsh,* and announcing that *Pendennis* "now commences, I hope it will turn out as well as its predecessor" (*Letters* 2:444). The inference is that the check was for *Vanity Fair.*

Tauchnitz's response to the hint about *Pendennis* came in due course, and Thackeray agreed on 23 April 1849 to send the numbers of the new novel as they appeared. In August he wrote again warning that the novel was to be extended to twenty-four numbers; he did not expect more money in consequence, "but I thought it would be right to make the change known to you so that you may accommodate the Leipzig edition to the proposed arrangement."[27] The accommodation was simple: the third volume is thicker. The first volume of *Pendennis* and the first volume of *Miscellanies* (with *The History of Samuel Titmarsh* and *The Book of Snobs*) appeared in 1849.

In 1851 Charles Jugell, of Frankfurt am Main, issued *The Kickleburys on the Rhine* along with *Tales for the Road* by William Howitt, apparently without agreement with the authors. Thackeray did have an agreement with Tauchnitz, who included the work in volume 2 of *Miscellanies.* This incident of competition between European publishers was brought up the next year by Williams and Norgate in a letter that is characteristic of Tauchnitz's business dealings with British authors: open and generous but firm. Thackeray had written in October 1851 proposing his next novel, *Esmond,* which he anticipated would be published in February of the next year, and noting that "though not so large as Pendennis, I shall expect the same price wh. I received from Mr. Tauchnitz for the foreign copyright of that work; as it will be published all at once, and as soon on the continent as in London" (*Letters* 2:806). Presumably what Thackeray meant by the last phrase was that the Tauchnitz edition would be a simultaneous publication, not a later reprint, and would therefore have the advantage of competing with the English edition on an even basis on the Continent. However, the novel was not published in England until October 1852, and

---

[27]*Der Verlag Bernhard Tauchnitz,* p. 122.

in the meantime Thackeray had had an offer for *Esmond* from a French publisher—probably Galignani[28]—which depended on Thackeray's undertaking to keep the Tauchnitz edition out of France. Thackeray raised the matter with Williams and Norgate, whose response explains several aspects of Continental publishing.

> *I shall forward your letter to Mr. Tauchnitz but I may mention that to the best of my knowledge all the previous agreements are in the same terms as the present.—They do not secure Mr. Tauchnitz any copyrights in France but they enable him to sell his editions there, and that is of consequence to him for to be restricted to the sale in Germany alone would I fear hardly enable him to print at all, much less to give any sum worth mentioning for the continental copyrights—I do not think he cares to have the exclusive copyright for any other part of the Continent except Germany, but he must have the right of selling his editions all over the continent and particularly in France.*
>
> *I have drawn up a rough memorandum which if you please we will add to the contract and I will undertake either to sign it for Mr. Tauchnitz (as I have a general authority) or to get him to sign it.—*
>
> *I am not quite certain what is Mr Tauchnitz's intention as to the future, but I am inclined to think that he will prefer giving a little more and securing the entire copyright for the Continent if it will be possible for him as a stranger to hold a copyright in France—At all events I believe if Mr Tauchnitz is a competitor with others for the copyrights in France he will have a preference (upon otherwise equal terms) with those authors with whom he has been in correspondence hitherto—*
>
> *P.S. I would mention that in selling Mr. T. copyright for Germany only, you do not even sell him any* right *except in Prussia or Saxony or about one fourth part of Germany—that for instance some of your works were reprinted at Frankfort without let or hindrance from Mr Tauchnitz.*[29]

The proposed memorandum was given in both German and English: "Though according to the laws in force hitherto, Mr Tauchnitz can claim no exclusive copyrights except in Saxony and the states united with her, he is however expressly hereby permitted to sell copies of his edition everywhere on the continent, particularly in France.—" How much this addi-

---

[28]In September, Thackeray wrote to Smith suggesting, "And Galignani Might he not be induced to give something for the English reprint in France?" (NLS).

[29]Copy of letter supplied by Gordon Ray.

tion cost the baron is not recorded, but there were no other Continental editions of *Esmond* in English in the period.

Bernhard Tauchnitz's domination of the Continental market seemed to suit Thackeray well. He wrote friendly letters from time to time, commenting in July 1855 that people in Baden and Frankfort had reported reading and enjoying *The Newcomes* with the Tauchnitz imprint and offering *Barry Lyndon* and the English *Miscellanies*. Tauchnitz replied with a check for an undisclosed sum and a remark about his poor English. Thackeray reassured him: "A letter containing . . £ is always in a pretty style. You are welcome to the *Miscellanies* for that sum." Thackeray went on to reveal the perfectly casual and trusting nature of his relations with the baron's firm when he remarked, "I don't think I ever sent you the sealed paper investing you with the right over *The Newcomes*—I fear I have lost it: but you need not fear that I shall shrink from my bargain." Further evidence of Thackeray's satisfaction with the baron appears in his 1856 recommendation that Charles Reade's novels should be included in the Tauchnitz collection, adding, "I have no doubt our friend of Leipzig will deal as liberally with Mr. Reade as he has with other men of our craft." And in 1857 he left "the agreement for the new book [*The Virginians*] to your discretion entirely, premising that my publishers here pay me twice as much as for the *Newcomes*. . . . Send me over any agreement and I will sign and return it."[30]

When Thackeray signed with George Smith in 1859, he signed away his interests in foreign contracts, but Tauchnitz continued to publish Thackeray's works in agreement with Smith. Some problem arose in September 1861 causing Smith to reduce an expected payment to Thackeray. The author sent the publisher a drawing of a long face—"because your speculation is not so good as it might be, not for the personal loss to yours always, W. M. T." The ledgers do not reveal the problem, but it seems in part to have involved Tauchnitz, for Thackeray in a cryptic postscript said, "In respect of Tauchnitz (as in some other cases) to be thankful for what I can get is my maxim."[31]

Translations of Thackeray's works developed another small but significant Continental market. As with the English-language reprints, no records survive about actual income, though one offer for the rights to translate *Esmond* into French came in March 1852 from Armand François

---

[30]*Der Verlag Bernhard Tauchnitz*, p. 123.

[31]NLS. Ray, reprinting from the Biographical Edition, did not include the postscript (*Letters* 4:246).

Léon de Wailly, translator of, among other works, *Tom Jones, Evelina,* and *Tristram Shandy.* Thackeray's reaction was enthusiastic on two grounds: "M de Wailly is the very man of all France I would like to translate me but is it possible he can give as much as 4000 francs to me?—there must be some mistake I fear. Nevertheless I empower you to act, and get what you can for me."[32] In September, Thackeray wrote Smith that "the Paris publisher who made that fabulous offer of 4000 francs has declared off as I expected: and I shall now be very glad to take what ever the Gods will send me. Will your acquaintance still give [£]50? it is [£]110 worse than 4000 francs: but it is 1250 francs better than nothing" (NLS). In the end Wailly undertook the work, but what the gods sent Thackeray in compensation is not known.

Others who translated Thackeray's works into French include G. Guiffrey (*Snobs*), Edouard Scheffter (*Pendennis*), William Hughes (*Yellowplush*), and Amédée Pichot (*Samuel Titmarsh* and *Pendennis*). To the latter, whom he had known for several years, Thackeray wrote: "I would counsel no publisher to reproduce Vanity Fair it is too long for any body's reading nowadays.[33] I thought part of it very well translated in the Union but it fell off at the last and was also 'arranged.' Wh. you gentlemen are perfectly authorized to do and wh. you especially (who know much more about our literature than English literary men themselves do) do very well—but here is the difficulty with an author—I can't say that yours are faithful translations—that I would not prefer to have them *more* faithful:— but you may be sure that I wish your little project every success."[34] *Vanity Fair* appeared in French as *La foire aux vanités,* in 1855.

Translations in book form appearing in Thackeray's lifetime include Russian (*Snobs*), Swedish (*Esmond* and *Samuel Titmarsh*), Hungarian (*Esmond*), German (*Pendennis*), Dutch (*Yellowplush*), and Spanish (*Vanity Fair*).[35] To an unknown German translator concerning an unknown title, Thackeray wrote: "To be sure I am but a poor judge of German style—but

---

[32]*Letters* 3:23–24. Ray noted that "though Wailly later translated Thackeray's *Barry Lyndon,* he did not try his hand at *Esmond,*" but the British Library catalogue lists a copy of *Esmond* "trans. into French by Léon de Wailly" and dated 1856.

[33]The letter is undated but may be from 1854 during the war in the Crimea about which Thackeray wrote to another correspondent, "The trade will be dead in another year in England I fear, if this war continues of wh. the dreadful interest so far surpasses all our fictions" (*Letters* 3:410).

[34]The letter breaks off, and Ray speculated that it was never finished or sent (ibid., 3:411).

[35]To my knowledge there has been no systematic search for or listing of translations of Thackeray's works, though many of them must have been excerpted in Continental periodicals.

your translation reads very pleasantly, & seems to me very correct. I hope you and Mr. Cotta will be able to make terms." As an afterthought he added, "You can of course make use of this letter if it is likely to forward your wishes" (NLS).

The Works under George Smith

Thackeray died on 23 December 1863, leaving two unmarried daughters and a mentally ill wife who would survive for thirty more years, dependent on an estate that consisted of one large Queen Anne–style house and contents in Kensington, another house in Brompton, some investments, and his copyrights. As things turned out, the house in Kensington was the most valuable of these commodities, bringing £10,000; the copyrights brought £5,000. In all the correspondence and contracts relating to the copyrights, it was assumed that Thackeray had a half interest only. This was in part because most of the works already published and currently in print were covered by contracts or agreements involving half shares in profits. The contract for *Vanity Fair,* the only one with Bradbury and Evans that survives, actually ends with the clause "That the Copyright of the said Work shall be the joint Property of the aforesaid William Makepeace Thackeray and William Bradbury and Frederick Mullett Evans."[36] All of the other surviving contracts have similar clauses. The obvious implication is that no collected edition of Thackeray's works could be arranged by a publisher without dealing with all of Thackeray's partners.

George Smith had always acted the good friend of Thackeray and his family. He seemed to feel responsible for helping the bereaved young ladies conduct their affairs and consolidate their finances. Their neighbor and old friend Sir Henry Cole enlisted in the same cause, and together Cole and Smith engineered a scheme for a collection of Thackeray's works which they did not waste time implementing. On 13 February, just one and a half months after the author's death, Cole wrote to Bradbury and Evans on Smith's behalf:

[Beinecke]   *It is so obviously for the interests of Mr. Thackeray's daughters that the publication of his works should be with one publisher that I am induced to ask you out of old friendship to Mr. Thackeray, to let me know at your early convenience if you are disposed to treat for purchasing his other copyrights; to say what you would give for Miss Thackerays interest—or if you will sell your own, with the remaining stock and on what terms for cash.*

---

[36]Ray, *Adversity,* p. 434; see Appendix A.

> *Your immediate attention will be a favour & oblige all parties interested.*

The partners gave the matter their immediate and disapproving attention. Though Cole had not mentioned a uniform or collected edition, Bradbury and Evans knew immediately that such a scheme lay somewhere behind the proposal. The first draft of their response, dated 15 February, began bluntly; but trouble composing a suitable conclusion developed:

> *We do not altogether agree with you as to the obvious advantage to the Miss Thackerays of having their fathers works in the hands of one publisher.—If it were thought expedient (which at present is more than doubtful) to print an uniform Edition, this might easily be done by a very simple arrangement.—Neither do we think it would be to their interest to part with their share of their father's copyrights; which are becoming more and more valuable.*
>
> *For ourselves we are content to remain as we are; and whilst we certainly decline to buy;* ⟨*should prefer not to sell.—*⟩ ↑ *are equally indisposed to sell.—* ↓ ⟨*At the same tim*⟩ ⟨. *Nevertheless if the point is pressed, and an offer should be made us, we shall not refuse to entertain it.*⟩[37]

A second effort, dated the following day, began more formally and diplomatically but carried the same message:

[Beinecke]   *We are in receipt of yours of the 13th inst. It was hardly necessary, to us, to advert to by-gone days to induce attention; for our relations with Mr. Thackeray—of some thirty years' standing—were ever based on mutual friendship & confidence throughout all engagements, including even those most dear to him—*

Fully sharing in the desire to further Miss Thackeray's true interests, we cannot ⟨*but express our*⟩ ↑ ⟨*however*⟩ *withhold the expressing of our* ↓ *sincere belief that, for the present, it would be inexpedient on their part to dispose of their share in their father's* ⟨*works*⟩ ↑ *copyrights* ↓ *: Whether, hereafter, under different circumstances,* ↑ *possibly* ↓ *may be worthy of consideration—but at all events it does not appear to us so "obviously for the interests of Mr. Thackeray's daughters that the publication of his works should be with one publisher," as to require immediate decision—*⟨*the daily sales having been considerable—*⟩

---

[37]Beinecke. These major cancellations and insertions are made in pencil in another hand.

> *For ourselves we are content to remain as we are: and whilst disinclined to buy, are equally indisposed to sell. When the time comes— as it will—to publish a handsome Library Edition of Mr. Thackeray's Works complete, a simple customary trade arrangement may* ↑ *easily* ↓ *be made. Or in the event of its being then considered desirable to be in the hands of one publisher, we dare say we should not be indisposed to negociate—reducing it to a simple question of terms.*

No doubt a fair copy, perhaps revised some more, and omitting the potentially betraying reference to daily sales having been considerable, was sent to Cole, intended for Smith's ears. Bradbury and Evans combined a cautious wisdom, moral high ground, and offhanded nonchalance about ordinary trade agreements to combat what suddenly looked like eager grabbing on Smith's part and perhaps to hide some of their private thoughts on the matter. It is tempting to see in the first drafted response and canceled passages of the second response Bradbury and Evans's own conflicting interests. Unable or unwilling to launch an ambitious publishing campaign with Thackeray's still warm corpus, they also did not want to lose any of their grip on the action. A glance at the firm's ledgers reveals that in the preceding three years, during which it published nothing new, the value of Thackeray's copyrights shared by Bradbury and Evans had yielded £154.19.2 in 1861, £244.13.11 in 1862, and approximately £150 by February 1863. February may have been too early in the year for Bradbury and Evans to know that the company's share of Thackeray's copyrights would profit it £914.16.5 in 1864, but they were experienced in publishing by this time and knew the value of an author's death to his copyrights.

On the other hand, Bradbury and Evans were probably right that the obviousness of the move on behalf of the Misses Thackeray was not apparent. Smith and Cole's enthusiasm for the project prevailed, nevertheless, and the girls sold out for £5,000. We do not know if Smith told them that their father had earned approximately three times that much in his few years as Smith's writer or that the firm of Bradbury and Evans was about to realize one-fifth of that in one year of pumping its half of the old copyrights. Suffice it to say that Anne and Minnie were happy with the transaction and are not known to have ever uttered a word of regret or suspicion about George Smith.

Having purchased Thackeray's share of the copyrights from the estate, Smith did a little homework before turning once again to the other partners. He sent his solicitor to the Stationers' Hall to check the register there concerning the status of Thackeray's copyrights. What he found was that Chapman and Hall had never registered anything and that Bradbury and Evans had registered its publications all on the same day in 1857 but had omitted to register *The Virginians*. A new round of letters, this time omitting any mention of past friendships, went out to the two other firms. Smith claimed full ownership of all unregistered works on the grounds that he had purchased Thackeray's share of all copyrights and the Stationers' Register did not indicate that anyone else had an interest in them. Smith asked to see any contracts that might alter his reading of the situation.[38]

Needless to say, Chapman and Hall and Bradbury and Evans did not see the logic of this reasoning. Chapman and Hall pointed out that while it had no contracts, it had maintained a long-standing gentleman's verbal agreement with the author and it had semiannual ledger accounts to prove that the agreements had been carried out. Bradbury and Evans seem to have declined to discuss the matter with Smith who threatened both publishers with legal action. Meanwhile, both publishers found themselves having to deliver semiannual reports and profit shares to Smith, who now owned Thackeray's shares. Finally in July 1865 a negotiated settlement was reached in which Smith paid £400 to Chapman and Hall for all Thackeray copyrights and £95.13.2 for the back stock, which included six books partly in quires, partly bound, and plates, drawings, and woodblocks for all six books. It is not difficult to see why Chapman and Hall would sell so cheaply; the company had earned only £20.17.2 in 1864 because it was unprepared for the sudden demand and had to reprint heavily, but things were already looking better in 1865, for it had netted £190 by July. Chapman and Hall's dealings with Thackeray had always been cautious if not downright niggardly, and the partners never saw the full potential of his works.

Bradbury and Evans was a different case and a harder nut for Smith to crack. That company, too, threw in the towel, selling out for £3,750 for copyrights and back stock. The threat of court action, though it might well have won, was apparently enough to make it negotiate. But why it sold so cheaply is a mystery: not only had it made £915 in 1864; by June 1865 it had made another £428.14.11. Its ledger accounts kept careful record of the fact that in spite of these profits, the two-volume edition of *The Virginians* was still technically £3,256.12.5 in arrears. One could say that Bradbury and Evans let Smith pay that back "debt" on *The Virginians*

---

[38]This account derives from unpublished correspondence held by John Murray, Publishers, which absorbed the Smith, Elder company in this century.

in exchange for the whole lot. In a way, it was not untypical of the alternating hot and cold enthusiasms of that firm.

Once in charge of the whole affair, Smith immediately reprinted everything from the stereotypes he had just acquired. His own cheap edition of *Esmond* had to be reset because he had not ordered stereotypes in 1858. And having set the back stock in order, he turned his attention to a new uniform Library Edition of the works, the first of a long series of collected editions of Thackeray's works that Smith would orchestrate, which included a Cheaper Illustrated Edition, an Edition Deluxe, a Standard Edition, each consisting of twenty-two to twenty-four volumes, and culminated in the Biographical Edition of 1899 in thirteen volumes and the Centenary Biographical Edition of 1910, which came after Smith's own death but still bore his company's name as the imprint.

The power of Thackeray's copyrights is attested not only by Smith's collected editions but by the competing editions published between 1889 and 1908 in Boston by Houghton Mifflin and in London by Macmillan (17 vols.), Dent (30 vols.), Caxton (13 vols.), and Oxford (17 vols.). One cannot help wondering if the Misses Thackeray were better off with the £5,000 Smith paid them for their share of the copyrights in 1865, or if they would have done better with a half share in the profits of Smith's enthusiastic publishing campaign that did not even end in 1890 when *Vanity Fair* entered the public domain or 1905 when the last of the works published in the author's lifetime became public property.

V

Book Production: Manufacture and Bookkeeping

The Production House

THERE ARE MORE QUESTIONS than answers about the production of books in Victorian England. Thackeray dealt with some of the most prominent publishers in the business, about whom books have been written, and yet not enough is known about the detailed work methods or the economic network of book production.[1] The problem stems in part from the fact that histories of publishing have focused on the glamorous workings of the shop front—the relations between publishers and authors and booksellers, many of whom were publishers themselves. Frank Mumby and Ian Norrie's *Publishing and Bookselling* recounts the origins and highlights of publishing and the progression of publishing firms through inheritance and mergers, but just what happened to a manuscript when it came into a publishing house and how it was transformed into a book is a story never told straight through. Instead it tells how anonymous manuscripts turned out to be by so-and-so, how such and such an author felt about the copyediting, how another was interested in the choice of type fonts or binding, how decisions were made about another title page, and so on. Such anecdotes are valuable in suggesting the processes involved, and they suggest questions about who designed the title pages, who did the copyediting, what training and education were common among compositors and pressmen, and what specific production tasks, if any, were undertaken by the business partners.

In addition, histories of printing have concentrated on machinery, guild rules, trade unions, and papermaking and have recounted these matters in terms of trade and economic forces separate from the roles of individual workers in the production of individual works. The generalizations are very useful for an overall picture but frustratingly short on

---

[1]The names missing from Thackeray's business relations include some who were just as famous: Longman, Macmillan, Moxon, Bohn, Routledge, Cassell, Constable, Collins, and Eyre and Spottiswood. And he came close to doing business with John Murray and John Blackwood, whom he counted among his friends.

specific information for specific printers in specific years. The idea that not much changed in the practice of printing from the seventeenth through the nineteenth centuries in spite of the advent of machine presses and steam power allowed Marjorie Plant in *The English Book Trade: An Economic History of the Making and Sale of Books* and Philip Gaskell in *A New Introduction to Bibliography* to omit detailed analysis of the passage of a manuscript through production in a Victorian publishing and printing house. Indeed, such specific information seems not to exist anywhere to be recounted. The works of these students of printing history do, however, indicate the questions to be asked.

The first major question has to do with division of labor. What jobs were related to the publishing, printing, and bookselling businesses, and who did them? These three divisions were just emerging as separate businesses in the nineteenth century, and they merged almost as often as they separated. The firm of Bradbury and Evans, for example, began as a printery and developed publishing as a later part of its growing business. Smith, Elder began as a trading company, supplying books as well as other materials to the colonies, then developed publishing, and fifteen years later acquired a printery.

The importance of other related businesses becomes apparent from the question of division of labor. At the two ends of book production there must, obviously, be writers and book purchasers (one supposes the latter to be readers, too, but for trade purposes it does not matter what is done with the book once it is purchased). Between these two stands an industry requiring financial backing and a multitude of skills.

How publishers dealt with authors and, to a degree, with booksellers is fairly well documented.[2] How they dealt with the manufacturers of paper and ink and with typefoundries, who did the purchasing, how much

---

[2] In addition of Frank Mumby and Ian Norrie's *Publishing and Bookselling* (London, 1974), other general works include James J. Barnes, *Free Trade in Books: A Study of the London Book Trade since 1800* (Oxford, 1964); Collins, *Profession;* N. N. Feltes, *Modes of Production of Victorian Novels* (Chicago, 1986); Hepburn, *The Author's Empty Purse;* and Sutherland, *Victorian Novelists and Their Publishers.* Additional works on specific publishers include Glynn, *Prince of Publishers;* Huxley, *House of Smith, Elder;* Frank Mumby, *The House of Routledge* (London, 1934); George Paston, *At John Murray's: Records of a Literary Circle, 1843–1892* (London, 1932); Arthur Waugh, *A Hundred Years of Publishing: Being the Story of Chapman & Hall, Ltd.* (London, 1930); Royal A. Gettmann, *A Victorian Publisher: A Study of the Bentley Papers* (Cambridge, 1960); and many other "official house histories." And finally there are a few books on specific authors: Patten's *Dickens and His Publishers;* Michael Anesko, *Friction in the Market: Henry James and the Profession of Authorship* (Oxford, 1986); Cohen and Gondalfo, *Lewis Carroll and the House of Macmillan;* and June Steffenson Hagen, *Tennyson and His Publishers* (London, 1979).

shopping around was involved, how many employees had regular work at the printshop and bindery is less well known.[3] It is difficult to know also whether traveling salesmen or agents worked for the publishers, for the book retailers, or for themselves. And yet all these questions concern the conditions of book writing, publishing, and reading and have a bearing on why books were written and published as they were and what markets were reached effectively.

From the anecdotes about publishing and book production and from the histories of publishing houses and of printing, bookbinding, and bookselling a list of jobs related to production can be made. What cannot be known is whether a different person performed each of these or whether one worker was employed for a combination of them.

Once a decision to publish was made, the manuscript was given to a compositor for typesetting. Surviving manuscripts for Thackeray's works, obviously used as setting copy, do not have copy editor's marks or book designer's specifications. Presumably, then, the publisher or the shop foreman or whoever acted as the book's designer talked it over with the compositors, who then implemented the plan as they set type. Each compositor imposed his own version of the house rules, if there were any, onto the portion of the manuscript assigned to him as he set it.[4] Compositors could set type directly into pages with running heads and page numbers or as galley slips of pure text. And then proofs would be pulled. We do not know, for Bradbury and Evans or Smith, Elder, precisely who read the proofs, but it seems clear that the compositor, who was paid by the amount of type he set, not by the number of hours he worked, was charged for any mistakes he had made. Since making corrections was not a profitable way to spend time, the compositor had to balance his desire for speed with the demand for accuracy and a need to anticipate corrections in the manuscript called for by the author or other proofreaders. Thus, a

---

[3]The best general sources are Marjorie Plant, *The English Book Trade: An Economic History of the Making and Sale of Books,* 3d ed. (London, 1974); Philip Gaskell, *A New Introduction to Bibliography* (London, 1972); and personal reminiscences like those of Charles Manby Smith, *A Working Man's Way in the World: Being the Autobiography of a Journeyman Printer* (London, n.d.), and Charles Knight, *Passages of a Working Life during Half a Century: With a Prelude of Early Reminiscences,* 3 vols. (London, 1864–65).

[4]I use the masculine pronoun because little is known about the role of women in the production house. Certainly in country presses in Australia, New Zealand, and America there are plenty of recorded instances of women compositors, often members of the proprietor's family, but to what extent large London firms employed women is not known to me. Plant, *English Book Trade,* noted that the jobs of folding and sorting in binderies often went to women, but illustrations of binderies in her book show only men.

good compositor had to be a good copy editor. Any eccentric authorial usage was likely, therefore, to be smoothed over by the compositors' editing instincts under conditions that required speed, not deliberation over textual nuances and innovations.

Proofreading, according to descriptions of some printeries, was often done by boys reading against copy. It is not known if that ever occurred with a Thackeray work. Though, with the exception of a few fragments of *Vanity Fair,* proofs for his works before 1857 do not survive, Thackeray did get proofs; he may have seen second corrected and even third corrected proofs before printing began. It is clear that he had frequent access to the premises of his major publishers, Chapman and Hall, Bradbury and Evans, and Smith, Elder, so it is possible that in the time-honored tradition recounted in *Henry Esmond* when Dr. Swift encounters Henry at the printer's house presumably on a similar errand, Thackeray often read proof in the shop.

The compositor would correct the type and turn it over to the pressmen for printing. Most of Thackeray's work up through 1857 was printed by Bradbury and Evans—even those works published by Chapman and Hall and Smith, Elder. We do not know how many presses the firm had or what kind they were. How fast, for example, could a number of *Vanity Fair* be produced? Markings on the manuscripts show that one installment would be divided up among as many as four or five compositors who could finish the work easily in a day. Proof corrections probably took longer to point out than to implement. If final corrections came into the printing house as late as the twenty-ninth of the month for a part that had to be available for sale on the first day of the next month, there were at most two days for the operation. Occasionally the ledgers show charges for night work. Pressing and binding and distributing were all that remained to be done. Two presses, each mounted with both inner and outer forms for one sheet, could print 2,500 copies on one side; the sheets were then turned end on end and perfected on the other side. Each printed sheet would then have two identical copies of a gathering for the book. Cut in half, 5,000 copies would result. If handpresses were used producing, say, 250 copies per hour, the work would take twenty-two hours. If some of the sheets were perfected before the full 2,500 copies were printed on one side, there would be copies available for binding well before the printing was completed. Presumably the wrappers, steel-plate illustrations, and advertising materials could have been prepared in advance or printed at other presses. Bradbury and Evans was obviously a substantial printing establishment, though perhaps not as big as Clowes's printing factory that in 1866 employed 568 men and had over fifty operational presses.[5] Many other firms had eight to ten presses, but Bradbury and Evans must have had more because it was publishing and printing *Punch* weekly, as well as serials by Dickens and Surtees at the same time it was bringing out *Vanity Fair,* and the company continued to be printers for other London publishers.

And so the printed sheets went to the bindery. It is very likely that there was a bindery on the premises at Bradbury and Evans. The practice up until the 1830s had been for publishers, whether or not they were also the printers, to announce to the trade that a work would be available in quires (unbound) on such and such a day. Wholesalers and agents would crowd in, buy, and take off to be bound the copies they hoped to sell to libraries and retail booksellers.[6] But by the 1840s most publishers were supplying books in their own cloth bindings. The ledgers show that to be the case with Thackeray's works published by Bradbury and Evans.

This summary would not be complete without commentary on stereotyping, for that process produced a number of bibliographical complexities of real interest. Eight years after the publication of *Pendennis,* Henry Bradbury, son of Thackeray's publisher, explained the increased use of stereotyping: "The demand for literature had so materially increased, that to print off large editions on speculation of immediate or eventual sale, or to keep whole works standing in type for indefinite periods to meet demands for reprints, was equally hazardous: in one case there was an uncalled-for outlay of capital invested in paper and print; in the other, there was an unnecessary accumulation of works standing in type, and the consequent loss of the repeated use of these types—a principle quite in opposition to the true spirit of the first invention of moveable types." Stereotyping, Bradbury contended, avoided both hazards. Earlier, however, T. C. Hansard had warned in a treatise on printing that an "extravagant notion prevails . . . of the exceeding economy of stereotyping; it would therefore be of advantage to give a fair view of the case. On an average, the cost of stereotyping may be taken as the same as that of composition, or even higher. It is quite clear, therefore, that if the first edition of a work is stereotyped, the speculator at once incurs the expense of printing two editions, minus the press-work."[7] In opposition to Han-

[5]Plant, *English Book Trade,* pp. 357–58.

[6]Mumby, *House of Routledge,* p. 19.

[7]Henry Bradbury, *Printing: Its Dawn, Day, and Destiny* (London, 1858), pp. 32–33; T. C. Hansard, *Treatises on Printing and Type-Founding,* from the seventh edition of the *Encyclopaedia Britannica* (Edinburgh, 1841), p. 130.

sard's estimate, number 1 of *Pendennis* cost £4.15 to compose, £3.17.6 to correct, but only £4 to stereotype. Furthermore, the phrase "minus the press-work" includes the savings in paper. The first pressrun of a work for which stereotypes have been cast can be much smaller, for additional printings can be produced at no extra cost in case of a sales hit. On the other hand, most books never reach a second printing, so Hansard was right to suggest that in many cases the stereotypes would prove to be an added and unnecessary expense.

While Bradbury seemed not to agree with Hansard, the actual practice in the printing of *Vanity Fair* and *Pendennis* was a compromise between the two views. Perhaps it was with an eye to economy that the printer prepared copies of the parts of these serials from type in insufficient numbers to see how sales went and if it would be worth plating the novels, but it is as likely that the printers, who had had years of experience with Thackeray, simply were not given enough time between the submission of copy and publication deadlines to allow for the plating process before the first printing. The results of the two methods of printing are visible in the quality of the product.

When a book is printed from standing type, particularly if the print run is relatively large, the type is liable to shift in the forms. The evidence of this shifting is easily revealed by machine collations done on the Hinman Collator. The fact that type was jostled and respaced during or between printings, as well as that type damage and corrections occurred, shows up as flickering images in an otherwise stable page. Some jostle of type is visible to the naked eye. Some examples, signifying nothing more than that *Pendennis* was printed from type, occur in volume 1 at page 97, lines 17, 18, 19, and 21, where the first two letters of each of these lines have dropped down in some copies, and at the page number for page 259, where the 9 is raised in some copies and lowered in others. Also at page 149.6 the line is loose and extends into the right margin; the letters move from side to side, leaving, in some copies, spaces with words; those noted are *w ith* and *th e*.

Stereotyping freezes such movement. Thus damage, corrections, and type shifting that show up in late printings from type often carry over into the plates. Also new changes and some restorations appear in the plates, for if the type has been used for printing, it must be cleaned and can be corrected or realigned before the casting molds are made. One surprising and at first baffling fact about *Vanity Fair* and *Pendennis* was that the type page of some copies were slightly smaller than others. This turned out to be due primarily to the difference between copies printed from type and copies printed from stereotyped plates. In *Pendennis,* for example, the type page (i.e., the size of the page measured from the top of the running head to the bottom of the last line and from margin to margin horizontally) was larger in some copies than in others (by 1½ mm horizontally and 2 to 4 mm vertically). In 1858 Henry Bradbury wrote, "The method of stereotype still in use—consists in making plaster-of-Paris moulds of pages of types, and casting plates in type-metal." The process of casting plates was given in greater detail by T. C. Hansard. A fine-grain plaster-of-paris is brushed on the types, and coarser plaster poured over that. When sufficiently set, the plaster mold is removed from the type and placed in an oven to dry and to raise its temperature to equal that of the molten lead used for the plate. In lectures on the subject, Thomas Bolas wrote, "Although plaster expands at the moment of setting, it afterwards contracts in drying, and a plaster stereotype is therefore smaller than the original by about 1–80th linear." Elsewhere J. Southward added: "The contraction in plates taken by the plaster process is much greater than by the *papier-mâché*. This is owing to the shrinkage of the mould in the baking, and in the dipping-pan. In the paper process, the baking is performed while the mould is on the type; but the plaster is put into the oven by itself, and the evaporation of the moisture causes the contraction. It may be safely stated that a page of crown quarto [about 19 by 25 cm] will shrink about a nonpareil in length [about 2 mm], and a thick-lead in width [about 1 mm]." Hence, a plate made from the contracted mold would print a smaller type page than would the standing type.[8]

Since books printed during this period—whether with type or with stereotyped plates—were printed on dampened paper, paper shrinkage during drying introduced dimensional changes that complicate simple measurement as a way to detect the use of stereotypes. In *Pendennis* horizontal type-page measurements vary from 9.45 to 9.8 cm. Copies printed from stereotypes range in width from 9.45 to 9.6 cm, and those printed from type measure from 9.6 to 9.8 cm in width, so that a page measuring 9.6 cm might result from either process. This problem is resolved by dealing with the evidence for one sheet or gathering at a time: in no case did a given leaf produce the 9.6 cm measurement in both its type-printed and plate-printed form. For a plate-printed sheet that varied from 9.45 to 9.55 cm, the corresponding type-printed copies usually varied from 9.6 to 9.7 cm or wider. I concluded that paper shrinkage

---

[8]Bradbury, *Printing*, p. 33; Hansard, *Treatises*, pp. 125–30; Thomas Bolas, *Cantor Lectures on Stereotyping* (London, 1890), p. 24; J. Southward, "Collection of MS. and Printed Matter relative to Stereotyping," p. 78, St. Bride Technical Reference Library, London.

variation amounted to a smaller difference than did the shrinkage caused by the stereotyping process.[9]

In *Vanity Fair* and *Pendennis* copies with the smaller type pages consistently show more type damage than the larger ones. The cases in which the smaller copies have superior readings show definite evidence of conscious rearrangement of type such as respacing. In identifying impressions, therefore, smaller pages (printed from plates) can be assumed to be later than the larger pages (printed from type). The undoubtedly linear progression from type to plates indicated by damage noted in copies of the books obviates the possibility of simultaneous printing from type and plates as T. C. Hansard indicated was the practice even before 1841 in the printing of the *Penny Magazine*.[10]

Whether it is worth the effort necessary to learn so little is—as Kathleen Tillotson says at the end of "*Oliver Twist* in three Volumes"—a matter of taste.[11] And as Mr. Foker says in *Pendennis,* there's no accounting for tastes.

Vanity Fair: *Production and Accounting*

In order to understand the publishing business as it affected Thackeray, one can follow *Vanity Fair* through production, accounting for prepublication advertising, the cost of paper, the cost of printing, everything associated with printing and binding the serial, and the way in which the publisher paid itself as well as the author. In order to focus on a production process that can no longer be reconstructed from accurate personal accounts, inferences from the printed books and data from the account ledgers must be used. Yet beginning with the printed books can easily cause confusion, for some of the standard bibliographical descriptions reveal ungrounded assumptions about the process.

For example, from time to time booksellers' catalogues offer *Vanity Fair* in parts with descriptive notes and references to Henry Van Duzer's 1919 description of his Thackeray library.[12] Occasionally the descriptions refer to other known copies of the novel for comparison. One such catalogue refers to "the Austin copy" as "the finest copy of '*Vanity Fair*' ever offered at auction in America" and ends its headnote on the current

[9]For further details, see my "Detecting Stereotype Plate Usage in Mid-Nineteenth Century Books," *Editorial Quarterly* 1 (1975): 2–3.

[10]Hansard, *Treatises,* pp. 133–34.

[11]Kathleen Tillotson, "*Oliver Twist* in Three Volumes," *Library* 18 (1963): 132.

[12]Van Duzer, *A Thackeray Library,* pp. 123–32.

offering as "ONE OF THE TWO FINEST COPIES EVER OFFERED AT AUCTION IN THIS COUNTRY."[13] Who owns the finest copy of *Vanity Fair* is a question likely to interest book collectors more than literary critics or book production historians. And as long as fineness is determined by references to the condition of the wrappers and the priority of advertisements unconnected with the novel's text, it will remain a question of little importance to the critic. But it is an important question to both collectors and critics when the significance of the connection between fineness and the text is explored in the production processes.

The basics are, of course, well known: the first edition consists of twenty numbers in nineteen separate installment parts, each with thirty-two pages of text, additional leaves of advertisements, and printed yellow paper wrappers.[14] The last installment contains numbers 19 and 20. The first number was published on 1 January 1847, and the final double number was published on 1 July 1848. Following completion of the serial issue, leftover sheets from that issue along with newly reprinted sheets from the same typesetting were used for publication of the novel in one volume. The publisher's accounts record multiple printings of this edition and continuous availability of the novel in parts and book form throughout the 1850s and 1860s.

This summary of the production of *Vanity Fair* gives a false impression of simplicity. Both scholars and book collectors have operated under certain naive assumptions that need dispelling—to wit: the idea that any given physical copy of *Vanity Fair,* whether in parts or volume form, might as a whole belong to a single printing (the production process of mid–nineteenth-century serialized novels makes this as likely to be untrue as to be true); or the idea that the "printing," "issue," or "state" of the text of a serialized novel can be ascertained by reference to points in the wrappers. Regardless of the literary significance of the textual variants in *Vanity Fair,* their existence and distribution have an important bearing on the question of fineness or priority. But the variants do, also, have literary significance and must attract the critics' notice. Among the printings within the first edition, there are 210 variant readings, of which 150 are

---

[13]Proofs from an unknown auction catalogue in the Lilly Library, Indiana University.

[14]By "first edition" I mean all printings of *Vanity Fair* using the type set for the book as it appeared in parts from 1 January 1847 through 1 July 1848 (see Fredson Bowers, *Principles of Bibliographical Description* [Princeton, N.J., 1949], pp. 379ff.). Some collectors use the term to mean only the "first printing," as seems to be the case in David A. Randall's "Notes towards a Correct Collation of the First Edition of *Vanity Fair,*" *PBSA* 42 (1948): 95–109.

substantive, 17 being the addition, deletion, or substitution of passages ranging in length from three to seventy-five words.

It would seem, for example, of some small importance to the literary critic to know that originally Mr. Jos Sedley in Vauxhall Gardens is referred to as a "fat bacchanalian" but that second thoughts led to the deletion of that description,[15] or that Miss Crawley had originally signified her intention of dividing her "fortune equally" between Sir Pitt's second son and the family at the rectory, but that in revision the fortune is described merely as an "inheritance" to be divided without reference to proportion (p. 72, l. 25). And it must be of some interest to the followers of Becky's fortunes that in the original text the reason Colonel Crawley, though governor of Coventry Island, could settle on her only £300 a year (out of an annual income of £3,000) was that his revenues went to the "payment of certain debts and the insurance of his life," but that later the reference to life insurance was deleted (p. 579, ll. 7–8).

Indeed, both the critic and the printing historian stand to benefit as much as the book collector from the effort to determine who owns the finest copy of the first edition of *Vanity Fair;* for though there is probably no satisfactory answer, the attempt at one requires attention not only to book-collecting values but to the complex printing history of the book and the artistic effects of the author's continued interest in the composition of the work during the printing processes. It is possible to determine when those 210 variants first appeared in the text, who was responsible for them, and finally what significance they have to an understanding and assessment of the novel.

As David Randall has pointed out, there are five areas of concern for parts-issued books: front wrappers, back wrappers, inserted advertisements, plates, and text.[16] For *Vanity Fair*, by far the greatest interest to date has been lavished on the first three—the parts the author had the least to do with. Booksellers continue to identify their copies of *Vanity Fair* by reference to readings on the wrappers and by one or two famous "points" in the text, which are not in fact points, one of the most often used "points" remaining unchanged throughout all printings of the first edition.[17] But

---

[15] *Vanity Fair* (London: Bradbury and Evans, 1848), p. 50, line 11 up. Further references to this edition of *Vanity Fair* are made in the text. A detailed account of composition and revision and of publication variants can be found in my edition of the novel (New York: Garland, 1989).

[16] Randall, "Notes," p. 96.

[17] *Mr. Pitt* (p. 453, l. 31), which was not changed to *Sir Pitt* until the second edition (London,

these five concerns are merely the discrete parts of the product. Taken together they are the corporate results of the activities of publishing, printing, binding, and marketing, each of which affects the five-part product. Synthesizing all the evidence makes it possible to provide a satisfactory guide to the effects that its production history had on the novel, the specific result of production represented by a given copy of the book, and the significance that the vicissitudes of production have for the student of the text and for the book collector.

The basic task in producing *Vanity Fair* was to typeset thirty-two pages a month on two octavo sheets bearing sixteen pages each in such a way that all thirty-two pages would be decently occupied by letterpress or illustration and so that the last page of the last chapter of each number would end a respectable way down the thirty-second page. Important incidentals to this task involved preparing the yellow paper wrapper which had a dated and numbered title as well as an illustration on the front and advertisements of various sorts on the front and back of the back cover. A four-page advertiser was printed and added at the end. The two sheets of text and one of advertisements were then folded, the wrapper placed around them, and they were sewn by "stabbing."[18] Having manufactured the installment, the publisher had to distribute it for sale.

The production records for *Vanity Fair* were kept in several books, two of which are of primary importance and tedious complexity.[19] The first is an unlabeled book that details the production costs of serial publications by Bradbury and Evans. Totals from this book were carried over to the second, labeled "Paper and Print," which was the final accounting book for the firm. The first unlabeled ledger may well be a book made up from a no longer extant daily ledger, for the production costs detailed in the unlabeled book seem to summarize certain categories of costs. It is possible, however, that the sources for the entries in this book were individual billings.

1853), seems to be a favorite point, perhaps because its presence in every copy of the first edition makes every owner happy. Other "points" such as the use of roman type for the heading on page 1 and the absence of the Steyne illustration on page 336 first occurred in the third printing of the numbers containing them.

[18]Stabbing means sewing straight through from front to back very close to the spine, rather than sewing through the fold or gutter of the gathering from the inside to the back. Many books originally issued in this form were later rebound in the standard way when the whole book was collected. The stab holes in these books remain visible in the inner margins.

[19]The Bradbury and Evans ledgers are used by permission of *Punch Magazine* and its former publishers, Bradbury, Agnew.

The entries for incidentals and advertising relating to *Vanity Fair* began on 21 November 1846, though an initial attempt to begin publication of the book took place in March or April.

Nov 21	Advs. slips 4/6 5/. 4/6		67	14.—
28	Half Share 30,000 Demy 8vo bills	—		6.—.—
—	Printing 30,000 8vo Prospectuses	—		5. 5.—
—	—— 40,000 Demy 8vo Bills	—		12.10.—
—	Engravg line	—		7. 6
—	—— Cut for Cover	—		2. 4. 6
Dec 12	4000 Dble Demy Posters		70	17.10.—
—	Circulars 6/6 Subs. Slips 4/6	—		11.—
26	3000 Shew Boards red & blue	—		17.17.—
—	Posting 2000 Bills	—		4.—.—
31	Advertising to this date	119.7.6	131	52. 8. 6
—	Engraving Wrapper Block		111	2. 4. 6
1847				
Jan 9	Advs Slips 3/6 Posting 1500 Bills 60/		87	3. 3. 6
23	—— 1/4 3/6 3/6			
	Posting Bills March 27 10/.	—		18. 4
Mar 13	Posting 300 Bills		94	12.—
—	Advs. Slip 1/4 3/. 1/. 1/. 3/6 1/. 2/.	—		12.10
Jun 30	Advertising to this date		132	81. 9. 9
	P&P Book		39	208. 8. 5

The numbers in the column just to the left of the cash amounts column on the right are something of a mystery except for number 39 preceding the total; that is the page number in the second account book which is titled "Paper and Print," indicated in this entry as the "P&P Book." The Paper and Print book is the book where all the costs and income related to *Vanity Fair* are gathered and summarized. That is also the book in which the publisher figured its own income. If the other numbers in this column also refer to page numbers, they are references to ledgers no longer extant.

What these seven months of entries for incidentals and advertising show is the amount of effort that went into promoting the sale of *Vanity Fair* during the first six months of its run, which began on 1 January 1847. The costs may not seem much, but the effort of composing, printing, and distributing 30,000 prospectuses and 40,000 (or perhaps 70,000) bills (some of which were stitched into the serial parts), and 3,000 posters, which from the cost (£17.17) must have been in two colors each, seems quite satisfactory if not extraordinary. Advertisements are also entered separately in the Paper and Print book and must be additional to those recorded in this unlabeled listing.

Production costs for each number were detailed in the same unlabeled book just a few pages after the incidentals entries.

1846	[No.] 1	
Dec 28	Printing 5000	
	Compos. 2 sheets @ 60/	6.—.–
	Corrections ditto	1.15.–
	Working 10 Reams 12/.	6.—.–
	Pressing	1.5.–
	5,000 Wrappers	4. 4.–
	Stereoty	4.—.–
	Paper 10 Reams D Demy 35/.	17.10.–
	2½ wrappers 25/.	3. 2.6
	10 rms Plate 12/.	6.—.–
	Writing Plates	12.–
	Engravings 7/. 9/. 2/7/6 15/. 9/. 18. 17/6	
	14/. 17/6 9/. 28/. 17/6	10. 9.–
	Printing 5000 Plates (2) @ 2/6	12.10.–
	Bindg 5000—Bills & advs	7.18.4
	Compsg of Spec[?] pages & Sheets	7. 7.–
	Editing includg etchings & drawings	60.—.–
	Steels	13.–
	Biting in	2. 2.–
	Bindg 760	1.—.9
	Advs. sheet	
	Compsg 4 pp.	2.10.–
	Working 5000	2. 5.–
	Paper 2½ rms 15/.	1.17.6
		149.0.14
	Reprint 2000	
	Working 2/16/ Pressing 10.	3. 6.–
	1000 Wrappers 12/. 2000 Plates 2/6 5/./.	5.12.–
	4 Rms D Demy 35/.	7.—.–
	½—Wrappers 12/6 4 Rms 2/8 Plates	3.—.6
	P&P. 39	177.19.7

Production of 7,000 copies in two printings of number 1 of *Vanity Fair* cost £177.19.7. These costs are to be understood as follows: the compositors setting type for two sheets (i.e., thirty-two pages) received 60s. a sheet, which comes to £6. Corrections or alterations in the typesetting cost £1.15. Working ten reams of paper (i.e., 5,000 sheets) at 12s. per ream equaled £6. Five thousand copies of the number resulted because each double demy sheet produced two octavo sheets for the book. "Pressing," an operation clearly separate from "working," but which I cannot explain, cost £1.5. Five thousand wrappers or covers for the part cost £4.4. Casting the stereotype plates cost another £4. Paper for the text of the novel, ten reams of double demy at 35s. a ream, cost £17.10. Two and a half reams of wrappers at 25s. came to £3.2.6. (In order for 5,000 wrappers to be produced from 2½ reams, each sheet would have to contain four wrappers. To achieve this arrangement, the wrapper need be composed only once, and one stereotype cast made. These two sets of type, mounted all at once on a press and printed by the work-and-turn method, would produced four identical wrappers on each sheet.) The fact that ten reams of paper were required for the steel etched plates indicates that only two illustrations could be printed at a time. This paper was heavier than the text paper and cost 12s. a ream, or £6 for the number.

Writing on the steel etched plates cost 12s. This was probably done by a coppersmith; there is a charge for a coppersmith's alterations for the second number.[20] Twelve wood engravings also were paid for. While Thackeray did his own drawings, he did not engrave the woodblocks himself. Not all the engravings paid for were necessarily used in the book, a possibility that lends itself to the notion that engravings embedded in the text were used or not according to the demands of last-minute adjustments to the length of the number, each of which had to be precisely thirty-two pages long. The steel plates added a significant expense to the number; it cost twice as much to print 5,000 copies of the plates as it did to print 5,000 copies of the text, £12.10. Binding the number, including the bills and advertisements for the "advertiser" that went with it, cost £7.18.4. The cost of printing the bills was an entry on the incidentals page, and so was not repeated here.

That the next entry involved composing of type is clear enough, but just what was being composed is not clear. There is no corresponding entry in the accounts of other numbers. The amount, £7.7, is just over that for composing the first number. I think it is the charge for the first typesetting of number 1, undertaken in March or April 1846. That type-

---

[20]Bibliographers and book collectors might, therefore, do well to look for variant forms of the etched plates for number 2.

setting was abandoned after it had been proofread at least once and corrections made for a second set of proofs. The decision to abandon it stemmed at least in part from the difficulties Thackeray had in adjusting its length to the thirty-two-page requirement. That attempt, incidentally, had no engraved illustrations embedded in the text to help in those adjustments.[21]

A quaint feature of the *Vanity Fair* accounts is that the payments to Thackeray as author and illustrator are listed as "Editing including etchings and drawings." Thackeray received £60 per number. His payments are included as a cost of production. This is important to note; the cost of these payments would have to be recovered before any profits began to show. The steel plates cost 13*s*; biting in the drawing—which Thackeray would have etched directly onto the coated plate—cost £2.2. The next entry is a bit of a mystery; £1.0.9 for binding 760 looks like a binding order for 760 copies of the part, billed at a fraction less per copy than for binding the 5,000 copies. But there were no more copies to bind, unless this refers to a partial binding order for the 2,000-copy reprint reported farther down the column. Later in the long-drawn-out life of the first edition, binding orders for small numbers are common.

An advertisement sheet of four pages cost £2.10 for composing type, £2.5 for working at the press, and £1.17.6 for 2½ reams of paper (each sheet, again, producing two copies of the advertiser). The next entry, "149.0.14," is tucked into the record in smaller handwriting as a notation and serves as a subtotal (inaccurate by £10) for the production costs of number 1 before adding the costs of the reprint.

The 2,000-copy reprint cost £3.6 for working and pressing (there was no composition cost because the stereotyped plates were used), £5.12 for wrappers and plates, £7 for text paper, and £3.0.6 for wrapper and plate paper.

The initial production cost for number 1 (up through June 1847) came to £177.19.7, including the author's fee. This figure and the total costs for incidentals and advertising for November 1846 through June 1847, £208.8.5, detailed in the unlabeled ledger, were carried to page 39 in the Paper and Print book where they became single entries in a 30 June summary of costs. The total cost for each number of the serial was similarly computed and carried over to the Paper and Print ledger.

This ledger has debits and credits on facing pages. The debits or costs for *Vanity Fair* are listed on a verso.

---

[21]See chapter 1 above, and my "Textual Introduction," in *Vanity Fair* (New York: Garland, 1989), pp. 651–54.

```
1847
June 30    To Paper and Print No   1— 7000 177.19. 7
                                    2— 6000 168. 5. 6
                                    3— 5000 136.10.10
                                    4— 5000 136.18.—
                                    5— 5000 140. 1.—
                                    6— 5000 133.15. 3
                                    7— 4000 126. 2.—1019.12.2
                                       37000
         Incidentals & Advertising           (54)      208. 8.5
         Commissn. allowd. to Agents   210.5.9          21.—.7
                                                      1249. 1.2
```

The first entry is the £177.19.7 just detailed for the production of
7,000 copies of number 1. The next six entries are comparable costs for the
production of the next six numbers produced up through 30 June 1847.
The incidentals and advertising costs from page 54 in the unlabeled book
have already been discussed. The commission allowed to agents (probably
wholesalers, but possibly traveling salesmen) is figured at 10 percent of
£210.5.9—a sum that does not appear elsewhere in the ledgers, nor have I
been able to figure out how it was determined. The commission to agents
appears to be a separate arrangement from the one that is recorded on the
credits page in which the price of numbers was discounted 25 percent from
a shilling down to 9d. The production costs for the first seven numbers of
Vanity Fair during the first six months amounted to £1,249.1.2 including
seven payments of £60 each to Thackeray.

The credits for *Vanity Fair* appear on the facing recto.

```
1847
June 30    By 37000 Nos. printed of 1 to 7
              1225 Nos. presented
              6694 — on hand in quires
              2722 ——— sd.
               600 — on sale in Country
                42 — Mr. T. 6 cos 1 to 7
         37000 = 25717 sold as 23739 @ 9d.      890. 4.3
         By Nett Proceeds of Advts. 1 to 7       92.13.6
                       Balance down             266. 3.5
                                               1249. 1.2
```

Of the 37,000 copies of numbers 1 to 7 printed, 1,225 (the equivalent
of 132 copies of the first seven numbers) were given away as presentation

copies and for review; 6,694 (about 956 copies of the seven numbers) were still in hand unsewn (in quires); 2,722 were still in hand already sewn or bound; 600 were on consignment to agents in the country; and 42 (6 copies of the seven numbers) had been given to Thackeray. The other 25,717 numbers (3,674 copies of the seven numbers) had been sold.

Two kinds of discounts appear here. The 25,717 copies were sold as 23,739 (i.e., 1,978 thrown in free, or a 7.7% discount), and these were sold at 9*d*. each rather than the shilling retail price (another 25% discount). Total income in the first six months from sales came to £890.4.3 (though it must be remembered that these figures represent at most the first day or two of the sale of number 7). Income from advertisements included in the number came to £92.13.6, leaving a shortfall of £266.3.5.

By the end of the next six months, production costs for numbers 8–13 had amounted to £771.2.9, and incidentals and advertising cost £31.16.9. An error was detected in the credits for the last six months, since the price per number was 8¾*d*. rather than 9*d*, so £24.14.7 was added to the debits. Agents' commissions were allowed on £159, which amounted to £15.18, and an undetailed charge for "Assistance in Nos. 6 & 7" came to £2.2.

The final entry on the debits page for the July to December 1847 accounting is a "Comm. to Publishers on 1813.3.3" which was figured at 10 percent and came to £181.3.4. The corresponding credits page shows that sales brought in £773.2 and proceeds from advertisements came to £57.3.6, a gross income of £830.5.6. The sum of this income and that of the first six months, £982.17.9, is £1,813.3.3. Bradbury and Evans figured the firm's commission as 10 percent of gross income of sales and the net income of advertising. Thus, at the end of the first year of publication, after thirteen installments, *Vanity Fair* was running £467.18.4 in the red, though it had paid its author £780 and its publisher £181.3.10.

The story of production costs and income had yet to reach a climax. The financial accounts of *Vanity Fair* turned from red to black in 1848. There was, apparently, no half-yearly accounting, since the Paper and Print book shows sums for the whole year. In addition to the £462.18.4 debt remaining from 1847, production, incidentals, agents' commissions, etc., for numbers 14–20 came to £2,162.15.8. This amount includes the £420 paid to Thackeray for those numbers and £338.11.5 paid to the publisher as its 10 percent commission figured on an income for the year of £3,385.14.5. Not only did income in 1848 make up for the deficit, but there was a surplus of £760.0.3.

None of this apparent surplus reached the author. In 1849 the publisher paid itself commissions of £46.18.4 and £16.8.5. The surplus on hand increased to £1,003.10 after the expenses of reprinting the whole book twice and various numbers a third time had been met. In the first six months of 1850, production and incidental expenses fell to £48.2 (which included £17.11.4 to the publisher as commission) while income came to £175.13.3. This brought the surplus balance to £1,179.3.3. By this time Thackeray had earned £1,200, which had been paid to him in advance at the rate of £60 a month while he was writing the novel. His last income had been credited to him in July 1848. Bradbury and Evans matched that sum for the publisher's share in January 1850, more than wiping out the surplus. The total publisher's commissions by this time had amounted to £600.15.10. Thus, as of 1 July 1850, Thackeray had made £1,200; Bradbury and Evans had made £1,800.15.10; and the account was £68.18.9 in the red. This accounting procedure was relatively common. It applied to Thackeray's arrangements with Smith, Elder as well. By equaling the score, so to speak, the way was paved to begin profit sharing.[22]

In the last half of 1850, the shortfall in the *Vanity Fair* account was reduced to £49.12.10, and in the first six months of 1851 the book showed its first sharable profit, £39.13.6 divided equally between author and publisher. The publisher continued to draw its 10 percent on sales before figuring profits, but for years publisher and author reaped small amounts of profit at six-month intervals: £12.19.8 each in December 1851, £28.3 each in June 1852, £30.12.4 each in December 1852. The income then dipped to £1, £2, or £3 in some years but jumped to £33.10.5 each in the first six months after Thackeray's death. It is not a macabre note to strike, since Thackeray repeatedly said he was working to leave his girls £10,000 apiece, and his copyrights—weak as some of them were—were among the greatest of his possessions.

Some traditional collectors of *Vanity Fair* might think much of this investigation unnecessary. One assured me that a useful bibliography is one that identifies the printings in a simple straightforward way for book collectors. But identifying the printing or state represented by any given

---

[22]One should note, however, that though Bradbury and Evans began accounting procedures for *Pendennis* in the same way, raking off 10 percent of gross income as a publisher's commission, they put the money is escrow and restored the whole amount to the credit side in December 1850, thereafter never again deducting a commission from Thackeray's accounts—not for *Pendennis* or *The Newcomes* or *The Virginians*. They even stopped deducting it from the *Vanity Fair* account in 1854. One might note that Smith's contracts specified that he would charge a 5 percent commission on sales income, but that the *Vanity Fair* contract (the only surviving Bradbury and Evans contract with Thackeray) does not mention a commission.

copy of *Vanity Fair* is seldom possible. It is often possible to identify the printing or state of each sheet or gathering within a given copy of the book, but most copies of *Vanity Fair* as wholes represent hybrids or mixtures of sheets from different printings, the natural result of the methods of manufacturing and marketing the book.[23] When each monthly part was published, a certain number of copies of the part were printed from type. As the stack of printed sheets for each number dwindled in the bindery, it was replenished by reprinting. The result was that some parts were reprinted more often than others (see Appendix C, chart 1). The book was available in parts for years after it had also become available in book form, and the book form itself was bound in small lots as needed for distribution; hence sheets from one printing can appear indiscriminately mixed with sheets from other printings in any given book—regardless of its present form, whether parts or volume. If a particular copy of the book has an early title page and prefatory material, the rest of the book may yet consist of sheets printed late or a mixture of early and late. Even if the issue of parts had ceased once the book as a whole became available, one need only be reminded that eighteen months elapsed between the printing of number 1 and the printing of the title page and that, according to the publisher's records, during those eighteen months numbers 1 and 7–13 were each reprinted once.

Though I have been able to identify the order in which variant readings were introduced to the text and have given them in that order in the appended table (Appendix C, chart 3) they may appear in confusing disorder in any given copy of *Vanity Fair*. Thus, in using the variants lists as a means of identifying a given book, each gathering must be identified separately. Furthermore, the *Vanity Fair* owner must be warned that the difference between parts and book-form issues was created by the bindery, not the press. In other words, the mere fact that a copy was issued in parts is no guarantee that the text is an early printing, nor does the fact that a copy is in book form mean that it is composed of later printed sheets.

Following the completion of the parts issue on 1 July 1848 and during the succeeding fifteen years, Bradbury and Evans issued the first edition of *Vanity Fair* continuously in parts and volume forms. Each monthly part was printed at least six times, twelve parts were printed seven times, and two parts were printed eight times—prepared according to the schedule in

---

[23]The terms *sheet, signature,* and *gathering* all refer to the same basic unit of the book produced at the printing press. In *Vanity Fair,* first edition, each gathering consists of sixteen pages (eight leaves) and is signed at the foot of the first and third pages.

Appendix C, chart 1. The novel was stitched into parts and bound in book form for distribution according to the schedule in Appendix C, chart 2.

1. The *first printing* of each number was run off from standing (movable) type. Positive identification of printings from type can be made by measuring the length of any printed line extending from margin to margin. If the measurement equals or exceeds 3¹³⁄₁₆ inches (9.7 cm), the page was printed from standing type; copies printed from stereotyped plates measure 3¾ inches (9.6 cm) or less.

States of the first printing were created when certain changes were effected in the standing type before stereotyped plates were cast. Though it is not clear whether these changes were stop-press corrections producing two states of the first printing or if they represent second printings from type, the former seems the more likely in view of certain evidence concerning the stereotyping. The changes in the standing type are listed in columns 1 and 2 of Appendix C, chart 3. In one instance, that of signature X in number 10, three states of the first printing are distinguishable (see chart 3, entries 309.3 and 309.11).

In the publisher's account books, charges for stereotyping were entered at the same time as those for initial composition and corrections, and it is conceivable, perhaps even probable, that the stereotypes were cast immediately after the first printing from standing type. If that were the case, one would expect to find relatively commonly copies of *Vanity Fair* in parts with numbers 1 and 7–13 printed from stereotypes since these numbers were reprinted months before their reissue in book form (see Appendix C, chart 1). In fact, however, both the normal complexities of original production and the rapacity of unscrupulous bookmen have produced copies of *Vanity Fair* in parts with sheets printed from stereotypes. An egregious instance of the latter is the Heineman copy in the Pierpont Morgan Library, which was expertly repaired so that only careful examination reveals that seven of the gatherings were made up by combining pages from at least two different copies—one printed from type and one from stereotyped plates—and that three additional whole gatherings printed from stereotypes were probably supplied surreptitiously: a classic case of collecting wrappers and advertisements rather than texts. However, not all "mixed copies" are aberrations; the publisher's records show that *Vanity Fair* was always available in parts so that as the years went by, new-sold parts would contain late-printed sheets. Similarly, copies in volume form sometimes contain early, maybe first-printing, sheets either as a normal result of binding schedules or because some purchaser of early parts had his copy rebound in volume form. Nevertheless, certain copies (not all in parts) composed mostly of sheets printed from type have been noted with numbers 1 and 7–11 both printed from stereotyped plates and sharing all the readings characteristic of the last state of the printing from type.[24] Not only does this pattern correspond with the publisher's records, but it demonstrates that the major alterations in *Vanity Fair,* for these numbers at least, were effected after stereotyping. It is likely that similar copies of the book in parts also exist with numbers 12–13 printed from stereotypes but with readings corresponding to the final state of the first printing.

It is misleading to speak of a second printing of *Vanity Fair,* for not all parts reached a second printing at the same time. There was, nevertheless, a short time in which the publisher was producing books with a characteristic combination of first-printing sheets and second-printing sheets which it is tempting to refer to as a second stage of production.[25]

2A. The *second printing* of numbers 1 and 7–13, apparently issued in combination with first-printing sheets of the rest of the book, was printed from stereotyped plates but shares the readings of the final state of the printing from type (see column 3 in Appendix C, chart 3). Numbers printed from stereotypes but with readings agreeing with the printing from type can be distinguished from type-printed numbers by the measurement described above (i.e., type-printed pages measure $3\frac{13}{16}$ inches or more horizontally from margin to margin while stereotype-printed pages measure $3\frac{3}{4}$ inches or less). This second printing of numbers 1 and 7–13 can sometimes be distinguished from other, later stereotype printings by the readings in column 3 of Appendix C, chart 3.

Though the publisher's records give no clear indication of when the majority of the substantive variants were introduced, the existence of numbers 1 and 7–11 printed from stereotypes with unaltered readings proves conclusively that changes in those numbers postdate the stereotyping and suggests a similar pattern for the rest of the book.[26] In addition, the

---

[24]See copy 5 in parts (part 1 only) and copy 1 in bound form (formerly belonging to Charles Dickens—numbers 1, 7–8, and 10–11) in the Berg Collection, NYPL, and the only copy in the Mitchell Memorial Library, Mississippi State University (numbers 1 and 7–11).

[25]See the similar circumstance noted in the account of *Pendennis,* below.

[26]The records do show that "correction and alteration" of numbers 19–20 cost £3.10 on 15 July 1848, that unspecified plate "repair" cost £1.10 on 24 Feb. 1849, and that unspecified "mending" of plates cost 15 shillings on 28 Feb. 1857. These charges probably refer to stereotyped plates of text rather than the steel engraved plates of full-page illustrations, for in a separate record of reprints there are standard charges for "bringing up plates and cuts." But it seems unlikely that the record of plate alteration is complete or that the cost of

evidence of machine collation, though inconclusive, seems to suggest that in numbers 2, 3, and 5 a few changes not actually noted in any copy of the book printed from type may in fact predate the stereotyping.[27] It is possible that these changes were made in standing type which was not then used again before the stereotypes were cast and that the further changes, made after stereotyping, were effected in the stereotype plates before they were used the first time. Hence, there may never have been copies of the book with the earlier changes only. The importance of the machine-collation evidence is that is suggests a chronology of changes and supports the notion that Thackeray's interest in changing the text was continuous, not merely a onetime or haphazard concern. The changes that appear to predate stereotyping are all corrections or alterations of some magnitude and are probably authorial.

2B. The *second printing* of numbers 2–6 and 14–20 was made from stereotyped plates incorporating considerable alteration and seems to have occurred at about the time of the third printing of numbers 1 and 7–13. See Appendix C, chart 1, for the rapidity of reprinting during the eight months following the serial's conclusion (July 1848 through February 1849). This second printing of numbers 2–6 and 14–20 can be distinguished from the first printing by the measurement indicated above (i.e., the first printing is from type, the second from stereotypes) and by the readings listed in chart 3, column 3.

3. The *third printing* of numbers 1 and 7–13 was made for the most part from corrected stereotyped plates. However, the "correction" of signature

---

altering stereotyped plates totaled only £5 or £6, particularly when original corrections and night work on parts 19–20 alone came to £11.6.

[27]When an alteration in standing type involves the substitution of only one character for another, the effect on the rest of the line is usually too small to be noticeable even under careful examination, but larger changes, particularly if the total number of characters in the line is affected, cause alterations in the arrangement of words contiguous to the change which are readily seen in a collating machine. Often the corrector changes the spacing of contiguous words to achieve an even balance of spacing along the line. When similar alterations are made in stereotyped plates, such aesthetic considerations are a luxury generally out of reach. The line (indeed the page) is a solid piece of metal which cannot be moved and pushed about; the new reading replaces the old reading and contiguous words remain frozen in place. The offending letter or word is chiseled off and a replacement "sweated" (soldered) in its place. If the resulting disproportionate spacing is too obvious, the whole line or perhaps two or three lines are reset, and the original plate is cut away to make way for the new material, which can be plated first or can be mounted in the press as standing type along with the plates. Most of the alterations in numbers 2–6 and 14–20 of *Vanity Fair* have an appearance compatible with the effects of changes in plates. Those that do not (confined to numbers 2, 3, and 5) are discussed further in the text and identified with an asterisk in Appendix C, chart 3.

Y entailed the removal of a woodcut from the text. The result was that the text from that point to the end of the chapter had to be moved up 9.7 centimeters. Rather than trying to cut and move stereotyped plates, the printers reset the whole of pages 336–40. Thus, the first pages of the next signature, Z, are also reset. At least one printing, probably the third, was run off from corrected plates except for pages 336–40, for which reset type was imposed along with plates. The readings characteristic of this printing are recorded in chart 3, column 4.

4. The *fourth and later printings* by Bradbury and Evans are not distinguishable from one another and are only occasionally identifiable at all. The publisher's records show six printings for each of the nineteen parts, seven printings for twelve parts, and eight printings for two parts. Signatures Y and Z are again significant, for the pages printed from type in the third printing were then stereotyped for subsequent printings, and though there are no distinguishing readings, the type-page measurements indicate stereotyping.

The title page, printed with part 19-20, is the only page that can be distinguished in more than four printings. According to the publisher's records, the final part (containing numbers 19–20, the preface, and title page) was printed seven times by Bradbury and Evans before Smith, Elder and Company acquired the stereotypes and back stock in 1865. The Bradbury and Evans printings occurred three times in 1848, once each in 1849 and 1855 and twice in 1864. Unlike the text, the title page seems to have been reset for each printing, and six different settings have been identified. Though it is impossible to determine the precise order in which the title pages were prepared, it is beyond question that the first one given in Appendix C, chart 4, is the first printing. It seems likely that the two printings dated 1849 precede some if not all the others dated 1848 because the books they belong to have some readings predating those in copies with the 1848 date. However, the mixtures of early and late sheets by the bindery makes it impossible to use the state of one sheet as evidence for the state of other sheets in the same book.

Since each of the title pages was entirely reset, the apparent carryover of a characteristic from one to the next would be fortuitous, not indicative of chronology.

When Smith, Elder and Company acquired the copyrights and the back stock of stereotypes and printed sheets from Thackeray's other publishers in July 1865, they acquired from Bradbury and Evans 5,001 copies of "various numbers" of *Vanity Fair* in parts and 2 copies bound up. Over the next eight months they printed enough "various numbers" to bring the total to 17,392 which were made into 865 copies of the book bound in cloth with 92 numbers left over. Though I have not yet encountered a copy dated 1865, a charge for new titles was entered in the account books for November of that year. A copy dated 1866 is at the Simon Fraser University Library.[28] The records also show an August 1868 printing of 250 copies, again with a new title page dated 1868; there is a copy (not personally examined) in the British Library. That Smith, Elder reprinted the first edition of *Vanity Fair* in 1868 (the same year in which they brought out an entirely new edition of the book as part of a collected edition of Thackeray's works) is a clear indication that Smith saw separate rather than overlapping markets for the various formats of a single title.

What does it all mean? For the book collector the historical record reveals the true nature of the copies of *Vanity Fair* one already owns, and it establishes a range of representative copies that can be added to one's collection. For the historian of printing, the record with its combination of evidence from publisher's records and the books themselves confirms the complexity of the economic, technological, and artistic confluence that commercial book publishing had become. For the textual editor the implications are patently clear: it takes a lot of collating to find the true state of textual variation. For the literary critic and student of Thackeray's works, the record of variants provides a basis for further understanding Thackeray's attitude toward his text and supplies evidence leading to a clearer understanding of his concerns in the novel. Some changes seem to have relatively obvious motives: the elimination of Dobbin's lisp (all but one instance) at pages 50.18 and 105.18-19 was clearly intended to improve the image of the book's only gentleman. And the deleted reference to life insurance at 579.7-8 was the mere correction of an error, since at 501.3-4 Rawdon was unable to qualify for life insurance at all. But other changes suggest more subtle motives. Why, for example, did Thackeray find it inappropriate, at 50.11up, to call Jos a "fat bacchanalian"? And why, at 75.29, did he change Lady Muttondown to Lady Southdown and then decide, at 500.35, that is was also inappropriate to refer to Lady Southdown as Lady Macbeth? Some changes can be understood by reference to the manuscript, as in the case of the deletion of the sentence at 40.10-11: "And what can Alderman Dobbin have amongst fourteen?" Though vaguely and puzzlingly reminiscent of St. John's account of the feeding of

---

[28]It appears to have been usual practice with publishers then, as now, to postdate works published late in the year; so the Simon Fraser University copy probably belongs to the November 1865 printing. I have not actually seen that book, which is noncirculating.

the five thousand, the sentence is unclear. The manuscript has "leave," not "have," a perfectly clear reading which does not recall the miracle feeding at all. But perhaps there was self-censorship, not correction, in the fact that Mrs. Blenkinsop, at 55.14-15, was no longer allowed to opine to Pinner, apropos of Becky, that governesses are "neither one thing nor t'other." If nothing else, the alterations focus attention on passages that were, somehow, not right and for which the new readings are, somehow, better.

The History of Samuel Titmarsh and the Great Hoggarty Diamond

Production processes affected single-volume publications in ways different from those attending serial publications. Though the importance of publisher's records in establishing printing history has long been recognized, the potential uses are exemplified particularly well in a study of the records for Thackeray's short novel *The History of Samuel Titmarsh and the Great Hoggarty Diamond*. Not only do these records reveal a hitherto unidentified edition of the book, but combining the information from the records with analytical examination of multiple copies of the books themselves reveals the processes of typesetting, stereotyping, imposition, pressruns, bindings, and sales of the book. As was the case with *Vanity Fair,* the total production picture has significance to textual analysis and gives insight into the influence of publishers on the book market as well as the book market's influence on publishers.

Thackeray wrote *The History of Samuel Titmarsh* in January and February 1841. He posted the manuscript to *Bentley's Miscellany* by 25 February and, having had no word from the publisher by June, reclaimed it rather angrily.[29] It was first published in *Fraser's Magazine* in installments from September to December 1841. In June 1848 Thackeray, having just completed *Vanity Fair,* suggested to his publisher, Bradbury and Evans, that the firm reprint *Samuel Titmarsh* in book form. He wrote his mother the same month that he was to receive £100 for the reprint (*Letters* 2:382). Although the first charges for *Samuel Titmarsh* in the Bradbury and Evans records are entered for 30 June 1848, the first edition in book form was the one published, without authorization, by Harper and Brothers of New

[29]The details were given by Ray in *Adversity*, pp. 261, 478. It is probably not true that the book was turned down by *Blackwood's Magazine* as Sir Theodore Martin inferred in his *Memoir of William Edmondstoune Aytoun* (Edinburgh and London, n.d.), p. 132. Robert Colby speculated that Thackeray may have intended it as a companion to *Comic Tales* (1841) in *Thackeray's Canvass of Humanity*, p. 197, n. 10.

York in November or December 1848 as *The Great Hoggarty Diamond.*[30] The first English edition, published by Bradbury and Evans, finally appeared in January 1849 (see figs. 1 and 2) and was followed immediately in February by a second edition from the same firm (see fig. 3). These two editions have always been referred to collectively as the first edition in book form (a label which ignores the New York edition) or the first English edition. The second of these two English editions, not selling well, was reissued with a new title page and slightly altered preliminaries by Bradbury and Evans in 1852 (see fig. 4) and then again in 1857 and finally by Smith, Elder and Company in 1872 (see fig. 5). A fourth edition, published by Bernhard Tauchnitz, of Leipzig, may precede the second English edition, for its setting copy consisted of proof sheets from the first English edition sent from Bradbury and Evans to Williams and Norgate, Tauchnitz's British agents.[31] Tauchnitz published the book together with *The Book of Snobs* as *Miscellanies: Prose and Verse,* volume 1, in 1849. A fifth edition was issued in two formats simultaneously. It was published in 1857 by Bradbury and Evans separately in paper wrappers as *The History of Samuel Titmarsh and the Great Hoggarty Diamond* and in cloth as part of the contents of *Miscellanies: Prose and Verse,* volume 4, a title borrowed from the Tauchnitz firm. The sheets for both of these issues were printed from the same setting of type; but they represent separate printings, for their pagination and signing differ.

On the basis of publisher's records, I conjectured in 1973 the existence of an unrecognized English edition of *The History of Samuel Titmarsh.*[32] Subsequently I found five copies and can show the distinctions between the two editions that had always been listed together simply as "London: Bradbury and Evans, 1849." The second of these editions went so long

---

[30]The month of publication is conjectured in *Catalogue of an Exhibition of the Works of William Makepeace Thackeray . . . Held at the Library Co., of Philadelphia . . . 1940* (Philadelphia, 1940), item 36. The earliest recorded review is in the *Literary World* 3 (9 Dec. 1848): 896; see Flamm, *Thackeray's Critics,* 59. Among surviving Harper and Brothers records (owned by Harper and Row, Inc., but now housed at Columbia University Library) is a manuscript titled "'Harper's Catalogue' 1817–1879" which lists *The Great Hoggarty Diamond* with the date 8 Dec. 1848.

[31]At least this was Thackeray's intention when he wrote to Williams and Norgate on 24 Oct. 1848 that "Messrs. Bradbury and Evans will send you proofs of my little story 'The Great Hoggarty Diamond' wh. I shall be glad to see published by Mr. Tauchnitz, and shall trust him for the terms" (*Letters* 2:444). However, Thackeray's letter of 11 Aug. 1849 to Tauchnitz suggests that the *Miscellanies* which was to contain the story was not yet published (*Der Verlag Bernhard Tauchnitz,* p. 122).

[32]Shillingsburg, "Thackeray and the Firm of Bradbury and Evans," *Victorian Studies Association* (of Ontario) *Newsletter,* no. 11 (March 1973): 13.

undetected because its preliminary pages and last gathering of text are identical with those in the first English edition, and the rest is virtually a line-for-line resetting which imitates the first edition in every respect, suppressing anything that would easily call attention to itself.[33] It is not surprising to find owners of the second edition who think they have the first: the covers are also replicas of the first-edition covers.[34]

According to the publisher's records, 2,000 copies of *The History of Samuel Titmarsh* were printed on 27 January 1849. The records show charges of £40.5.6 for typesetting the first edition, but there is no entry for stereotyped plates. The record's next entry shows a printing of 2,000 more copies on 17 February, referred to as the second edition, entered this time at the cost of £36 for "composing and working" and adding charges for stereotyping. The obvious conclusions to draw are that stereotyped plates were not made for the first English edition, that most of the type was redistributed before a need for the second edition was recognized, and that type had to be recomposed for the second edition only twenty-one days after the printing of the first edition. Composition for the second edition was less expensive because the preliminary twelve pages and one gathering of text type were saved from the first edition for reuse and because line-for-line resetting was probably cheaper than typesetting from the magazine version. Ironically, sales of *Samuel Titmarsh* dwindled rapidly, and the

---

[33]Line-for-line resetting of new editions is not unusual. The main reason for it in this case was probably to ensure that the reset gathering M would mesh with the preserved setting of gathering N. But other advantages have a bearing: resetting line for line means that end-of-line word divisions and line justification problems are already worked out. Most deviations from exact line-for-line resetting were attempts to improve the look of especially crowded or tight lines.

From time to time the compositor(s) working on the second edition failed to make the new lines match the line breaks in the first edition. On at least one occasion a textual variant caused the line-break difference (see Appendix D, table 1, item 55.9), but for the most part carelessness was the apparent cause, or else the knowledge that if one line did not match, the text could easily be brought back to the proper line ending within a line or two. Differences could result from attempts to loosen a tight line; almost as often, however, new tight lines were created in bringing the lines back to the proper endings.

Other examples of line-for-line resetting occur in Thomas Babington Macaulay's *Critical and Historical Essays,* vol. 1 (London: Longmans, 1843), entirely reset line for line for the second edition and again for the third edition, and in Thackeray's *The English Humourists of the Eighteenth Century* (London: Bradbury and Evans, 1853), which was printed at least three times in 1853 with substantial revisions and considerable line-for-line resetting.

[34]One copy in original paper-covered boards is in the Fales Collection, NYU. Two copies, both rebound, are at the Library Company of Philadelphia. A fourth copy, also rebound, is in the British Library (C.71.b.12). A fifth copy, rebound and extra-illustrated but with the original covers bound in, is at the Huntington Library. A special note of thanks is due to Mrs. Lillian Tonkin of the Library Company for her cooperation.

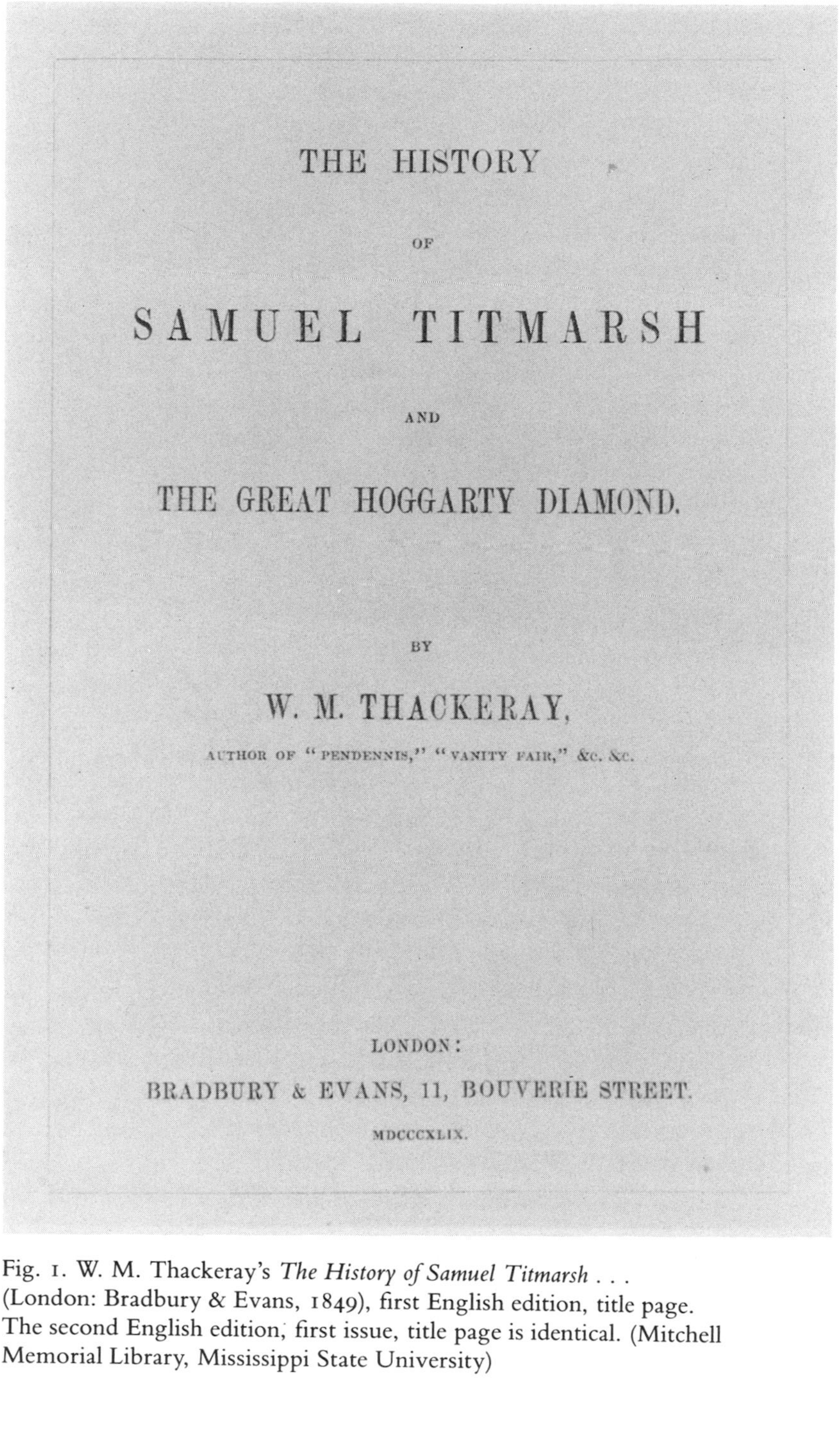

THE HISTORY

OF

SAMUEL TITMARSH

AND

THE GREAT HOGGARTY DIAMOND.

BY

W. M. THACKERAY,

AUTHOR OF "PENDENNIS," "VANITY FAIR," &c. &c.

LONDON:

BRADBURY & EVANS, 11, BOUVERIE STREET.

MDCCCXLIX.

Fig. 1. W. M. Thackeray's *The History of Samuel Titmarsh* . . .
(London: Bradbury & Evans, 1849), first English edition, title page.
The second English edition, first issue, title page is identical. (Mitchell
Memorial Library, Mississippi State University)

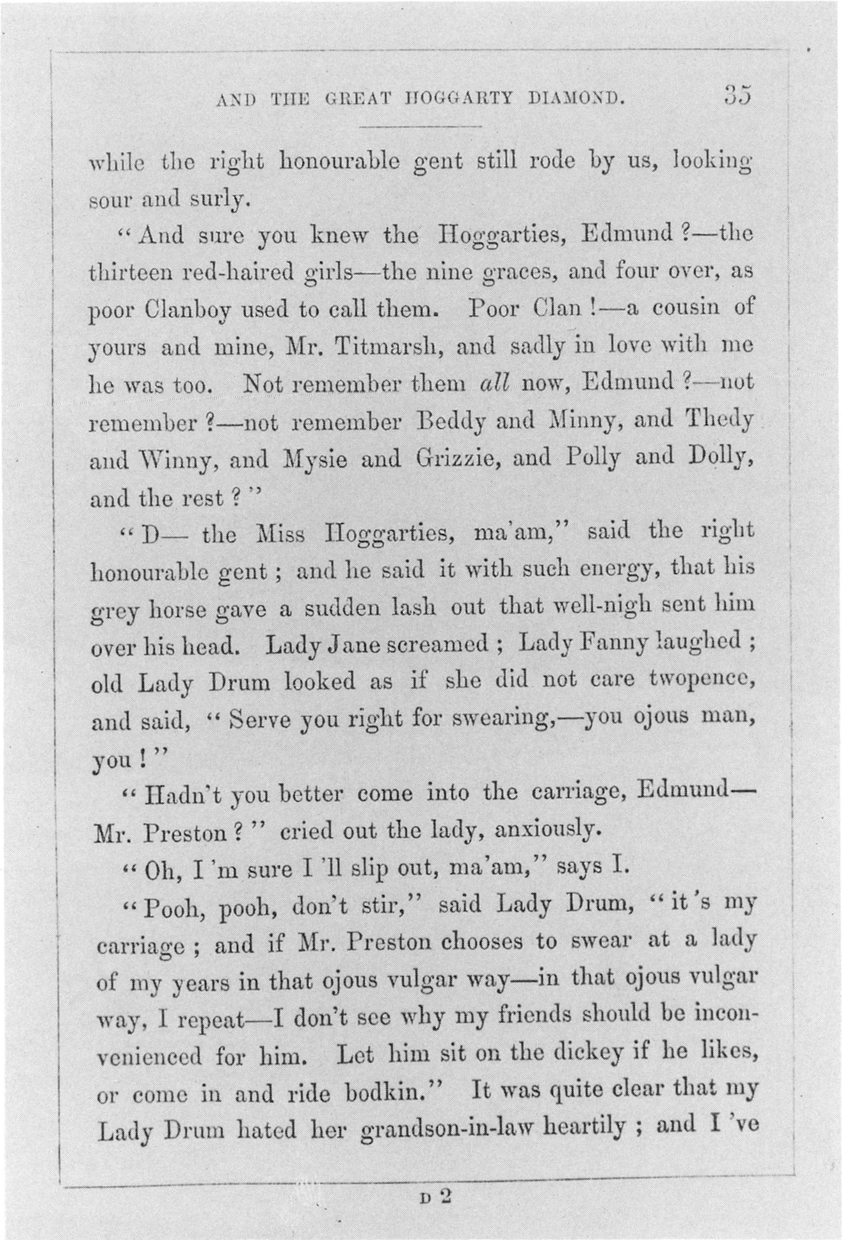

while the right honourable gent still rode by us, looking sour and surly.

"And sure you knew the Hoggarties, Edmund?—the thirteen red-haired girls—the nine graces, and four over, as poor Clanboy used to call them. Poor Clan!—a cousin of yours and mine, Mr. Titmarsh, and sadly in love with me he was too. Not remember them *all* now, Edmund?—not remember?—not remember Beddy and Minny, and Thedy and Winny, and Mysie and Grizzie, and Polly and Dolly, and the rest?"

"D— the Miss Hoggarties, ma'am," said the right honourable gent; and he said it with such energy, that his grey horse gave a sudden lash out that well-nigh sent him over his head. Lady Jane screamed; Lady Fanny laughed; old Lady Drum looked as if she did not care twopence, and said, "Serve you right for swearing,—you ojous man, you!"

"Hadn't you better come into the carriage, Edmund— Mr. Preston?" cried out the lady, anxiously.

"Oh, I'm sure I'll slip out, ma'am," says I.

"Pooh, pooh, don't stir," said Lady Drum, "it's my carriage; and if Mr. Preston chooses to swear at a lady of my years in that ojous vulgar way—in that ojous vulgar way, I repeat—I don't see why my friends should be inconvenienced for him. Let him sit on the dickey if he likes, or come in and ride bodkin." It was quite clear that my Lady Drum hated her grandson-in-law heartily; and I've

Fig. 2. W. M. Thackeray's *The History of Samuel Titmarsh* . . . (London: Bradbury & Evans, 1849), first English edition, page 35. (Mitchell Memorial Library, Mississippi State University)

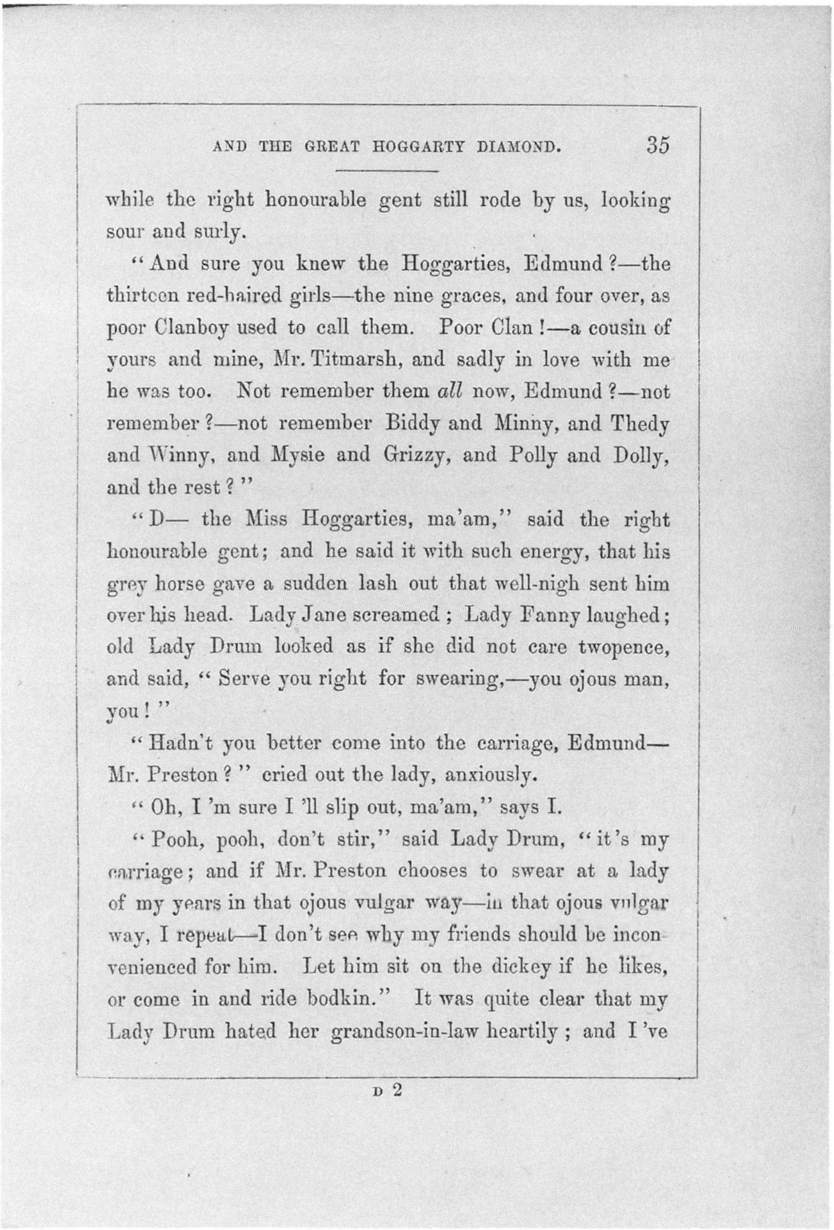

while the right honourable gent still rode by us, looking sour and surly.

"And sure you knew the Hoggarties, Edmund?—the thirteen red-haired girls—the nine graces, and four over, as poor Clanboy used to call them. Poor Clan!—a cousin of yours and mine, Mr. Titmarsh, and sadly in love with me he was too. Not remember them *all* now, Edmund?—not remember?—not remember Biddy and Minny, and Thedy and Winny, and Mysie and Grizzy, and Polly and Dolly, and the rest?"

"D— the Miss Hoggarties, ma'am," said the right honourable gent; and he said it with such energy, that his grey horse gave a sudden lash out that well-nigh sent him over his head. Lady Jane screamed; Lady Fanny laughed; old Lady Drum looked as if she did not care twopence, and said, "Serve you right for swearing,—you ojous man, you!"

"Hadn't you better come into the carriage, Edmund— Mr. Preston?" cried out the lady, anxiously.

"Oh, I'm sure I'll slip out, ma'am," says I.

"Pooh, pooh, don't stir," said Lady Drum, "it's my carriage; and if Mr. Preston chooses to swear at a lady of my years in that ojous vulgar way—in that ojous vulgar way, I repeat—I don't see why my friends should be inconvenienced for him. Let him sit on the dickey if he likes, or come in and ride bodkin." It was quite clear that my Lady Drum hated her grandson-in-law heartily; and I've

D 2

Fig. 3. W. M. Thackeray's *The History of Samuel Titmarsh . . .* (London: Bradbury & Evans, 1849), second English edition, page 35. (British Library C.71.b.12)

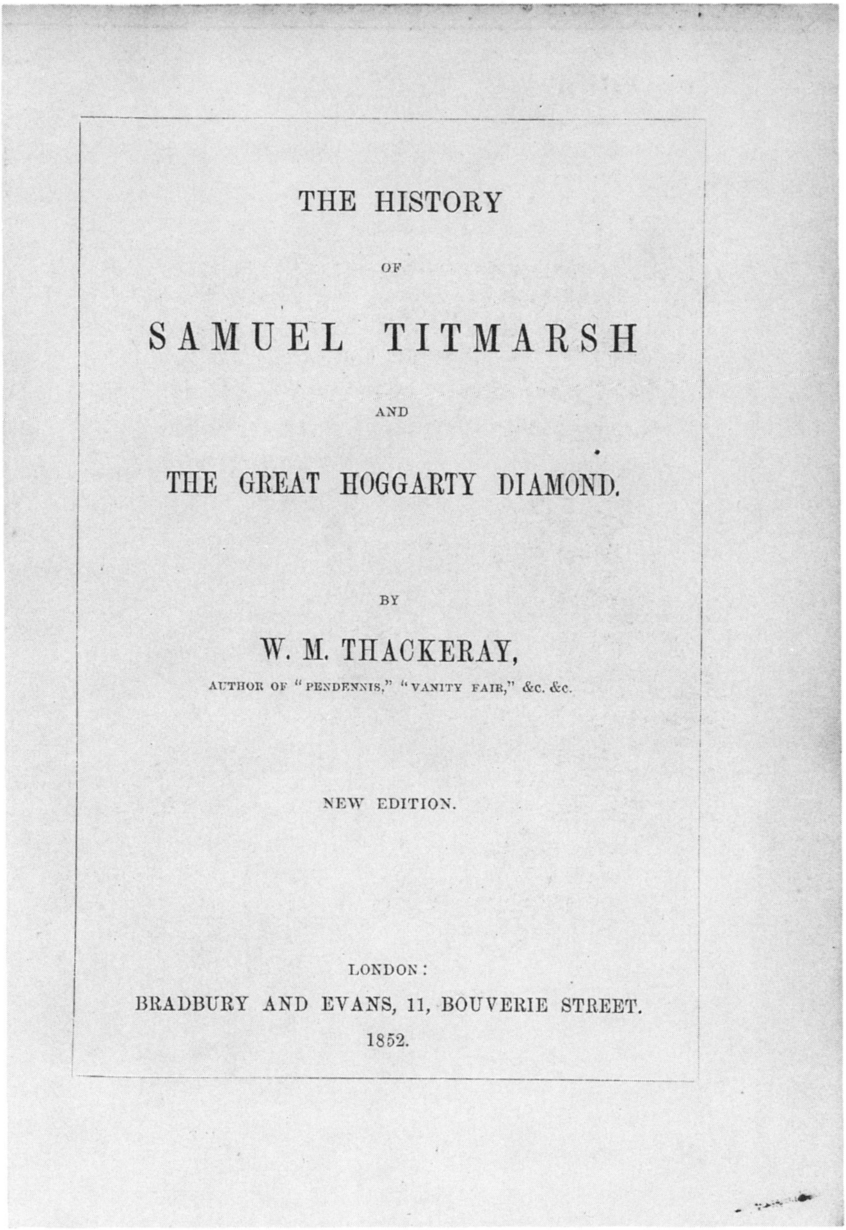

THE HISTORY

OF

SAMUEL TITMARSH

AND

THE GREAT HOGGARTY DIAMOND.

BY

W. M. THACKERAY,

AUTHOR OF " PENDENNIS," "VANITY FAIR," &c. &c.

NEW EDITION.

LONDON:

BRADBURY AND EVANS, 11, BOUVERIE STREET.

1852.

Fig. 4. W. M. Thackeray's *The History of Samuel Titmarsh . . .*
(London: Bradbury & Evans, 1852), second English edition, second issue, title page. (British Library 1608/2920)

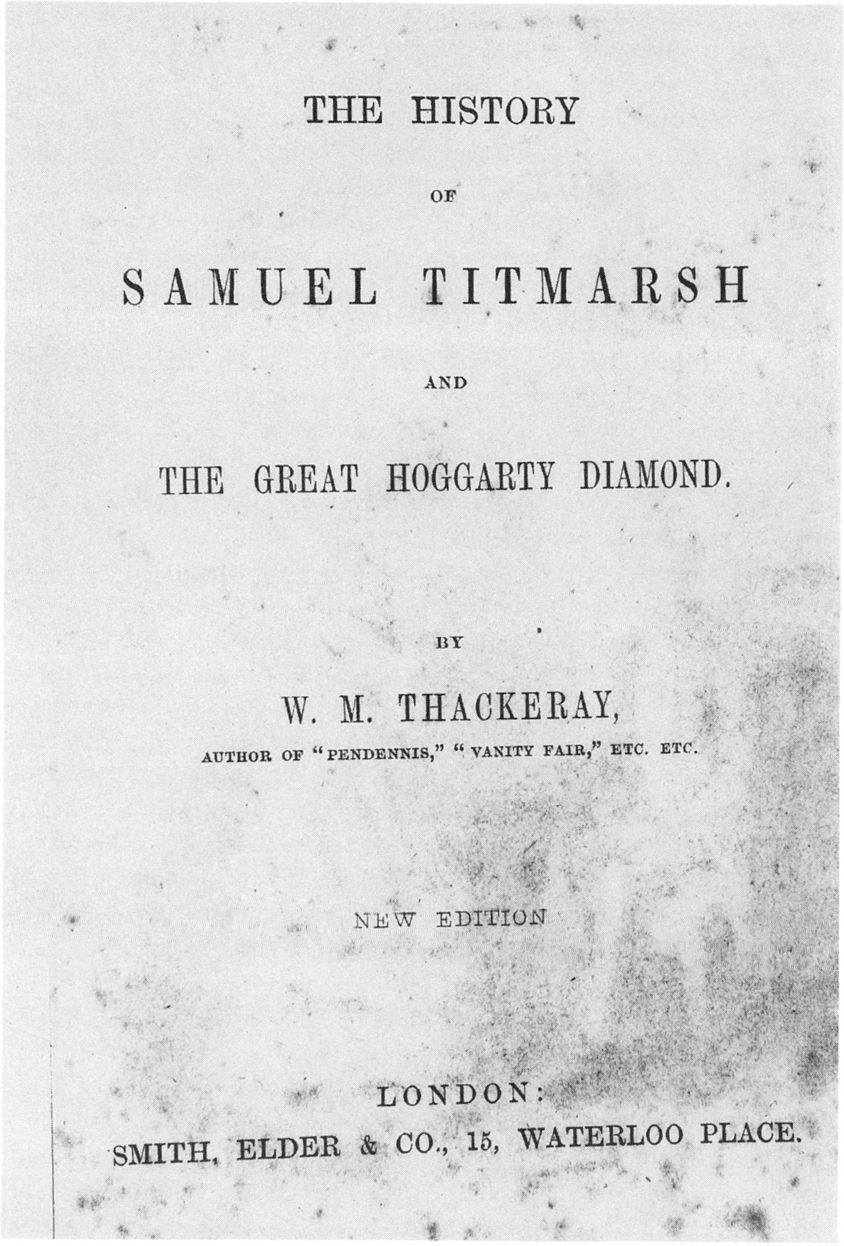

THE HISTORY

OF

SAMUEL TITMARSH

AND

THE GREAT HOGGARTY DIAMOND.

BY

W. M. THACKERAY,

AUTHOR OF "PENDENNIS," "VANITY FAIR," ETC. ETC.

NEW EDITION

LONDON:
SMITH, ELDER & CO., 15, WATERLOO PLACE.

Fig. 5. W. M. Thackeray's *The History of Samuel Titmarsh . . .*
(London: Smith, Elder & Co., n.d.), second English edition, fourth issue, title page. (North Carolina Collection, University of North Carolina at Chapel Hill)

stereotypes from the second English edition were never used either by Bradbury and Evans or by Smith, Elder, which acquired them in 1865.

The publisher's records and an analysis of copies of the two 1849 editions of *Samuel Titmarsh* show how the books were produced, explain the carryover of the first-edition typesetting of the preliminaries and last gathering, expose the odd alterations made by Bradbury and Evans in 1852 for the second issue of the second edition, and demonstrate how Smith, Elder altered the remaining sheets for reissue in 1872.

The entry for the first edition on 27 January 1849 reads: "Printing 12 Sheets 12pp Sup Ryl 16° *2000;* 6 Sheets @ 6.6. 12pp 2.9.6 40.5.6." Later the entry records a charge for twenty-six reams of paper. The entry shows that the twelve gatherings of the book's text were printed on super royal sheets of paper (measuring about 80 by 50 cm). The book itself measures about 17.7 by 12.4 cm per leaf, and each super royal sheet would make sixteen book leaves. Since the book's text is composed of twelve gatherings of eight leaves each, this means that each super royal sheet used in printing contained two gatherings of the book. Hence the reference to six sheets, since six sheets run through the press in 16mo imposition would produce twelve octavo sheets or gatherings for the book when properly cut apart. Composition of six sheets was charged at £6.6 each, or £37.16; there is an added charge of £2.9.6 for twelve pages (six leaves) of preliminaries, which makes the total cost of composition come to £40.5.6. This interpretation of the records is supported by the entry for paper. If one is to get 2,000 copies of a book which has twelve gatherings of eight leaves each and one preliminary gathering of six leaves from twenty-six reams of paper, one must get two gatherings from each sheet of paper. Figuring 26 reams x 500 sheets per ream = 13,000 sheets of paper ÷ 13 gatherings per book = 1,000 copies, so that to get 2,000 copies, there must be 2 gatherings per sheet.

There are two ways this can be done. The sixteen pages of each gathering can be imposed so that both the inner and outer forms print together in the work-and-turn method, or the sixteen pages of the inner forms of two gatherings can be printed together and perfected by printing the outer forms of the same two gatherings. In both cases the sheets would be divided after printing. Each method requires the same amount of presswork, so neither method is more likely to have been used in this case.[35]

---

[35]For a description of the work-and-turn method and diagrams suggestive of the impositions mentioned, see Gaskell, *A New Introduction to Bibliography* (London, 1972), p. 83, figs. 52 and 60.

The entry for the second edition is complicated. Composition costs were entered at £36, as explained above. Stereotypes, costing £15.18.9, were entered for "six sheets 12pp." I have not seen stereotypes referred to as "sheets" before, and the plaster-cast method of stereotyping apparently used by the Bradbury and Evans printers at the time would not allow the production of a stereotyped plate of even octavo size, let alone any larger size that might explain the "six sheets" entry as a plate. It is most likely, therefore, that the "six sheets" refers to paper rather than to stereotyped plates. If so, six sheets is the right number necessary for the text of the book (plus the "12pp." of prelims) if it was imposed as 16mo for division into octavo gatherings after printing. The key to the problem, as with the first edition, is that according to the ledger the number of reams of paper required for the 2,000-copy pressrun was twenty-six. The price of stereotyping is given as £2.10 per sheet, for £15, but the total cost is given as £15.18.9, so the twelve pages of preliminaries must have cost 18s. 9d. to cast.

The mutual carryover of the typesetting for gathering N and the preliminaries seems to indicate that the call for the second edition came after the type from signature M and all preceding gatherings of the text had been distributed but before distribution of type from N or the prelims was begun. It seems also to indicate that each gathering was printed separately on 16mo sheets, each sheet producing two copies of the same gathering. Otherwise, one would expect both M and N to be carried over. It seems certain, in any case, that the second edition was printed from type before the stereotypes were cast, for there is no characteristic shrinkage of the type page in printed copies of the second edition.

That the preliminaries were imposed in eights even though only a six-leaf gathering was bound into the book is highly probable. There is no indication in the records that paper of a different size was used. And a six-leaf gathering could be made more easily by printing an octavo and stripping away the outer fold than by printing quartos and folios to be united or even 12mos to be separated and the parts united. Neither machine collations nor charges for composition and stereotyping, in so far as they can be seen to apply to the preliminaries, give any reason to suspect duplicate settings run simultaneously.[36] Furthermore, the ragged top edges of A3 and A4 (the central fold in the prelims) have no interlocking partners in any copies examined; these two leaves in a normally folded octavo would

---

[36]Nor is there any reason to think that standing type and a stereotyped copy were imposed together to produce a single sheet with two copies. That method was used ten years later by Bradbury and Evans (with electrotypes) for the wrappers of *The Virginians*.

have been joined by their top edges to the outermost leaves. It seems clear, then, that the preliminary gathering was an octavo with its outer conjugate leaves stripped away. I do not know to what extent it was normal in a printing house to allow the wastage of four pages per gathering, but it is possible that these cast-off leaves were used for advertisements or for some other purpose unconnected with *The History of Samuel Titmarsh*.[37] Assuming, in any case, that the paper for the first edition preliminaries was of the same size as that for the rest of the book, one possible procedure would have been to cut two reams in half and print the resulting 2,000 sheets in an octavo imposition. This would have the disadvantage of doubling presswork (i.e., as much presswork for one gathering as was necessary for a sheet of two gatherings elsewhere).[38] The most likely possibility is that preliminaries were imposed as two half sheets of 16mo for printing by the work-and-turn method.

The first English edition of *Samuel Titmarsh* existed, then, in a single printing of 2,000 copies. This accounts, in part, for its rarity and for the difficulty of procuring copies for machine collation. Spot collation of several copies under difficult conditions revealed no variants within the first edition.[39] A representative sampling of the features that distinguish the first edition from its look-alike second edition are recorded in Appendix D, table 1. Examination of the textual variants leads one to suspect that though there are a few new readings that are superior and which one might like to see retained in a new edition, nevertheless, none of the changes is authorial. In the absence of external evidence, this conclusion is corroborated though not proven, I believe, by two bibliographical facts. First, though there are textual variants in every reset gathering, no alterations appear in the preliminaries or in signature N. It seems likely that if Thackeray were responsible for the changes, he would be as anxious to alter readings in these two gatherings as in the reset ones. Second, if my analysis of the printing procedure for the second edition is anywhere near accurate and since some speed was evidently required in its production,

---

[37]Ronald B. McKerrow, *An Introduction to Bibliography* (Oxford, 1928), pp. 194–95, noted, for an earlier period, a dislike among printers for blank leaves.

[38]Graham Pollard in "Notes on the Size of the Sheet," *Library*, 4th ser., 22 (Sept.–Dec. 1941): 132ff., says that double impositions were introduced, as increased press sizes allowed, for the purpose of reducing presswork; hence, the increased presswork required by octavo imposition here seems unlikely.

[39]I used a photocopy of the copy in the Mitchell Memorial Library (Mississippi State University) to compare copies at the University of North Carolina, University of South Carolina, Duke University, Princeton University, and the Berg Collection, NYPL.

then compositors setting the new edition from a copy of the old with instructions to imitate its line configuration (so that ultimately signature N could be reused as it was) would be liable, by haste, to lapses of memory which can account for many of the variants. As for the rest, even the best changes are probably the result of the compositors' ingrained propensity to make unauthorized "improvements" in an attempt to forestall the need later for corrections. None of the changes is out of keeping with normal compositorial and editorial tampering.

The second edition, because it did not sell as well as the first, has a more varied publication history. After the initial printing of 2,000 copies from type on 17 February 1849, stereotyped plates were cast but remained idle even after Smith, Elder and Company acquired them in the general purchase of Thackeray's copyrights in 1865. But Bradbury and Evans published two reissues before Smith, Elder entered the picture.

The 1849 records show that only 3,500 sets of illustrating plates—including, presumably, the vignette title—were printed. Although in 1852 there were some 1,700 unbound copies still in stock, the records show a printing of 500 more vignette titles, bringing the total to equal that of the printed text, 4,000. At the same time 1,000 copies of letterpress titles were printed bearing the statement "NEW EDITION." Examination of three copies with 1852 title pages (see fig. 4) confirms the ledger account.[40] But it also reveals the odd extent to which the preliminaries were altered for this reissue: leaf 2 (the title page and the imprint on its verso) and leaf 6 (containing the last page of the list of contents and the page listing the illustrations) were reset and reprinted as conjugate leaves. The original leaves 2 and 6 were detached from their conjugates (leaves 1 and 5) and discarded. The new conjugate leaves 2 and 6 were inserted and the old leaves 1 and 5 were tipped in along with the frontispiece and vignette title. The reason for this apparently inefficient operation remains something of a mystery. No textual changes were required or effected in leaf 6. (For other changes, see Appendix D, table 2). Perhaps it was seen as desirable for binding purposes to have the two remaining conjugate leaves in the gathering next to each other rather than separated by the two tipped-in plates, new title page, and (now loose) leaf 5. The original binding arrangement, the 1852 arrangement, and the one that was avoided can be seen in figures, 6, 7, and 8.

---

[40]In the British Library (1608/2920); the Fales Collection, NYU; and the personal possession of Mr. Nicholas Pickwood. I wish to thank Mr. Pickwood for his advice on the investigation of the alterations in the preliminaries.

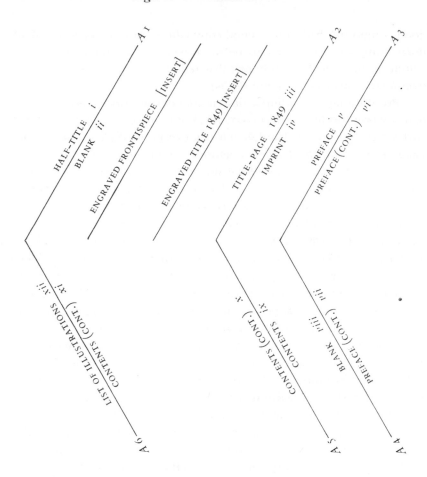

Fig. 6. First issue of the second English edition preliminaries, 1849. This is a six-leaf gathering with the engraved frontispiece and engraved title inserted following the first leaf. This format is identical with that in the first English edition.

By January 1852 when the first print order for 1,000 copies of the title page went in, there were just over 1,700 copies of the book in stock. It follows that at least 700 copies retained the 1849 title page. In 1857 when the next print order for titles went in, the stock had been reduced by about 400 to 1,300 copies. One would assume that those 400 odd copies bore the 1852, rather than the old 1849, title page.

A print order for 200 titles came in October 1857. I have seen no copies to determine the extent of alteration, but presumably they bear an 1857 date. There is, of course, no way to know if these replaced copies

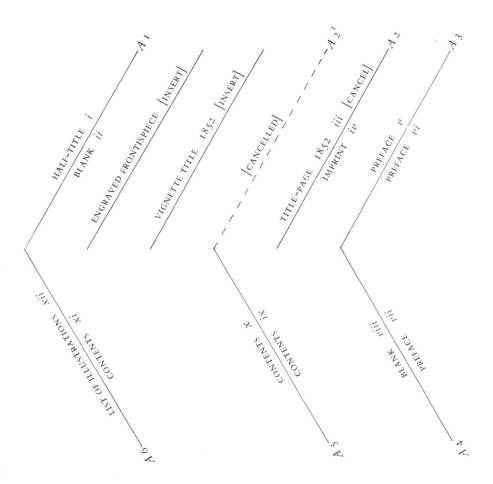

Fig. 7. This arrangement represents what would have happened in
1852 had only the title page been reprinted and tipped in in place of the
original. Note that four single leaves would have occurred between
the inner and outer folds.

with 1852 or 1849 title pages. By 23 June 1865 over 260 more copies had
been sold, no doubt depleting all stock of 1857 titles. There remained
unsold, at the last Bradbury and Evans accounting, 1,035 copies, of which
1,019 were in unbound quires.[41]

<hr />

[41]These figures are from the Bradbury and Evans ledgers kept at the *Punch* Office. The
Smith, Elder accounts of stock received, kept at John Murray, Publishers, record the receipt
of 1,039 copies—1,020 in quires and 19 bound.

Fig. 8. Second issue of the second English edition preliminaries, 1852. The second and sixth leaves have been replaced by conjugate cancels. This arrangement allows some of the strain of the inserts to be borne by the front free endpaper, thus reducing it on the sewing through the inner margin. It cannot, however, be known if this was the reason for the procedure followed. No textual changes were made in resetting leaf six.

The fourth issue by Smith, Elder in 1872 repeats this arrangement, except that the one copy I have seen omits the vignette title. I have seen no copy of the third issue, by Bradbury and Evans in 1857.

According to the Smith, Elder records, between August 1865 and January 1872 that company issued just over 200 copies using Bradbury and Evans title pages. In 1872, with 811 copies still on hand, Smith, Elder printed 800 undated cancel titles with their own imprint and again the imprecise statement "NEW EDITION." The one copy I have seen lacks the vignette title, which may have been omitted because it bore a dated Bradbury and Evans imprint.[42] The Bradbury and Evans imprint at the foot of page 190 remained unchanged: replacing it would have required reprinting a whole gathering or the bother of a cancel. In 1879 the last 538 copies were remaindered to Reeves and Turner for just over 2*d.* per copy. The original publisher's price was 4*s.* 11*d.* This issue had not attracted collectors; the only copy I have seen (in the North Carolina Collection of the University of North Carolina at Chapel Hill Library; see fig. 5) was acquired because of the Zebulon Vance autograph on the flyleaf.[43]

With no known copies of the 1857 reissue and only one copy of the Smith, Elder undated but probably 1872 reissue, it is impossible to make general statements about the form the preliminaries took in these issues. But the Smith, Elder issue apparently repeated the format of the 1852 issue (see fig. 8). While it is likely that the 1857 titles were sold out before Smith, Elder purchased the stock and rights in 1865, there would have been some of the 1852 titles left at the time. Whether the 1852 format was imitated to facilitate use of front matter already altered in 1852, or if binding requirements again were the deciding factor, I do not know. In any case the new title page is conjugate with A6 (pp. xi and xii), which therefore also had to be reset and reprinted. The changes introduced in the 1872 prelims are recorded in Appendix D, table 3.

It is fortunate that analytical bibliography need not justify itself by its usefulness to textual criticism, for the preceding discussion far exceeds the needs of that discipline, and the variants between the first and second edition are of negligible textual importance—unless the unsuspecting editor were to work at the British Library or the Library Company of Philadelphia, which have only the second edition looking very like the first. The variants between the first, second, and fourth issues of the second edition are of no textual significance whatsoever. They do, how-

---

[42]Smith, Elder did not always discard Bradbury and Evans engraved title pages when reissuing the books. The single copies I have seen of the Smith, Elder reissues of the first edition of *Pendennis* and *The Newcomes* in 1866 both have new Smith, Elder title pages but retain the engraved titles showing the Bradbury and Evans imprint.

[43]Zebulon Vance was governor of North Carolina, 1862–65 and 1876–79.

ever, illustrate a point about the reputation of the book itself as well as of its author: 2,000 enthusiastic readers of *Vanity Fair* grabbed up the new offerings, and then it took thirty years to dispose of the remaining 2,000 copies. Nevertheless, in 1857 the same publisher who was having such a hard time moving the books he already had in stock brought out a new edition of *Samuel Titmarsh* in two different formats.[44] The success of that seemingly bold venture demonstrated the existence of alternative markets; the reprints did not simply reach more of the same market targeted by the first edition.

Pendennis

The combined examination of printed book and account ledger unravels secrets about *The History of Pendennis* also. The first edition exists in several impressions and substates.[45] A superficial comparison of any copy in parts with any copy bound in two volumes shows that the book issue is composed of sheets printed from the same typesetting used for the parts issue. The two forms of the book, however, incorporate many differences. While the particular changes themselves are of little critical significance (and seem to be editorial in origin), the evidence they provide concerning printing practices is significant to bibliographers both textual and descriptive, to book collectors, and to printing and publishing historians.

In brief the situation is this: *Pendennis* in parts was first printed from type. Stereotype plates were subsequently cast from the same setting of type in anticipation of the printing for the issue in two volumes. During this process intentional changes were introduced (see Appendix E, table 2) and unintentional damage occurred. Finally, in 1865—ten years after Bradbury and Evans had brought out a revised, cheap edition of *Pendennis* and nearly two years after Thackeray's death—Smith, Elder and Company acquired the plates of the first edition, repaired a few damaged pieces of type, furthered the unintentional damage, and printed the novel several more times. These last impressions are distinguishable from other printings by the substitution of the Smith, Elder imprint for the Bradbury and

---

[44]It appeared as pp. 327–451 of *Miscellanies,* vol. 4, and separately in paper wrappers as *The History of Samuel Titmarsh and the Great Hoggarty Diamond.* The sheets for both formats were printed from the same setting of type, but their pagination and signing differ.

[45]*The History of Pendennis* (London: Bradbury and Evans, Nov. 1848–Dec. 1850, twenty-four numbers in twenty-three parts, and 1849–50 in two volumes). My conclusions are based on the machine collation of five copies: three sets of parts and two book issues. In addition I have examined nine other copies.

Evans imprint at the foot of the last printed page in each volume.[46] The title page and dates remained unaltered in all printings.

That summary glosses a multitude of complexities. Because the idiosyncrasies of bindings-up often resulted in mixtures of impressions within single copies of the novel and because new impressions of single numbers, as well as new general impressions,[47] could occur, the printing history of *Pendennis* must be approached on the level of sheets. One cannot say categorically that a copy of *Pendennis* in parts represents the first printing or that a copy in two volumes with Bradbury and Evans imprints represents the second or third. Furthermore, in dealing with the printing history of the novel, it is not possible to take the publisher's records at face value, for they do not tell the whole story. Stereotyping is entered with the initial cost of printing *Pendennis,* but machine collations show beyond doubt that the first printing was from type. In fact, variants in copies of numbers 2 and 5 printed from type seem to indicate separate printings from the same setting of type before stereotyping. In addition, while I have seen one copy of the issue in book form composed partially of sheets printed from type (definitely not issued previously as parts), I have also seen four copies issued in parts with scattered sheets printed from plates.[48] To complicate matters, I have noted four copies of the book issue of volume 1 composed of sheets printed from plates except for number 12—

---

[46]The Smith, Elder records show that Bradbury and Evans turned over 5,217 copies of various numbers in August 1865 to Smith, Elder, who printed 3,663 more numbers on 18 Oct. and 10 Dec. 1865. Not until 3 April 1866 is there a record that repairs were made in the stereotypes, after which 5,969 more numbers were printed. This gave a total of 14,849 numbers, which were bound into 613 copies of the novel, leaving only 111 numbers after having also sold 26 loose numbers. The plates of the first edition, not used again, were sold as old metal on 1 July 1868.

[47]For lack of a better term I have used "general impression" to mean the series of printings of separate numbers, often separated by months and even years, that constitutes a separate and distinguishable printing of the book as a whole. Thus, while the publisher's records indicate that number 2, for instance, was printed six times between 1848 and 1866, only three impressions of the book as a whole have been distinguished.

[48]The one copy of the book-form issue composed partially of sheets printed from type is the presentation copy to Peter Rackham in the Berg Collection, NYPL. Of the four sets of parts with some sheets printed from plates, two are in the British Library; one in the Cooper Library, University of South Carolina; and the fourth is in my own collection.

Many copies of *Pendennis* bound in two volumes without wrappers or advertisements were originally issued in parts and are distinguished from the book issue by the three stab holes in the gutter margins where the parts were sewn. Apparently this is not generally known: three of the seven copies of *Pendennis* in the Berg Collection, NYPL, described as "in book form" are actually bound sets of parts.

the last two sheets in the volume—which was printed from type.[49] The problem that remains is to reconcile the records with the evidence of collation and to determine when the stereotyping occurred.

The one copy of the first book-form issue containing some sheets printed from type (other than those in number 12) is the most crucial in settling these problems. That this book belongs to the first issue in book form is not absolutely certain from external evidence though it is a presentation copy from Thackeray to Peter Rackham. The distribution records of the publisher show Thackeray receiving presentation copies early in 1851; in fact, Thackeray's presentation copy to Dr. Elliotson is dated 1 January 1851. However, it is certain that the Rackham copy is not a bound set of parts, for there are no telltale stab holes in the gutters. The records and the evidence of this book suggest an answer to the question of when stereotyping took place.

By 31 December 1849 the total number of copies printed of part 1 was 10,000 (in one printing); part 2, 9,500 (in two printings); parts 3–4, 10,000 (in two printings); and parts 5–12, 9,000 (in one printing).[50] The initial 8,000-copy printing of part 2 was exhausted by May 1849, and the initial 8,000-copy printings of parts 3 and 4 were exhausted by August 1849, for reprints were required on those dates. It can be assumed on this basis that an average of 8,000 copies per number had been issued in parts before volume 1 was ready to be bound in book form. If the assumption is correct, only 2,000 copies of the first printing of part 1, none of parts 2–4, and only 1,000 of numbers 5–12 could have remained to be issued in book form. One might expect, then, that about 1,000 copies of the book issue were composed of sheets printed from type with the exception of numbers 2–4 and that about 1,000 more contain number 1 as well as number 12 printed from type.

The presentation copy to Peter Rackham shows that, like all early issues in book form which I have examined, part 12 is printed from type. But, more significantly, unlike any other copy issued in book form which I have seen, volume 1 is composed mostly from sheets printed from type— the exceptions being numbers 2–4, which were reprinted before the first issue in book form. The evidence of the Rackham copy indicates that the initial printings entered in the publisher's records (10,000 for part 1, 8,000

[49]Of the four, one is my own; the others are in the Berg Collection, NYPL, described as "in book form" numbers 3, 4, and 5.

[50]Manuscript records of the Bradbury and Evans Company (Bradbury, Agnew).

each for parts 2–4, and 9,000 each for numbers 5–12) actually equal the number of copies printed from type before stereotypes were cast. Copies of volume 1 issued as parts sometimes contain numbers other than 2–4 printed from plates. Of those numbers printed from plates, the one most often noted in copies of the parts is number 9 (signatures S and T). There is the possibility, of course, either that sets of parts with sheets printed from plates were issued after the novel became available in book form[51] or, and this is more likely, that incomplete sets of parts were made up with later printed sheets.

As the novel established its popularity, which it did at a faster rate than did *Vanity Fair,* it apparently became necessary to print more copies of the early numbers to meet the demands of new readers picked up midway through the publication of the first volume, and these demands were met by reprints from the standing type. Variants in numbers 2 and 5 seem to indicate this. Then, perhaps anticipating the necessary reprinting for issue as a book but too rushed for time between Thackeray's submission of printer's copy and the publication deadline of each new part to allow for plating before any printing was done, the printer started plating immediately after the initial printing for the parts issue.[52] And the early parts

---

[51]For how long *Pendennis* and other serialized novels were available from the publishers in parts is not clear. It might seem that once the novel was available in book form, no more parts would be issued. However, the publishers' records seem to indicate otherwise. Reprints by Bradbury and Evans are recorded by part number, and those by Smith, Elder are recorded in one place as of "various numbers" and in another by specific number. In addition, Smith, Elder recorded the sale "as parts" of twenty-six numbers, a peculiar number equaling one copy of the whole book plus two numbers. The discovery of a copy issued in parts composed entirely of sheets printed from plates or with the Smith, Elder imprint would confirm the availability of the novel in parts after the appearance of the issue in book form.

[52]That Thackeray was often barely ahead of his printer is on record. Gordon Ray wrote: "Anny and Minny . . . were accustomed to the sight of 'the Printers devil waiting downstairs for copy.' Only when he was late with his number of *Vanity Fair* or *Pendennis* did he become preoccupied. 'Towards the end of the month . . . I get so nervous that I don't speak to anybody scarcely, and once actually got up in the middle of the night and came down & wrote in my night-shimee' " (*Wisdom,* p. 16). Henry Vizetelly, writing of *Vanity Fair,* said, "I know perfectly well that, after the publication commenced, much of the remainder of the work was written under pressure from the printer, and not unfrequently the final installment of 'copy,' needed to fill the customary thirty-two pages, was penned while the printer's boy was waiting in the hall at Young-street" (*Glances Back through Seventy Years* [London, 1883], p. 285). James T. Fields said Thackeray "liked to put off the inevitable chapters till the last moment" and told the well-known story of the author holding up one of his own parties while he was finishing an installment for the printers (*Yesterdays with Authors,* pp. 17–18). This may have been an embellishment, but the bibliographical

until then kept standing in type also were plated. This scenario would account for the entry in the extant records for stereotyping in the initial cost of publication.

When in September 1849 Thackeray's illness forced the suspension of publication until January 1850, only one number, the twelfth, was needed for the completion of volume 1. By this time plates of the first eleven numbers had been cast, and demands for back numbers may have been such that sheets printed from plates were sold as parts as early as 1849. (This is at least one explanation for the four sets of parts of volume 1 I have examined which contain sheets printed from plates.) Finally, when Thackeray had recovered sufficiently to write the twelfth number, sheets printed from type went into both the parts issue and the book issue. This accounts for the many book-form copies with only number 12, the last in volume 1, printed from type. It is impossible to hold that there were simultaneous printings from type and plates because in that case the plates would have had to have been cast from the type before the printings from type were run off. Collation shows that the printings from type were made before the plates were cast, for damage occurring in late copies printed from type is carried over into the plates, and corrections made for the plates do not occur in copies printed from type.

A given set of parts of volume 1, then, instead of being the first printing, may be composed of the second impression (from type) of early sheets, the second or third impression (from plates) of the middle sheets, and the first impression of the last number. On the other hand, the first book issue of volume 1 may be composed of the third impression of some early sheets, the second or third impression of the rest through number 11, and the first impression of the last number.

Volume 2 is not so complicated. The publisher's records indicate a single 9,000-copy printing of each number from 13 to 24. There is no reason to believe otherwise. If the sale of parts of volume 2 matched that of volume 1 (that is, about 8,000 copies distributed, or at least bound, as parts before issue in book form), there should have been about 1,000 copies of the first book-form issue of volume 2 made up of sheets printed from type. Three presentation copies in book form have been noted in each of which

evidence does not contradict him. Furthermore, when Thackeray on 17 Sept. 1849 "became suddenly ill" (Ray, *Wisdom,* p. 87), he had not finished writing the October number, which his publishers surely were anxious to receive on time since it would complete volume 1. As it was, Thackeray's habit of staying only a half step in front of the printer caused a three-month delay.

volume 2 is composed entirely from sheets printed from type.[53] The publisher's records of printings and distribution also tend to corroborate this hypothesis. First, only one entry is given for the 9,000-copy printings of numbers 13–24, and no reprint was required until 30 June 1853, two and a half years after the book-form issue. The distribution records are significant, even though they omit the record of sales at the date of issue in book form, December 1850, which would have made their use here much more precise. They show that by 31 December 1851 the publisher had disposed of 215,050 parts out of 228,500 printed. The number printed includes 11,000 copies of number 1, 10,500 of number 2, 10,000 each of numbers 3–12, and 9,000 each of numbers 13–24. If the 215,050 parts distributed were made up into as many copies as possible of the whole novel (not a likely occurrence), then about 8,950 copies of the book were out of the publisher's hands within one year after issue in book form. This figure, with a slight downward adjustment to allow for readers who may have discontinued the novel after a few numbers, fits in well with the 8,000-copy figure arrived at on the basis of the required reprints for numbers 2–4 mentioned above. Later copies of volume 2, of course, are composed entirely of sheets printed from plates.

As with sets of parts of volume 1, copies of volume 2 in parts have been noted time and again with sheets printed from plates. Again, I know of only two possible explanations—both of which may hold true. The first is that readers with incomplete sets of parts made up their copies after reprints from plates became available, and the other is that the publisher continued to promote the sale of the novel in parts even after the book-form issue.

The identification of impressions combined with the current practice of examining wrappers, bindings, and advertisements may make it possible to know with some certainty just what copy of *Pendennis* one has. But to elaborate Michael Sadleir's hypothetical case,[54] it is not only possible for the last 500 copies of sheets from one printing to remain for some time in the storeroom to come forth at a later date in an alternate binding or with new advertisements but also for, say, the last 200 copies of sheets of one impression to come forth dressed identically with, and mixed with, the first 200 copies of sheets from a new impression. In fact, as my

---

[53]Berg Collection, NYPL, copies "in book form" numbers 1, 3, and 4, presented to Rackham, Elliotson, and Surtees.

[54]Sadleir, *Trollope: A Bibliography,* p. xiv.

examination of *Pendennis* seems to show, the combination of sheets from different printings bound together could be almost endless. Even the one set of parts I have examined which is composed entirely of sheets printed from type is not a first printing, for in the case of at least three of the sheets, earlier printings (or at least earlier printed copies within an impression) are bound into other sets containing some sheets printed from plates.

The reprinting from type of isolated sheets of early numbers produced several variants. Like the readings which are defective in all examined copies but were apparently correct at one time (see Appendix E, table 1), some of these variants may be attributed to type batter. However, gathering D of number 2 does exist in three states, if not printings. Early printings read *where, in the* at page 42.27 and have a clear semicolon after *ear* at 43.46. The second state reads *where, i h e* at 42.27 but still has the clear semicolon at 43.46. The third state restores the correct reading at 42.27, but all copies of this state so far examined have a chip off the top of the semicolon at 43.46. This evidence may indicate a stop-press correction rather than separate printings, but gathering K of number 5 seems definitely to exist in two printings before plating. The lines at 143.2–6 and at 144.2–6 have been reset for no apparent reason; there are no textual variants in the reset lines, only respacing. On page 143 the printings are most readily identified by the position of the *L* of *London* at line 6 in relation to the space between the words *and frets* at line 5. In the first printing the *L* is under the space; in the second and all subsequent (including plated) printings the *L* is to the right under the *f* of *frets*. On page 144 the printings are identified by the position of the *y* in *they* at line 6 in relation to the space between the words *were by* in line 5. In the first printing the *y* is slightly to the left, half under the second *e* of *were;* in the second and all subsequent printings the *y* is to the right under the space. The distinction is an important one. By indicating the necessity for reprinting early numbers, it forms a partial basis for concluding that the readership of *Pendennis* was growing. One reason for this may have been pressure from readers made impatient by the three-month delay in the publication of volume 1 as a whole, imposed by Thackeray's illness.

Of less importance, perhaps, but of interest is the evidence the first edition of *Pendennis* presents for the fact that plating does not fix the text of a book. In addition to the damage sustained through reprinting and plating, there is evidence of activity in gathering H (pp. 97–112) of Volume 1. Just before or in the process of the second printing (from plates), resetting became necessary for the portion of page 100 below the illustration. At 100.1 (above the illustration) the first impression (from type) reads *Digby;* the second (plated) and all subsequent impressions read the correct *Derby.* In some copies printed from plates, the lower part of page 100 (below the illustration) exists reset (with respacing) and printed from type with no textual changes. Copies also exist reset a second time and plated, introducing three textual changes. The first impression of H, then, is from type and reads *Digby* at 100.1. The second impression, printed from plates and reading *Derby* at 100.1, exists in two states: (1) with the lower part of 100 plated without change: (2) with the lower part of 100 reset (respaced) without textual variants but printed from type.[55] A third impression of gathering H is from plates with the lower part of 100 reset again, plated, and introducing *champion"* for *champion,"* (100.10), *young"* for *young,"* (100.12), and *Milly!* (turned semicolon) for *Milly;* (100.13).

Only one oddity breaks the textual simplicity of volume 2. The two conjugate leaves at the center of gathering U in number 22 (pp. 295–98) are plated in one copy examined. The rest of the signature is from type. Type damage at 296.19b (defective *r* on *nor*) persists in the Smith, Elder impression, indicating that the same plates were used. This copy may be part of a late binding-up and issue in parts. And possibly it represents an anomaly created by an owner who replaced a torn page in this copy (printed from type) with a conjugate leaf taken from another, perhaps otherwise defective, copy (printed from plates).

While the foregoing description of impressions is necessarily imprecise, enough is known to avoid an editor's uncomfortable feeling "that in his bibliographical ignorance it is quite possible for him to base his text on . . . an unrecognized late impression containing possible alterations of dubious authority."[56]

Esmond *in Three Volumes*

Before discussing the production and cost-sharing arrangement for *Henry Esmond,* it would be good to review what is meant by the terms *impression, edition,* and *issue.* In modern bibliographical parlance, edition refers to all copies of a book printed from a single setting of type; impression refers to all copies of a book consisting of sheets printed in a single pressrun; and

---

[55]The only way to distinguish the two states of the second impression without a collating machine is to measure the length of the lines. Both states measure 9.55 cm horizontally at page 100.1. The first state measures 9.55 cm at lines 4, 7, and 8; the second state measures 9.7 cm at these lines.

[56]Bowers, *Principles of Bibliographical Description,* p. 359.

issue means all copies of a book marketed as part of a single publishing or marketing drive and (usually) bearing some distinguishing mark of that publishing drive, such as tipped-in title pages, different covers, or significantly different advertisements bound into the book itself. The terms were much more fluid in the nineteenth century. "Edition" was used sometimes to denote a new impression from the same typesetting, sometimes to mean a new impression from reset type, and sometimes to mean part of an old impression reissued with a new title page. "Impression" was used sometimes to mean the total number of copies specified in a contract, regardless of how many printings were required to produce them, and sometimes to mean any of the three things mentioned above as the meanings for edition, impression, and issue.

The *Esmond* contract specifies that the proceeds from the entire "first impression" of 2,500 or 2,750 copies (at George Smith's option) of the three-volume work were to belong to Smith, Elder and that "such impression may be published in one edition or divided into two or three editions as he may consider expedient" (NLS; see Appendix A). Confident but not knowing in advance how well the book would do, Smith was hedging his bets. By specifying the number of copies he could print and call his own, he seemed to commit himself to print at least 2,500 copies, but he left himself with a little cushion in case the sales went well. By allowing himself up to three "editions" in which to dispose of the "first impression," he allowed for the possibility that it would take years and several marketing efforts to dispose of the first printing.

The publication records for *Esmond* are sketchier than for any other of Thackeray's major works. The ledgers in which Smith, Elder kept accounts up until December 1852 have been misplaced or lost. The first entry for *Esmond* in the new ledger is for May 1853. Fortunately, one of the few surviving financial reports from Smith, Elder to Thackeray is for *Esmond,* but, of course, it begins with the "second edition" because Thackeray had parted with all rights to the "first impression." (Smith called it a second edition, and in this case it seems, in fact, to have been a true second edition, entirely reset, though at least 500 copies of it seem to have been issued with title pages identical to the first edition.)

Although there is no surviving ledger record for the first printing of *Henry Esmond,* the contract agreement indicates that Smith, Elder paid Thackeray £1,200 in three installments. The contract further specifies that Smith, Elder and Company was to have the total income on a "first impression" of 2,500 or 2,750 copies according to the publisher's discretion. If the first impression was of 2,750 and sold out within eighteen months, Smith was, by contract, to pay Thackeray an additional £100. The first impression, published in October 1852, just as Thackeray was headed to America on his first lecture tour, was completely sold out within six weeks. Thackeray wrote to James Field on 29 November, "Smith writes to me from London that the whole of the first edition of Esmond is disposed of, an edition of 3000 at a guinea & a half!"[57] Thackeray wrote at the same time to friends in England that Smith had indicated a second edition was being undertaken (*Letters* 3:135). There was no need for a special agreement about the new edition because the original contract specified a straight profit-sharing system for subsequent editions. Since there are no extant records of the first-edition production or of any of the payments to Thackeray for the first edition, there is no way to determine whether Smith printed 2,500 or 2,750 or whether Thackeray got the extra £100.[58] Whatever the case may be, if Smith sold 2,250 copies of the first impression (leaving 250–500 as gratis, promotion and review, and discounted copies) at 22s. 6d. each (the price commanded by the first 600 copies of the second edition), he would have grossed about £2,500. Mrs. Proctor wrote to Thackeray on 23 November that "Mudie says. 400 Copies of Esmond not being sufficient 100 more are added."[59] It is likely that Mudie's Circulating Library did not pay 22s. 6d. per copy; hence, the generous allowance for discounts in my calculations. According to the terms of the contract, £1,200 and possibly £1,300 of that £2,500 went to Thackeray; at least £700 went into production costs (judging from the cost of the second edition, which involved a resetting of all the type, and by a rough comparison with the production costs of Charles Dickens's comparable *Great Expectations* in three volumes). John Sutherland, remarking on the frequency and prominence of contemporary advertisements and notices of *Esmond,* suggested that an expensive promotional effort was mounted for the book.[60] The relevant ledger evidence is not available. No special advertising effort is evident in the ledger accounts for the second edition. Smith, Elder could easily have made a profit of about £500 on the

---

[57]Huntington. Thackeray often rounded out figures and is therefore unreliable for specific information. The edition was either 2,500 or 2,750, not 3,000. Smith's letter, no longer extant, must have been written around 15 November.

[58]Edgar Harden conjectured in the absence of evidence for the £100 payment that Smith printed only 2,500 copies ("The Writing and Publication of *Esmond,*" p. 92).

[59]*Letters* 3:126. John Sutherland claimed Mudie's Circulating Library purchased 430 copies (*Victorian Novelists and Publishers,* p. 113); he cited no source.

[60]Sutherland, *Victorian Novelists and Publishers,* p. 113.

first edition—perhaps more if a greater number of the 250–500 other copies were actually sold.

Smith's financial statement to Thackeray begins in December 1852 with production and promotion costs for the "second edition," which consisted of 1,000 copies. Production costs included composing type, paper, pressing, and a charge for 250 "third edition" title pages, all coming to £379.2.6. A note by the entry for the third-edition title pages says "not used," and in May 1853 the production of 250 "second edition" title pages is recorded. No other record of title-page production or reprinting of this edition exists in the ledgers; however, copies of the book with second-edition sheets have been noted with first-edition titles, second-edition titles, and third-edition titles. In addition, a few copies with second-edition titles have first-edition sheets—which indicates that Smith may have projected the sellout of the "first edition" before all copies were out of the bindery and that "second edition" titles were produced before all "first edition" sheets were bound. In any case, it seems clear that of the 3,500–3,750 copies of *Esmond* in three volumes that were produced, no more than 250 have "second edition" title pages, and no more than 250 others have "third edition" titles.

Be that as it may, by 30 June 1853, 668 copies of the new edition were reported sold for £662.5, from which Smith deducted £33.2.3 as his 5 percent commission on gross income. That left a credit balance of £250.0.3, from which £46.18 was spent in September 1853 to purchase back 67 copies "returned from America" in order "to protect stock in this country" (100 copies had been sold to Appleton in New York, but Harper had produced a much cheaper authorized edition for which it had paid Thackeray $1,000). At this point, September 1853, Smith divided the remaining balance of £203.2.3 with Thackeray, the author getting the odd penny. In 1854, 53 more copies were sold for £57.7.6; Smith deducted the firm's 5 percent commission (£2.17.4) and £10.16 for promotion costs, etc., and divided the remaining £43.14.2 evenly with Thackeray. In February 1855 author and publisher cheerfully (or solemnly) divided the proceeds from the sale of two more copies, each receiving 8s. 9d. after Smith had deducted the company's 2s. 3d. commission. And so the story goes, until by 1864 only 124 copies were left and the selling price had fallen to 10s. 6d.

From the approximately 3,750 copies printed of *Esmond* in three volumes, Thackeray made about £1,360, Smith made an estimated £640, and production costs equaled around £1,100. Gross sales brought in, then, about £3,100. By comparison, ten years later Charles Dickens's *Great Expectations* in three volumes cost just over £1,000 to produce the same number of copies (3,750), grossed £3,250, of which about £1,960 went to Dickens and about £250, including a commission of 7.5 percent and profits, went to the publisher, Chapman and Hall.[61]

Most of Thackeray's books fell off in sales relatively quickly after the first year of publication; sales of *Esmond* in three volumes dipped to an average of ten copies a year from 1855 to 1863. Smith had gambled safely on the first printing, knowing that he could rely on the circulating libraries, and he no doubt banked on Thackeray's newly established reputation as author of *Vanity Fair* and *Pendennis*.[62] When the first edition sold out in one and a half months, *Esmond* proved to be a best-seller, but a second printing of 1,000 copies was still a shrewd decision by Smith. True, he had not anticipated a second printing and, therefore, had not asked the printer, Bradbury and Evans, to prepare stereotyped plates; consequently, he had to pay for recomposition for the second edition. Because the ledgers show that stereotyping cost nearly as much as composition, however, it is clear that except for the savings resulting from smaller print runs, stereotyping did not become economical until a third printing was required. No third printing was at all likely for a novel in three volumes, selling at a guinea and a half and readily available from the circulating libraries—and none was required for *Esmond*. (Copies of the book with title pages indicating a third edition are merely new title pages attached to second-edition sheets.) Smith might have done better to order a second edition of 750 copies (many three-deckers had first printings no larger), but that could have been too conservative a figure. Within two months 600 copies of the new edition were sold, and already there was a small profit to share between author and publisher. Renewed sales, spurred by the news of Thackeray's death in December 1863, nearly carried off the remaining copies in 1864.

Although Thackeray complained several years after the publication of *Esmond* that a review by Samuel Phillips in the *Times* in 1853 had stopped its sales (*Letters* 4:125), the three-volume edition had been a very good venture, exceeding Smith's original expectations and far outstripping the sales and profits of most three-decker novels.[63] The few hundred copies remaining and slow sales match the residual sales of all Thackeray's

---

[61]Patten, *Dickens and His Publishers*, p. 385.

[62]See Sutherland, *Victorian Novelists and Publishers*, pp. 12–30, esp. 15–17, for an account of the stabilizing influence of the circulating libraries.

[63]Compare the £2,000 profit from *Esmond* with the dismal tale of novel after novel in the same format described by Sutherland, in *Victorian Novelists and Publishers*, with single print runs of 600 to 1,000 copies and profits of £300 or less. Many of those authors sold their copyrights and had no hope of sharing in any profits that might accrue from cheap editions.

first editions and is remarkably like the sales record of Charles Dickens's *Great Expectations* in three volumes, which sold 3,461 copies in the first year, 39 the next, and then stopped dead with 247 copies remaindered at 2*s.* 3*d.* apiece three years later.[64]

Esmond *in One Volume*

In 1857 Smith knew he was not making the money he could for himself or his author with this valuable dormant property. Bradbury and Evans was reprinting Thackeray's early magazine pieces in the *Miscellanies;* successful cheap editions of *Vanity Fair* and *Pendennis* were out, and *The Newcomes* had already proven to be a substantial money-maker. Smith was ready to work the property and took his cue from Bradbury and Evans.

The cheap edition of *Esmond* in one volume has 464 pages of text and 16 pages of preliminaries. It is composed of thirty octavo gatherings (eight leaves, sixteen pages per gathering). The book was printed on paper large enough to accommodate two octavo sheets (sixteen pages) at a time. It took 300 reams of long primer paper or double octavo (both terms appear in the record) to produce 10,000 copies of the book. Either of two methods of printing could have been used: work and turn with both forms of one gathering or with the inner forms of two gatherings imposed together and the outer forms together. In either case, each sheet would have been cut in two before binding. It should be noted that Smith, Elder acquired its own printing shop in 1857, having previously depended on other printers, notably Bradbury and Evans, for book production. *Esmond* was reprinted on Smith's own presses. Publication was announced on 17 October 1857,[65] though the ledger accounts are dated November and the book itself bears the date 1858.

It might be said that Smith overestimated the demand for a cheap edition of *Esmond,* since in June 1863 the firm's warehouse still held 3,320 copies out of a first printing of 10,000. Yet there was every reason to bet high on Thackeray in 1857. Although Bradbury and Evans lived to rue the euphoria of that year, claiming to have lost thousands on *The Virginians,* the amazing thing is that Smith did not lose a penny. In the first month and a half the company had sold 3,528 copies, enough to pay all its costs for the cheap edition of *Esmond* and divide £6.17 with Thackeray. In the next year author and publisher divided a profit of £88.9, and in the next they shared an even £100, after which they still had half the edition in hand. Far from

[64]Patten, *Dickens and His Publishers,* p. 385.
[65]Harden, "The Writing and Publication of *Esmond,*" p. 87.

being a drug on the market, the remaining stock was like money in reserve, for the author was Thackeray and the publisher had a long-term commitment to the property. Thackeray's unexpected death sent sales soaring, and by January 1866 Smith was preparing a new edition for a new printing of 1,000 copies. By hindsight one could say that Smith did not bet high enough in 1857, for he failed to order stereotyped plates, which he could have used for the January 1866 edition and for a second printing of 1,000 more copies in September of the same year. By 1866 Smith had completed his acquisition of the Thackeray literary empire by purchasing copyrights from all other owners, so he did not have to share profits with anyone. In eighteen months, by June 1867, he had recovered costs on the 1866 edition of *Esmond* and made another £57.12, plus the publisher's 5 percent commission figured on total income.

The available records are incomplete, but one can estimate that the cheap edition of *Esmond* made between £800 and £1,200 of profit from 12,000 copies produced in three printings over an eight-year period on an investment of under £700, all of which was recovered within two months. By comparison, the profits for Bradbury and Evans's cheap edition of *Vanity Fair* over a thirteen-year period came to about £1,300 on 22,000 copies produced in eleven printings and a remainder in 1865 of 681 copies.

VI

The Artist and the Marketplace

The Shaping Influence of the Marketplace

AMONG THE CONCLUSIONS a study like this one reveals is that books are shaped by the demands they are intended to fulfill. If one is writing for money, as Thackeray quite clearly was, one must write that which will be accepted by publishers. Likewise, this study shows that the production of a book is a multifaceted cooperative affair and that the resulting printed text is not attributable to the author solely. One is led inevitably, then, to a number of fundamental questions concerning literary works: about competing authorities for the verbal content and visual design of the books, about the authenticity of the text in any given book, about the relative claims as "best text" that could be made for competing editions. Fundamental to any answers is another rather metaphysical question: At what point or points in a continuum from pure, free authorial autonomy to rigid social determinism does the production of literary art take place? If one thinks art is the product of the artist exercising creative freedom to write as he or she pleases, then the answers to the questions about authority, authenticity, and "the best text" will tend to be answered differently from the way they are answered by one who thinks art is the product of social forces fulfilling external demands for a market. These concepts are more easily adjudicated in the abstract than in specific cases; so this chapter is devoted to an effort to understand the consequences of various answers as they relate to a specific work, Thackeray's *Henry Esmond.* I try to demonstrate that the questions raised here are of crucial importance to any reader of the novel, not just an editor trying to determine the textual details of a new edition.

A brief orientation regarding theories of textual criticism will help establish their importance. The authority of the text, or more accurately, the authority for the text, is the person, persons, or "force" that has the final responsibility for "getting the text right." Among common notions about authority are, first, that of the author, who originated the linguistic text and read proof, giving authorial approval to additions, deletions, and alterations introduced by other hands. A second center of authority is the production personnel, for they create the combination of verbal text and visual book that "for the first time really" constitutes the "public work." A third idea is that regardless of romantic ideals, the final object, often referred to reverentially as "the text itself," is its own authority and, regardless of its provenance, must be treated as "the work." And a fourth is that any thinking, careful, sensitive, knowledgeable person can, through close reading and/or research into the developing text, find and correct flaws and improve the work to better represent its potential ideal artistic form. These views are basically incompatible with one another and appeal variously to different people.

Once a notion of the "properly responsible" authority has been settled, questions about the authenticity of the text in any particular copy of the work can be asked. Identifying typographical errors and unauthoritative interpolations starts the effort to authenticate the text. Locating and restoring or incorporating authoritative readings that "belong" in the text complete the authentication.

Some works, however, do not fit easily into the procrustean bed created by the concepts of authority and authenticity. Authors sometimes revise, or the works become significantly altered in other ways, so that alternate authoritative and authentic versions vie for attention. Persons who think a literary work should be one thing usually push for one text. They would like for statements about a work of art to have a stable referent. In the case of *Henry Esmond,* such a goal is easier to wish for than to have.[1]

There is no one answer to these questions. What needs to be recognized is that every reader answers them, perhaps not explicitly, in the act of reading by placing some credence in the symbols for the text on the page and by formulating some concept of what kind of thing is being read and what source or sources produced it. It has been usual for readers to assume that Thackeray wrote *Henry Esmond,* that Thackeray wrote what is printed on the pages of the book, and that what the readers understand and experience in reading the book came from Thackeray. Some readers, of course, do not have a very clear notion of Thackeray and may think that the text before them is its own authority. More sophisticated readers may wish to discount Thackeray's authority over meaning and choose instead to read "against the grain" for meanings revealed inadvertently by the text

---

[1] I have discussed these related concepts in more detail in *Scholarly Editing in the Computer Age* (Athens, Ga., 1986), pp. 11–95. These questions are discussed in a considerable additional literature, which is surveyed in *Scholarly Editing: A Research Guide,* ed. David Greetham, scheduled for publication by the Modern Language Association in 1992.

about the author or about his society or about the means of production that created the physical book. All of these are common and legitimate readerly acts, and all require some act of faith regarding the authenticity and authority of the text.

One of the objects of this book is to explore the foundations for such acts of faith, to see more than is normally seen about the processes, aims, and social forces that influence the particular sequence of symbols on the page. The problem with this objective is that any historical construct is just that, a construct. Constructs are influenced not just by the evidence of history put together objectively but by the historian's answers to metaphysical questions like, Are works of art the product of individual artistic talent, or are they social acts? For that reason this chapter does not argue in behalf of one point of view, but rather explores the consequences of adopting two or three different points of view.

A working proposition here is the idea that the persuasiveness of any historical construct and of any accommodation of the questions of authority, authenticity, and authorial autonomy or social determinism depends on the context identified as relevant to the construct. Of course, everything is a context for everything else, but historians, editors, and readers usually focus narrowly on "truly relevant" contexts selected from the narrow range of material that survives as evidence.

It is necessary, therefore, to identify the various contexts in which *Henry Esmond* has been seen and to show the differing consequences to readers and editors. Implicit in the procedure is the idea that coherent explanations can be attempted within defined contexts. In everyday practice the meanings of verbal utterances are guided heavily, if not actually established, by contexts. In *The History of Henry Esmond,* Thackeray, writing in 1851–52, had a mid-nineteenth-century audience consisting of book reviewers, circulating-library readers, his mother, his publishers, his friends, and his ex–lady love Jane Octavia Brookfield. These people can be seen as having been addressed by the novel. But Thackeray said not one word in *Henry Esmond,* for his narrator, the aged Esmond, and the memoir's editors and commentators, Esmond's wife and daughter, do all the writing. The writing is understood to take place in the second and third decades of the eighteenth century and records events said to have occurred between 1670 and 1720. Esmond's memoirs are addressed to his grandsons, but his audience clearly includes his wife, who is thought by most critics to resemble Jane Brookfield. The speakers in the novel, in passages of dialogue, also produce their utterances in contexts that help identify their meanings. One can ask what the character meant, what Esmond meant by reporting the character's speech, and what Thackeray meant by having Esmond report it. One can ask what the passage may have meant to a Victorian totally ignorant of the author and what it may have meant to Jane Octavia Brookfield. And, of course, modern readers produce their own responses to these meanings by contrasting them with their own sense of acceptable beliefs and behaviors. Thus readers contextualize the text in various specific ways as a means of producing what they think are appropriate understandings of the text.

This is only the tip of an iceberg of contexts within which the novel's words can be set and understood. Each context illuminates the text in a different way. Readers know this and act upon that knowledge almost without reflection—they are that good at using and understanding language. And when a scholar/critic points out to readers an aspect of context they had not considered, they gratefully add it to the mix of factors that influence their understanding of the text. The study of genre, the author's other works, biography, cultural history, the history of ideas, all these are understood to extend the readers' awareness of the contexts within which texts create and convey meaning. Even the physical embodiments of texts, the books themselves as paper, ink, and bindings, influence interpretations.[2]

There is, however, a major flaw in the ordinary idea of authentic texts. If it is assumed that the text of a work is stable, that is, if we work with a text that is thought to have been established, we use the principle of contexts to produce "readings of the text" for contemplation. But if it is recognized that the text itself is not stable, we tend to use the principle of contexts to produce a "reading of the text" that will help establish what the text is by leading us to the right critical choices among variants. That is clearly circular reasoning and leads to predictable texts that best fulfill the editor's particular contextual construct. But the situation is worse than that. It does not matter that no variant survives at a given point in the text; each word or mark of punctuation is potentially an erroneous witness to the context identified for use in interpreting the text. That may seem good to the editor, for that is what makes emendation of errors possible. Editors tend to think that some errors, like typographical errors and scribal errors, are "demonstrable," and they emend them. But they may be too quick to

---

[2]D. F. McKenzie, particularly in *The Sociology of Texts* (London, 1987), and Jerome McGann, particularly in *A Critique of Modern Textual Criticism* (Chicago, 1983), develop this idea, which owes much to the influence of ideas current in the so-called new historicism.

believe an error to be demonstrable because they are not sufficiently aware of the influence of the contextualization that they are using to determine the meaning which identifies the textual anomaly as a demonstrable error.

To illustrate the consequences of this approach, a useful example is *The History of Henry Esmond,* which for these purposes will have to be examined in the original edition, published in London by Smith, Elder and Company in 1852 in three volumes. In what follows I speak as an editor of *Henry Esmond,* but I mean to imply that in order for an editor to know what is being edited and why it is being edited, he or she must first be a reader, must know how to read, and must know what effect the editing is having on reading. Consequently, everything I say about the editor is applicable also to any careful reader.

To do a contextual reading, one must try to draw together the historical details of authorship as a profession and printing and publishing as a complex of economic traditions and interests in a continuous struggle with innovation—both technical and moral—and with attitudes toward gender, family, and moral conventions, particularly as they reflected the audiences for lending libraries in order to see what *Henry Esmond* was. Then, perhaps, it can demonstrate more clearly what the reader's and editor's task is, or, at least, what purposes modern scholarly editions serve. While not forgetting that authors attempt to create something original that will fulfill their own purposes (including the purpose of making money), we will have to examine bibliography, printing history, papermaking, taxes on books and newspapers, copyright law, labor relations, trade guilds relating to printing, publishing, and bookselling, marketing associations, professional societies, the apprentice system, lending libraries, the three-deckers in relationship to parts publication and magazine serials, the growth of the literate public, the development of authorship as a profession, and the developing division of labor into literary agents, publishers, printers, wholesalers, and booksellers. Each of these can be thought of as a force field influencing what the work became, limiting what the work could say, shaping the work, and thereby influencing reactions to and understandings of the final product. (Incidentally, one of the nice things about scorning historical reconstructions is that there is less work involved.)

Now obviously all of that cannot be detailed here, but it has been done, and its salient details can be summarized.[3] *The History of Henry*

---

[3]The basis for this summary can be found in the following works: Feltes, *Modes of Production of Victorian Novels;* Sutherland, *Victorian Authors and Publishers;* Edgar Harden's edition of *The*

Esmond is Thackeray's only book to appear originally as a three-decker. It was published by a firm whose head, George Smith, was an executive member of the Bookseller's Association. It was Thackeray's second book with Smith, Elder and Company—his first major book with that publisher—and it represented the first significant step in an attempt by George Smith to make Thackeray one of his authors—an object he accomplished thoroughly and completely in 1859. Smith descended into publishing from the banking business by way of substantial reference works and scientific publications. His literature list, his fiction, was respectable, yet he was bold and aggressive. He published Charlotte Brontë's *Jane Eyre* and later went on to acquire as his authors Anthony Trollope and George Eliot. *Esmond,* therefore, by virtue of its publishing house belongs to a tradition of book production controlled by establishment wealth and power. To be published by Smith implied certain standards of literary and moral content that Thackeray had never been clearly subject to before, though he was subject in a general way to the Mrs. Grundy censorship affecting all Victorian publications above pulp street literature. [4]

Thackeray rose to the Smith, Elder house from his major publisher, Bradbury and Evans, which in turn had risen into publishing from bookselling, newspaper publishing, and being proprietor of that low comic magazine, *Punch,* and other comic and sporting publications. In spite of the firm's industry and success, Bradbury and Evans belonged to a decidedly antiestablishment point of view, and in the 1840s Thackeray was one of its chief writers. Thackeray's sojourn in bohemia as an art student in Paris and as a writing hack in London were social and financial descents from which the economic success of books like *Vanity Fair* and *Pendennis* were raising him. Those works and the bulk of his writings in the 1840s (*The Book of Snobs, Novels by Eminent Hands, Barry Lyndon, Catherine, The Yellowplush Papers, The Reminiscences of Major Gahagan*) all reflect the satirical, antisnob, antiestablishment attitudes of *Punch* and *Fraser's Magazine,* the main outlets for his writings.

History of Henry Esmond (New York: Garland, 1989); Richard Altick, *The English Common Reader* (Columbus, Ohio, 1957); Patten, *Dickens and His Publishers;* Guinevere L. Griest, *Mudie's Circulating Library* (Bloomington, Ind., 1970); Nowell-Smith, *International Copyright Law and the Publisher in the Reign of Queen Victoria;* and James L. W. West, "Book Publishing, 1835–1900: The Anglo-American Connection," *PBSA* 84 (1990): 357–75, and "The Chace Act and Anglo-American Literary Relations," *Studies in Bibliography* 45 (1992): 303–11, which explore the development of literary agents and crosscurrents in book production and author/publisher relations between England and America.

[4] See Louis James, *Fiction for the Working Man* (Harmondsworth, 1974).

Esmond was to be different. The author of *Esmond* was a man financially and socially restored to the level of his upbringing. He was a popular writer and successful public lecturer, having delivered his urbane lectures on the eighteenth-century English humorists to receptive and aristocratic audiences in London, Edinburgh, Oxford, Cambridge, and the larger industrial cities. *Esmond* was to be his calling card and proof that he could write a thoroughly good, artistically complete, and serious work of art. By and large, *Esmond* has been seen, both by his contemporaries and by generations of literary critics up to our own day, as a peak in Thackeray's rising career as a writer and artist.

The book belongs to the establishment in other ways, too. The three-decker was in mid-Victorian England a thoroughly establishment commodity, an expensive book made possible and necessary by circulating libraries whose large guaranteed prepublication purchases made three-decker production a book publisher's staple. It was nearly impossible for a book publisher to lose money on a three-decker that had been adopted by Mudie's library, but the discounts Mudie demanded and the price regulations that kept most ordinary customers from purchasing their own copies instead of subscribing to Mudie's made it equally difficult for a publisher to make very much money on a three-decker. The price-maintenance system for three-deckers worked to the benefit of publishers and the circulating libraries from the mid-1840s to the mid-1890s by providing stability; no one was making an inordinate amount of money, but the system could be counted on. This stability depended not only on control of prices but also on certain simple controls over the content and size of the books. These constraints imposed by Mudie's are now relatively easy to document; their primary focus was on the length of the book and the moral character of the plot and characterizations. An author and publisher who could work within the library constraints and win selection could count on a sound though not spectacular financial return.

But the respectability of the publisher and the library demands are not the only determining or constraining forces observable. *Esmond* is a historical novel created within a tradition of historical fiction which Thackeray may be said to have modified but not to have invented. Among these constraints was the demand for historical plausibility and the historical research which that demand entailed.[5] Plausibility was judged by the depth and breadth and accuracy of the historical detail surrounding the

---

[5]See "The *Esmond* Notebook" in Edgar Harden's edition of *Esmond* (New York: Garland, 1989), pp. 429–34, for a record of Thackeray's historical reading.

fictional characters and events. It was not necessary, however, to maintain historical perspective in moral and intellectual concerns or issues; Sir Walter Scott had made the historical novel both respectable and relevant to current moral and political concerns. But the freedom offered by historical fiction within the establishment contours of the three-decker published by Smith, Elder was a narrow freedom indeed.

N. N. Feltes, in considering *Esmond* in its marketplace context, has noted that the Booksellers Association and the circulating libraries were fighting a losing battle against an encroaching democratizing, proletarian invasion of the world of books and literature represented by cheap books, serializations in shilling parts, and shilling magazines. The booksellers' battle was to save the commodity which three-deckers epitomized and thereby save the economic control and stability which they enjoyed primarily through the three-decker. Feltes saw the three-decker as symbolic of the upper-class resistance to progressing economic forces and finds in the three-decker morality and traditional structures a corollary conservatism and reactionary spirit. He found in *Esmond,* a historical novel redolent with nostalgia for a past age, the same conservatism and establishment resistance to mass values, mass mores, and mass tastes. He found in *Esmond*'s literary reputation a confirmation of conservative tastes and socioeconomic politics. In the social history of the last half of the nineteenth century, on the other hand, Feltes saw the slow but irresistible subversion of the commodity book by the new cheap, democratizing commodity text. The triumph of this movement was the demise of the three-decker novel in the 1890s. For Feltes, therefore, *Esmond* represents a reactionary, establishment work. As such it represents a change or an anomaly in Thackeray's role, which for *Vanity Fair* and the early journalism was that of satirist of the establishment. Feltes posited the explanation that within the constraints of the three-decker, Thackeray was determined by cultural forces greater than himself and that an examination of these cultural contexts proves that the language and the culture speak the author, that the autonomous author is a figment of the romantic imagination; "reality" is the reality of social determinism.

If this discussion were to stop here, the weight of the social contract might seem irresistible; the social theory of texts would convincingly vest authority for the linguistic text and the meaning of the work in the social context. And the editorial solution for *Esmond* would be to select the first edition as the copy-text, emend nothing, and present the novel as a commodity book with large margins, heavy paper, and expensive packaging, thus perpetuating its role as representative of the establishment, standing as an anomaly in Thackeray's literary corpus. But the author, his text, and his meaning need not disappear behind this sociological arrangement of historical details. It is a significant shortcoming in Feltes's work that he did not apply his critical apparatus to a reading of the text.

Careful rereading of *Esmond* suggests a conclusion opposite to the one Feltes reached. He skated over the elements in the book that do not confirm his social deterministic theory of book production. The flaw of his approach is the rigidity with which his view of the social contract theory of texts controlled and limited his reading of the work by paralyzing his belief in authorial intentionality. Social determinism apparently obviates autonomy in Feltes's way of looking. Although all that Feltes pointed out about the cultural milieu surrounding *Esmond* is true, it is hardly as comprehensive or constraining a view as he suggested. Though the novel was hailed by many of its original readers (particularly its better-educated and better-heeled readers) as a critical triumph, and though it for many years has been held in high regard even by readers who do not generally admire Thackeray's works, it was and is a profoundly troubling book to many others.

Many of its first readers and reviewers were shaken and angered by the ending, in which Esmond marries the woman he has long treated as his mother. That that denouement was Thackeray's intent from the beginning is perfectly clear on rereading with close attention to Rachel's character—she knew her heart's true relation to Henry well before her husband died and years before naive Esmond himself recognized it. It shows in her nearly hysterical reaction to the news that Henry has exposed himself to smallpox by visiting Nancy Sievewright, the blacksmith's daughter, although a superficial reading allows one to think that she is reacting merely as a social snob and doting mother (bk. 1, chap. 8). It also shows in her behavior to Henry on his third visit home from college when young Frank reveals that she has been fussing over Henry's room for days, having worked a new counterpane for his bed and put fresh-cut roses in his window in anticipation of his arrival, though she pretends not to know if the housekeeper has prepared his room (bk. 1, chap. 11). It shows in her reaction to the news that "Henry" has been killed in a carriage accident, though the Henry involved turned out to be Mohun, not Esmond (bk. 1, chap. 13). It shows in the nearly psychopathic rejection scene in prison after Lord Castlewood has been killed in a duel (bk. 2, chap. 1). And it shows in the news that she has sneaked off to Southampton to watch from hiding as Esmond returns from the Continental wars (bk. 2, chap. 7). Rachel clearly believes that God has punished her for her disaffection to her husband and her secret affection for Henry by allowing her husband to be killed. She tells Esmond years later when they meet again that God has forgiven her sin: "But I would love you still—yes, there is no sin in such a love as mine now; and my dear lord in heaven may see my heart; and knows the tears that have washed my sin away" (bk. 2, chap. 6). Rachel's secret love was even more disturbing to the Victorian consciousness than the apparent though not real incest at the end of the book, for it portrays a good woman—the heroine angel in the house—in the grip of a powerful and lifelong illicit passion she must and does suppress with visible effort. Morally the book's psychological realism, though delicately handled, is profoundly subversive to the establishment. It is a measure of Thackeray's artistry that he portrayed these telling scenes in ways susceptible to more conventional interpretations, though to read them as such is to believe Thackeray has overwritten them.[6]

But the book is subversive in an even more important way, for Esmond's ostensibly weak character, his apparent vacillation and inability to cast himself passionately and unreservedly behind any cause, religious, political, economic, or amorous—though goodness knows he tries—arguably stems not from a psychological weakness but from a fundamental philosophical uncertainty and humility that is very dangerous to establishment mentality. The elderly narrator of the book, recounting Esmond's youthful naive enthusiasm for Father Holt's Catholicism, Rachel's Anglicanism, the Dowager Castlewood's Jacobitism, Beatrix's concepts of heroism and honor, constantly reveals Esmond discovering himself in an assumed and uncomfortable role-playing. Esmond spends his life fulfilling or trying to fulfill other people's expectations for himself and repeatedly discovering that the goals were not worth winning. He ends ashamed of himself as a soldier witnessing his fellows attack nuns, of Father Holt's tawdry lies and deceptions, of Frank Esmond's subjugation to Clotilde, of Beatrix's head-hunting selfishness as courtesan, and ultimately of his own complicity in these other shames he has participated in as a role player rather than in *propia persona*.

The measure of Esmond's superiority over other characters is that he recognizes his self-delusions and those of his fellow actors. Esmond's way of thinking and suiting action to thought is antiestablishment. That is why Beatrix has no permanent use for him. Esmond is constantly giving away

---

[6]A particularly good assessment of Thackeray's "philosophy" and the way it influenced how he wrote is provided in Geoffrey Tillotson, *A View of Victorian Literature* (Oxford, 1978), pp. 152–86.

the store on the grounds of scruples; he loses ground for honor and principle without any compensating social or economic or political gain. He is ultimately anti-imperialist and antiroyalist, and he rejects the optimism of the intellectual rationality for which his age, the eighteenth century, is known. At the end of the book he retreats happily enough to the margins of the empire, where he establishes a domestic kingdom of his own.

The question about Thackeray's "intentions" with regard to *Esmond* and its potentially antiestablishment meanings can be pursued a bit further in two directions. They both bring to bear on the reading of *Esmond* other contexts than the Marxist economic contexts just examined.

The first is the biographical background and in particular the events in the year immediately preceding the writing of *Esmond* concerning Thackeray's love life.[7] By 1851 Thackeray's wife had been confined under special care for insanity for seven years. In the three years before the writing of *Esmond* his love for Jane Octavia Brookfield, the wife of his best friend, the Reverend William Brookfield, had gotten as heated as a platonic relationship can get. Thackeray was clearly in love, though he was fully aware of the impossibility of the situation. He imagined that Jane suffered under a sense of repression and lack of appreciation by her husband, which may have been greater in Thackeray's mind than in reality. Whatever the case, in September 1851 William Brookfield, who had tolerated Thackeray's attentions to Mrs. Brookfield with increasing wariness, put his foot down, banning Thackeray from the society of his home and wife. It is not hard to trace Thackeray's melancholy in the Henry Esmond/Rachel Castlewood relations in the book he was then commencing.

Though he had not written any part of the book, he signed the contract for *Esmond* in June 1851. It was a story he claimed was boiling up within him as early as January, though his work on his lectures on eighteenth-century English humorists came first. That the rupture with the Brookfields affected the story there can be no doubt. Thackeray complained to Smith as late as December that he could not get on with the book under the effects of an ailment which time alone could mend. In the book itself there is a romanticized version of what could have been: Lord Castlewood's insensitivity to his wife may be read as William Brookfield's insensitivity to Jane writ large; Rachel's deep love for Esmond, suppressed and denied but tortured and irrepressible, may be Thackeray's portrait of what he saw or wished to see in Jane Brookfield's relation to himself.

[7]See *Letters* and Ray, *Wisdom,* passim.

Thackeray seems to have been much more interested, to judge also from his letters, in assuaging his own sorrow than in upholding establishment social mores. And in the character of Henry Esmond, Thackeray was able to make Rachel suffer the jealous pangs of seeing her unattainable love object throw himself at the feet of another—Beatrix, who was Rachel's daughter. Nor is it hard to see Thackeray beating his own breast and exploring the ecstasies of rejection while describing the perpetual and nearly unstiflable but unrequited love of Esmond for Beatrix. The psychological realism of a complicated and confusing network of love and jealousy involving mothers and sons and other forbidden attractions is carefully handled, for in Victorian fiction serious and troubling life passages could be explored only in code.

And finally, to focus on the way in which interpretation bears on editing, the rhetorical context of *Esmond* must be considered. It is a memoir: *The History of Henry Esmond, Esq., a Colonel in the Service of Her Majesty Q. Anne. Written by Himself.* It has all the rhetorical characteristics of an extended dramatic monologue, addressed by Esmond to his grandsons. Thackeray, the author, said not one word in *propia persona* in the whole book; even the introduction is written by Esmond's daughter. As with any first-person narration, the potential for irony and for misapprehending irony is great. Traditionally, critics have read Esmond's narrative as something like the preachments of the author's alter ego. Esmond's opening comments, on the nature of history, strike readers as honest and commonsensical. "Why shall History go on kneeling to the end of Time? I am for having her rise up off her knees, and take a natural posture: not to be for ever performing cringes and congees like a Court-chamberlain, and shuffling backwards out of doors in the presence of the sovereign. In a word," Esmond writes engagingly, "I would have History familiar rather than heroic." It sounds like the sort of attitude Thackeray would adopt; it is like his reviews of pictures in the Academy, knowledgeable but unimpressed. Esmond seems to reflect Thackeray's own attitude also by placing himself and his neighbors on the stage of history and comparing them with the figures normally found there: "I have seen too much of success in life to take off my hat and huzza to it, as it passes in its gilt coach: and would do my little part with my neighbours on foot that they should not gape with too much wonder, nor applaud too loudly. Is it the Lord Mayor going in state to mince-pies and the Mansion House? Is it poor Jack of Newgate's procession, with the sheriff and javelin-men, conducting him on this last journey to Tyburn? I look into my heart and think I am as good as my Lord Mayor, and know I am as bad as Tyburn Jack." In short, the book abounds with reasons not to draw a sharp distinction between the narrator and the author.

Moreover, Esmond has a basic distrust of absolutes—that is, of other peoples' absolutes—he does not trust the judgment of priests, military leaders, political leaders, or kings. His love and his loyalty are always tinged with sardonic self-detachment. As one critic has noted, "Like *Vanity Fair, Henry Esmond* is a sustained argument against the reality of moral absolutes. Esmond himself does much of the arguing, for he is proficient at identifying illusory values and beliefs. His sophisticated skepticism, however, is itself founded on a dedication to one surviving absolute: truth."[8] This personal truth of Esmond's is the foundation of his appeal to the reader in his autobiography. And, as with most monologists, Henry constantly asks the reader to share in his personal recognition and judgment of the self-deception of others. Furthermore, he seldom expects the reader to take him very seriously, and he appears to be disingenuous when he does.

Feltes probably would not rejoice over this coup d'état within the camp of the dying establishment, for the book does not subvert the establishment on behalf of the rising proletariat. Instead, the subversion emanates from the principles of a small intellectual elite, the freethinkers of England's Victorian intellectual class. Some of those freethinkers were ideologues, but Thackeray's religious and philosophical ideas did not develop in a cell of like-minded philosophers or so-called freethinkers (though it was not insignificant that he was a close friend of Edward FitzGerald, the translator of Omar Khayyám's *Rubáiyát*). Thackeray's philosophy is revealed in his letters and private papers as a deep and fundamental individual skepticism about causes of every sort. It got him into trouble with many proponents of causes in need of money or moral support who approached Thackeray. If the cause was individual, to honor an admirable writer's family, to provide charity on nonsectarian bases, Thackeray was a patsy. But if it was to establish a guild for literature or to propose an evangelical school or cause, his purse and ear alike were closed. He did not trust institutionalized schemes. *Esmond* is subversive to the establishment it represents, but not on behalf of emerging socioeconomic ideologies. Even the fact that both Thackeray and his publisher made a good bit of money from *Esmond,* which was an unusually good seller despite its price, does not indicate that its themes or its production was

[8]Elaine Scarry, "Henry Esmond: The Rookery at Castlewood," *Thackeray, Hawthorne and Melville, and Dreiser,* ed. Eric Rothsheim and Joseph A. Wittreich, Jr., Literary Monographs, vol. 7, Madison, Wis., 1975), p. 3.

determined or dominated by either a vested production tradition or an emerging public taste. Both of those "ideologies" claim the book by ignoring its subversive elements.

So much for Feltes's establishment interpretation of *Esmond;* this "establishment" book has a strikingly antiestablishment text—it is a wolf in sheep's clothing. And this interpretation makes the social contract solution to the editorial problem unacceptable. To take the first edition as copy-text for the linguistic text of an edition would be to accept the work of the minions of the establishment. Now, it so happens that in 1852 George Smith did not own his own printing establishment, so he sent Thackeray's manuscript to Bradbury and Evans to be typeset and printed. There may be comfort to be found, then, in the fact that the compositors of Thackeray's "proletarian serial novels" also typeset his "establishment commodity book," but the principle of authorial autonomy which the antiestablishment interpretation tends to support leads one to question the whole production process. That is to say, belief in the possibility of authorial autonomy, even of a limited sort, requires the rejection of any blanket rules for editing.[9]

Rejecting Feltes's conclusions about the meaning of *Henry Esmond* in three volumes and rejecting the conclusion that a social contract requires special respect from an editorial view I do not mean that the three-volume format and the production process are unimportant. Quite the contrary. The book could not be a wolf in sheep's clothing without the sheep's clothing, and such a wolf means far different things from regular wolves or regular sheep. The novel is quite definitely a collaboration, or at least a joint venture between the author and the social institutions of book production and marketing. And that identifies serious editorial problems.

A close look at *Esmond* reveals an extensive network of evidence suggesting an intentional subversion of the narrator by the author. Thackeray seems not to have trusted Esmond's foundation rock of personal truth. Elaine Scarry in a 1975 article compiled an extensive list of errors in the book.[10] These she invariably attributed to Esmond, claiming that Thackeray put them there on purpose. Scarry was not the first to notice that Es-

---

[9]It is true, of course, that subversive acts are in a sense both authorized and determined by the establishments they subvert, for, on the one hand, subversive acts fall into two categories, those tolerated and those not. *Henry Esmond* dutifully remains tolerated. And, on the other hand, subversive acts must be of a kind relevant to the establishment being subverted, else there would be no point. These meanings of determinism are much looser than those invoked by Feltes, who imagined Thackeray under the sway of social and economic powers inevitably producing a novel bearing the establishment stamp in both form and content.

[10]Scarry, "Henry Esmond: The Rookery at Castlewood."

mond occasionally contradicts himself or forgets what he has said earlier in the narrative, but she was the first to attribute these errors to Esmond instead of to Thackeray or to the publishers. John Sutherland's Penguin edition annotations, for example, point out scores of historical and plotting errors, but Sutherland encouraged the readers to ignore them as understandable though regrettable characteristics of Thackeray's fiction.

Scarry identified an astonishing array of errors and anomalies, including an undermining of the rhetorical force of Esmond's own protestations—as when, having renounced the doctrine of divine right of kings and declared himself a republican, he nevertheless couches his adoration for Beatrix in the language of subjugation to royalty—and other more direct contradictions—as when he declares that an event so impressed him that memory would never fail him, whereupon he recounts the event in such a way as to contradict or distort his own earlier account of it. I believe Scarry is right to say that Esmond, "who has taken truth for his motto," was ironically undercut by Thackeray, "who has taken the absence of truth for his theme."

J. Hillis Miller, following a different line of reasoning altogether, arrived temporarily at the same conclusion Scarry reached. Miller brilliantly revealed the older Henry's ironic stance with respect to the younger Henry and then showed the ironic self-destruction of the self that Henry Esmond the narrator has constructed. Miller saw Thackeray's presence behind the narrator undercutting his claims to memory's sovereignty and the basis upon which Esmond allows himself to become "king" of the Virginia Castlewood and to accept the "worship" of Rachel and his daughter. Miller did not use any references to the "narrative errors" in the book to detect this irony. But his view of Thackeray undercutting the narrator was a temporary stop on Miller's deconstructive way through the novel, for he then undercut or deconstructed this third level of irony by arguing that Thackeray was trying to "understand and control his life by taking ironic authority over that assumed role and by showing the imagined person to have made a false interpretation of himself."[11]

Miller was more interested in his theory of irony as "infinite absolute negativity" than he was in the meaning of *Henry Esmond,* the book being in the final analysis only an illustration for what Miller had to say about irony. Furthermore, his conclusion about the novel could not stop with resolution, for it is the nature of deconstructive criticism to deconstruct

---

[11]J. Hillis Miller, "*Henry Esmond:* Repetition and Irony," in *Fiction and Repetition: Seven English Novels* (Cambridge, Mass., 1982), p. 106.

the deconstruction. Resolution would put an end to the fun and games. However, Miller's point is not without seriousness. Resolution—say, the conclusion Miller considered at one point, that Thackeray undercut the narrator through telling references to Oedipus Rex and Hamlet which the reader with the help of Freud's *Interpretation of Dreams* can use to see Thackeray's ironic distance from his narrator—cannot be reached with any conviction if one is fully cognizant of the slippery ground such a resolution must take for its base. Miller implied that Thackeray, like his narrator, revealed himself rather than justified himself in the endless cycle of ironic undercuttings. This view makes *Henry Esmond* "one of the best texts in English fiction by means of which to explore the workings of irony in narrative." But in order to get boxed up, as Miller wanted the reader to be, one must agree that Thackeray was seeking "authority over his own life by way of a detour representing that life in ironically displaced form in a fiction." Miller's conclusion that Beatrix is a sad mirror image of Esmond, revealing unconsciously the "corrosive power" of both characters and of their author, was based on the idea that Thackeray was seriously trying to present a "pretense of mastery."[12]

It would be possible—in fact, preferable—to conclude that Thackeray was not trying any such thing.[13] Instead, he was demonstrating the inability to exercise any such mastery. Beatrix, in her cold-blooded, calculating attempts, which from the cynic's point of view should succeed, fails just as truly as does Esmond, whose machinations the reader is led to believe are wholly unconscious. The melancholy nihilism of the book can and has been seen as Thackeray's cynicism. But it is one thing to recognize the lack of control implied by nihilism and quite another to give in to it. Beatrix recognizes it and gives in to it. Henry Esmond recognizes it up to a point; that is, he recognizes it for others but not for himself, and the sensitive reader of his memoirs is bruised by Esmond's lack of self-awareness, revealed, for example, in the way he punishes Rachel for "unfaithfulness" to him in the prison while excusing his own blatant and egregious "unfaithfulness" to her during the years of his infatuation with Beatrix. It is inconceivable that Thackeray failed to see Esmond's self-deception or the dual view of nihilism implied by Beatrix's and Esmond's stories. Thackeray did not give in to it, as the cynical view would have it,

---

[12]Ibid., pp. 106, 114.

[13]One could turn Miller's argument on himself, showing that his attempt to master Thackeray's unconscious agenda reveals Miller's, perhaps equally futile, attempts to master his own life. Instead, it seems more likely to me that both Thackeray and Miller were operating out of the assumption that absolutes are all illusory and unstable.

nor did he close his eyes to it, reverting blindly to an assertion of good that would be no more than a repetition of Esmond's quest for something worth believing in at one further level of self-deception. Anyone who has read Thackeray's own story—in the *Letters* and Gordon Ray's two-volume biography—can see the melancholy acceptance of uncertainty, as opposed to mastery, that characterized his mature years. But two things mitigate against Miller's reading of *Esmond,* which was after all based on a reading of the text alone. One is Thackeray's determination expressed in conversation to John Chapman in 1851, thirteen days before he signed the contract to write *Henry Esmond,* that he did not feel "called upon to martyrise himself for the sake of his views" by expressing them too clearly to his reading public.[14] The second is, that Thackeray's personal reaction to his nihilistic ideas was to resist the temptation to give in. His personal intense desire not to hurt anyone, not to take advantage of anyone, not to manipulate others out of a sense that his version of "the truth" was the right version of it all reveals the light in which he created in *Esmond* the views Miller has described.

That is to say, in view of the emptiness of institutionalized values such as royalty, inherited rank, honor, party and country loyalty, marriage, and institutional religion, Thackeray chose not to sneer and not to pontificate, but to assert a sardonic kindliness and gentleness that are as far from sentimentality as those qualities can get. Nihilism in Thackeray bred humility about his politics, religion, and responsibilities. It did not, of course, keep him from reacting rather dangerously when his dignity was bruised by Edmund Yates's caricature of him in 1858. That episode may appear to give the lie to the portrait sketched here, but in spite of what the episode ultimately turned into, Thackeray's actions began as self-defense against what he saw as unprovoked attack. That, at least, is not antithetical to the view that Thackeray, in *Henry Esmond,* was giving up mastery over his life rather than desperately trying to gain control of it.

The Force of Chosen Contexts

Now the point of all that is this: The contexts we identify as relevant to the text we read determines our interpretation, and the interpretation that is adopted determines the text we establish or edit. If N. N. Feltes's interpretation is adopted, one chooses the first edition as copy-text and makes the reading text ape the result of the social contract that originally produced it. The emendations policy will be documentary and conservative.

---

[14]Chapman's MS diary, Beinecke.

If, however, John Sutherland's interpretation is adopted, one selects the manuscript (or possibly the first edition) and emends the text to conform as closely as possible to one's notion of Thackeray's intentions by correcting as many errors as possible and writing notes for all the rest to explain them away or de-emphasize any damage they might do to the reader's enjoyment of Thackeray's tour de force historical pastiche. And if Elaine Scarry's interpretation is adopted, one chooses the manuscript as copytext and emends the text so that it effectively undermines the narrator's credibility, thus emphasizing Thackeray's rejection even of Esmond's attachment to personal truth. But if J. Hillis Miller's interpretation is adopted, there is no need to edit the text since his reading is untrammeled by information of any sort from Thackeray's life, the period in which he lived, the production institutions which enabled the book to become a book, or the genesis of the text.

If our goal is to read the text as a finished product, edited according to a "better way," then we must take a stand or abide by the editor's stand on answers to the following questions: To what extent was the author aware of and in control of the book's potential ironies? Did Thackeray intend to undermine Esmond's trust in personal truth, or did he share Esmond's view? Did Thackeray deliberately undercut Esmond's credibility by introducing obvious errors and memory lapses into Esmond's memoirs, or are the errors those of the novelist, Thackeray? To what extent did the production crew understand the author's intention and enhance or inhibit it? These questions are to be answered by critical inquiry, not by ascertaining discoverable facts. This situation illustrates well what is critical about critical editing. But it also illustrates the way any single text edition of the book is capable of distorting it and hiding its possible meanings by privileging one context over others as the determiner of meaning. It does not take genius to see that an editorial approach to *Esmond* which sets about correcting errors may well be thwarting the author's intentional and meaningful introduction of those errors. On the other hand, not to correct the errors also may thwart authorial intention. Only persons who regard their personal solutions to these imponderables as universally acceptable would say that editing can be done by anyone correctly.

The economic, biographical, and rhetorical contexts in the cultural envelope where *Esmond* became a three-decker historical novel all influenced what that book became; but it is a gross oversimplification to conclude that the book became inevitably what it is through determining forces over which the author had no control. A concept of the editorial task is not helped by the glittering generalities that suggest "the language speaks the artist" or "the social complex employs authors to produce books" or "the author is dead." These conclusions are half-truths. Likewise, it does not help one to understand the business of editing if one concludes that the author is autonomous, the sole authority over text. That view tends to cast the editor in the role of rescuer and restorer. But the illustration just detailed demonstrates that it is impossible to say with any certainty what Thackeray is to be rescued from or what needs to be restored.

This brief survey of the complexities of *Esmond*'s text seems to indicate that the author's communication to the reader is not only individual and free but constrained and directed by external forces. That is not a contradiction, nor is it a tragedy. It is a fact. Nothing understandable can be said or thought without the contextual frame of language and society and genre and custom and economic realities. But all establishments and power structures have within them the capacity to be satirized, subverted, criticized, and amended—that is to say, the author is free within the limits allowed by the medium. The power of some texts is that their subsurface purposefully subverts the surface meanings. The question about the reader's and editor's dual responsibility to authorial intention and the social contract can be answered by saying they are both operative. It follows that a critical theory that ignores either is a lopsided theory, and it also follows that an editorial practice that edits away the evidence of either is equally lopsided.

The concept of editions which emphasize the importance of process and avoid extravagant claims for the correctness of the product is gaining ground, but not without resistance—resistance stemming from editors who are reluctant to give up power over the texts, from critics who want a stable text, and from publishers who, market driven, wish to save expense. Editions such as Hans Gabler's of *Ulysses,* Michael Warren's of *King Lear,* and the Garland Thackeray edition are attempts in different ways to emphasize alternative texts, or multiple texts, or indeterminate texts, but all these editions are controversial. Resistance to them in preference for editions with supposedly unproblematic, stabilized texts accounts for the polemics of textual theory. Any single solution requires commitment to one of several orientations toward texts which are mutually exclusive. At that level there is considerable debate among editors about the right way to edit or the right goal or end product to present as the established text.

The alternative to a single text solution represents not an extension of polemic but a resolution. It represents a more comprehensive view of textual criticism, which, though probably not stable, at least does not stagger distractedly from one polemic to another.

What then is the function of a scholarly edition? In the Garland edition of *Vanity Fair,* the famous last paragraph of chapter 32, in which Jos takes flight and the war is brought to a close, reads: "No more firing was heard at Brussels—the pursuit rolled miles away. The darkness came down on the field and city, and Amelia was praying for George, who was lying on his face, dead, with a bullet through his heart."

The effect is both thrilling and chilling, and even first readers of this passage as it appears here can feel the tear of opposing passions as the pleasure of seeing George dead combats the sorrow for sudden death and for poor Amelia, while at the same time the reader feels she is a sap for turning on the ever-ready waterworks for what one already knows is a "selfish humbug," a "low-bred cockney-dandy," and "padded booby," though Becky does not provide these words to describe George till chapter 67. First-time readers will also, no doubt, sense the clean, crisp, efficient, and flat (i.e., nonpejorative, nonheroic) diction which gives the account its force and gives free play to the reader's conflicting feelings.

If readers were inclined to contemplate the passage, they might note that the phrase "The darkness came down" probably means primarily that night fell, but it allows the potential reverberations of the thought that "the darkness" has ominous symbolic overtones. There is little to encourage such a speculation, however, except the juxtaposition of Amelia's own sorrow—which one can only partially share—and perhaps a twentieth-century propensity to see symbols everywhere. Should these readers turn to the "Record of Composition and Revision" in the Garland edition, they will find that the printed text reflects the reading of the first edition (1847) and that in 1853 someone (it is not entirely definite that it was Thackeray) revised the phrase to "Darkness came down."

Now, if the revised reading had been in the text in the first place, the sense of potential ominous symbolic overtones to the descent of "Darkness" (now fortuitously capitalized) might have struck readers more forcibly. Some might say, because this reading is "stronger," it should have been chosen for the Garland edition. It was not chosen because such aesthetic judgments were not part of the editorial strategy. To choose readings that correspond with the historical integrity of Thackeray's text at the time of first publication is not to reject the 1853 revisions. The point is not which of these readings is the correct one. The fact is that no one knows if either is correct or if both are correct.

The point is that in a scholarly edition both are available and have their various effects on the reading of *Vanity Fair.* Having read "The darkness came down," readers then find that a change was made to "Darkness came down." Either reading, by itself, conveys the fall of night, and both reveal the potential for a symbolic reading, the revised reading perhaps more so. But discovering that the reading was revised is the strongest indication that something was being attempted here beyond indication that night fell. The changing itself is a stronger indication of meaning than either phrase is alone.

That is a crucial point in understanding the importance of a scholarly edition. The aim of the editorial work should not be to produce a pristine, correct, reliable text, a product. It should instead be to trace the growth and development of the work and to place the reading text in its developing context, a process. The effect is lost on readers who insist on reading the text as product, but the potential is there for serious, sensitive reading directed in part by reaction to what the author did—as opposed just to what the author said.

This paragraph from *Vanity Fair* reveals a flaw in the Garland edition. The edition fails to include a parallel account of George's death from a letter Thackeray wrote to his mother who had complained about Amelia's selfishness. Thackeray's response is pretty well known, but it all should have been quoted in the edition, including his anticipation of the time two months ahead when Amelia's "scoundrel of a husband is well dead with a ball in his odious bowels" (*Letters* 2:309). With that highly inflammatory and emotionally laden phrase ringing in one's ears, one cannot read the printed passage in the book without trying to account for the clean, flat, efficient diction found there in terms of Thackeray's narrative strategies and, perhaps, the demands of serial publication.

Scholarly editions should encourage and make possible such intertextual readings. The richness and satisfaction of such reading complexities go up when the countertexts are understood for what they are: parallel texts in letters, revisions in manuscripts, or alternative printed texts emanating either from revision or from compositorial or editorial intervention. The sources and relative dates of countertexts have a great deal to do with a reader's assessment of their significance. It seems, then, that the duty of a scholarly edition is not arbitrarily (and stealthily) to reduce the complexity and richness of a work of art to one correct and established standard text, but rather to lay out the materials as clearly and usefully as possible.

VII

An Epilogue on Prefaces

AFTER THIS SURVEY of production and market conditions and after this argument about the consequences of ideological positions to the specifics of texts, one could well ask whether Thackeray and his publishers were producing a commodity to be sold or a text to be read. Putting the question in this way emphasizes the controversy over whether in fulfilling expectations Thackeray was a pawn in the larger social order or an independent artist pushing against the limitations of a social order he was refusing to bow to. Any answer given will depend on how one looks at the evidence. I think it is possible to see Thackeray as both, playing opposing roles at once. Thackeray the writer was making a living by producing commodities for a marketplace; Thackeray the author was creating texts indicative of the lives of characters and societies in a fictive reality embodying the artist's view of the world. If the social order shaped how he did both of these things, he also shaped the social order he left behind at his death.

Both of these ways of looking at the question suggest that readers should be influenced in their response to a text by the conditions under which that text was produced. They suggest that the intention of the author or the conditions of production (perhaps the "intention" of the society that produced both author and text) somehow should determine the meaning or significance of the text. It would, however, be possible instead to read the text "against the grain" and to find its significance in what it reveals unintentionally. Thus, *Henry Esmond* can be read to see how Thackeray's or his age's biases are revealed in those aspects of the described fictive lives that go unchallenged or go without saying. One could examine and become critical of the unequal male-female relationships that form the assumed ideal against which are judged the unequal male-female relations that form the normal experience. Thus the author may be seen as having "intended" to criticize a relationship (such as Lord Castlewood and Rachel's) by showing its failure to fulfill an assumed ideal (represented, perhaps, by Esmond and Rachel's marriage). But the reader could choose to be critical of that ideal by describing the paradise on the banks of the Rappahannock River with which the book ends as a male-dominated fiefdom on the margins of the empire. Such a comment disregards the apparent "intentions" of the author and of his social order.

And yet, to read a work against the grain requires first that the grain itself be discovered or constructed. The significance of such a description requires a knowledge of the conventional view of a retreat to paradise, which constitutes the grain. Therein lies the value of the close examination of historical evidence about authors and the means of production. It is not to establish what was meant, or what was intended, or even what was not intended. Rather, it is to set up a variety of contexts against which to place formulated critical insights. One needs as much evidence as possible about the historical circumstances of the text before one can remark cogently upon Thackeray's acquiescence in the conventional values of his day or his distancing himself from Henry Esmond's acquiescence in them. Even then, one has only posited alternative ways of reading the text.

The basic idea arising from this study is that Thackeray was very conscious of two fundamental roles that did not always have the same goals and rules. That is not the idea with which I began. In the beginning I set out to show a creative genius at work; what I have found is a genius in traces pulling a rather heavy load and trying to do so with grace and integrity. Though Thackeray himself did not refer to the distinction in any consistent terms, these roles might be distinguished by considering the difference between being a writer and being an author: the writer making a living and the author creating fictive worlds as an exploration of life and ideas.

One way to see how the writer influenced the author is to read the prefaces to Thackeray's works. They constitute confidential communications from the writer to the purchaser about the problems of writing, publishing, and marketing commodities. The author, in the body of the fictions, frequently addressed the reader about the problems of understanding the world of the characters and of being an author. The audience for these two speakers was equally distinct, sometimes acting as purchasers and sometimes as readers. Of course, Thackeray may well have thought of the terms *author* and *writer* as synonyms, and he occasionally spoke of readers as purchasers of books. Such confusions are only natural, since the distinctions are conceptual and since it was Thackeray's business to meld the two.

That Thackeray was keenly aware of these distinctions is evident, however. Dedicating *The Irish Sketch-Book* "To Dr. Charles Lever, of Templeogue House, Near Dublin," Thackeray distinguished between that personage and the ones of the same name and location who created Harry

Lorrequer and who edited the *Dublin University Magazine,* neither of whom, Thackeray imagined, would be very happy with the dedication. Dr. Lever of Templeogue House, on the other hand, addressed as a hospitable and good Irishman and friend of Mr. William Makepeace Thackeray, had every right to the dedication.

Notes of a Journey from Cornhill to Grand Cairo came to have three introductory notes by the writer. The first dedicates the book to Samuel Lewis, captain of the tour ship, offering the book as a "commodity" in token of the writer's gratitude for a safe voyage. The second, written in the voice of Mr. Titmarsh, details the circumstances that led to the voyage. The crucial question, he says, was, "Could he afford it?" The clinching fact, he tells us, was that the directors of the company "would make Mr. Titmarsh the present of a berth for the voyage." It might seem that this Mr. Titmarsh was the same as the author of the text of the work, but the preface ends with a recommendation that "all persons who have time and means . . . make a similar journey," not through reading his book but in person in real life. There may be no frigate like a book, but it seems that this appeal is directed to the purchasers of the book by the writer of the book, rather than to the readers by the author. The personal communication from writer to purchaser is reopened in the "Postscript to the Second Edition" where the writer hopes "that in its present and cheaper form, my little volume may be found welcome to those of another class, who were deterred hitherto, perhaps by the price, from reading it." The context and conventions of the prefaces and dedications dictate that the speaker be a seller and the audience be a buyer or a person to whom a gift is offered.

The preface to *Rebecca and Rowena* toys with the roles of writer, illustrator, and author more than with the differences between purchaser and reader. Thackeray in the voice of M. A. Titmarsh refers to his illness and to Dr. Elliotson's injunction "ON NO ACCOUNT to put pen to paper" and adds, as an explanation for the employment of Richard Doyle as illustrator, that it "need scarcely be said, that the humble artist who usually illustrates my works fell ill at the same time with myself." That there is no reference to the reader as purchaser in this book may suggest Thackeray's affection for the story, an indication that he offered it primarily to his readers rather than to purchasers, or at least pretended so for this preface.

The Kickleburys on the Rhine originally went forward without dedication or preface, but a supercilious and pompous review in the *Times* prompted a rejoinder signed by M. A. Titmarsh published in the second edition, which followed so closely on the heels of the first as to be ordered by the publishers on the same day of the *Times*'s review. The review is remarkable for two objections, both relevant to the distinctions drawn here. The first objection is that

> *there is another motive for these productions, locked up (as the popular author deems) in his own breast, but which betrays itself, in the quality of the work, as his principal incentive. Oh! that any muse should be set upon a high stool to cast up accounts and balance a ledger! Yet so it is; and the popular author finds it convenient to fill up the declared deficit, and place himself in a position the more effectually to encounter those liabilities which sternly assert themselves contemporaneously and in contrast with the careless and free-handed tendencies of the season by the emission of Christmas books—a kind of literary* assignats, representing to the emitter expunged debts, to the receiver an investment of enigmatical value.*[1]

In short, the first objection is that the motive for the work was to make money. Of course, what is being invoked here as a standard for judgment is the romantic notion of the priestly function of the hero as man of letters—a position Thackeray mocked and rejected and modified over and over.

Ten years earlier, when Thackeray in the voice of Yellowplush accused Bulwer Lytton of writing for money, the intention of the accusations was opposite to that of the reviewer of *Kickleburys* in the *Times*. There the fact of writing for money is a natural and correct motive, not a shameful one:

> *You wrote it for money,—money from the maniger, money from the bookseller,—for the same reason that I write this. Sir, Shakspeare wrote for the very same reasons, and I never heard that he bragged about serving the drama. Away with this canting about great motifs! Let us not be too prowd, my dear Barnet, and fansy ourselves marters of the truth, marters or apostels. We are but tradesmen, working for bread, and not for righteousness' sake. Let's try and work honestly; but don't lets be prayting pompisly about our "sacred calling." The taylor who makes your coats (and very well they are made, too, with the best of velvit collars)—I say Stulze, or Nugee, might cry out that their motifs were but to assert the eturnle truth of tayloring, with just as much reazn; and who would believe them?*[2]

---

[1] The review is quoted in full in the preface to the second edition, titled "An Essay on Thunder and Small Beer." My quotations are from that essay.

[2] "Epistles to the Literati," *Yellowplush Papers* (1840; New York, 1991), p. 123.

The second objection in the *Times*'s attack on *Kickleburys* is that the delineations of character ostensibly offered up for enjoyment are unpleasant, though the illustrations are "spirited enough." But the praise is faint and damning: "Mr. Thackeray's pencil is more congenial than his pen. He cannot draw his men and women with their skins off, and, therefore, the effigies of his characters are pleasanter to contemplate than the flayed anatomies of the letter-press." In short, the reviewer claimed, not only was the purchaser being offered a bill of goods, the reader was being offered an unpleasant experience. Perhaps the two, in this case, amounted to the same thing.

Thackeray didn't think so. In the voice of Titmarsh he warned his readers that "the *Times* newspaper does not approve of the work, and has but a bad opinion both of the author and his readers. . . . if you happen to take up the poor little volume at a railroad station, and read this sentence, lay the book down, and buy something else. You are warned. What more can the author say? If after this you *will* buy,—amen! pay your money, take your book, and fall to." As for the charge that he wrote for money, nothing could be more natural; the critic in the *Times* did as much. Thackeray likened himself and the publishers to publicans brewing and serving beer, "and it is liked by customers: though the critics (who like strong ale, the rogues!) turn up their noses." The irony was, he continued, that on the very day of the review the author received a notice from the publishers which he quoted:

> "*My dear Sir,—Having this day sold the last copy of the first edition (of x thousand) of the 'Kickleburys Abroad,' and having orders for more, had we not better proceed to a second edition? and will you permit me to enclose an order on,*" &c. &c.?

This letter is not in George Smith's style, though the facts are accurate enough—there was a bonus check, and there was a second edition. So whether or not the critic was pleased, the public seemed content; and as usual with Thackeray, he was happy to let the public decide. Besides, he pointed out, the critic at the *Times* had not been given the book by the publisher or the author in hopes of a puff, nor had the critic paid for his copy. The critic, having asked for a copy, disdained what cost him nothing on the grounds that it wasn't worth the price. "Every farthing you have paid," Titmarsh taunts the critic, "I will restore to your lordship, and I swear I shall not be a halfpenny the poorer."

So much for the first objection and its various implications. Thackeray and Titmarsh say nothing about the second one. It seems to have been a principle with Thackeray that readers and critics were welcome to their opinions about the texts—these were matters of taste—but beware of any comments on the writer and his motives. As he had said in the second preface to *Cornhill to Cairo,* "It becomes writers [he means authors] to bear praise and blame alike meekly; and I think the truth is, that most of us get more of the former, and less of the latter, than we merit."

The difficulties Thackeray had in twining the roles of author and writer are alluded to in the preface to *Pendennis.* Remarking on the surprising number of readers he had attracted, Thackeray disclaimed any right to say to them, "You shall not find fault with my art, or fall asleep over my pages"; but he did ask that they consider him an individual following his own lights: "I ask you to believe that this person writing strives to tell the truth. If there is not that, there is nothing." So spoke the artist, the author. But two paragraphs later the writer admitted that there were restraints: "Even the gentlemen of our age—this is an attempt to describe one of them, no better nor worse than most educated men—even these we cannot show as they are, with the notorious foibles and selfishness of their lives and their education. Since the author of Tom Jones was buried, no writer of fiction among us has been permitted to depict to his utmost power a MAN. We must drape him, and give him a certain conventional simper. Society will not tolerate the Natural in our Art." Thackeray did not spell out why, in its fiction, society "will not hear . . . what moves in the real world, what passes in society, in the clubs, colleges, news'-rooms,—what is the life and talk of your sons." One must conjecture that the demands of the marketplace prevented such frankness and that the role of the author was being curbed by the role of the writer, that the individual was not entirely free to say as much as he would like in society.

A contrasting way to put this conflict is revealed in the preface to *Vanity Fair* where the Manager of the Performance surveys the fair of which he was himself a player in competition with "quacks (*other* quacks, plague take them!)." Thackeray here seemed to take a sad responsibility for his own performance, which he had "brilliantly illuminated with the Author's own candles," but at the same time he seemed to disavow responsibility for what his puppets had done and said. They are controlled by what society does and says; the author merely reported, as when one comes home from the fair and sits down "in a sober, contemplative, not uncharitable frame of mind" to reflect on what was seen. In other words, the author may be seen as constrained by the facts of the society in which he lives to describe what he sees and knows; forced, as author, to do the very thing the author of *Pendennis* complains that, as writer, he cannot do: to say more than he finds pleasant to report.

Prefaces are prefatory only for readers; they are the author's and writer's last words. Thackeray invariably used his last words to reflect on the discrepancy of values between the author's pursuit of truth and the writer's obligation to the trade, or at least to present realities. The preface to *The Newcomes* remains literally an epilogue to the novel in which the writer seems to come out of a daze in which he is not sure whether the reality lies before or after the horizontal rule drawn at the end of the story. But the shift in role from storyteller to book writer was clearly in his consciousness. The image of Pegasus in harness is Thackeray's own, and he seems never to have escaped a feeling akin to that expressed by W. B. Yeats:

> *There's something ails our colt*
> *That must, as if it had not holy blood*
> *Nor on Olympus leaped from cloud to cloud,*
> *Shiver under the lash, strain, sweat and jolt*
> *As though it dragged road metal.*[3]

That Thackeray came to accept this condition as par for the course need not suggest that he did not chafe at the bit.

In a way, the message of this study is that the controlling force determining what a book means and what effects it will have resides with the reader, and with the contexts by which meaning is constructed that the reader chooses or has chosen for him or her. The experience of those constructions is richer for readers with a greater knowledge of text generation and text reception than it is for those with more limited access to the range of relevant contexts. It is not to establish the meaning of Thackeray's works or even the meaning of Thackeray's career that I undertook this book, but to open still further the range of responses that readers can make to the man, as author and as writer, and to his work, as art and as commodity.

---

[3]W. B. Yeats, *The Collected Poems* (London, 1950), p. 104.

APPENDIXES

WORKS CITED

INDEX

Appendix A
The Contracts

The Irish Sketch-Book[1]

Memorandum of an agreement entered into between William Thackeray Esqe. of 13 Great Coram Street Brunswick Square on the one part and Edward Chapman & William Hall, publishers on the other part.

The said William Thackeray agrees to write a work to be called Titmarsh in Ireland to consist of two volumes of the size & somewhat of the nature of the Paris Sketch Book—& the said Edward Chapman & William Hall agree to purchase the copyright thereof on the conditions following—

Wm. Thackeray engages to write the work, and deliver it into the hands of Chapman & Hall by the 31st. December & to execute the plates both designs & etchings for the same

Chapman & Hall engage to pay for an unlimited right and interest in the sale of an impression of fifteen hundred copies as follows.—

£120 to be paid down this day

    50 on the delivery of the MSS.

40	*on the sale of the first*				*250*	*copies*
35	*"*	*"*	*"*	*" second*	*250*	*"*
35	*"*	*"*	*"*	*" third*	*250*	*"*
35	*"*	*"*	*"*	*" fourth*	*250*	*"*
35	*"*	*"*	*"*	*" fifth*	*250*	*"*
35	*"*	*"*	*"*	*" sixth*	*250*	*"*
£350					*1500[2]*	

And in case of a Second Edition being required, half the profits of the same to be divided between the said William Thackeray & Edward Chapman & William Hall.

That subject to these conditions Mr. Thackeray will assign to Chapman & Hall the entire copyright of the first & second editions of the work entitled Titmarsh in Ireland, when called upon so to do—
London 8th. September 1840

                               W. M. Thackeray.
                               Edward Chapman
                               William Hall."[3]

---

[1]Reprinted from *Letters* 1:470–71.

[2]The total income on 1,500 copies should be £385.

[3]The terms of this agreement are nearly identical except in wording to the proposal Thack-

Vanity Fair[4]

*Memorandum of agreement made this Twenty fifth day of January 1847[5]
between William Makepeace Thackeray Esqe of 13 Young Street Kensington, and William Bradbury and Frederick Mullett Evans, copart-
ners, Printers & Publishers, Whitefriars—*

*The said William Makepeace Thackeray hereby agrees with the
said William Bradbury and Frederick Mullett Evans, to publish a work
in Monthly Parts to be called "Vanity Fair, Pen & Pencil Sketches of
English Society"—*

*The said William Makepeace Thackeray undertakes to furnish by
the 15th of every month sufficient matter for at least Two printed Sheets
with two Etchings on Steel, and as many drawings on Wood as may be
thought necessary—*

*The said William Bradbury and Frederick Mullett Evans agree to
pay to the said William Makepeace Thackeray the sum of Sixty Pounds
every month on the Publication of the Number—*

*It is then agreed that after the whole Expenses of the Work are paid
(including the above named sum of £60—)[6] that the said William
Bradbury & Frederick Mullett Evans shall receive out of the first profits,
the sum of £60, and that whatever further profits shall arise shall then be
equally divided between the aforesaid William Makepeace Thackeray
and William Bradbury and Frederick Mullett Evans—*

*That the Copyright of the said Work shall be the joint Property of
the aforesaid William Makepeace Thackeray and William Bradbury and
Frederick Mullett Evans—*

[signed] W M Thackeray—

---

eray submitted to the publisher, except that Thackeray specified explicitly that there would
be twelve plates "besides vignettes wood-cuts &c." and an escape clause in the event of
"illness or any domestic calamity," a poignant reference to his wife's depression.

[4]Reprinted from Ray, *Adversity*, pp. 433–34.

[5]If this date is accurate, the agreement was signed as the second installment was being
prepared for press and at least a month and a half after the subtitle used in this contract had
been changed to "A Novel without a Hero." On the other hand, the correct date cannot be
January 1846, for while that is probably the date of the first verbal agreements between
Bradbury and Evans and Thackeray, leading to the first, aborted publishing effort in April
or May of that year, Thackeray did not come up with the main title used in the contract,
Vanity Fair, until sometime in the autumn. Furthermore, this contract calls for both etchings
on steel and drawings on wood, whereas all the physical evidence from the aborted
serialization of 1846 indicates that drawings on wood had not been contemplated at that
time.

[6]Among the expenses apparently intended but not specified here was a 10 percent commission on gross income, which is revealed by the ledgers and which meant that over the life of
the contract the publisher earned considerably more than the author. See above, chapter 5.

The History of Henry Esmond[7]

Memorandum of Agreement between William Makepeace Thackeray Esqr. of Young Street Kensington and Mr George Smith Publisher trading under the firm of Smith Elder & Co. of Cornhill London made this Twenty Seventh of June 1851.

Mr W. M. Thackeray agrees in consideration of the sum of Four Hundred Pounds the receipt of which he hereby acknowledges to write an original work of fiction forming a continuous narrative in three volumes Post 8vo. to consist of not less than One Thousand pages of the usual novel size and to place the Manuscript of the same in the hands of Mr George Smith complete and ready for publication on or before the first day of <November> ↑ December ↓ next ensuing.[8]

Mr George Smith agrees to print and publish the said work and on receipt of the Manuscript thereof to pay to Mr W. M. Thackeray another sum of Four Hundred Pounds and on the publication of the said work to pay to Mr W. M. Thackeray a further sum of Four Hundred Pounds.—

It is agreed between Mr W. M. Thackeray and Mr George Smith that the first impression printed of the said work shall consist either of 2500 or 2750 copies at the option of Mr George Smith and that such impression may be published in one edition or divided into two or three editions as he may consider expedient. In the event of Mr George Smith Printing 2750 copies he agrees to pay to Mr W. M. Thackeray One Hundred Pounds if the whole of such impression be sold within eighteen months from the date of the publication of the first edition.—

It is further agreed that in consideration of the above mentioned payments the whole of the profits arising from the sale of the first impression of 2500 or 2750 copies of the work shall belong to Mr George Smith, that all future impressions of the said work shall be published by Mr George Smith at such times and in such manner as he may think advantageous and that one half of the net profits derived from them shall be paid by Mr George Smith to Mr W. M. Thackeray as follows viz: an account of the expenses and proceeds of each future impression shall be made up and rendered to Mr W. M. Thackeray every six months (Five Per Cent being allowed to Mr George Smith upon the amount of sales as guarantee [sic] commission) and Mr George Smith shall pay to Mr W. M. Thackeray one half of the balance appearing at the credit of the account.—

---

[7]Original in NLS. Titled on the reverse: "Agreement between W M Thackeray & Mr. George Smith for Copyright of a Novel in 3 Vols. June 27 1851."

[8]The cancellation and insertion were done in a different shade of ink.

It is also agreed by Mr W. M. Thackeray that he will not print or publish any serial or other work within six months of the date of publication of the above mentioned work and that any profit that may be derived from the sale of early proof sheets for publication in America shall belong to Mr George Smith.—

[signed] W M Thackeray

George Smith

"Tour on the Continent"[9]

Memorandum of an Agreement made on 3rd of June 1852 between W. M. Thackeray Esqre and Smith Elder & Co

In consideration of Two Hundred Pounds now paid to him by Smith Elder & Co Mr Thackeray agrees to write an account of the Tour he is about to make on the Continent to form a volume containing not less matter than the First Edition of his "Journey from Cornhill to Cairo" and Illustrated with designs on wood, and to deliver the manuscript of the work complete & ready for publication to Smith Elder & Co by the First of October next and prior to Mr Thackeray's departure for America.

Smith Elder & Co agree to publish the book on the following terms—1st. The size, price, and manner of publication to be decided by Smith Elder & Co—

2nd. On the work being placed in the hands of Smith Elder & Co an estimate is to be made by them of the cost of printing, paper, engraving, binding, advertising and other necessary expenses of the publication of the First Edition and also of the probable proceeds of the sale of the Edition[.] In this estimate Seventy five copies are to be allowed for gratuitous distribution—the remaining copies are to be counted 25 as 24 and are to be valued at the Trade Sale price, (being Twenty nine per cent less than the retail price) and Five per cent is to be allowed from the estimated proceeds to cover the risk of bad debts—

3rd Upon the above-mentioned estimate being made up, Smith Elder & Co are to pay Mr Thackeray the difference between the amount of Four Sevenths of the estimated profit of the First edition & the Two Hundred Pounds already received by him.

Smith Elder & Co are to be at liberty to publish a Second or any

---

[9]Original in NLS. Titled on the reverse: "*Agreement* For the Publication of Thackeray's 'Tour on the Continent'——& acknowledgment of the receipt of £200.—3rd June 1852." The work contracted here was never written; Thackeray eventually "refunded" the cash advance with other work.

subsequent edition of the work on the same terms as the First (except as regards the Two Hundred Pounds already paid Mr Thackeray). An estimate of the cost and net proceeds of each Edition being made on the plan above specified and Four-Sevenths of the estimated Profit of each Edition being paid to Mr Thackeray. But payment for the Second and subsequent Editions is to be made one half on publication and the other half when two thirds of the Edition have been sold.

Smith Elder & Co are to have the sole right of printing and publishing the work until Four Years after the publication of the First Edition. After that period Smith Elder & Co are to have no interest in the Copyright. But Mr. Thackeray agrees not to publish or authorize the publication of any new Edition of the work until any copies that may then be in the hands of Smith Elder & Co shall have been sold.

Smith Elder & Co
[signed] W M Thackeray

Tauchnitz Miscellanies, *Vol. 3*[10]

Vertrag zwischen W. M. Thackeray Esq. . . . London *und Herrn Bernhard Tauchnitz Verlagsbuchhändler, Ritter des Königl. Sächs. Albrechtsordens und mehrerer anderer Orden, zu Leipzig.*

1. Es überträgt Herr Thackeray *an Herrn Bernhard Tauchnitz das ausschliessliche Recht, das Werk:* "Miscellanies" Volumen 3 *bis* 8 *der Leipziger Ausgabe in englischer Sprache für den Continent zu verlegen.*

2. Es macht sich Herr Bernhard Tauchnitz verbindlich in keiner Weise seine Ausgaben des erwähnten Werkes nach England oder dessen Colonieen zu verkaufen.

3. Es zahlt Herr Tauchnitz an Herrn Thackeray *für Uebertragung dieses Verlagsrechtes ein für allemal die Summe von* Ein Hundert Pfund Sterling.

4. Dieser Vertrag ist in zwei gleichlautenden Exemplaren von beiden Theilen vollzogen worden.

Leipzig und London, den 25 August 1857.

[signed] Bernhard Tauchnitz[11]

---

[10]Original in Gordon Ray's collection, Pierpont Morgan Library. This contract is a printed form; the handwritten portions are in roman type, but I have not imitated the typography and format of the form. Thackeray did not sign this copy of the contract and might not have signed and returned another copy. The contract had no legal standing and represented a gentleman's agreement which Thackeray and many of his compatriots dealing with Baron Tauchnitz took to be as good as any piece of paper.

[11]Since the signature is in the same hand that filled in the form, it may not be Tauchnitz's own.

Cornhill *Memorandum, First Draft*[12]

Smith, Elder, & Co. have it in contemplation to commence the publication of a Monthly Magazine on January 1st, 1860. They are desirous of inducing Mr. Thackeray to contribute to their periodical, and they make the following proposal to Mr. Thackeray:

1. That he shall write either one or two novels of the ordinary size for publication in the Magazine—one-twelfth portion of each novel (estimated to be about equal to one number of a serial) to appear in each number of the Magazine.

2. That Mr. Thackeray shall assign to Smith, Elder, & Co. the right to publish the novels in their Magazine and in a separate form afterwards, and to all sums to be received for the work from American and Continental Publishers.

3. That Smith, Elder, & Co. shall pay Mr. Thackeray 350£. each month.

4. That the profits of all editions of the novels published at a lower price than the first edition shall be equally divided between Mr. Thackeray and Smith, Elder, & Co.

65 Cornhill: February 19th, 1859.[13]

First Cornhill *Agreement*[14]

Memorandum of an agreement made the ninth day of April 1859 between William Makepeace Thackeray Esqre and Messrs Smith Elder & Co Publishers of 65 Cornhill London.

Mr. Thackeray in consideration of the engagements of Smith Elder & Co contained in this agreement agrees to write two novels the scenes of which are to be descriptive of contemporary English life society and manners, each novel to form as much printed matter as is contained in sixteen numbers of thirty two pages each of Mr. Thackeray's work

---

[12]The only copy known of this memorandum is in Smith's manuscript autobiography, "George Smith, A Memoir," pp. 106–8. It has been printed by Leonard Huxley in *House of Smith, Elder* and in *Letters*, 4:130, which is the source of the text printed here. Smith gave the memorandum to Thackeray in February 1859, saying, "I wonder whether you will consider it, or will at once consign it to your wastepaper-basket?"

[13]Smith recalled that "Thackeray read the slip carefully, and, with characteristic absence of guile, allowed me to see that he regarded the terms as phenomenal. When he had finished reading the paper, he said with a droll smile: 'I am not going to put such a document as this into my wastepaper-basket.' " Thackeray wrote to his mother that he was to have "8500 in the next 2 years from Smith & Elder—prodigious!" (*Letters*, 4:130).

[14]Original in NLS.

entitled "The Virginians" and Mr. Thackeray agrees to place in Smith Elder & Co's hands a sixteenth portion of the Manuscript of one of the novels before the first of December next, and to continue to furnish them before the first of each succeeding month with a further sixteenth portion of Manuscript of the first novel until its completion. Also after an interval of four months shall have elapsed from the last portion of the first novel being placed in Smith Elder & Co's hands to furnish them with a sixteenth portion of the Manuscript of the second novel and thereafter to continue to place in their hands before the first of each succeeding month a further sixteenth portion of the Manuscript of the second novel until its completion.

Mr. Thackeray further agrees to furnish Smith Elder & Co with not less than twenty four original drawings for etchings on steel each of the size of a demy 8vo. page for the illustration of each of the two novels.

In consideration of the engagements of Mr. Thackeray contained in this agreement Smith Elder & Co agree to pay to him on receipt of each sixteenth portion of the Manuscript of each of the novels the sum of three hundred and fifty pounds and it is further agreed that Smith Elder & Co are to be at liberty to publish each of the above mentioned novels in a periodical to appear monthly and also in two or more different forms as a separate work: but neither of the first two publications of either of the novels as a separate work is to be published at a lower retail price than twenty shillings per copy.

And it is further agreed that the copyrights of each novel so far as is requisite for the publication of it in a periodical and also as a separate work in two different forms is to belong exclusively to Smith Elder & Co and their assigns, the whole of the profit of these publications to belong to them, but that the profits of the third and subsequent publications in different forms and sizes from either of the two first separate publications of each novel are to be equally divided between Mr. Thackeray and Smith Elder & Co or their assigns after allowing publisher's commission of five per cent from the amount of the sales to Smith Elder & Co.

Mr. Thackeray agrees not to publish any other writing of his either in a periodical, or in a separate form until after the completion of the publication of the above mentioned two novels in the periodical in which they will be published by Smith Elder & Co, without their consent.[15]

---

[15] A large curly brace occupies the left margin of this paragraph. It points to the opposite page, now torn away, on which Thackeray objected to the stipulation made here (see above, chapter 3).

And it is further agreed that all sums which may be received for facilitating the priority of publication in the United States of America or on the Continent of Europe or for the assignment of the Continental copyright or for the right of translating one or both of the above mentioned novels into any other language than English shall belong to Smith Elder & Co.

And Mr. Thackeray agrees to execute any necessary assignments to them. But Smith Elder & Co agree that in the event of the net sum received by them for facilitating early republication in America of the two novels exceeding the sum of four hundred & eighty pounds for each novel they will pay to Mr Thackeray two thirds of any amount in excess of such sum of four hundred and eighty pounds for each novel.

[signed] W M Thackeray[16]

Second Cornhill Agreement[17]

Memorandum of an agreement made on the 20th. of August 1859 between W. M. Thackeray Esqre. and Smith Elder & Co.

Some of the conditions of the agreement made on the 9th. of April 1859 between Mr. Thackeray and Smith Elder & Co. are to be varied as follows—1st. the two novels therein referred to are to be published as separate serial works in monthly parts in place of in a Magazine. 2nd. Mr. Thackeray is to furnish the first portion of of [sic] the Manuscript of one of the novels to Smith Elder & Co on the 1st. of June 1860 in place of on the 1st. of December 1859. 3rd. Mr. Thackeray is to have the option of furnishing Twenty instead of sixteen portions of each novel[.] 4th. Mr. Thackeray is to furnish for each portion two drawings for etchings on steel and drawings for the initial letters of the chapters. 5th. the copyright of each novel as far as is requisite for the publication of it as a serial work and also afterwards in a volume is to belong exclusively to Smith Elder & Co and their assigns, the whole of the profits of these publications to belong to them, but the profits of any subsequent publication in a different form are to be equally divided between Mr. Thackeray and Smith Elder & Co and their assigns, after allowing publishers commission of five percent to Smith Elder & Co from the amount of the sales.

Mr. Thackeray further agrees to contribute to a monthly magazine

---

[16]Smith did not sign this copy; presumably there was another, given to Thackeray, which Smith did sign.

[17]Original in NLS. This agreement was signed when Thackeray was rather ill and despairing of his work on *The Virginians*.

to be published by Smith Elder & Co a story of six sheets of sixteen pages each and to place the manuscript for the first sheet in Smith Elder & Coy's hands on the 1st. of December 1859 and the Manuscript for the other five sheets on the first of each succeeding month, at the rate of one sheet per month. Mr. Thackeray also agrees to furnish to Smith Elder & Co the manuscript of his lectures on the Four Georges to be published in successive numbers of their Magazine. The copyright of each of these two works as far as is requisite for the publication of it in a periodical and also as a separate work in one form and size is to belong exclusively to Smith Elder & Co and their assigns, but should it be published in more than one separate form, the profits of its publication in such other separate form or forms shall be equally divided between Mr. Thackeray and Smith Elder & Co after allowing publishers commission of five per cent from the amount of the sales, to Smith Elder & Co.

Smith Elder & Co agree to pay to Mr. Thackeray Fifteen hundred pounds for the above two works in the following manner £500 on the 1st. of January 1860—£500 on the 1st. of April 1860 and £500 on the delivery to them of the Manuscript of the Lectures on the Four Georges[.]

[signed] *W M Thackeray*

The Roundabout Papers[18]

Agreement between W. M. Thackeray Esqre and Smith, Elder, & Co.—
    The Roundabout Papers in the "Cornhill Magazine" are to consist of 24 papers[19] of five pages each on an average with an initial Woodcut to each. Smith Elder & Co are to pay Mr Thackeray £1,000 for the right of publishing them in the Magazine, and in either one or two separate forms (at their option) afterwards. If published in more than two separate forms then the profit on its publication in such other separate form is to be equally divided by Mr. Thackeray and Smith Elder & Co.

[signed] *W M Thackeray*

The Adventures of Philip[20]

Agreement between W. M. Thackeray Esqre and Smith Elder & Co for the publication of "Philip."
    "Philip" is to be published in sixteen consecutive numbers of the

---

[18]Original in NLS. Thackeray's copy, signed by Smith, is in Gordon Ray's collection, Pierpont Morgan Library.

[19]The copy signed by Smith reads: "24 pages, of five pages."

[20]Original in NLS.

"Cornhill Magazine." Mr Thackeray is to furnish for each number Twenty four pages of letterpress, a Drawing for a Page Illustration, and two Initial vignettes. Smith Elder & Co are to pay Mr Thackeray Two Hundred & Fifty Guineas for each number, and are to have the Copyright so far as is necessary for the publication of "Philip" in the "Cornhill Magazine" and also separately in two different forms, neither of which is to be published at less than Fifteen Shillings. The profits of all other Editions are to be equally divided between Mr Thackeray and Smith Elder & Co. All Sums received from America and the Continent are to belong to Smith Elder & Co—

[signed] *W M Thackeray*

London. December 8th 1860.

The terms of this agreement apply to "Philip" as about to be extended to twenty numbers of the Magazine[.][21]

[signed] *W M Thackeray*

Second Roundabout Papers *Agreement*[22]

Agreement between W. M. Thackeray Esqre. and Smith Elder & Co. August 5th. 1862.

Smith Elder & co are to have the right of publishing "Roundabout Papers" Nos. 1 to 19, "Nil Nisi Bonum" and "A Roundabout Journey" in either one or two separate forms (at their option.) If published in more than two separate forms then the profit on their publication in such other separate form is to be equally divided between Mr Thackeray and Smith Elder & Co[.]

Smith Elder & co are to have similar rights in regard to "Roundabout Papers" Nos. 20 to 23 which have already appeared and in regard to any other "Round-about Papers" which may hereafter appear in the "Cornhill Magazine[.]"

The "Round-about Papers" which may hereafter appear in the "Cornhill Magazine" are to be paid for at the rate of £12.12.0 per page. They are not to exceed seven pages in length—and either Mr Thackeray or Smith Elder & co are to be at liberty to terminate this Agreement as far as it relates to the publication of further "Round-about Papers" in the "Cornhill Magazine" at any period after the end of the present year[.]

The entire copyright of three pages entitled "The Last Sketch"

---

[21]This statement is added in a smaller script but apparently the same hand as the main text of the contract.

[22]Original in NLS.

written by Mr Thackeray which appeared in the "Cornhill Magazine"
No 4 as an introduction to the fragment of a Story by Charlotte Brontë is
hereby assigned to Smith Elder & Co[.]

[signed] *W M Thackeray*

Denis Duval[23]

Agreement between W M. Thackeray Esqre and Smith Elder & Co

Mr. Thackeray agrees to contribute to the "Cornhill Magazine" a
story of eight parts of twenty four pages each, and to place the manuscript
for the first part in Smith Elder & Co's hands on or before the 1st. of
March and the Manuscript of each of the other seven parts on the first of
each succeeding month. Mr. Thackeray is to make a Drawing on wood
for an initial letter for each part.

Smith Elder & Co are to pay Mr Thackeray on the delivery of the
Manuscript for each part two hundred and fifty pounds and are to have the
copyright of the work so far as is necessary for it's publication in the
"Cornhill Magazine" and in two separate forms. If published in more
than two separate forms then the profit of the publication in such other
separate forms is to be equally divided between Mr. Thackeray and Smith
Elder & Co. The date of the commencement of the work in the Cornhill
Magazine is to be decided by Smith Elder & Co, and the sums received
from America and the Continent are to belong to them[.]

[signed] *W M Thackeray*

London
   February 11th 1863[24]

---

[23]Original, reproduced here, and scribal copy in NLS. A third copy, signed "Smith Elder & Co" is in Gordon Ray's collection, Pierpont Morgan Library.

[24]An agreement for *Denis Duval* between Smith and Bernhard Tauchnitz was signed on 30 April 1867. Tauchnitz paid £50.

Appendix B
A Census of Imprints to 1865

This remains a working list of imprints of Thackeray's separately published works. Although I have examined a large number of the books cited here, the list was compiled from library and rare-book catalogue entries, secondary reference works, publishers' records, and reports sent me by other scholars. The list, therefore, requires verification and was compiled for the purpose of facilitating verification and as a preliminary step toward a descriptive bibliography.

The list includes imprints after 1865 for editions that first appeared by 1865. It excludes collected editions of Thackeray's works—specifically, the collected edition begun by Smith, Elder and Co. in 1867. (By 1968 that edition had published volumes containing *Vanity Fair, Pendennis, The Newcomes, Esmond, The Virginians, Philip, A Shabby Genteel Story*, and *The Paris Sketch-Book and Yellowplush*. Also excluded is *The Loving Ballad of Lord Bateman*, often attributed to Thackeray and Dickens; Thackeray's version of the story was a separate effort from that of Dickens and Cruikshank, published in 1839 and 1851. Thackeray's *The Famous History of Lord Bateman* was first published in *Harper's Magazine* in 1892, and again in the Biographical Edition of his works. All other omissions are unintentional.

Library locations are given when known; the failure to list a library under a given imprint cannot be taken to mean that the library does not own it. Nor are the number of copies reported for a given library necessarily all the copies owned by that library.

The list of imprints was compiled from manuscript publishers' records of the Bradbury and Evans Co. (B&E), the Smith, Elder and Co. (S,E), the Harper and Brothers Co., and the Carey and Hart Co.; from the Thackeray exhibitions and checklists compiled by John D. Gordan (NYPL), M. L. Parrish, the Grolier Club, F. S. Dickson, Lewis Melville, R. H. Shepherd, and H. S. Van Duzer; from booksellers' catalogues in my files; from the catalogues of the libraries listed below and/or from their reports to the National Union Catalogue; and from the reports of personal libraries of individuals whose initials are listed below.

Additional locations and additional imprints are requested. Send information to the author in care of the publisher.

Abbreviations for Locations

Arents	Arents Collection, NYPL	InU	Indiana Univ.
An-C-TU	Univ. of Toronto	KU	Univ. of Kansas
ArU	Univ. of Arkansas	KyLx	Lexington Public Lib.
AzU	Univ. of Arizona	KyU	Univ. of Kentucky
Berg	Berg Collection, NYPL	Lilly	Lilly Library, Indiana Univ.
BM	British Library	LNT	Tulane Univ.
CaAEU	Univ. of Alberta	LU	Louisiana St. Univ.
CaBVa	Vancouver Pub. Lib.	MB	Boston Public Lib.
CaBVaS	Simon Fraser Univ.	MBU	Boston Univ.
CaBVaU	Univ. of British Columbia	MH	Harvard Univ.
		MU	Univ. of Mass.
CaBViV	Univ. of Victoria, BC	MWA	Am. Antiquarian Soc.
CLSU	Univ. of So. Calif., LA	MWelC	Wellesley College
CLPhFB	Central Lib., Philo. Fac., Brno, Czech.	MWiW-C	Chapin Lib., Williams College
CLU-C	Clark Lib., UCLA	MdBJ-G	Garrett Lib., Johns Hopkins
CSmH	Huntington Lib.	MdBP	Peabody Institute, Baltimore
CSt	Stanford Univ. Lib.		
CU	Univ. of Calif., Berkeley	MeB	Bowdoin College
CU-A	Univ. of Calif., Davis	MeU	Univ. of Maine
CoU	Univ. of Colorado	MiU	Univ. of Michigan, Ann Arbor
CtU	Univ. of Conn.		
CtY	Yale Univ.	MnU	Univ. of Minnesota
DGU	Georgetown Univ.	MoSU	St. Louis Univ.
DLC	Library of Congress	MoSW	Washington Univ., St. Louis
DeU	Univ. of Delaware		
EDB	English Dept., Brno	MoU	Univ. of Missouri
Fales	Fales Collection, NYU	MsSM	Mississippi State Univ.
FMU	Univ. of Miami, Coral Gables	NBC	Brooklyn College
		NBu	Buffalo and Erie Co. Pub. Lib.
FTaSU	Florida State Univ.	NBuG	Grosvenor Ref., Buffalo Co. Pub. Lib.
FU	Univ. of Florida		
GEU	Emory Univ.	NBuU	SUNY, Buffalo
GU	Univ. of Georgia	NIC	Cornell Univ.
ICN	Newberry Lib., Chicago	NN	New York Public Library
ICU	Univ. of Chicago	NNC	Columbia Univ.
ICarbS	So. Ill. Univ.	NNU	New York Univ., Washington Sq.
IEN	Northwestern Univ.		
IEdS	So. Ill. Univ., Edwardsville	NNUT	Union Theological Sem.
INS	Ill. St. Univ., Normal		
IU	Univ. of Illinois	NRU	Univ. of Rochester, NY
IaU	Univ. of Iowa	NSyU	Syracuse Univ.

NWM	US Milt. Acad., West Point	PPL	Library Co. of Phila.
NcCuW	Western Carolina Univ.	PPLas	La Salle College, Phila.
		PPPrHi	Presbyterian Historical So.
NcD	Duke Univ.	PPT	Temple Univ.
NcU	Univ. of North Carolina at Chapel Hill	PPWe	Westminster Theological Seminary
NjP	Princeton Univ.	PPiU	Univ. of Pittsburgh
NjR	Rutgers Univ.	PSt	Penn State Univ.
OC	Cincinnati Public Lib.	PU	Univ. of Pennsylvania
OCU	Univ. of Cincinnati	RPB	Brown Univ.
OCX	Xavier Univ., Cincinnati	Robarts	Robarts Lib., Univ. of Toronto
OCl	Cleveland Pub. Lib.	SW	Saffron Walden Lib., Saf. Wal., Essex
OClMA	Cleveland Mus. of Art		
OClW	Case Western Reserve Univ.	ScU	Univ. of South Carolina
		TNJ	Joint Univ. Libraries, Nashville, TN
OClWHi	Western Reserve Historical Soc.		
		TxHR	Rice Univ.
OKentU	Kent State Univ.	TxHU	Univ. of Houston
OO	Oberlin College	TxU	Univ. of Texas
OOxM	Miami Univ. of Ohio	TxU-HR	Hum. Res. Ctr., Univ. of Texas
OU	Ohio State Univ.		
OWoC	College of Wooster	Vic	Victoria College, Univ. of Toronto
Or	Oregon State Lib.		
OrCS	Oregon State Univ. Lib.	VPI	Virginia Poly. Inst.
OrPR	Reed College	ViLxW	Washington & Lee Univ.
OrU	Univ. of Oregon	ViU	Univ. of Virginia, Charlottesville
Parrish	Parrish Collection, Princeton		
		ViW	College of William and Mary
PBm	Bryn Mawr College		
PHC	Haverford College	WU	Univ. of Wisconsin
PHi	Historical Society of Pennsylvania	WaPS	Washington State Univ.
		WaSpG	Gonzaga Univ., Spokane
PMA	Allegheny College		
PP	Free Library of Philadelphia	WaU	Univ. of Washington
		WaWW	Whitman College, Walla Walla, WA
PPDrop	Dropsie College, Phila.		
PPG	German Soc. of Pennsylvania		

Personal libraries of: RAC, JEG, DH, EFH, JK, HL, JM, RWO, NP, GR, PLS

The Adventures of Philip

London: Smith, Elder, 1862. 3 vols.

BM, NN, Berg(6), NNC(2), Parrish(5), OU, MsSM, CU, CaBVaS,

Lilly(2), CaAEU, Fales(2), ICN, CSmH(2), INU, ViU, CtU, NcU, OrPR, ScU, IEN, WU, MH, CtY, IU, OU, ICU, CLU-C, IaU, NIC, PLS, JM, GR(3)
Reprinted, 1863.
AzU
Reissued by Lippincott, Phila., 1866.
MH
New York: Harper & Brothers, 1862. 1 vol.
DLC, NN, Berg, Parrish, Fales, INS, NcU, ScU, MiU, PPL, MH, PU, PLS
Leipzig: Tauchnitz, 1862. 2 vols. British Authors nos. 629, 630.
BM, CSmH, MH
Columbia, S.C.: Evans and Cogswell, 1864.
BM, CSmH, ViLxW, ViW, ViU, GEU, OClWHi, NcD
[with *A Shabby Genteel Story*.] London: Smith, Elder, 1868. 2 vols.
NN, MB, MH, MdBP, PP, CSmH, IU

Ballads
London: Bradbury and Evans, 1855.
BM, Berg(3), Parrish, CU, NN, NNC, Lilly, TxU-HR, CSmH, MH, MeU, DGU, CU-A, MiU, CtY, IU, PLS, JM, GR
Reprinted, 1856.
Fales, PLS
Reprinted, 1857.
Fales
Reprinted, 1859. (Source: B&E records)
Reprinted, 1862. (Source: B&E records)
Reprinted, 1864. (Source: B&E records)
Reprinted by Smith, Elder, 1865. (Source: S,E records)
Reprinted by Smith, Elder, 1866.
WU, NcU
Reprinted by Smith, Elder, 1868. (Source: S,E records)
Boston: Ticknor and Fields, 1856.
DLC(2), NN(2), Berg, Fales, Parrish, InU, CSmH, OU, MH, NBuU, PPL, PHC, MiU, OClW, OO, MB, NcU, PU, NcD, PPT, TxU, KyLx, WaU, MeB PLS(3), RWO, GR

The Ballymulligan Polka. As Danced at Mrs. Perkins's Ball.
London: H. Tolkien, n.d. [Van Duzer suggests 1847].
Berg

Barry Lyndon. See *The Luck of Barry Lyndon*

The Bedford Row Conspiracy. See *A Little Dinner at Timmins's*

The Book of Snobs
London: Punch Office, 1848.
Berg(4), Parrish, NN, Fales, ICN, CSmH, Lilly, CaAEU, NcU, OOxM, AzU, TxU, PPL, MWiW-C, MH, IU, OrU, CtY, EFH, GR(2)

New York: D. Appleton, 1852.
   Berg(2), Parrish, NN, Fales, NNC(2), CSmH(3), NWM, MB, CtY, MoSU, ViU, MH, PU, FTaSU, DeU, GR, JK
  Reprinted, 1853.
   IaU, MoU
London: Bradbury and Evans, 1855.
   BM, Berg, Parrish, NN, Fales, MsSM, CtY
  Reprinted, 1856.
   Berg, MH
  Reprinted, 1857. (Source: B&E records)
  Reprinted, 1858. (Source: B&E records)
  Reprinted, 1860. (Source: B&E records)
  Reprinted, 1864. (Source: B&E records)
  Reprinted by Smith, Elder, 1865.
   PLS
  Reprinted by Smith, Elder, 1866 and 1868. (Source: S,E records)
New York: Appleton, 1864.
   BM, DLC, NcU, MnU
[as *Le livre des snobs.* Trans. G. Guiffrey.] Paris, [1857].
   BM, MH
[as *Snoby.*] Petersburg, 1860.
   BM
See also *The History of Samuel Titmarsh*

Burlesques: A Legend of the Rhine *and* Rebecca and Rowena
London: Bradbury and Evans, 1856.
   Berg(3), Parrish, NN, Fales, CSmH, TxU-HR, ICN, NIC, WU, NcU, ICU, CtY, MH, IU

Christmas Books
London: Chapman and Hall, 1857. 1 vol.
   BM, Parrish, Berg(2), Fales, CsMH, INS, CtY, NcU, IU, PP, PPL
  Reprinted, 1864.
   PLS
London: Smith, Elder, 1866. (Source: S,E records)
  Reprinted, 1868.
   NN, MH, MdBP, PP

Comic Tales and Sketches
London: Hugh Cunningham, 1841.
   BM, Berg(5), NN(2), Fales, CSmH(2), ICN, An-C-TU, CaAEU, Lilly, TxU-HR, MsSM, OrU, NcD, ScU, MH, PPL, CtY, IU, NcU, IEN, GR
  Reissued, n.d. [1848; title page mentions *Vanity Fair*]. (Source: Grolier)
   MoSW, ScU, GR

Confessions of Fitz-Boodle and Some Passages in the Life of Major Gahagan
New York: Appleton, 1852.

BM, DLC, Berg, Parrish, CU, Fales, CSmH(2), NN(2), MB, NWM, ViU, PU, PPT, LU, PSt, OOxM, DeU, MH, ICarbS, WaWW, NBu, CtY, NcD, OClW, PLS

Reprinted, 1853.

BM, NcU, NjP, MiU, PPL, PHi

Reprinted, 1859.

ViU

[as *Fitzboodle Papers and Men's Wives.*] London: Bradbury and Evans, 1857.

BM, Berg(2), Parrish, Fales, CSmH, CtY, IU, OClW, MH, MB

Denis Duval

New York: Harper and Brothers, 1864.

NN, Fales, Parrish, CSmH, ViU, TxHU, MH, PPL, PU

London: Smith, Elder, 1867.

BM, NN, Berg(2), Fales, NNC, Parrish(2), CU(2), CSmH(2), ICN, InU, CaAEU, CaBVaS, MH, CtY, AzU, ICU, OrU, IU, MdBP, NcU, PLS, GR

Leipzig: Tauchnitz, 1867. British Authors no. 907.

BM, NRU, MB, NIC

The Diary of C. Jeames de Plushe, Esq. See *Jeames's Diary* and *Yellowplush Correspondence*

Doctor Birch and His Young Friends

London: Chapman and Hall, 1849.

BM, DLC, NN, Berg(3), Fales(2), NNC(2), Parrish, CSmH(2), ICN, CU, Lilly, An-C-TU, CaAEU, CaBVaS, MoU, NcU, ScU, NIC, CtY, CLU-C, MoSW, MH, MWiW-C, IaU, MsSM, WU

Reprinted, 1864.

NIC, MH, PLS(2), JM, GR

Paris: A. and W. Galignani Co., 1849.

Fales

New York: D. Appleton, 1853.

NN, CSmH, CU, ViU, PP, NRU, PPiU, CtY, OClW, MB, PPL

Reprinted, 1856.

MH, CSt

Reprinted, 1857.

Parrish, PU, MB, PHC, ICU

Early and Late Papers

Boston: Ticknor and Fields, 1867.

BM, DLC, NN(2), Berg, NNC, Fales, Parrish(2), CSmH, CU, ICN, Lilly, MsSM, CaBViV, CaAEU, MB, ViU, NIC, ICU, PP, MiU, PU, PPL, PBm, PHC, GEU, TxU, WaPS, OrCS, MeB, DGU, LU, MH, NcD, OU, OClW, OCU, PLS, GR

The English Humourists

London: Smith, Elder, 1853.

BM, DLC, Berg(4), Fales(4), NNC, Parrish(2), ScU(2), NcU, MsSM, CSmH(2), PHi, CtY, MH, PPL, TxU, ScU, NcU, CU, InU, OrPR, OrU, MoSW, IU, ICU, KU, ICN, CaAEU, PLS, EFH, JM, RAC, RG

Reprinted, 1853. "Second Edition, Revised."

BM, NN, Berg, NNC, CSmH, InU, Lilly, PLS, EFH, GR

New York: Harper and Brothers, 1853.

BM, NN, Fales, Parrish(3), CSmH(2), CU, GU, OU, PSt, Lilly, CtY, MU, PPG, NcU, MB, NIC, MWelC, OKentU, NcD, WU, OrCS, NRU, MH, OCX, OU, IU, ScU, ViW, MWA, IaU, MeB, PLS(2), GR

Reprinted, 1854.

DLC, NN, ICN, Lilly, OCl, MH, DGU, PPG, PPLas, NjP, ViU

Reprinted, 1858.

NNC

Reprinted, 1860.

NIC, MWA, MH, OO

Reprinted, 1864.

OClW

Reprinted [with *The Four Georges*], 1862.

ICN

Reprinted [as *Lectures,* Complete in One Volume], 1867.

NcU, MH, OCX, PU, CtY

Reprinted, 1868.

FMU, ICN, PP, TxU, MeB

London: Smith, Elder, 1858.

BM, NN, NNC, WU, WaSpG, NIC, TxU, OCl, TNJ, NBuU, CtY, MiU, PLS

Reprinted, 1863. (Source: S,E records)

Reprinted, 1866.

DLC, PSt, OKentU, CtY

Reprinted, 1867. (Source: S,E records)

Leipzig: Tauchnitz, 1853. British Authors no. 277.

NN, Berg, EDB, GU, MB, NjP, MH, CtY

New York: Leypoldt Holt, 1867.

NN

An Essay on the Genius of George Cruikshank

[London]: Henry Hooper, 1840.

BM, DLC, NN(2), Fales(3), Berg(3), NNC, CSmH(5), Lilly, NcU, MWiW-C, IU, MB, NjP, OrPR, OrU, WU, MWA, ScU, MH, CtY, PU, GR(2)

The Exquisites[?]

London, [1839].

CSmH

The Fatal Boots, and Cox's Diary

London: Bradbury and Evans, 1855.

BM, NN, Berg(3), NNC, Fales, Parrish, Lilly, IU, IEN, CtY, MH, JM

Reprinted, 1856.
    ICN, MH, NcD
Reprinted, 1857.
    BM, IaU, PLS
Reprinted, 1857.
    ViU, WU
Reprinted, 1860. (Source: B&E records)
Reprinted by Smith, Elder, 1866, 1868. (Source: S,E records)

Fitzboodle Papers and Men's Wives. See *Confessions of Fitzboodle*

Flore et Zéphyr by Theophile Wagstaff
    London and Paris: J. Mitchell, 1836.
        BM, Berg(5), Fales, CSmH, MH, IU, CSt, NSyU, CtY, GR

The Four Georges
    New York: Harper and Brothers, 1860
        DLC, Berg, Fales, NNC, Parrish(4), Lilly, CSmH, CaAEU, MoSW,
        MH, OCX, NcU, PPL, CaBVaU, MB, TxU, MWA, NcD, INS, NcU,
        ViU, CtY, MeB, FTaSU, GR
    Reprinted, 1862.
        NN, FU, PP, MH, NjP
    Reprinted, 1864.
        OClW
    New York: James O. Noyes, 1860. Noyes Ten Cent Serials, no.1.
        NN(2), Fales, Parrish
    London: Smith, Elder, 1861. With title-page subtitle.
        BM, NN, Berg(5), Fales, Parrish(2), CU, CSmH, ICN, OU, PSt, Lilly,
        NIC, CtY, ViU, CLU-C, DLC, CoU, ScU, MoSW, WU, MH, TxU,
        GR, EFH
    Reprinted, 1861. Without title-page subtitle.
        BM, Parrish, Fales, PLS, EFH
    Reprinted, 1862. Without title-page subtitle.
        CaBVaU, PLS(2), JM
    Reprinted, 1866.
        OClMA
    [with *Lovel the Widower.*] Leipzig: B. Tauchnitz, 1861. British Authors
        no. 580.
        BM, CSmH, InU, CLPhFB, MH, OO, MB

Gorilla Fight
    London: T. McLean, n.d. [ca. 1860?].
        Berg(3), Fales, Parrish(2), ICN, MH, IU, CtY

The Great Hoggarty Diamond. See *The History of Samuel Titmarsh and the
    Great Hoggarty Diamond*

The History of Henry Esmond
    London: Smith, Elder, 1852. 3 vols.
        BM(2), Berg(6), Parrish, NN, Fales, NNC(2), MsSM, CaBVaS,
        ICN(2), Lilly, OU, PSt, PPL, NIC, PHC, MiU, IU, MWiW-C, ScU,

CLU-C, ViU, CtY, KU, FTaSU, OKentU, TxU, OrU, ICU, NcU,
MoSW, CtU, OO, FU, OrU, PPT, INS, EFH, JM, GR
Reprinted, 1853. "Second Edition" on title page.
BM, NN, Fales, IU, WU, ICU, NcU, MdBP, PLS
Reprinted, 1853. "Third Edition" on title page.
CU, FMU, GR

London: Smith, Elder, 1858. 1 vol.
BM, NNC, GU, IU, MH, PLS, EFH, GR
Reprinted, 1866.
MH, MB, PP, NN, MdBP, DLC
Reissued by Lippincott, Phila., 1866
MH

New York: Harper and Brothers, 1852.
Parrish, WaPS, PLS
Reprinted, n.d.
Fales

Leipzig: Bernhard Tauchnitz, 1852. 2 vols. British Authors nos. 245,
246.
BM(2), NN, Fales, CU, CLPhFB, MiU, MU, ViU, OClW, MB, CtY,
PPL, MH

[trans. into French by Léon de Wailly.] Paris: [1856].
BM

[as *Esmond Henrick.* 2 vols.] Pest, Hungary: 1862.
BM

[as *Die Geschichte Heinrich Esmonds.*] Buda: Wien, 1852.
Fales

[as *Henrick Esmond*] Stockholm: Bonniers, 1868.
Fales

The History of Pendennis
London: Bradbury and Evans, 1849–50. 24 nos. in 23 pts.
DLC, Berg(6), Fales, NNC, Parrish, ScU, CSmH(2), ICN, Lilly,
CaAEU, OU, PSt, GU(2), MWiW-C, NcU, ICU, NBu, OO, OCU,
ViU, JM, GR
London: Bradbury and Evans, 1849, 1850. 2 vols.
BM(2), DLC, Berg(7), NN, NNC, Parrish, Fales(2), ICN, CU(2),
CaBVaS, CaAEU, AN-C-TU, ScU(3), CaBViV, GU, IaU, INS,
PHC, ViU, CoU, MH, MBU, OU, NIC, PPiU, OCl, NcU, AzU,
OOxM, CtY, TxHU, FU, CU-A, OrU, NRU, MsSM, OrPR, TxU,
DeU, MiU, MoU, NcD, FTaSU, CLSU, PLS(4), EFH, JM, RAC,
GR
Reprinted by Smith, Elder, 1866.
PLS

New York: Harper and Brothers, 1849–50. 8 nos.
Berg, Parrish, CSmH, NNC
New York: Harper and Brothers, 1849, 1850. 2 vols.

DLC, NN, Fales, Parrish, ScU, MsSM, ICN, PSt, ViU, OO, PPLas, OCX, MB, NNU, KU, OKentU, PHi, NWM, PLS, GR
Reprinted, 1854.
Berg, ViU
Reprinted, 1855.
ICN
Reprinted, 1858.
CU, MB, MiU
Reprinted, 1860.
NBuU
Reprinted, 1863.
MB, OClW, OCU, NBuG
Reprinted, 1867.
NN, OClW, TxU, OCl, OCU, PU, ViU, IEdS
Leipzig: Bernh. Tauchnitz jun., 1849–50. 3 vols. British Authors nos. 167–69. Post-1852 issues read: Bernhard Tauchnitz, 1849.
CtY, MH, BM, NN, CU, MdBP, PHi, PU, NRU, WaWW, TxU, PPL, DGU, MH, GR
London: Bradbury and Evans, 1856. 1 vol.
BM, ScU(photocopy), DH, JEG
Reprinted, 1858.
MH
Reprinted, 1860. (Source: B&E records)
Reprinted, 1863.
NNC
Reprinted, 1864.
IU
Reprinted by Smith, Elder, 1865. (Source: S,E records)
Reprinted by Smith, Elder, 1866. (Source: S,E records)
Reissued by Lippincott, Phila., 1866.
MH
Reprinted by Smith, Elder, 1867. (Source: S,E records)
Reprinted by Smith, Elder, 1868. (Source: S,E records)
Reissued by Lippincott, Phila., 1868.
MB, PP
New York: M. Doolady, 1867.
NN, PPDrop, MH, MB
[as *Histoire de Pendennis*. Trans. E. Scheffter.] Paris: L. Hachette, 1858. 3 vols.
BM
Reprinted, 1866.
DLC
Reprinted, 1869. (Source: Bibliothèque Nationale)
Reprinted, 1875. (Source: Bibliothèque Nationale)
[as *Die Geschichte von Arthur Pendennis*.] Leipzig: Weber, 1851.
Fales, ViU

The History of Samuel Titmarsh and the Great Hoggarty Diamond
   London: Bradbury and Evans, 1849.
      BM, NN, Berg(3), NNC, Fales, CSmH, CU, MsSM, Parrish, Lilly,
      CaBViV, CaAEU, MoSW, ICU, CLU-C, MB, IU, CtY, MWiW-C,
      PPT, OrU, MoU, NcD, NcU, MH, TxU, CU-A, NIC, ScU, AzU,
      KU, NBu, EFH, JM
      Reprinted, 1849. *See* Appendix D
      Fales, PPL(2), BM, CSmH
      Reissued, 1852. With new title page.
      BM, Fales, NP, GR
      Reissued, 1857. With second new title page. (Source: B&E records)
      Reissued, by Smith, Elder, n.d. [1865]. With third new title page.
      NcU
   London: Bradbury and Evans, 1857.
      BM, Berg, NN, Fales, Parrish, ICN, MH, OC, IU, PPiU, CtY
   [as *The Great Hoggarty Diamond.*] New York: Harper and Brothers, n.d.
   [1848].
      NN(2), Berg(2), Fales(2), Parrish, CaAEU, MH, CtY, NcU, CSmH
      Reprinted, 1864.
      CSmH
      Reprinted, 1865.
      NN, IU
   [with *The Book of Snobs.*] Leipzig: B. Tauchnitz, jun., 1849.
      NRU
   [as *The Great Hoggarty Diamond, and The Book of Snobs.*] New York:
   Leypoldt & Holt, 1866.
      MH, CtY
   [as *Le diamant de famille et La jeunesse de Pendennis* par M. Thackeray,
   avec une notice biographique et littéraire par Amédée Pichot.] Paris:
   L. Hachette, 1855.
      IU, RAC
   [as *Samuel Titmarsh och den stora Hoggarty-Diamond.*] Stockholm: Tryckt
   Hos L. J. Hjerta, 1850.
      Fales
An Interesting Event
   London: David Bogue, 1849. A T. J. Wise forgery.
      Berg(3), Fales, CSmH, ICN, MsSM
The Irish Sketch-Book
   London: Chapman & Hall, 1843. 2 vols.
      BM, NN, Berg(6), Fales, NNC, CSmH(2), Lilly, ICN, CaAEU, NcD,
      MeB, MB, WU, MH, IU, OrPR, ICU, PPL, NcU, CtY, PPiU, ScU,
      MoU, KU, GR
      Reissued, 1845. With new title page saying "Second Edition."
      BM(2), CU, WU, KyU, ICU, IU, UU, OrU, PLS, HL

London: Chapman & Hall, 1857. "New Edition" on title page; a true
new edition.

>BM, IU, PU, HL

Reprinted or reissued, 1860. "Third Edition" on title page.

>FMU

Reprinted or reissued, 1863. "New Edition" on title page.

>IU, CU

New York: J. Winchester, New World Press, n.d. [1844; Van Duzer
says 1843].

>NN(2), NcU, ViU, CSmH

New York: Berford & Co., 1847.

>PLS

Philadelphia, 1864.

>PPL

[as *Thackeray's Irish Sketch-Book*.] Philadelphia: T. B. Peterson, n.d.
[1864].

>CSmH, MB

[as *Irländische Zustande* geschildert von M. A. Titmarsh.] Stuttgart:
Franckh, 1845.

>CSmH

Reprinted, 1848.

>BM

London: Smith, Elder, 1865. A reprint of the Chapman and Hall, 1857,
edition.

>PSt

Jeames's Diary; or Sudden Riches

New York, Philadelphia, and Baltimore: William Taylor and Co., 1846.

>NN, Fales, Parrish, TxU, MH, GR

[with *A Legend of the Rhine* and *Rebecca and Rowena*.] New York: Appleton, 1853.

>BM, DLC, NN(2), Berg, Fales, Parrish(2), CSmH, CU, OClW, ViU,
>MB, MWA, MeB, MH, LU, PBm, PPL, NcU, PLS

Reprinted, 1859.

>Vic, OClW

The Kickleburys on the Rhine

London: Smith, Elder, 1850.

>DLC, Berg(5), NN(2), NNC, Fales, Parrish, CSmH(4), Lilly, ICN,
>TxU-HR, MsSM, CaBVaS, CaBViV, CaAEU, GU, NcU, MoSW,
>CoU, MdBJ-G, CtY, MH, MWiW-C, OrU, WU, CLU-C, OrPR, PPL,
>ScU, DGU, CU-A, DeU, MoU, GR

Reprinted, 1850. "Second Edition" on title page.

>NP

Reprinted, 1851. "Second Edition" on title page.

>BM(2), Berg, Fales, Parrish, CSmH, CaAEU, NcU

Reprinted, 1851. "Third Edition" on title page.
NNC, PSt
Reprinted, 1856.
CSmH
London: Smith, Elder, 1866. A new edition.
BM, Fales, GU, WU, FTaSU, NcD, NcU, CtY, PLS, JM
New York: Stringer & Townsend, 1851.
DLC, NN(3), Fales, Parrish, CtY, PP, NNU, ICU, MeB, MB
Frankfort o. M.: Charles Jugell, 1851. Jugell's Pocket Edition, No. 29.
NN, Parrish(2), CSmH, MH, CtY, PU, PLS
[as *The Kickleburys Abroad.*] Leipzig: Tauchnitz, 1851. British Authors no. 197.
NN, PSt, MH, GR
New York: Leypoldt & Holt; Leipzig: Tauchnitz, 1867.
TxU

A Leaf Out of a Sketch Book
London: Emily Faithfull & Co., 1861. A T. J. Wise forgery.
BM, Berg(3), Fales, Parrish, CSmH, ICN, TxU, MH, CtY, NSyU, MB
A Legend of the Rhine. See *Jeames's Diary*
A Little Dinner at Timmins's and The Bedford Row Conspiracy
London: Bradbury and Evans, 1856.
NN, Berg(4), Fales, Parrish, CSmH, ICN, CaBViV, TNJ, NIC, CtY, ICU, MH, OC
Reprinted, n.d.
BM
Reprinted, 1857. (Source: B&E records)
Reprinted, 1863. (Source: B&E records)
Leipzig: Tauchnitz, 1857.
CtY
New York and Leipzig, 1867.
CtY

Lovel the Widower
New York: Harper & Brothers, 1860.
DLC, Fales, Parrish, CSmH, CaAEU, MH, OClW, PPPrHi, PPL, NNU, CtY, NB, GR
London: Smith, Elder, 1861.
BM, DLC, Berg(4), NN, NNC(2), Fales(2), Parrish, CSmH(2), CU, ICN, TxU-HR, CaBVaS, CaAEU, GU, OU, MoU, CtY, CLU-C, MH, WU, OrPR, PLS, GR
Reprinted, 1866. (Sources: S,E records; Anthony Garnett Cat.)
See also *The Four Georges*
The Luck of Barry Lyndon
New York: D. Appleton, 1853. 2 vols.
BM, NN, Berg, Fales(2), Parrish(2), CSmH, ICN, Lilly, PSt, DeU,

MsSM, NWM, CtY, PPL, NcU, OClW, MoSU, KU, IaU, DGU, MeB, ICU, MH, NcD, MB, ViU, PU, GR

[as *The Memoirs of Barry Lyndon.*] London: Bradbury and Evans, 1856.
  NN, Berg(2), Fales, Parrish, CSmH(2), ICN, NIC, IU, MH, PPiU, CtY, NcU, MB, PLS
  Reprinted, 1861. (Source: B&E records)
  Reprinted by Smith, Elder, 1866. (Source: S,E records)
  Reprinted by Smith, Elder, 1868.
  NN, MH, MdBP, CtY

[as *Mémoires de Barry Lyndon*] Paris: [Bibliothèque des milleurs Romans étrangers, 1857].
  BM

[as *Mémoires de Barry Lyndon, du royaume d'Irlande,* trans. Léon de Wailly.] Paris: L. Hachette, 1865.
  MH, RAC

The Mahogany Tree
  [London]: Office of the Music Book, [1847?].
  CSmH

Memoirs of Major Gahagan. See *Tremendous Adventures of Major Gahagan*
The Memoirs of Mr. Charles J. Yellowplush. See *Yellowplush Correspondence*
Men's Wives
  New York: Appleton, 1852.
  NN(2), Berg, NNC(2), Fales, BM, DLC, Parrish, CSmH, ICN, InU, OU, NNU, NCU, NWM, WaWW, NIC, KyU, MB, ViU, DeU, DGU, MoSW, PBm, PU, PPL, OrPR, PLS
  Reprinted, 1853.
  BM, DLC, NcU, CtY, PHi, NIC
  Reprinted, 1864.
  DLC
  Reprinted, 1868.
  ViU

[with *Mr. and Mrs. Frank Berry* only.] New York: G. P. Putnam, 1864.
  PLS

[with *Mr. and Mrs. Frank Berry* only.] New York: Office of the Rebellion Record, 1864.
  Berg, Parrish, MH, OCl

Miscellanies: Prose and Verse
  [Vol. 1.] London: Bradbury and Evans, 1855.
  BM, NN, Berg, NNC(2), Fales(2), Parrish, CSmH, InU, CaAEU, Robarts, NBC, ScU, CoU, LU, CtY, Or, NBuU, WU, NIC, MB, OClW, MH, PLS, GR
  Reprinted, 1856.
  CSmH
  Reprinted, 1857. (Source: B&E records)

Reprinted, 1858.
MH
Reprinted, 1861.
PLS
Reprinted, 1864. (Source: B&E records)
Reprinted, 1865.
CU
Reprinted by Smith, Elder, 1866.
CaBVaS, LNT
Reissued by Lippincott, Phila., 1866.
NNC
Reprinted by Smith, Elder, 1867, 1868, 1870. (Source: S,E records)
Reissued by Lippincott, 1868.
InU

[Vol. 2.] London: Bradbury and Evans, 1856.
BM, NN, Berg, NNC(2), Fales(2), Parrish, CSmH(2), InU, CaAEU,
NBC, ScU, CoU, LU, An-C-TU, CtY, Or, NBuU, WU, NIC, MB,
OClW, MH, PLS, GR
Reprinted, 1857.
MH
Reprinted, 1860.
PLS
Reprinted, 1864. (Source: B&E records)
Reprinted by Smith, Elder, 1865.
CU, Robarts
Reprinted by Smith, Elder, 1866.
CaBVaS, LNT
Reissued by Lippincott, Phila., 1866.
NNC
Reprinted by Smith, Elder, 1867, 1869, 1871. (Source: S,E records)

[Vol. 3.] London: Bradbury and Evans, 1856.
BM, NN, Berg, NNC(2), Fales(2), Parrish, CSmH(2), InU, Robarts,
CaAEU, NBC, ScU, CoU, LU, CtY, Or, NBuU, WU, NIC, MB,
OClW, MH, PLS(2), GR
Reprinted, 1857.
MH
Reprinted, 1863. (Source: B&E records)
Reprinted by Smith, Elder, 1865.
CU
Reprinted by Smith, Elder, 1866.
LNT
Reissued by Lippincott, Phila., 1866.
NNC
Reprinted by Smith, Elder, 1868, 1871. (Source: S,E records)

[Vol. 4.] London: Bradbury and Evans, 1857.
BM, NN, NNC(2), Berg, Fales(2), Parrish, CSmH(2), InU, CaAEU,

Robarts, MH, NBC, ScU, CoU, LU, CtY, Or, NBuU, WU, NIC, MB, OClW, MH, PLS, GR
Reprinted, 1860, 1864. (Source: B&E records)
Reprinted by Smith, Elder, 1865.
CU
Reprinted by Smith, Elder, 1866.
LNT
Reissued by Lippincott, Phila., 1866.
NNC
Reprinted by Smith, Elder, 1867, 1869, 1871. (Source: S, E records)

Miscellanies: Prose and Verse
Leipzig: B. Tauchnitz, 1849–57. 8 vols. British Authors nos. 171, 197, 345, 353, 354, 369, 379, 408.
BM, NN, CaBVaS, CLPhFB(vols. 1–2 only), MB, ViU, MH, ViW, MdBJ, PPL, PP, NjP
New York: Leypoldt & Holt, 1866. 8 vols. This may be a reissue of the Leipzig edition.

Miscellanies
New York: D. Appleton, 1864. 6 vols. (Source: Dickson)

Morgiana, le chevalier dès herité
Paris: Michel Lévy Frères, 1864.
GR

Mr. Brown's Letters . . . and The Proser and Other Papers
New York: Appleton, 1853.
BM(2), DLC, NN(2), Berg(2), Fales(2), CSmH, CU, Parrish(2), GU, PSt, OClW, OrPR, MH, ViU, NcD, NWM, MB, MU, NcU, ScU, MWA, DeU, NIC, CtY, PHi, PBm, PPL, PLS, GR
Reprinted, 1859.
ICN
Reprinted, 1866.
ViU, ICN

Mrs. Katherine's Lantern[?]
[N.p., n.d.]
Berg, CSmH

Mrs. Perkins's Ball
[London]: Chapman and Hall, n.d. [published in Dec. 1846].
BM(2), DLC, NN(2), Berg(8), NNC, Fales(4), Parrish, CSmH, CU, TxU-HR, CaBVaS, CaBViV, Lilly, ScU, CLU-C, PPT, TxU, CtY, MoU, MWiW-C, AzU, NcD, INS, MH, DeU, OrU, IaU, NcU, NIC, PLS, JM, GR. Note: Van Duzer distinguishes three printings; the copies listed here may on examination prove to be any of the three.
Reprinted, 1847.
Fales

Reprinted by Smith, Elder, 1866.
   WaSpG

The Newcomes

   London: Bradbury and Evans, 1854–55. 24 nos. in 23 pts.
      BM(2), DLC, NN, Berg(6), Fales, Parrish, CSmH(2), CU, MsSM, Lilly,
      CaAEU, Arents, FU, ViU, MWiW-C, WU, OC, CaBVa, IU, PBm,
      OkentU, NRU, CaBVaU, OrU, GR

   London: Bradbury and Evans, 1854, 1855. 2 vols.
      BM(2), DLC, Berg(4), NN(2), NNC(2), Fales(2), CSmH(2), CU(3),
      CaBVaS(2), TxU-HR, InU, Lilly, ICN, CaBViV, CaAEU, An-C-TU,
      MsSM, OU, PSt, GU(2), AzU, NjP, PU, LU, OCL, INS, CLU, IaU,
      TxU, NRU, TxHU, NcD, NcU, KU, FU, MH, ScU, ICU, NIC, CtY,
      PPL, KyU, OOxM, ICN, OrU, CLSU, ViU, MB, PPiU, MU, RPB,
      PLS(4), EFH, JM, RAC, GR
   Reprinted by Smith, Elder, 1866.
      PLS

   New York: Harper and Brothers, 1855. 2 vols.
      BM, NN, Fales, CSmH, CU, ICN, PPLas, ViU, MB, NWM, DLC,
      WaWW, IaU, TNJ, MoU, PHi, NcD, PLS, GR
   Reprinted, 1856.
      NN, Fales
   Reprinted, 1859.
      MB, PU, OClW
   Reprinted, 1865.
      PMA
   Reprinted, 1868.
      MH

   London: Bradbury and Evans, 1860. 1 vol.
      BM, PLS
   Reprinted, 1863. (Source: B&E records)
   Reprinted, 1864.
      NNC
   Reprinted by Smith Elder, 1865, 1867, 1868, 1869, 1870. (Source: S,E rec-
   ords)
   Reissued by Lippincott, Phila., 1866.
      MH, PU

   Leipzig: Tauchnitz, 1854–55. 4 vols. British Authors nos. 290, 306, 315,
   332.
      BM, DLC, NN(vols. 2–3 only), Berg, Fales(2), EDB, PPL, MH, ScU,
      MB

   New York: Doolady, 1867.
      Vic, DLC, NBuU, PPDrop, MH, OClW, MoU, NN

Notes of a Journey from Cornhill to Grand Cairo

   London: Chapman and Hall, 1846.
      BM(2), Berg(7), NN, NNC(2), Fales, Parrish, Arents, CSmH, CU,

ICN, Lilly, TxU-HR, CaAEU, GU, CLU-C, WU, NcU, MH, CaB-VaU, ScU, OrU, JM, GR
Reprinted, 1846. "Second Edition" on title page.
BM(2), Berg, Fales, Parrish, PLS, GR
Reprinted, 1850. (Source: Wm. Allen Cat.)
Reprinted, 1864. "Third Edition" on title page.
TxHR, MH, PPiU
Reprinted, 1865. "Third Edition" on title page.
BM, CU, PSt
Reprinted by Smith, Elder, 1865.
SW, CU, ViU
New York: Wiley and Putnam, 1846.
DLC, NN(2), Fales, Parrish(2), MWa, MB, MH, PPL, TxU, OO, OClW
Reprinted by George P. Putnam, 1848.
DLC, NN, Parrish, MB, OKentU, PP
Reprinted, 1850.
PLS
Reprinted, 1852.
NN, MH, NjP, NNUT
[as *Aufzeichnungen von Cornhill nach Gross-Cairo.*] Grimma. Verlags-Comptoir, 1851.
NN

Novels by Eminent Hands and Character Sketches. See *Punch's Prize Novelists*
Our Street
London: Chapman and Hall, 1848.
MB, DLC, NN, Berg(4), NNC(2), Fales(2), Arents, Parrish, CSmH(2), CU, CaBVaS, ICN, Lilly, CaAEU, DeU, CLU, ScU, OrU, OOxM, GEU, MB, MoU, WU, CtY, PPiU, MH, NcU, MWiW-C, CLU-C, NcD, MiU, FTaSU, PLS, JM. Note: A "second issue" is claimed by Berg(2) and Fales, and a colored copy dated "MDCCCXLVII" is claimed by MH.
Reprinted, 1848. "Second Edition" on title page.
GR, NP(2), NN, CSmH, MH, ICU
Reprinted, 1864.
CSmH

The Paris Sketch Book
London: John Macrone, 1840.
BM, NN(2), Berg(7), Fales, NNC, CSmH, CU, ICN, Lilly, CaAEU, GU, MH, IU, ICU, WaU, AzU, PP, PPiU, MB, PPL, NcU, CtY, WU, IEN, OC, GR(4)
London: Smith, Elder, 1866.
CU, NcU
Reprinted, 1867, 1868, 1870. (Source: S,E records)
New York: D. Appleton and Co., 1852. 2 vols.

NN, Berg, Parrish, CSmH, InU, Lilly, ViU, CtY, NcD, NcU, PHi,
PU, PPL, PPG, MB, WaWW, DLC, RAC, PLS (vol. 2 only)
Reprinted, 1853.
NjP, PPWe, MiU
Reprinted, 1865.
OClW

Punch's Prize Novelists

New York: Appleton, 1853.
BM(2), DLC, NN(3), Berg, Parrish(2), Fales, CSmH, CU, PSt, ViU,
NcU, MB, TxU, AzU, MeB, CaBVaU, DGU, DeU, IaU, MH, CtY,
NcD, PHi, PPWe, PPL, OCX, OClW, PLS(2)
Reprinted, 1859.
ICN
Reprinted, 1865.
OClW
Reprinted, 1868.
ViU

[as *Novels by Eminent Hands and Character Sketches.*] London: Bradbury
and Evans, 1856.
NN, Berg(3), Fales, Parrish, CSmH, ICN, Lilly, OU, PSt, LU, DGU,
MH, MB, IU, OC, CtY, NIC, MWiW-C, JM
Reprinted, 1858. (Source: B&E records)
Reprinted, 1861. (Source: B&E records)
Reprinted by Smith, Elder, 1865. (Source: S,E records)
See also *Sketches and Travels in London*

Rebecca and Rowena

London: Chapman and Hall, 1850.
BM, DLC, NN(2), Berg(8), Arents, NNC(2), Fales(2), Parrish, CSmH,
ICN, Lilly(2), An-C-TU, MsSM, MoSW, MdBJ, INS, WU, PP, OCL,
NIC, FTaSU, MWiW-C, NBuU, ICU, CtY, PPT, OC, NSyU, MoU,
NcU, MH, CLU-C, KyU, IU, PLS, JM, GR
Paris: A. and W. Galignani & Co., 1850. (Source: Melville)
Leipzig: Tauchnitz, 1852.
BM

See also *Jeames's Diary* and *Burlesques*

The Rose and the Ring

London: Smith, Elder, 1855.
BM, DLC, NN, Berg(4), Arents, NNC(2), Fales(2), Parrish(2),
CSmH(2), CU, Lilly, CaAEU, INS, MH, CLU, MoSW, MdBP, MoU,
PPL, OCL, OrU, ScU, CtY, MWiW-C, JM, GR
Reprinted, 1855. "Second Edition" on title page.
Berg, EFH
Reprinted, 1855. "Third Edition" on title page.
BM

Reprinted, 1866. "Fourth Edition" on title page.
  BM, PLS
Reprinted, 1867. "Fifth Edition" on title page.
  NcD
New York: Harper and Brothers, 1855.
  NN, NNC, Fales, Parrish, MH, CtY, WU, NcD, PLS

The Roundabout Papers

London: Smith, Elder, 1863.
  BM, NN, Berg(5), Fales, NNC, Parrish, CSmH, CU, CaBVaS, ICN,
  NSyU, AzU, PPiU, MU, ICU, DGU, NcD, CtY, OCl, PP, PLS, GR
Reprinted, 1864.
  PLS
New York: Harper and Brothers, 1863.
  DLC, NN, CSmH, CU, ICN, OClW, PPL, OrU, NcU, MH, MB,
  NjP, ViU, NSyU, MWA, KyU, MsSM, OrU, PBm, GR
Reprinted, 1864.
  MH, OO

The Second Funeral of Napoleon

London: H. Cunningham, 1841.
  BM, DLC, NN(2), Berg(4), Fales(2), CSmH(3), ICN, Lilly, PPTiIIi,
  MdBP, MB, CtY, MoU, MH, OClWHi, ICN, NRU, MiU, OrCS,
  GR. Note: An undated facsimile edition exists. *See* Van Duzer item 194.
Leipzig: Tauchnitz, 1851. British Authors no. 197.
  NN

A Shabby Genteel Story

[with *Other Tales.*] New York: D. Appleton and Co., 1852.
  BM, DLC, NN(2), Berg, NNC, Fales, Parrish, PSt, CSmH(2), CaAEU,
  MnU, CtY, NWM, MB, MH, NcU, NRU, ViU, PU, NIC, PPL, NcD,
  DGU, TxU, WaWW, MsSM, OCl, OrU, JM, GR
Reprinted, 1853.
  Parrish, CSmH, CtY, MB, MiU, NcU
Reprinted, 1864.
  NcCuW
London: Bradbury and Evans, 1857.
  NN, Berg(2), Fales, Parrish, CSmH, IU, MH, CtY
Reprinted, 1864. (Source: B&E records)

Simple Melodies

Choisy le Roi: for E. Torre, 1832 [according to NUC, probably 1896].
  Berg, CSmH, GR

Sketches and Travels in London

London: Bradbury and Evans, 1856.
  DLC, NN, Berg(4), NNC, Fales, Parrish, CSmH, MsSM, MH, WU,
  NcU, CtY, PLS, JM
Reprinted, 1858. (Source: B&E records)

Reprinted, 1863. (Source: B&E records)
Reprinted by Smith, Elder, 1865.
  ViU

[with *Novels by Eminent Hands.*] New York: Leypoldt Holt; Leipzig:
  Tauchnitz, 1867.
  NN, Berg, CtY

Sketches by Spec (No. 1, "Britannia Protecting the Drama"; No. 2, "No
  Accounting for Taste")
  London: H. Cunningham, [1840]. (Source: Van Duzer)
    Facsimiles made in 1885 are at MH, CtY, NRU.

The Snobs' Trip to Paris; or the Humours of the Long Vacation [from *The Snob*]
  Cambridge: W. H. Smith, [1829?].
    Berg(2), CSmH(2), Lilly

Specimens of a New Process of Engraving for Surface-Printing
  London: W. J. Linton, 1861.
    CSmH, CtY

Stubbs's Calendar: or, The Fatal Boots
  New York: Stringer and Townsend, 1850.
    NN, Berg(2), Fales, Parrish, CSmH(4), MH, DGU, CLU-C, CtY, PPL,
    OrPR, MB, NWM

The Tremendous Adventures of Major Gahagan
  [as *Memoirs of Major Gahagan* or as *Major Gahagan's Reminiscences.*]
    Published in America ca. 1838–40. (Sources: Preface to *Comic Tales;*
    Dickson)
  London: Bradbury and Evans, 1855.
    NN, Berg(3), Parrish, CSmH, ICN, GU, DGU, IU, ICU, CtY, MH,
    NcU, JM
  Reprinted, 1856.
    CaBVaS, PLS, RAC
  Reprinted, 1858.
    IEdS
  Reprinted by Smith, Elder, 1865, 1866. (Source: S,E records)
  New York: Leypoldt and Holt, 1866.
    NN, CtY

  See also *Confessions of Fitzboodle*

Vanity Fair
  London: Bradbury and Evans, 1847–48. 20 nos. in 19 pts.
    Berg(5), Arents, Parrish(2), CSmH(2), ScU, Fales, ICN, Lilly, CSt,
    PBm, ViU, MWiW-C, IU, MH, GR(2)
  London: Bradbury and Evans, 1848. 1 vol.
    BM(2), DLC, Berg(9), Fales, NNC, NN, CSmH, CU, ScU, NcD, VPI,
    An-C-TU, MsSM, GU, PSt, MoSW, MH, CLU-C, OC, MoU, DGU,

INS, OrPR, CaBVaU, OCU, OrU, NIC, IEN, LU, CtY, IU, MnU, ICU, ViU, GEU, PLS(2), JM, GR
Reprinted, 1849.
BM, Fales, ScU(2), MiU, GU, MH, NIC
Reprinted by Smith, Elder, 1865. (Source: S,E records)
Reprinted by Smith, Elder, 1866.
CaBVaS
Reprinted by Smith, Elder, 1868.
BM

New York: Harper and Brothers, 1848. In 2 pts.
CSmH, Arents, GR

New York: Harper and Brothers, 1848. 1 vol.
NN, Parrish, CaBVaS, ICN, CSt, PPL, MiU, OU, TxU, OClW, NNU, PPT, PHi, MH, MB
Reprinted, 1849.
BM, Lilly, ViU, MH, MdBP, PPL, PLS, GR
Reprinted, 1857.
NN, MH, NjP, ViU
Reprinted, 1860.
OC, NjP
Reprinted, 1865.
Berg
Reprinted, n.d.
BM, DLC, MsSM, NN (second half only), OU, InU, MiU, AzU

New York: Harper and Brothers, 1865. 2 vols.
NjR

New York: Harper and Brothers, 1865. 3 vols.
PMA, NcD, IaU, PPL, MH, CtY
Reprinted, 1868.
Fales

London: Bradbury and Evans, 1853. Cheap edition.
BM, CU, GR(2), EFH
Reprinted, 1854.
BM
Reprinted, 1856.
PHi
Reprinted, 1857. (Source: B&E records)
Reprinted, 1859.
MH
Reprinted, 1861, 1863, 1864. (Source: B&E records)
Reprinted, 1865.
IU
Reprinted by Smith, Elder, 1865.
IU
Reprinted by Smith, Elder, 1866, 1867. (Source: S,E records)

Reprinted by Smith, Elder, 1868.
    MH
Reissued by Lippincott, 1868
    MH, OCU
Reprinted by Smith, Elder, 1869, 1870, 1871. (Source: S,E records)
Cambridge [Mass.]: Sever and Francis, 1865.
    DLC, NN, CSmH, OCU
Leipzig: Tauchnitz, 1848. 3 vols. British Authors nos. 157, 158, 159.
    BM, NN CLPhFB, NRU, OCX, KU, PPL, PHi, CtY, MB, MdBP,
    MH, PLS
New York: Leypoldt and Holt; Leipzig: Tauchnitz, 1866.
    CSmH
[as *Der Jehrmarkt des Lebens.* Trans. Christoph F. Grieb.] Stuttgart:
    Franckh, 1850.
    ViU
[as *La foire aux vanités.* Trans. Georges Guiffrey]. Paris: Hachette, 1855.
    2 vols.
    BM, Fales
Reprinted, 1859.
    Lilly
Reprinted, 1865.
    WU
[as *La Feria de las Vanidades.*] Mexico, 1860.
    BM

The Virginians

London: Bradbury and Evans, 1858–59. 24 nos. in 24 pts.
    DLC, NN, Berg(6), Arents, NNC, Fales, CSmH(2), Parrish, Lilly,
    MsSM, CaAEU, MoSW, GR
London: Bradbury and Evans, 1858, 1859. 2 vols.
    BM, DLC, Berg(6), NNC(2), Fales(2), Parrish, CU, CaBVaS, ICN,
    TxU-HR, MsSM, CaBViV, CaAEU, An-C-TU, Robarts, PSt, GU,
    MH, FU, ViU, OU, CLU-C, GEU, KU, FTaSU, LU, PU, CSt, MnU,
    IU, MiU, NcU, CtY, MoU, CLSU, NcD, ScU, NIC, OrU, DeU,
    CLU, INS, OOxM, IaU, MWiW-C, CoU, DGU, WU, ArU, CtU,
    PLS(2), EFH, GR
Reissued by Smith, Elder, 1866. (Source: S,E records)
Reissued by Lippincott, Phila., 1866.
    MH, PU
New York: Harper and Brothers, 1859.
    NN(2), CSmH, DLC, MH, NcD, PU, PP, ViU, TNJ, INS, CtY, FU,
    MB, MU, MiU, MoU, NBuG
Philadelphia, 1866.
    NNC
Leipzig: Tauchnitz, 1858, 1859. 4 vols. British Authors nos. 425, 441,
    470, 477.

BM, NN, ViU, CtY, PPL, MH, MB, TxU
London: Bradbury and Evans, 1863. 1 vol.
    NNC, Fales
William Makepeace Thackeray at Clevedon Court
N.p., n.d. [ca. 1860 according to Van Duzer; 1870s or 1880s according
    to MH card].
    CSmH, MH
The Yellowplush Correspondence
Philadelphia: Carey & Hart, 1838.
    BM, NN, Berg(5), Fales, MsSM, CSmH, ICN, MWA, InU, PPT, TxU,
    CtY, NRU, NcD, MB, MH, GR
[as part of C. Dickens, *Master Humphrey's Clock (to Which Is Added Papers
    of Mr. Yellowplush).*] Paris: Baudry's European Library, 1841.
    DLC, BM
[as *Gedenkschriften van den Heer Yellowplush.*] Arnhem: Is. An. Nijoff,
    1848.
    BM, Arents
[as *The Yellowplush Papers.*] New York: Appleton, 1852.
    NN(2), Berg, Fales, Parrish, CSmH, Lilly, GR, PSt, PPiU, PPL, ViU,
    PHi, MH, MB, NNU, MoSU, WaWW, ICarbS, CtY, OCX, MiU,
    NBuG, TxU, NRU, NWM
Reprinted, 1853.
    NN, NNC, CU, OCL, IU, ViU, NIC, MeB, OWoC, MH, NcU, PLS
[as *The Memoirs of Mr. Charles J. Yellowplush and the Diary of C. Jeames de
    la Plushe, Esq.*] London: Bradbury and Evans, 1856.
    NN, Berg(3), Fales, Parrish, CSmH(2), IU, CtY, ICU, PPiU, WU,
    OrPR, INS, NcU, MH, PLS, JM
Reprinted, 1859. (Source: B&E records)
Reprinted by Smith, Elder, 1865. (Source: S,E records)
Reprinted by Smith, Elder, 1866.
    NIC
[as *Memories of Mr. Charles J. Yellowplush.*] Leipzig: Tauchnitz, 1856.
    NjP
[as *Mémoires d'un valet de pied.*] Paris: A. Bourdillat, 1859.
    Bibliothèque Nationale
[as *The Yellowplush Papers* (including *Jeames's Diary*).] New York: Ley-
    poldt and Holt; Leipzig: Tauchnitz, 1866.
    CtY
[as *Mémoires d'un valet de pied.* Trans. William L. Hughes.] Paris: Michel
    Lévy Frères, 1865.
    CSmH

Appendix C
Vanity Fair

THE FOLLOWING CHARTS are referred to in chapter 5.

Chart 1. Vanity Fair *Printing Schedule*

Basically there were six printings of *Vanity Fair:* the original printing, 1 January 1847 through 1 July 1848; a second comprehensive printing in July 1848; a third in September 1848; a fourth in February 1849; the fifth, scattered out

Part #	1st Printing Mon/Yr: Size	2nd Printing Mon/Yr: Size	3rd Printing Mon/Yr: Size	4th Printing Mon/Yr: Size	5th Printing Mon/Yr: Size	6th Printing Mon/Yr: Size	7th Printing Mon/Yr: Size	8th Printing Mon/Yr: Size
1	12/46: 5000	Same: 2000	7/48: 1250	9/48: 1500	2/49: 2000	11/54: 500	5/61: 500	None
2	1/47: 6000	7/48: 1000	9/48: 1500	2/49: 2000	2/55: 500	12/63: 250	6/65: 250	None
3	2/47: 5000	6/48: 500	7/48: 1000	9/48: 1500	2/49: 2000	2/55: 500	12/63: 250	6/64: 250
4	3/47: 5000	7/48: 1250	9/48: 1500	2/49: 2000	2/55: 500	12/63: 250	6/64: 250	None
5	4/47: 5000	7/48: 1250	9/48: 1500	2/49: 2000	9/56: 500	2/64: 250	None	None
6	5/47: 5000	7/48: 1000	9/48: 1500	2/49: 2000	11/54: 500	5/61: 500	None	None
7	6/47: 4000	1/48: 1000	7/48: 1000	9/48: 1500	2/49: 2000	2/55: 500	12/63: 250	6/65: 250
8	7/47: 4000	1/48: 1000	7/48: 1000	9/48: 1500	2/49: 2000	2/56: 500	1/64: 500	None
9	8/47: 4000	2/48: 1000	7/48: 1000	9/48: 1500	2/49: 2000	2/57: 500	4/64: 500	None
10	9/47: 4000	2/48: 1000	7/48: 1000	9/48: 1500	2/49: 2000	2/57: 500	4/64: 500	None
11	10/47: 4000	3/48: 1000	7/48: 1000	9/48: 1500	2/49: 2000	2/57: 500	4/64: 500	None
12	11/47: 4500	3/48: 500	7/48: 1000	9/48: 1500	2/49: 2000	2/57: 500	4/64: 500	None
13	12/47: 4500	3/48: 500	7/48: 1000	9/48: 1500	2/49: 2000	2/57: 500	4/64: 500	None
14	1/48: 5000	7/48: 1000	9/48: 1500	2/49: 2000	2/57: 500	4/64: 500	None	None
15	2/48: 5000	7/48: 1000	9/48: 1500	2/49: 2000	2/57: 500	4/64: 500	None	None
16	3/48: 5000	7/48: 1000	9/48: 1500	2/49: 2000	8/56: 500	2/64: 250	None	None
17	4/48: 5000	7/48: 1000	9/48: 1500	2/49: 2000	8/56: 500	2/64: 250	None	None
18	5/48: 5000	7/48: 1000	9/48: 1500	2/49: 2000	8/56: 500	2/64: 250	None	None
19								
20	6/48: 5000	7/48: 1000	9/48: 1500	2/49: 2000	2/55: 500	1/64: 500	4/64: 500	None

TOTALS per number: 1 = 12750; 2 = 11500; 3 = 11000; 4 = 10750; 5 through 18 = 10500 each; 19/20 = 11000

over the years 1854 to 1857; and the sixth, scattered through 1861 to 1864. In addition numbers 1, 3, and 7–13 were printed an extra time in 1847–48, and numbers 1–4, 7, and 19–20 were printed an extra time in 1864–65. Thus, numbers 3 and 7 were printed eight times; numbers 1, 2, 4, 8–13, and 19–20 were printed seven times; and the rest only six times.

Chart 2. *Vanity Fair Schedule of Disbursement*

There are various ways to read the publisher's records to gain an idea of the rate at which books left the publisher for the public—and none produces the same result. All the records account for the book by parts, so that a single bound book is treated as twenty parts. There are records of payments made for stitching copies (no telling if for parts or book issue), but apparently some copies were sold unstitched. There are half-yearly summary reports of numbers sold (no telling whether as parts or book form), but these figures were determined, apparently, by subtracting the number currently in hand, presented, given to the author, etc., from the number in hand at the beginning of the six-month period plus any new printings; hence, the number "sold" seldom if ever equals a number divisible by twenty parts, which if that were the case might indicate all sales were of whole books. So it is not clear whether the number recorded as sold accurately reflects the sale of partial runs in parts or simply approximates the numbers sold in book form. Finally there are six-month records of the form of copies remaining in hand: so many parts in quires, so many stitched, so many in cloth binding, and so many "P.O." (a label I do not understand, identifying figures which sometimes are divisible by twenty, sometimes not, and ranging from 3 to 242).

The following chart provides half-yearly summaries of the records of disbursement and analysis of stock in hand in parts in order to demonstrate the ways any bound copy of the book might combine sheets from separate printings as a normal product of the manufacturing process—making it, incidentally, solecistic to speak of the "impression" or "state" of a given copy of *Vanity Fair* as a whole. The usually discrete production stages of book publishing (printing, binding, selling) intermingle in serial publication to produce bewildering combinations.

Ending Date of Half-Year Reporting Period:	June 47	Dec 47	June 48	Dec 48	June 49	Dec 49	June 50	Dec 50	June 51	Dec 51	June 52	Dec 52
Number of Parts												
In Hand at Beginning:	—	10016		10868	4245	30304	25425	20206	19258	15605	14418	11953
Printed During Period:	37000	25000		92250	40000	—	—	—	—	—	—	—
Total Parts Available:	37000	35016		103118	44245	30304	25425	20206	19258	15605	14418	11953
Sold:	25717	22972		96961	13941	4879	5219	948	3653	1187	2465	2411
Otherwise Disposed of:	1267	1176		1912								40
Total Parts Disbursed:	26984	24148		98873	13941	4879	5219	948	3653	1187	2465	2451
Number of Parts												
In Hand at End: Quired:	6694	8450		3145	28289	24187	19245	17897	15067	12729	11165	8506
Stitched:	2722	1718		558	460	231	331	411	251	426	198	226
Bound:	—	—		300	1420	900	580	900	200	1220	540	660
P.O.:	—	—		242	135	107	50	50	87	43	50	46
Other:	600	700										64
Total Parts Remaining:	10016	10868		4245	30304	25425	20206	19258	15605	14418	11953	9502

Ending Date of Half-Year Reporting Period:	June 53	Dec 53	June 54	Dec 54	June 55	Dec 55	June 56	Dec 56	June 57	Dec 57	June 58	Dec 58
Number of Parts												
In Hand at Beginning:	9502	7338	6536	4470	4753	6662	6069	5362	6785	8415	7956	7310
Printed During Period:	—	—	—	1000	3000	—	500	2000	3500	—	—	—
Total Parts Available:	9502	7338	6536	5470	7753	6662	6569	7362	10285	8415	7956	7310
Sold:	2144	802	2066	717	1091	573	1207	577	1870	459	646	485
Otherwise Disposed of:	20					20						
Total Parts Disbursed:	2164	802	2066	717	1091	593	1207	577	1870	459	646	485
Number of Parts												
In Hand at End: Quired:	6629	6022	2762	3788	5675	5583	4896	6284	8125	7554	6696	5562
Stitched:	276	191	214	188	177	66	102	117	170	80	74	58
Bound:	280	160	1340	620	500	320	240	200	60	260	440	560
P.O.:	89	99	90	93	90	60	64	84	—	42	40	65
Other:	64	64	64	64	220	40	60	100	60	20	60	580
Total Parts Remaining:	7338	6536	4470	4753	6662	6069	5362	6785	8415	7956	7310	6825

Ending Date of Half-Year Reporting Period:	June 59	Dec 59	June 60	Dec 60	June 61	Dec 61	June 62	Dec 62	June 63	Dec 63
Number of Parts										
In Hand at Beginning:	6825	5687	5228	4585	3724	3991	3743	3646	3429	3286
Printed During Period:					1000					1000
Total Parts Available:	6825	5687	5228	4585	4724	3991	3743	3646	3429	4286
Sold:	1098	459	643	861	733	248	97	217	143	602
Otherwise Disposed of:	40									20
Total Parts Disbursed:	1138	459	643	861	733	248	97	217	143	622
Number of Parts										
In Hand at End: Quired:	5437	4776	4166	3458	3698	3498	3430	3110	3058	3356
Stitched:	60	182	54	71	33	27	65	64	84	63
Bound:	60	180	220	80	140	100	40	180	80	180
P.O.:	70	50	65	55	60	58	91	55	44	65
Other:	60	40	80	60	60	60	20	20	20	
Total Parts Remaining:	5687	5228	4585	3724	3991	3743	3646	3429	3286	3664

Ending Date of Half-Year Reporting Period:	June 64	Dec 64	June 65	30 June 65
Number of Parts				
In Hand at Beginning:	3664	5833	5251	5005
Printed During Period:	6500		500	
Total Parts Available:	10164	5833	5751	5005
Sold:	4331	582	746	5005
Otherwise disposed of:				
Total Parts Disbursed:	4331	582	746	5005
Number of Parts				
In Hand at End: Quired:	5389	4942	4965	——
Stitched:		42		——
Bound:	420	220	40	——
P.O.:	24	47		——
Other:				——
Total Parts Remaining:	5833	5251	5005	——

The Smith, Elder and Company account books record 5,001 parts including 2 bound copies received from Bradbury and Evans in June 1865. In 1865 Smith, Elder printed 7,391 more parts, and in 1866 the company printed 5,000 more, yielding 17,392 parts available. These were bound into 865 bound copies, leaving 92 odd parts. In 1868 it printed 250 more copies of the whole book. The Smith, Elder accounts of the first edition of *Vanity Fair* were closed out in 1883.

Chart 3. *Variants within the First Edition of* Vanity Fair

This chart provides a means of identifying the printing and sometimes the state within a printing of individual sheets in *Vanity Fair*. The variants are grouped under part numbers and, within parts, under signatures. The first two columns represent the first and second states of the first printing of each sheet (a third state of signatures X and FF is distinguishable as indicated in notes under these signatures in the chart). Columns 3 and 4 represent the second and third printings of each sheet. A fourth printing is distinguishable for signatures C, L, M, R, Y, Z, and QQ (as indicated in notes under each of these signatures in the chart).

The second printing is always distinguishable from the first, even when no variants occur (as in signature B), because it was printed from stereotyped plates. When the illustration in signature Y (336.2-3) was removed, text was reset and moved up to fill the gap—moving in the process some text from Z to Y, hence the jagged delimiter between these signatures in the chart. The third and fourth printings of signatures Y and Z are distinguishable even though there are no variants because pages 336–40, newly reset for the third printing, were printed from type whereas in the fourth printing plates were used.

When a reading remains unchanged from one state or printing to the next, it is represented in the next column by a dash. When for a given signature a printing is identifiable only by a change from type to stereotype as a means of printing, the column will contain no changed readings but will be represented by dashes. If the state or printing represented by a column is not distinguishable in any way for a given signature, the column is left blank. For example, for signature B, only one state of the first printing can be distinguished, hence column 2 is blank; on the other hand, because no variants were introduced in the second printing, made from stereotyped plates, the second-printing column has dashes.

Anyone discovering a copy of a signature in the book which contains changes in a pattern not fully represented by any one column (or its attending notes) will have discovered a hitherto unknown printing or state for that signature.

Entries marked by an asterisk (*) record changes which machine collation suggests may have been made in the type before stereotyping; however, no copy of the book printed from type with altered readings has been seen confirming the priority of asterisked readings (see chap. 5, n.27).

	First Print. (from type)		Printings from Stereo Plates	
Page.Line	First State	Second State	Second Print.	Third Print.
Part #1				
Sig. B				
1.[Title]	[Rustic Type]			[Roman Type]
1.[Sub-Title]	[Roman Type]			[Gothic Type]
8.17	only fifty			five and fifty
9.42	had			with
10.11	and her father			her father,
10.16	pupil,			pupil;
10.17	seen,			seen;
10.17	free;			free,
13.[run-title]	WITHOUT A			WITHOUTA
13.24	that she			as she
13.1up	Horse			Life
15.14	harm trying."			harm in trying."
Sig. C				
18.2up	measure;			
19.23	Stycorax			Sicorax
24.23	"and		'and	
24.6up	26,			96,
24.3up	roguish;			roguish,
24.3up	Amelia,			Amelia,
26.10	dining-room,			dining-room,—
26.12	society,			society;—
26.21	Christmas;			Christmas:
26.22	remembered			he remembered
27.35	great sigh.	great / sigh.		
28.8	howdah			seat
28.1up	[printer's widow]	[end of ¶]		
29	[19 lines]	[20 lines]		
30.5	hearth			roof
31.2up	Joseph:			

NOTE: *A fourth printing agrees with the third except at 18.2up* measure, *and at 31.2up* Joseph;

| | First Print. (from type) | | Printings from Stereo Plates | |
Page.Line	First State	Second State	Second Print.	Third Print.
Part #2				
Sig. D				
34.1up	other.			other
40.10–11	face? And what can Alderman Dobbin have amongst fourteen?"		face?	
43.1up	gaberdine,		gabardine,	
45.4	Devonshire		D——	
45.8	Cupids,		Cupids	
45.14	*Trent emille*		*Trente mille*	
45.19	Devonshire!"		D——!	
Sig. E				
50.18	fooltll"		fools!"	
50.11up	this fat bacchanalian		Mr. Jos Sedley	
52.34	Glauber		Gollop	
53.19	Glauber		Gollop	
54.14	ran:—		ran—	
55.14	Pinner, they're neither one thing nor t'other.		Pinner, she remarked to the maid.	
55.3up	James,"		James,'	
*58.1–2	Crawley's son, the		Crawley, son of the	
*58.42	Shiverly		Gaunt	
*60.2	I be		I'm	
*60.3	baynt.		aynt.	
*60.17	Crawley,		Tinker,	
*61.31	orphan,		baronet,	
*62.9	noise		nose	
63.12	hath		has	
63.14	What		Where	

Part #3		
Sig. F		
*66.17	Mudbury	Leakington
*66.36	Leakington	Mudbury
*66.45	Leakington	Mudbury
74.10	about	about,
75.29	Muttondown's	Southdown's
77.25	fortune equally	inheritance
Sig. G		
83.11	as Cornet and	in the Life
	Lieutenant Crawley.	Guards Green.
*88.6	Crawley	Crawley's
*92.4	Petty	Rawdon
94.30	Rincer,	Bowls,
Part #4		
Sig. H		
97.24	gift	knack
99.6up	it's	it is
99.6up	There's	There is
101.6up	that	that
101.1up	to Heaven	Te Deum
104.40	correspondence	correspondent
105.18	alwayth	always
105.18	nonthenth	nonsense
105.18	thcandal	scandal
105.19	Othborne	Osborne
105.19	ith	is
108.30	carpenter	weaver
109.35	Maria:"	Jane:"
110.18	Maria."	Jane."
Sig. I		
113.9	Hulker	Hulker's
116.32	Fisher	Firkin
122.2	chicken that day.	chicken.
128.6	vort.	vor't.

	First Print. (from type)		Printings from Stereo Plates	
Page.Line	First State	Second State	Second Print.	Third Print.
Part #5				
Sig. K				
129.1up	siad	said		
144.25	use		used	
Sig.L				
145.sig	L [centered]			
147.sig	L2			2
149.23	Young Cornet and Lieutenant		And young Lieutenant	
151.page	[Chapter heading has normal top margin]			
152.8–9	this worthy		the worthy	
152.33	honest, kind		trembling	
152.36	kind		sad	
153.3	good mother		old mother	
153.25	good old		old	
154.1	good kindly		humiliated	
156.5	done;			done,
*156.38	Miss A.		Miss Ann	
*156.1up	improved		uproused	

NOTE: A fourth printing agrees with the third except at 145.sig L [is on the right] and 147.sig L2 [is restored] and 151.page [Chapter heading flush with top margin] and 156.5 done

	First State	Second State	Second Print.	Third Print.
Part #6				
Sig. M				
165.22	all the particulars she could		sundry strange particulars	
167.13	know		know,	
173.14	ready;			
175.1up	three		and three	

NOTE: A fourth printing agrees with the third except at 173.14 where the semicolon has been replaced in heavier type.

Ref			
Sig. N			
180.5	Mahogany Charmer		mahogany charmer
*188.26	Osborne		Sedley
*188.32	Osborne		Sedley
191.12	marriage. And		marriage; and
191.15	here		there
Part #7			
Sig. O			
202.35	stately	———	state
203.17	commission:	———	commissions:
206.20	young, favourite	young favourite,	———
Sig. P			
223.15up	are	ar	
Part #8			
Sig. Q			
227.16	mother		parents
232.15	friends		friend
236.25	Flanagan's		Flanahan's
236.27	Major-General		Major-General
Sig. R			
242.11	This		The
244.3up	soldier		orderly
247.35	of		with
247.37	company		society
248.4	"Near [normal quote]		"Near [first quote lower]
252.1up	get	gain	———
254.9	shall	shawl	

NOTE: A fourth printing agrees with the third except at 248.4 'Near

Page.Line	First Print. (from type)		Printings from Stereo Plates	
	First State	Second State	Second Print.	Third Print.
Part #9				
Sig. S				
259.19	below			above
266.9up	Allée-Vertél		————	Allée-Vertel
Sig. T				
280.32	in her			in their
280.4up	Crawley had		Crawley's horses had	————
Part #10				
Sig. U				
289.20	be Captain and Lieutenant-Colonel		————	be Lieutenant-Colonel
293.11	given up all			but faint
293.19	report says was once			was secretly
294.4up	the Grand Duchess			the Duchess
295.7	[Randall reports the word *worldty* on this line; I have not seen it in any copy examined.]			
296.4up	worldty		————	worldly
Sig. X				
305.5	buzz.		————	'buzz.'
309.3	Osborne	Sedley		
309.11	knicknacks,		knick-knacks,	
310.13up	of —		————	of the
312.1	fight			fights
313.1	chance		a chance	

NOTE: A third state of the first printing agrees with the second state except at 309.11 knick-knacks,

Part #11
Sig. Y

328.29–34   [¶] After a stay at Brussels, where they lived in good fashion, with carriages and horses, and giving pretty little dinners at their hotel, the Colonel and his lady again quitted that city, from which slander pursued them as it did from Paris, and where it is said they left a vast amount of debt behind them. Indeed, this is the way in which gentlemen who live upon nothing a-year, make both ends meet. [¶] From Brussels, Colonel   ] [¶] And so, Colonel

Line	Reading	Variant
331.3up	salon	salons
333.28	St.	Ste.
333.37	Susan's	Jane's
334.13	Mr.	Mr
334.14	orphan;	orphan,
336.1– end of sig.	[original typesetting]	[plated]

[reset and printed from type]

Line	Reading	Variant
336.1	silk;	silk:
336.2–3	[woodcut illustration of Lord Steyne]	[omitted]
336.18	too; he's	too: "he's

| Page.Line | First Print. (from type) | | Printings from Stereo Plates | |
	First State	Second State	Second Print.	Third Print.
Sig. Z				
337–340	[original typesetting]			336–340 [reset and printed from type]
337.10	"Yes,		——	336.30 "Yes,"
337.10	I		——	336.30 "I
338.2	loud;		——	337.22 loud:
338.15	Minor		——	337.35 minor
338.19	Father		——	337.39 father
338.31	patronizingly		——	338.2 patronisingly
338.16up	fragrance,		——	338.5 fragrance
338.45	splendor		——	338.16 splendour
338.46	pink,		——	338.17 pink
339.8	Minor		——	338.28 minor
339.36	literary, and that		——	339.7 literary and that,
339.41	to night		——	339.12 to-night
340.15	said,		——	339.34 said
340.29	Minor		——	339.48 minor
342.3	horse		——	horse,
342.3	rode		——	rode,
350.8up	IOU		——	IOU's

NOTE: A fourth printing of Signatures Y and Z agrees with the third printing except that pages 336–340 are printed from stereotyped plates.

Page.Line	First State	Second State	Second Print.	Third Print.
Part #12				
Sig. AA				
363.23	Mr. Glauber, the surgeon,		The family surgeon	
Sig. BB				
371.11up	in		n	
373.3	upon		that	
376.17	her. The		her: &c: the	

Part #13
Sig. CC

385.19	away	and
386.14	and that if	and, if
391.25	Dobbins	Dobbin
391.30	"dearest William"	dearest William
394.8	Briggs'	Briggs
395.12–11up	to to his	to his
399.1up	" It 's	" It 's

Sig. DD

403.31	Cabine	Cabinet
405.18	sneaked	bolted
405.6–5up	[¶] Hunters arrived, from time to time, in charge of the boy Jack species—the young	[¶] Many young
405.5up	hacks	hacks,
406.13	Will	Tom
409.7up	submission,	submission.
	and Dalilah	Dalilah
	restlessly, still	restlessly still,
414.8	dinners,	dinners:
414.30		

Part #14
Sig. EE
[No alterations]

Sig. FF

| 434.1up | tired of | tired o | tired of [restored] |

NOTE: *A third state of the first printing reads:* tired

Part #15
Sig. GG

| 458.14–13up | Agamemnon | AGAMEMNON |
| 459.1 | an d [#] | an d a |

Page.Line	First Print. (from type)		Printings from Stereo Plates	
	First State	Second State	Second Print.	Third Print.
Sig. HH [No alterations]				
Part #16				
Sig. II				
481.1up	read		made	—
482.22	gentleman,—		gentleman,	—
482.22	word,		word,—	—
482.36	tattoo		tune	—
483.17up	Jane		Jane,	—
484.4-3up	the the suburbs			the suburbs
Sig. KK				
497.4	Behanged] these	——	Behanged to these	
499.10	a—fool	——	a d—fool	
500.35	Macbeth	——	Southdown	
502.3up	in his pompous manner,	——	in pompous orations	
508.9up	leaving	——	he left	
505.7	cost, as to his mother, saying he to her.		cost, saying that he to his mother.	
505.8	thram	thram		
510.1	miserable		faded	
510.19		——		
Part #17				
Sig. LL				
514.2	"it		(it	
514.3	window."		window.)	
514.5up	wages. Sisters		wages,—sisters	
517.27	youngster		youngsters	
521.24	that perennially		which perennially	
523.9	Ten		Long	

Sig. MM		
536.3	an harsh	a harsh
536.27	cot; Miss	cot as Miss
536.41	time;	time
543.7	dandy	dandies
Part #18		
Sig. NN		
550.8up	was affected	was pleased
555.3up	Mr.	Mrs.
560.1up	the German	German
Sig. OO		
561.1	Palatinate: in	Palatinate. In
571.6up	the Elephant,	the Pariser Hof,
Part #19–20		
Sig. PP		
579.7–8	certain debts and the insurance of his life;	certain outstanding debts and liabilities,
579.17	make	take
580.5up	Hornby	Horner
585.3	à *vipère*	a *vipère*
587.5–4up	and at his lordship's side was	and near his lordship was
588.18up	Fenouil,	Fiche,
588.10up	Fenouil,—	Fiche,—
589.1	Fenouil's	Fiche's
589.21	in the cushions	on the cushions
589.29	Fenouil	Fiche
589.33	Fenouil	Fiche
589.35	Finelli	Ficci
590.2	Grey	White
590.20	Fenouil,	Fiche,
592.1	sonorous	*sournois*
592.3up	94,	90,

time,

| | First Print.
(from type) | | Printings from Stereo Plates | |
Page.Line	First State	Second State	Second Print.	Third Print.
Sig. QQ				
593.1	92,			92
593.7	Fitz		Fritz	
598.1–2	such as		like	
598.5up	acceptances,		acceptance,	
601.7up	seemed to be		also was	
601.6up	might have		certainly	
602.4	William, he was		William was	
602.29	look,		look;	
602.29a	and		and,	
602.30	place;		place,	
603.11up	pure,		pure,—	
604.8	Jos eagerly		Mr. Sedley hearing the	
605.12up	hearing—Tufto,		tale. Tufto,	
605.7up	Mrs. Sedley		Mr. Sedley	
607.10	even			
607.12	Major			

NOTE: A fourth printing agrees with the third except at 607.10 eve and at 607.12 Majo

Sig. RR				
617.21up	Captain		and Captain	
617.20up	day at		day on	
617.9up	him		*him*	
621.15	scenes;		scenes,—	
623.11up	payment: invited		payment. They invited	
623.10up	examination: declared		examination, they declared	
624.imprint	[present]			[omitted]

Chart 4. Six Title Pages for Vanity Fair

Though the characteristics of the first title page listed below are definitely those of the first printing, the order of the subsequent printings is conjectural. Smith, Elder and Company reissued the first edition with two relatively accurate title-page dates: 1866 and 1868.

Line	First T-p[1]	Second(?) T-p[2]	Third(?) T-p[3]	Fourth(?) T-p[4]	Fifth(?) T-p[5]	Sixth(?) T-p[6]
2	Novel [$3\frac{1}{4}$ inches]	Novel [$3\frac{1}{16}$ in.]	Novel [$3\frac{3}{16}$ in.]	Novel [$3\frac{11}{16}$ in.]	Novel [$3\frac{3}{16}$ in.]	Novel [$3\frac{13}{16}$ in.]
5	STEEL AND WOOD					WOOD AND STEEL
5						&
7	AND	AND	AND	&	AND	
7	[$3\frac{3}{8}$ in.]	[$3\frac{1}{4}$ in.]	[$3\frac{1}{4}$ in.]	[$3\frac{1}{16}$ in.]	[$3\frac{5}{16}$ in.]	[$3\frac{3}{16}$ in.]
8	1848	1849	1849	1848	1848	1848

[1] Copies examined: Univ. of South Carolina, parts; Berg Collection, NYPL, parts copies 1, 2, 3, and 4; Univ. of North Carolina at Chapel Hill, Whittaker copy; Pierpont Morgan Library, copies 1 and 2; and two personally owned copies.

[2] Univ. of South Carolina, V28/1849.

[3] Univ. of South Carolina, V28/c2/1849.

[4] Univ. of South Carolina, V2/1848.

[5] Duke Univ. Library, only copy.

[6] Pierpont Morgan Library, copy 3.

Appendix D
The History of Samuel Titmarsh

THE FOLLOWING TABLES are referred to in chapter 5

Table 1. Textual Variants

Recorded here are representative textual variants between the first and second English editions of *The History of Samuel Titmarsh*, both published by Bradbury and Evans in 1849. The preliminary pages and signature N (pp. 177–92) are identical in all respects except that at 181.15 the *t* of *the* has dropped somewhat out of line in the first edition but is in line in the second edition in all copies checked. Signatures B to M (there is no J) have been entirely reset but in a virtual line-for-line reproduction of the first edition.

Signa-ture	Page Ref.	First Eng. Ed.	Second Eng. Ed.
B	8.12	wereΛ	were,
	9.26	church yard	churchyard
C	18.16	Though,	ThoughΛ
	20.23	shew	show
D	33.15	galloped	gallopped
	35.8	Beddy	Biddy
	35.9	Grizzie	Grizzy
	36.12	shewed	showed
	39.4	Λif	"if
E	51.10	M'Whirter	M'Whirter
	55.9	must look	must have looked
F	71.8	Paxon	Paxton
	72.26	Snodgras	Snodgrass
G	88.13	centΛ,	cent.,
	92.26	Mac Whirter	M'Whirter
H	107.1	*immence*	*immense*
	107.23	Everything	Every thing
I	120.title	OFF	HOFF
	127.20	Edward	Edmund
K	129.7	connexion	connection
	144.27	plays	played
L	145.6	*Old-clo*	*OldΛClo*
	145.10	shentlemensh	gentlemensh
M	160.13	talking,"	talking?"
	171.3	to sleep	asleep

Table 2. The 1852 Reissue

Recorded here are the differences between the first issue of the second English edition (February 1849) and the second issue with a new title page (1852). The second issue is in a green pebble-grain cloth. The front cover has a decorative border stamped in blind and, in the center, a gilt-stamped medallion resembling the central decoration on the front cover of the first edition. (Copies in original binding are in the British Library [1608/2920] and in the personal collection of Mr. Nicholas Pickwoad. A rebound copy is in the Fales Collection, New York University Library.)

	Second English Edition	
	First Issue	Second Issue
Ref.	(1849)	(1852)
t.-p.9	[blank]	New Edition
t.-p.11	BRADBURY & EVANS,	BRADBURY AND EVANS,
t.-p.12	MDCCCXLIX.	1852
verso t.-p	PRINTERS,	PRINTERS˄
xi.5, 7, 10	[the dots preceding page numbers end in a direct line below last letter of line above]	[the final dots are all nearer to the number]
xii	[diamond under title is square]	[diamond under title is pointed or slightly flared]
xii.6	Mr. [slab serifs on cap M]	Mr. [bracketed or tapered serifs]
xii.7	Mr. [slab serifs on cap M]	Mr. [bracketed on right side]

Table 3. The Smith, Elder Reissue

Recorded here are the variations between the second Bradbury and Evans issue of the second English edition (1852) and the Smith, Elder issue (1872). (I have located no copy of the 1857 Bradbury and Evans reissue.) The only variants occur in the text of the preliminaries, for the rest of the Smith, Elder issue consists of unaltered sheets from the Bradbury and Evans printing. The one copy I have seen of the Smith, Elder issue has a brown bubble-grain cloth binding. The front cover has a triple plain rule border in blind within which is a broad ornamental border also in blind. Centered and stamped in gilt is the brooch portrait of a military gentleman (Mick Hoggarty), identical with that on the front cover of the first English edition and the 1852 reissue. The spine has a double plain rule at the top, a double but spaced rule at the bottom, and four spaced ornamental rules in blind with the title stamped in gilt between the top and second ornamental rules. The back cover is like the front save for the omission of the center vignette.

Ref.	Second Issue (B &E; 1852)	Fourth Issue (S, E; 1865)
t.-p. 4	*and*	AND
t.-p. 8	&c. &c.	ETC. ETC.
t.-p.10	LONDON	LONDON
t.-p.11	*[B &E imprint]*	*[S,E imprint]*
t.-p.12	1852	*[blank]*
xi.5	[2 dots *following Ch title*]	[1 dot *following Ch title*]
xi.7	ACQUAINTANCE |	ACQUAINT- |
xi.10	BEST DIAMOND |	BEST |
xii	[rule under title *has a single centred solid diamond*]	[rule under title *has centred hollow diamond flanked by 2 smaller solid ones*]
xii.2	Frontispiece *[roman, flush right]*	*Frontispiece [ital., does not reach right margin]*

Appendix E
The History of Pendennis

THE FOLLOWING TABLES were referred to in Chapter 5.

Table 1A

Readings listed here are apparently defective but occur in all copies printed from type so far examined. In each case there is evidence—usually a blank space—that type was set but damaged. Presumably, therefore, very early copies of the first printing will supply the missing type. As copies incorporating correct readings are found, the entries from this table should be transferred to table 1B.

VOLUME I

22.title INDEED∧

33.35-34.1 money∧/taker's [faint hyphen]

34.19 hearse∧feather [faint hyphen]

38.15 companion∧

45.27-28 commanders∧/in-chief [faint hyphen]

55.39 "Stranger." [broken comma]

58.30 made∧

59.14 coat∧buttons [faint hyphen]

90.23 bed∧

92.25 conversation∧

95.27b a∧year [faint hyphen]

110.17 shoes∧

120.33 true∧

121.20 Mr∧

122.31-32 heart∧/broken [faint hyphen]

124.16 play∧bills [faint hyphen]

141.39 breakfast∧table [Both the Leipzig and New York editions show a hyphen.]

153.11 cried; [malformed tail on semicolon; may be a colon as in the revised edition of 1855 and the Leipzig edition; the New York edition has a semicolon]

159.15 soldier∧

168.25 college∧life [faint hyphen]

183.26-27 dragoon∧/regiment

222.41 Mr∧

243.21-22 gene∧/rously [faint hyphen]

257.23a her∧

261.2 Strong∧

272.18 Mr∧

295.22 know∧

317.3 Indeed!∧

319.47 Mr∧

377.40 Pen∧

378.1 aloud; [faint tail on semicolon; the revised and Leipzig editions have a colon; New York shows a semicolon]

382.21 Mr∧

34.47	∧and [malformed parenthesis]	202.34-35	good∧/humour [hyphen in vertical position]
45.1	morning∧		
73.24	children∧ [faint point]	209.15	son-in∧law [faint hyphen]
84.17	beauty∧	223.20	Mr∧
93.15-16	sim∧/plicity [faint hyphen]	278.head	XXVII∧
104.37-38	summer∧/houses	283.6	hand∧
116.32-33	hand∧/writing	307.24	dining∧room
119.1	duty∧	314.11	sherry∧
128.9-10	grey∧/headed	321.12-13	cham∧/bers
128.22	speaking∧	323.9	away∧
135.28	sitting∧room [faint hyphen]	327.10	smoking∧rooms
140.29-30	regard∧/ing	329.33	forgotten∧
142.10-11	morn∧/ing [faint hyphen]	354.9	Bart∧, [faint point]
151.20-21	Ar∧/thur's [faint hyphen]	355.17	Esq∧, [faint point]
158.47	gloomily∧	366.3	me∧
170.17b	sir∧		

Table 1B

Readings listed here are damaged in some copies printed from type, but correct readings have been noted.

VOLUME I

	Original reading	*Damaged reading*
8.41	green-baize	green baize
9.14	up-stairs	up stairs [faint hyphen]
42.27	where, in the [Note: see discussion, Part II, above]	where, i h e
43.46	ear;	[top of semicolon broken]
69.2	daughter-in-law	[second hyphen faint]
69.47	manuscripts.	manuscripts
114.title	CRISIS [faint point]	CRISIS
159.38	bed room [faint hyphen]	bed room
186.15	school-days	school days [faint hyphen]
216.6	Ostrolenka.	Ostrolenka
251.47	effect.	effect

VOLUME II

	Original reading	*Damaged reading*
33.18	shine.	shine
48.20	angry.	angry
84.16-17	mantel-/piece	mantel /piece [faint hyphen]
88.26	so.	so
92.6-7	at-/tends	at-/tends [faint hyphen]
93.32-33	him-/self	him /self
136.27	there.	there
209.15	son-in-law [second hyphen faint]	son-in law
286.48-287.1	affec-/tions	affec-/tions [hyphen lowered]
307.24	dining-room	dining room
337.29-30	con-/tents	con /tents

Table 2

Listed here are the intentional changes made during plating. In all but four cases the change of punctuation represents a restoration of apparently dropped-out marks. For example, at 114.title the period exists in early runs of the sheet; it is dropped out of later copies and was restored during plating. The four exceptions are 117.23, 175.13, and 187.13 in volume 1 and 91.11 in volume 2, all of which are new readings involving the resetting or partial resetting of the lines.

VOLUME I

Reference	Late impression from type	Early impression from plates
22.title	INDEED	INDEED.
33.35-34.1	money /taker's	money-/taker's
90.23	bed	bed.
100.1	Digby	Derby
114.title	CRISIS	CRISIS.
117.23	that	"that
149.6	[line extends beyond right margin]	[line is flush with margin]
159.38	bed room	bed-room
175.13	Rembrandt etching	Rembrandt-etching
179.41	tacid	tacit
182.5	dandyfied	dandified
183.26-27	dragoon /regiment	dragoon-/regiment
187.13	sevens	seven's
187.22	*Vingt-et-un*	*vingt-et-un*
192.7	Boundell	Bloundell
251.47	effect	effect.
261.2	Strong	Strong.

VOLUME II

Reference	Late impression from type	Early impression from plates
34.47	and [faint parenthesis]	(and
62.11	nuns [in margin]	nuns [aligned]
62.12	sacredquiet	sacred quiet
84.17	beauty	beauty.
91.11	"Pen	Pen
116.32-33	hand /writing	hand-/writing
128.9-10	grey /headed	grey-/headed
128.22	speaking	speaking.
140.29-30	regard /ing	regard-/ing
219.33	scoundrel.	scoundrel."
286.48-287.1	affec_/tions	affect/tions
288.22	qu ickly	quickly
307.24	dining room	dining-room
347.46	m e."	me."
366.3	me	me.

Works Cited

Altick, Richard. *The English Common Reader.* Columbus: Ohio State Univ. Press, 1957.

Anesko, Michael. *Friction in the Market: Henry James and the Profession of Authorship.* Oxford: Oxford Univ. Press, 1986.

Barnes, James J. *Authors, Publishers, and Politicians: The Quest for an Anglo-American Copyright Agreement, 1815–1854.* London: Routledge and Kegan Paul, 1974.

——. *Free Trade in Books: A Study of the London Book Trade since 1800.* Oxford: Clarendon Press, 1964.

Bolas, Thomas. *Cantor Lectures on Stereotyping.* London: W. Trounce, 1890.

Bowers, Fredson. *Principles of Bibliographical Description.* Princeton, N.J.: Princeton Univ. Press, 1949.

Bradbury, Henry. *Printing: Its Dawn, Day, and Destiny.* London: Bradbury and Evans, 1858.

Catalogue of an Exhibition of the Works of William Makepeace Thackeray . . . Held at the Library Co., of Philadelphia . . . 1940. Philadelphia: priv. ptd., 1940.

Cohen, Morton N., and Anita Gandolfo, eds. *Lewis Carroll and the House of Macmillan.* Cambridge: Cambridge Univ. Press, 1987.

Colby, Robert. *Thackeray's Canvass of Humanity.* Columbus: Ohio State Univ. Press, 1979.

Collins, A. S. *The Profession of Letters: A Study of the Relations of Authors to Patron, Publisher, and Public, 1780–1832.* London: Routledge and Kegan Paul, 1928.

Collins, Philip, ed. *Thackeray Interviews and Recollections.* 2 vols. London: Macmillan, 1983.

Cozzens, James Gould. *Morning Noon and Night.* New York: Harcourt, Brace & World, 1968.

Cross, Nigel. *The Royal Literary Fund, 1790–1918.* London: World Microfilms, 1984.

Crowe, Erye. *With Thackeray in America.* London: Cassell, 1893.

de Groot, H. B., and Walter Houghton. "The *British and Foreign Review;* or, *European Quarterly Journal,* 1835–1844: Introduction." In *Wellesley Index to Victorian Periodicals.* Ed. Walter E. Houghton and Esther Rhoads Houghton. 5 vols. Toronto: Univ. of Toronto Press, 1966–89, 3:62–76.

Eddy, Spencer. *The Founding of the* Cornhill Magazine. Ball State Univ. Monograph no. 19. Muncie, Ind., 1970.

Exman, Eugene. *The Brothers Harper.* New York: Harper & Row, [1946].

Feltes, N. N. *Modes of Production of Victorian Novels.* Chicago: Univ. of Chicago Press, 1986.

Fields, James T. *Yesterdays with Authors.* 1871; rpt. Boston: Houghton Mifflin, 1925.

Flamm, Dudley. *Thackeray's Critics*. Chapel Hill: Univ. of North Carolina Press, 1967.

Fraser, Sir William. *Hic et Ubique* (1893), excerpt rpt. in Philip Collins, ed. *Thackeray Interviews and Recollections*. London: Macmillan, 1983.

Gaskell, Philip. *A New Introduction to Bibliography*. London: Oxford Univ. Press, 1972.

Gettmann, Royal A. *A Victorian Publisher: A Study of the Bentley Papers*. Cambridge: Cambridge Univ. Press, 1960.

Glynn, Jenifer. *Prince of Publishers: A Biography of George Smith*. London: Allison and Busby, 1986.

Gordan, John. *William Makepeace Thackeray: An Exhibition*. New York: New York Public Library, 1947.

Greetham, David, ed. *Scholarly Editing: A Research Guide*. New York: Modern Language Assoc., forthcoming.

Griest, Guinevere L. *Mudie's Circulating Library*. Bloomington: Indiana Univ. Press, 1970.

Gulliver, Harold Strong. *Thackeray's Literary Apprenticeship*. Valdosta, Ga.: priv. ptd., 1936.

Hagen, June Steffenson. *Tennyson and His Publishers*. London: Macmillan, 1979.

Hansard, T. C. *Treatises on Printing and Type-Founding*. From the seventh edition of the *Encyclopaedia Britannica*. Edinburgh: Adam and Charles Black, 1841.

Harden, Edgar. *The Emergence of Thackeray's Serial Fiction*. Athens: Univ. of Georgia Press, 1979.

——. "Historical Introduction" to *The History of Henry Esmond*. New York: Garland, 1989.

——. "Thackeray: 'Rebecca and Rowena': A Further Document." *Notes and Queries* 24 (1977): 20–22.

——. "Thackeray and the Carlyles: Seven Further Letters." *Studies in Scottish Literature* 14 (1979): 165–77.

——. "Thackeray's *Miscellanies*." *PBSA* 71 (1977): 479–508.

——. "The Writing and Publication of *Esmond*." *Studies in the Novel* 13 (1981): 79–92.

——. "The Writing and Publication of Thackeray's *English Humourists*." *PBSA* 76 (1982): 197–207.

Harper, Joseph Henry. *The House of Harper*. New York: Harper & Bros., 1912.

Hepburn, James. *The Author's Empty Purse and the Rise of the Literary Agent*. London: Oxford Univ. Press, 1968.

Hodder, George. *Memoirs of My Time*. London: Tinsley, 1870.

Howes, Craig. "*Pendennis* and the Controversy on the 'Dignity of Literature.'" *Nineteenth Century Literature* 41 (Dec. 1986): 269–98.

Huxley, Leonard. *The House of Smith, Elder*. London: priv. ptd. 1923.

Jackson, R. V. "The Structure of Pay in Nineteenth-Century Britain." *Economic History Review*, 2d ser., 40 (1987):561–70.

James, Louis. *Fiction for the Working Man*. Harmondsworth: Penguin, 1974.

Knight, Charles. *Passages of a Working Life during Half a Century: With a Prelude of Early Reminiscences*. 3 vols. London: Bradbury & Evans, 1864–65.

Lund, Michael. "Novels, Writers, and Readers in 1850." *Victorian Periodicals Review* 17 (Spring-Summer 1984): 15–28.

McGann, Jerome. *A Critique of Modern Textual Criticism*. Chicago: Univ. of Chicago Press, 1983.

McKenzie, D. F. *The Sociology of Texts*. London: British Library, 1987.

McKerrow, Ronald B. *An Introduction to Bibliography*. Oxford: Clarendon Press, 1928.

Mackinnon, Sir Frank. "Notes on the History of English Copyright." In *The Oxford Companion to English Literature*. London: Oxford Univ. Press, 1967, pp. 921–31.

McLean, Ruari. *Joseph Cundall: A Victorian Publisher*. Pinner: Private Libraries Association, 1976.

Martin, Sir Theodore. *Memoir of William Edmondstoune Aytoun*. Edinburgh and London: W. Blackwood, n.d.

Melville, Lewis. *William Makepeace Thackeray: A Biography Including Hitherto Uncollected Letters and Speeches and a Bibliography of 1,300 Items*. 2 vols. London: John Lane, 1910.

Miller, J. Hillis. "*Henry Esmond*: Repetition and Irony." In *Fiction and Repetition: Seven English Novels*. Cambridge: Harvard Univ. Press, 1982, pp. 73–115.

Monsarrat, Anne. *An Uneasy Victorian: Thackeray the Man*. London: Cassell, 1980.

Mumby, Frank. *The House of Routledge*. London: Routledge, 1934.

——, and Ian Norrie. *Publishing and Bookselling*. London: Jonathan Cape, 1974.

Nowell-Smith, Simon. *International Copyright Law and the Publisher in the Reign of Queen Victoria*. Oxford: Clarendon, 1968.

Paston, George. *At John Murray's: Records of a Literary Circle, 1843–1892*. London: John Murray, 1932.

Patten, Robert. *Charles Dickens and His Publishers*. Oxford: Clarendon, 1978.

——. Review of Nigel Cross's *The Common Writer*. *Review* 9 (1987): 1–34.

Peters, Catherine. *Thackeray's Universe*. London: Faber & Faber, 1987.

Plant, Marjorie. *The English Book Trade: An Economic History of the Making and Sale of Books*. 3d ed. London: Allen & Unwin, 1974.

Pollard, Graham. "Introduction." In I. R. Brussel. *Anglo-American First Editions, 1826–1900, East to West*. London: Constable, 1935, pp. 3–31.

——. "Notes on the Size of the Sheet." *Library*, 4th ser., 22 (Sept.–Dec. 1941): 105–37.

Randall, David A. "Notes towards a Correct Collation of the First Edition of *Vanity Fair*." *PBSA* 42 (1948): 95–109.

Rawlins, Jack. *Thackeray's Novels: A Fiction That Is True*. Berkeley: Univ. of California Press, 1974.

Ray, Gordon N. *The Buried Life: A Study of the Relation between Thackeray's Fiction and His Personal History*. Cambridge: Harvard Univ. Press, 1952.

——. *Thackeray: The Age of Wisdom*. New York: McGraw-Hill, 1958.

——. *Thackeray: The Uses of Adversity*. New York: McGraw-Hill, 1955.

——. "*Vanity Fair*: One Version of the Novelist's Responsibility." *Essays by Divers Hands* 25 (1950): 87–101.

——, ed. *The Letters and Private Papers of William Makepeace Thackeray*. 4 vols. Cambridge: Harvard Univ. Press, 1946.

Sadleir, Michael. *Trollope: A Bibliography*. 1928; rpt. London: Dawsons, 1964.

Saintsbury, George. "Introduction" to *Pendennis*. London: Oxford Univ. Press, [1908].

Scarry, Elaine. "Henry Esmond: The Rookery at Castlewood." *Thackeray, Haw-thorne and Melville, and Dreiser.* Ed. Eric Rothsheim and Joseph A. Wittreich, Jr., Literary Monographs, vol. 7. Madison: Univ. of Wisconsin Press, 1975, pp. 3–43.

Shillingsburg, Peter. "Detecting Stereotype Plate Usage in Mid-Nineteenth Century Books." *Editorial Quarterly* 1 (1975): 2–3.

———. "*Pendennis* in America." *PBSA* 68 (1974): 325–29.

———. *Scholarly Editing in the Computer Age.* Athens: Univ. of Georgia Press, 1986.

———. "Textual Introduction" to *Vanity Fair* (New York: Garland, 1989), pp. 651–54.

———. "Thackeray and the Firm of Bradbury and Evans." *Victorian Studies Association* (of Ontario) *Newsletter,* no. 11 (March 1973): 11–14.

Smith, Charles Manby. *A Working Man's Way in the World: Being the Autobiography of a Journeyman Printer.* London: William and F. Cash, n.d.

Smith, Constance. "The Henry Silver Diary: An Annotated Edition" (Ph.D. diss., St. Louis Univ., 1987).

Smith, George. *Chapters from Some Memoirs.* London: Macmillan, 1894.

———. "The Recollections of a Long and Busy Life." 2 vols. Typescript. Quoted by Edgar Harden. "The Writing and Publication of *Esmond.*" *Studies in the Novel* 13 (1981): 80–81.

Southward, J. "Collection of MS. and Printed Matter relative to Stereotyping." St. Bride Technical Reference Library, London.

Spielman, M. H. *Hitherto Unidentified Contributions of W. M. Thackeray to* Punch. 1900; rpt. New York: Haskell House, 1971.

Strebigh, Fred. "Keeping the Hacks and Geniuses Out of Debtors Prison," *Smithsonian* (May 1985):121–29.

Sutherland, John. *Thackeray at Work.* London: Athlone, 1974.

———. "The Thackeray-Smith Contracts." *Studies in the Novel* 13 (1981): 168–83.

———. *Victorian Novelists and Publishers.* Chicago: Univ. of Chicago Press, 1976.

Thackeray, W. M. *Flore et Zéphyr; The Yellowplush Correspondence; The Tremendous Adventures of Major Gahagan.* Ed. Peter L. Shillingsburg. New York: Garland, 1991.

——— *The History of Henry Esmond.* Ed. Edgar Harden. New York: Garland, 1989

———. "Lever's *St. Patrick's Eve*—Comic Politics." *Morning Chronicle,* 3 April 1845; rpt. in *Thackeray: Contributions to the* Morning Chronicle. Ed. Gordon N. Ray. Urbana: Univ. of Illinois Press, 1966.

———. *Vanity Fair.* Ed. Peter L. Shillingsburg. New York: Garland, 1989.

Thackeray Newsletter, nos. 6 and 7 (1977).

Tillotson, Geoffrey. *A View of Victorian Literature.* Oxford: Clarendon, 1978.

Tillotson, Kathleen. "*Oliver Twist* in Three Volumes." *Library* 18 (1963): 113–32.

Trollope, Anthony. *An Autobiography.* New York: Harper and Bros., 1883.

———. *Thackeray.* London: Macmillan, 1879.

Van Duzer, Henry S. *A Thackeray Library.* 1919; rpt. New York: Kennikat Press, 1965.

Der Verlag Bernhard Tauchnitz, 1837–1912. Leipzig: Tauchnitz, 1912.

Vizetelly, Henry. *Glances Back through Seventy Years.* London: Kegan Paul, Trench, Trübner and Co., 1883.

Waugh, Arthur. *A Hundred Years of Publishing: Being the Story of Chapman & Hall,
     Ltd*. London: Chapman and Hall, 1930.
West, James L. W. "Book Publishing, 1835–1900: The Anglo-American Connec-
     tion," *PBSA* 84 (1990): 357–75.
——. "The Chace Act and Anglo-American Literary Relations," *Studies in Bibli-
     ography* 45 (1992): 303–11.
Wilson, James Grant. *Thackeray in the United States, 1852–3, 1855–6*, 2 vols.
     London: Smith, Elder, 1904.
Wilson, R. Jackson. *Figures of Speech*. New York: Knopf, 1989.
Yeats, W. B. *The Collected Poems*. London: Macmillan, 1950.

Index